THE GAY DECAMERON

THE GAY DECAMERON

Christopher Whyte

VICTOR GOLLANCZ

LONDON

First published in Great Britain 1998
by Victor Gollancz
An imprint of the Cassell Group
Wellington House, 125 Strand, London WC2R 0BB

A catalogue record for this book is
available from the British Library.

ISBN 0 575 06505 2

Typeset by Rowland Phototypesetting Ltd
Bury St Edmunds, Suffolk
Printed in Great Britain by
St Edmundsbury Press Ltd, Bury St Edmunds, Suffolk

97 98 99   5 4 3 2 1

1

Seen from the windows of Edinburgh's New Town, the northern sky in June is never completely dark. Bars of light traverse it long after midnight has passed. It was not quite eight o'clock when Dougal paused at the dining-room door of the top floor flat where he lived with Kieran. The quality of the evening light, its intensity of vibration as midsummer approached, did not concern him in the slightest. He barely glanced beyond the panes at the Fife hills, too busy scrutinizing the starched tablecloth for any trace of dirt or creasing, and checking the symmetry of wineglasses, cutlery and napkins at each of the ten places he had set. Ceramic baskets containing a tasteful selection of cut flowers stood at either end of the table. On the sideboard the red wines he had fixed upon after considerable hesitation were uncorked and breathing, ready to be poured. The bottles of white were neatly stacked on the lowest shelf of the fridge in the butler's pantry.

He was at a loss to explain why he should put himself through an ordeal of this kind. Only just past forty, already a senior partner in a prosperous city law firm, the days when formal dinners had been an obligatory part of his working life were long gone. He could afford to look back on their dreadfulness with rueful amusement. He had not come out until late in his thirties and had forced a longsuffering (and not infrequently lovesick) train of women friends to furnish him with the needed alibi on such occasions. The sex he had survived on then, if plentiful, was furtive and unsatisfactory. His life today was far less complicated, yet there were times when he accused himself of merely having exchanged one form of social servitude for another. Within an hour the candles would be ablaze and ten gay men would be seated round the table. The prospect, as always, filled him with trepidation.

He went back into the kitchen. Kieran was busy over the gas hob.

'They'll start arriving any minute now!' he spluttered. 'What are you doing, cooking?'

Kieran was unperturbed. Peering over his shoulder, Dougal saw that the saucepan he was stirring contained the most flawless of white sauces. He watched with fascination, as a delicate pink glow spread out from the centre and suffused the whole.

'What on earth is that?

'A *sauce aurore.*'

Kieran's facility with languages always made Dougal feel excluded.

'In other words?'

'A dawn sauce, as in Homer. You know, rosy fingers lighting up the eastern sky.'

His tones were slow and wondering, as if he were no less entranced than Dougal by the progress of the sauce.

'Remember the holiday we had in that castle near Carcassonne? You got sunstroke lying by the pool on the second day and had to spend the rest of the week in bed. It was really boring. I couldn't leave you in the house alone and there was absolutely nothing for me to do. So I persuaded Madame Aubert the house-keeper to come over and give me cooking lessons. She only charged four pounds an hour. It was so hot we both wore bathing suits. Quite a lady, that Madame Aubert. I think it crossed her mind to teach me something more than recipes but she didn't get the chance.

'This is for eating with fish. You have to skin ripe tomatoes, chop the pulp up as finely as you can, then stir them into the sauce. It's looking pretty good, don't you think?'

Dougal's attention had already wandered. He dried and tidied away the saucepans and utensils littering the draining board. Kieran was the more gifted cook of the two but he made a dread-ful mess in the kitchen. Dougal could not bear to run a dinner party unless everything was in the right place from the very start. He would even wash up between courses. He popped a pyrex dish into a wall cupboard and swung the door shut, then turned to gaze at his partner from behind. Kieran was delicately built. The hair at the nape of his neck was getting long and needed cutting. Dougal's eyes dropped to the backside he so much admired: neither too big nor yet too small. It was not sexual excitement, more a kind of proprietorial familiarity. I am happy now, he thought all of a sudden.

The doorbell rang.

'Bloody hell! It's not even eight o'clock yet!'

He picked up the entryphone then realized they were already climbing the stairs. It made him so angry when one of their neighbours forgot to shut the main door. Did no one other than himself appreciate the security risk? There was a scuffling of feet on the stone landing outside. Straightening his tie, he opened the door to find a bunch of huge orchids thrust right under his nose.

'Still fucking the Catholic, then?'

Dougal nearly dropped the orchids he was so appalled. Mark and Alan stepped across the threshold without waiting to be invited. Mark was Kieran's ex and invariably found a way of getting under Dougal's skin the moment they set eyes on one another.

He gave Alan his coat and sauntered off, humming, to see what Kieran was doing. Alan contemplated the lawyer with a mixture of compassion and derision.

'Where shall I put these?'

He was holding two coats now. Dougal gestured towards the spare bedroom and went to the butler's pantry to get a vase for the orchids. He resolved to keep out of the kitchen until more people had arrived.

The decoration of the bedroom, Alan observed, was as stunning as the rest of the flat. The pale blue wallpaper had undoubtedly been handprinted. The curtain material was Chinese in style, with peacocks strutting next to a pond and diminutive human figures beyond it laughing, playing instruments and singing. The light from a single lamp on one of the bedside tables caught the curtains at an angle, sending a golden sheen across them, like a faint dust haze.

'So what's on the menu?' asked Mark.

He had already found the bubbly in the fridge, opened a bottle and filled four glasses. Alan called in for his. Nobody thought to take one through to Dougal. Kieran took time off from his preparations to sip his wine. He enjoyed the atmosphere of mischief and transgression Mark invariably brought with him. The circumstances he lived in now were vastly different from the chilly bohemian room in southern Edinburgh he had shared with Mark several years before. He was familiar with Mark's scepticism concerning his translation to the New Town. The glint that entered Mark's eyes when they discussed it was compounded of irony and envy. Kieran was never quite sure which predominated.

'Watercress soup,' he began. 'Dougal made it. That reminds me, I'd better heat the tureen. Then there's baked monkfish with a French sauce.' He fixed a point on the ceiling as he concentrated on getting everything in the right order. 'Next comes a lemon sorbet, then a selection of salads. The main course is pork baked with plums and apples, served with roast potatoes and a julienne of carrots.'

'And the puddings?' Mark enquired.

He well knew puddings were Kieran's soft spot although, and he glanced at his waistline, he kept a very trim figure notwithstanding. Mark was convinced he should have been a dancer. And instead he was teaching Communication Studies in one of the new universities.

'That would be telling,' said Kieran, shaking a glass bottle with a dressing in it next to his ear and tilting his head, as if it could produce a musical note to inform him of its quality.

'He says these things deliberately to rile you,' said Alan, who had wandered into the dining-room.

Dougal had his back to him and was adjusting the orchids with the help of the reflection in the mirror above the sideboard. His heart was still pounding. The cheek of the man! He should have thrown the orchids in his face and shut the door on both of them.

Mark embodied several of the features he most disliked in gay men. He gelled his hair and, Dougal could have sworn, used make up. His cheeks were just a bit too tanned to be convincing. He was chief supervisor in a rainwear shop on Princes Street and could be seen raving it up every Friday night at one of the more respectable discotheques. Unable to act his age, frozen in a dream world from his early twenties. Alan, being an air steward, was away flying a lot of the time. If Dougal had been talking to Kieran,

Kieran would have commented, with his usual astuteness, that in the lawyer's eyes neither had a proper job, and would have asked him what a proper job involved. He might also have suggested that Mark's assiduity at the disco was in direct proportion to Alan's absences from home. Mark was not one to get a video and sit alone with a glass of wine in front of the television.

Dougal's silence had begun to embarrass Alan. He toyed with the idea of asking if he really *did* fuck Kieran. Acquainted with certain titbits hidden from Dougal, he was aware that not fucking had been a problem in Kieran's previous relationship. Mark's devil-may-care exterior was misleading. The nonchalance vanished once he got into bed. It's just as well we aren't into that, thought Alan. At any rate, Mark isn't.

Dougal was merely playing with the flowers to win himself more time to calm down. What incensed him was that the words Mark had greeted him with were true, but in defining something they soiled it, turning it into what it was not, or at least into what it would mean to the person who had said them.

He remembered the state Kieran had been in when they first got together, barely seven months after the final farewells with Mark. Dougal had found himself with a lot of repair work on his hands. Kieran automatically assumed that if they did not spend Friday night in each other's company, Dougal would be waking up next to another man on Saturday morning. He found it practically impossible to believe that, if Dougal told him he had to have dinner with his mother on Saturday night, then stay over and go to church with her on Sunday morning, that was exactly what he intended to do. It was as if Kieran had received a very powerful blow and still vibrated painfully from the impact. In those first months Dougal had had the clear sensation of tissue forming over a wound. Part of him resented the process because it was not a wound of his own making. He was constantly afraid something he might say or do would open it again. Thankfully that had not happened.

It was like protecting a young sapling so that it could grow straight and healthy. Dougal had a way with plants and longed for the time when they would have a garden. Odd, he reflected. He had never thought this was the kind of expertise coming out properly was going to demand of him.

He did indeed fuck a Catholic. Kieran had come to lunch at his mother's in Barnton on several occasions. Nothing was explained. To this day he honestly had no notion as to whether she guessed at their relationship. He could hear her voice saying:

'McLaverty. Kieran McLaverty from Glasgow. From Drumchapel.'

It had lifted on the last syllable but one, as she pronounced the name of a council housing estate which was nowhere near as infamous as she imagined. As if coming from Glasgow were not enough, Kieran's parents did not even own the house they lived in.

Kieran had not got past the hall at that point. She extended a limp hand towards him as she repeated his name. Dougal wanted to touch him on the shoulder to give him courage, then thought better of it. His mother had once had a cleaning woman who was Catholic. That was as far as her acquaintance with other religious communities went. The woman arrived one morning with a black eye inflicted by her husband the previous night and was dismissed on the spot. Mrs Hamilton had no desire to bring her accountant husband or their offspring into the proximity of similar dramas. The unremitting anger which was no doubt the cause of her digestive difficulties, and which sent her reaching for the port at three in the afternoon, even while Dougal was still at school, had never been allowed to ruffle the thoroughly Presbyterian calm and decorum of her household.

'Is this strictly an affair for couples?' Mark was asking Kieran in the kitchen

'By no means. Rory's bringing his latest trade along.'

Mark gave a low whistle. Kieran would never have spoken of 'trade' in conversation with Dougal. With Mark, he fell back into old habits almost without noticing.

'He was on the phone last night so I know the story. They clocked each other at the Festival Theatre in one of the intervals of *Don Giovanni*. When Rory walked into the pub at the end of the show, there he was. A Catalan, from Barcelona. He's been here since October taking a postgraduate qualification at the university. Much younger than Rory. Usual style. You know what an intellectual snob he is. He insists they converse in a mixture of Spanish and French even though the Catalan guy has perfectly good English. We'll be able to talk to him. Rory just wants to demonstrate what a model European he is.'

'Did you get the other guy's name?'

'Why? How many Catalans have you slept with?'

Mark ignored the provocation.

'Ramon. Ring any bells?'

'Didn't Rory live in Barcelona for a while? Or am I getting him mixed up with somebody else?'

'No, you're right. He taught English there for five or six years after he graduated. Then he came home and started working as a journalist. Apparently they have long discussions about opera. They're both mad about *Don Giovanni.*'

The doorbell rang again. Mark dashed to the entryphone, beating Dougal to it by a narrow margin. Behaves as if he owns the place, thought Dougal, but with an inward smile, for his anger had evaporated.

'Who is it?'

'Gavin somebody,' said Mark and returned to the kitchen.

2

He awoke. He was on a train. It was moving. He panicked and tried to get up but his body was still numb with sleep. The woman sitting opposite him looked alarmed. The train pulled to a halt, throwing the weight of his body forwards. The pattern of raindrops on the windowpane resembled tears. Beyond the glass a sign said 'Girvan'. Doors slammed, and again the train lurched into motion. All he could see was dull moorland with stunted trees dotted across it and, approaching them from out at sea, a veil of rain. They must be heading for Stranraer to connect with the ferry for Larne. Last night came flooding back to him. The letter, packing a case, Glasgow at half past six in the morning. Make it not have happened, a voice inside him pleaded. Let this not be real.

The woman made a feint of reading a novel she produced from her handbag while observing Gavin's features closely from the corner of her eye. An interesting face, she thought, attractive enough, dark hair and beard, a fine, strong, slightly hooked nose. The lips were a bit thin and ungenerous. He looked shy, the kind of person who would avoid small talk with strangers. It was a pity. She felt ready for a chat.

'Here's the tea trolley at last.'

Aidan had written the letter. Gavin found it on the dresser in the hall when he got home from the hospital. He had lost touch quite deliberately with the people in Dublin, even with Dermot and Shevaun. And now that old world was lunging violently back at him.

'A coffee. Yes, with milk and sugar. Aren't you having anything?'

He registered her question, startled, and ordered a cup of tea and a piece of cake. The cellophane his slice had been wrapped in slipped noiselessly to the floor as he munched, dropping crumbs and raisins onto his trousers. He pressed the back of his head into the coarse upholstery. For this not to have happened, he repeated to himself. For it not to be real.

'We're running late.'

She was determined.

'Between twenty minutes and half an hour. I do hope they hold the ferry for us!'

'How long do we have before it leaves?'

'Only about a quarter of an hour. Mind you, if I have to wait till the next one, it's no real problem. I'm stopping in Belfast tonight. Will you be doing the same?'

The intonation of the question was casual, but she was gazing at him with particular intensity. Gavin's eyes widened and he fumbled for his ticket. The nightmare got its final confirmation. He stuffed it back into his coat pocket.

'I'm bound for Dublin, actually.'

He looked straight at her for the first time and asked, not without a touch of malice:

'Off to Belfast for a holiday break?'

She smiled. At last she had permission to talk.

'I'm going to visit an old schoolfriend in County Wicklow. But I have an aunt in Belfast and want to see her while I'm passing through. She's an old dear who doesn't get many visitors. It's not as bad in Belfast as everybody says. My aunt lives in a pros- perous part of the city and they never have any trouble. Are you going on directly to Dublin?'

'Yes, yes, that's right . . .'

'On business?'

Again the eyes grew keener. He glanced at her as if she were mad, spluttered and gazed out at the sea. Recovering himself after a moment, he smiled and answered:

'You must excuse me. I'm not properly wakened yet. Got hardly any sleep last night.'

Having terminated the conversation with such satisfying ease he folded his arms, closed his eyes, and started remembering. Surprised you weren't there, the letter said. Didn't the family inform you? I presumed you would have heard one way or another. Otherwise I would have got in touch at once. A small

13

village north of Sligo. Nasty way to go. Maybe we ought to have expected an ending like this.

They had given him a Catholic funeral. What a hypocritical family, reflected Gavin. He was unsure about Aidan's views on religion. Aidan adapted effortlessly to whatever circles he encountered, finding it worth his while to lavish charm on even the most boorish of clergymen. It made no difference whether they were Catholics or Church of Ireland. He had even managed to get into the good graces of Colin's mother, a feat which had always proved beyond Gavin's capacities.

If he didn't watch he would begin to cry, here, on the train, on a Thursday morning, in the midst of a pack of strangers. Breathing regularly, and trying to feel anger rather than pain, he opened his eyes for an instant. The woman opposite caught his glance, snapped her book shut and replaced it in her handbag.

'Have to look sharpish if we're not going to miss that ferry. We'll be there in ten minutes.'

A guard was passing. Gavin grabbed the edge of his sleeve.

'Don't worry, sir, the boat'll wait for you. And when you get into Belfast you have two hours till the Dublin train leaves. Station's other side of the city. I'd advise you to get a taxi across. You know what things are like there.'

Of course he couldn't shake her off. And to be honest, he didn't really want to. Her chatter was preferable to the company of his own thoughts. There would be plenty of time for those on the train to Dublin. The cafeteria filled up quickly, as the boat shuddered round the point and breasted St George's Channel. The popping of beer cans being opened and the acrid smell of stewing tea accompanied their conversation. Her name was Desirée Healy and she lived in Bearsden. Four years ago a small inheritance had allowed her to abandon teaching and devote herself full-time to writing romantic fiction. She was now making a discreet living under a name she initially refused to disclose. Her ease and fluidity of self-revelation amused and relaxed him, accustomed as he was to cajoling tongue-tied children cowed by illness and the hospital routine. Soon enough Desirée was explaining the plot of her current project.

'I wanted to try something different this time, not quite so conventional, although my agent is uneasy about it and keeps trying to put me off. The heroine is a mature woman who has lost her husband in a climbing accident in the Cairngorms. After the funeral she starts examining all his papers and belongings in the house in Edinburgh. She discovers that her husband was a spy but it takes her rather longer to realize he was a double agent. MI5 have set a man to watch upon her . . .'

At this point the first set of love scenes intervened. Desirée was no prude. Having kindled smouldering passions in the breasts of mysterious but promising suitors, her heroines invariably conceded everything and faced the consequences. She disposed of a limited but highly effective vocabulary to describe the groans and panting which accompanied these surrenders and the sensations they provoked. Somehow she thought Gavin would find this aspect of her work less interesting.

Looking up, she saw that his mind had wandered off again. Across from them, a group of football supporters broke intermittently into raucous song. An older man swung his beer can from side to side while another supplied percussion with his teaspoon and a saucer.

'You still haven't told me why you're going to Dublin,' she said, moving closer so he could hear her words above the din.

'It's to do with a funeral,' said Gavin. 'Or rather, the funeral's already happened and I'm going over . . .'

His voice tailed off, as he asked himself exactly why he was going over.

'I do hope it was no one you were close to,' said Desirée.

She had already noted the absence of a wedding ring.

'Not for some time, no. A chap called Colin.'

Gavin would never have dared name Colin in the hospital. Something in the woman attracted and irritated him at the same time. He added, almost without pausing:

'We were lovers for five years.'

Desirée rose. The fork she had used to eat her steak pie and chips clattered to the floor. She was a little breathless.

'Can I get you some more tea?'

She made her way gingerly to the counter. There was a swell coming from the sea. She needed time to think.

She had met gay people before now. She was pretty sure her agent in London was, and during her first trip southwards two months earlier she had watched, out of the corner of her eye, a group of men camping things up in an absolutely unequivocal way at a literary party. Then she experienced a mixture of fascination and repulsion. Now she was trying to decide whether or not she should feel insulted.

Turning round with the cups in her hands, she saw the empty table. She need not have worried. He had taken the opportunity to slip into the men's toilet. When he returned, she was sipping the boiling liquid with furrowed brows.

'Do you always blurt things out so boldly?'

He looked alarmed. He wondered if she had been trying to chat him up. He was hopeless at noticing these things.

'Go on telling me about your novel.'

'I've got the ending clear,' she continued stalwartly. 'Of course they get married, it's obligatory. The problem is how to wind the spy thing up. Which side they choose . . .'

'Are you married?' Gavin interposed.

'I almost was. We were at teacher training college together. He married someone else in the end. We still meet up from time to time and it's perfectly amicable.'

Encouraged by his preference for personal topics, she hazarded: 'How old was your friend?'

No dangers here, thought Gavin.

'Thirty-two.'

'What did he die of?'

Be considerate, he told himself.

'A heart attack.'

'At thirty-two?'

'He smoked a lot.'

Gavin was a hopeless liar and they both burst out laughing. A voice from the tannoy warned drivers to rejoin their cars on the garage deck, while foot passengers got their luggage ready. Soon Larne, with its peculiar air of a beleaguered holiday resort, its mixture of frivolity and tension, of arriving and not arriving in a different country, was behind them. Their compartment was nearly empty, the nearest people at a safe enough distance not to overhear their conversation.

'Tell me about him,' said Desirée. 'It'd do you good.'

'But I hardly know you. I don't want to embarrass you.'

16

'Just because I'm not married doesn't mean I'm ... doesn't mean I haven't...'

Desirée couldn't find the words, and Gavin laughed again.

He had met Colin in Glasgow, at a stage when he was at last beginning to enjoy his work in the hospital, to feel he had reached a plateau beyond the periodic panicking of the early years. Although he spent so much time within those walls, he again found space and energy for interests he had abandoned when a student.

That was how he came to find himself at a soirée in a Kersland Street flat one Sunday night. A mixture of Irish and Scottish people were present. An Irish harper and a poet had just finished a sponsored tour of the Highlands and were hanging on for a few days before returning home, guests of a lecturer named Sam. Sam's wife Nadia was a nursing sister and had invited Gavin along. He had published a couple of poems in a student magazine but couldn't remember whether he had told her this or not. The sitting-room, which had a huge bay window, was crammed with people. The furniture had been pushed up against the walls. Sam's concern, according to Nadia, was that the drink would release a flow of Republican oratory, antagonizing the cultural bigwigs he had encouraged to come through from Edinburgh. In the event, the atmosphere proved peaceable enough. About half past ten a space was cleared, and the readings started.

The more established figures read before the younger ones. Gavin could still remember a slim, pallid girl with almost no breasts and a mass of intricately plaited, hennaed hair who looked cold even in that stifling room. Gesturing wildly, she struck sculpted poses during brief silences which lulled her listeners into thinking she had ended.

Colin came next. Gavin fell for him there and then. He read a sequence of love poems without looking up so much as once from the smudgily typed sheets. Gavin could tell they were to another man, though they were sufficiently understated for a less attuned listener to overlook the fact. Even then he experienced a mixture of desire and jealousy. Who had Colin felt these things for? How had he achieved so much so fast? Were they projections, in that poet's way of knowing things without needing to live through them? Colin had an unmistakably Irish accent but he did not look out of place in those surroundings. Gavin knew the strong admixture of Irish that Glasgow blood contains. When he first visited Dublin, he realized that he was already acquainted with certain physical types from western Scotland, but diluted and adulterated, whereas here the lineaments were starker, purer, with a tight-boned, fragile beauty that alarmed him. Colin had a scattering of freckles and deep red pools, like shifting spotlights, on either cheek.

The poems were good and were enthusiastically received. A tense excitement took root in Gavin's bowels. His distraction from the conversations he pretended to engage in verged on rudeness. Then, quite unexpectedly yet naturally, he found himself in a group that included Colin. When it broke up, Colin hung on, wanting to be spoken to. Gavin was at a loss for what to say. Colin told him he looked like his cousin, hadn't they met before, they must have met before. They didn't separate, and the excitement became Gavin's daily and nightly bread for many months thereafter.

Some, but not all of this he told Desirée. Belfast was quick and ugly. Menacing soldiers touted rifles as Gavin's taxi circled the city centre, hedged in with road blocks beyond which stretched pedestrian tunnels of crudely matched planks topped with barbed wire. The familiarity of the shops, the buses and the language made it all the more grotesque.

He must have dozed off before the Dublin train pulled out, for he awoke to find the border behind him already. There was hardly anybody on the train, though he recognized a face or two from the ferry. It was early evening and they were just coming into Dundalk. The setting sun slipped down below cloud cover and illuminated the streets of the town, where a random cyclist hovered like a nonchalant fly, casting shimmering, watery shadows. The flatness and the silence of the landscape soothed him at last, calming his morning fears.

There was barely half an hour to go before they got to Dublin. He took his coat from the luggage rack above and extracted an envelope from the inside breast pocket. As he did so, a slip of paper with Desirée's address on it dropped to the floor. He picked it up and crumpled it into a ball, then paused and smiled.

18

Smoothing it out again, he read it meditatively, as if it were a message, folded it carefully and stored it in his wallet. Next he teased the contents from the envelope. He had intended to look through them earlier in the day, but had lacked the courage. Or rather, Desirée had relieved him of the need to find out whether he did or not. The envelope was dog-eared at the corners and gradually splitting open at the sides. Gavin made three separate piles on the table in front of him, just the way he sorted reports and mail on his desk in the hospital. He had a quick look round to ensure he was not observed. No one was even at an angle where they could see what he was doing.

He took a paper from the pile to his right and unfolded it, averting his gaze as if some winged creature were going to fly out from inside it and sting him in the eyes. It was a hotel bill. Neatly sheltered in its folds were two train tickets, in a style British Rail had not issued for many years now. Glasgow to Balloch Pier, they said. August 15th 1987. Off-peak return.

He replaced them and took two photographs from the central pile. The first showed Colin and himself leaning against the parapet of a bridge. It came up just above their waists and was made of roughly matched and mortared blocks of stone. A hillside dotted with olive trees could be seen in the background. Aidan had taken the shot on their second Italian holiday. Gavin had never taken to Aidan. For ten days they had shared a flat with him and his sister and the situation provoked constant quarrels between Gavin and Colin. Superficially at least, the reasons were social. Gavin found Aidan more English than Irish. Born just on the outskirts of Dublin, he had attended an English public school, then Oxford. What Gavin perceived as the insinuating arrogance of his manner needled him unbearably. Native courtesy prevented him from challenging a friend's friend openly, so he took his frustrations out on Colin instead, in private.

The second photograph was of a room in the Glasgow flat where Gavin still lived. It had been redecorated, and on the rare occasions when he took the photograph out, the old colours came as a shock to him. A party was in full flow to celebrate Colin finishing his Ph.D. Meg was there, and Gillian, Tom and Mike, a couple Gavin had known for years, as well as one or two colleagues from the hospital who knew he was gay. Some punky friends of Colin's could be seen too, along with people from the BBC he had been cultivating for some time, in the hope of eventually getting work there.

He shuffled the papers together and squeezed them back into the envelope without taking anything from the third pile. He knew what was at the bottom of it. Right now, such a long time after, he could visualize the page with Colin's handwriting, curiously awkward and deformed in that last year. Certain phrases had churned round in his head for so many months he did not need to read them to remember. His memory might even have altered them. 'Sense of common failure . . . unable to offer you anything better than this . . . much simpler . . . dearest.' The suburbs of Dublin swallowed the train up as he snapped his suitcase shut on the envelope, laying it crossways before him on the table.

He found himself alone when the crowd at the end of the platform cleared. Those who were to be met had been met, the others had hurried off for taxis or in the direction of the bus stop. Then he saw two figures coming from a side entrance. The halflight still concealed their faces. One carried a baby and the other, leading a small child by the hand, fell behind and turned to urge it on.

Two children! Time had certainly passed. As they came up, Dermot smiled and stuck out his hand. Shevaun shifted the baby to her other arm and peered critically into Gavin's face.

'So it took this to bring you back to us,' she said.

'Leave him alone, Shevaun,' said her husband. 'He's had a long day.'

'I always said that little runt wasn't worth a farthing. You were wasting your time with him and you're wasting it again now.'

'Shevaun, will you shut *up*?'

Gavin said hello to the little boy.

'How old's the baby?'

'Seven months.'

'Letting you sleep?'

'She's heaven compared to her brother.'

They reached the car, a slightly less battered, differently coloured version of the one Gavin had last seen them with. He got into the front seat while Dermot clambered into the back

20

with the children. Shevaun revved violently and the exhaust pipe gave a clatter as if eager to get going.

'It was pretty late when I phoned last night.'

'You sounded shattered. Had you just got the news?'

'We'd have told you if we'd had an address to contact,' Shevaun broke in, swerving suddenly to the right. There was nothing between the seats to plug the safety belt into. Gavin clutched it to his crotch, as if it could offer some protection in that position. It didn't seem worth explaining that his address was the same as ever.

'A letter from Aidan. Not the kind of courtesy you would expect from him.'

'He's not as bad as either of you make out. He's all right basically.'

'Yes, but I don't see the point of coming now. After the funeral, I mean, when it's all over and done with. That is, we're delighted to see you and all that . . .'

The little boy had finished his sugar stick and, as his father proved unable to produce another one, broke in with a deafening howl at this point. Shevaun swore copiously and wrenched the wheel to the right another time, then swerved again so that they came to an abrupt halt inches from a garage door whose red paint was peeling off. Gavin peered through the darkness at a semi-detached house behind an untidy garden. He extracted himself with difficulty from the front seat. It turned out that the little boy had been exhausted. Two hours later the children were soundly bedded and the meal over. Gavin wiped a last couple of dishes then Dermot turned the sound down on the television. He lit a cigarette and scanned the Scotsman's face with a kind of worried detachment. Shevaun, who had poured three whiskies, flumped into an armchair which received her with a resonant pyoing.

'How's the centre going then?

'Tough,' she answered. 'Tough, as usual. Only one angry hubbie called round yesterday.'

She outlined a bruise on her cheek which Gavin had failed to notice.

'Worse for your lot, though. All the places keep closing down.'

'I didn't come for entertainment.'

21

Dermot sipped at his whisky, letting it run delicately over his tongue. 'So tell us why you did come then.'

Gavin's eyes widened. 'That's a question I find hard to answer. Something about endings, maybe.'

'Suicide's not an end. Not even a way out. It just looks like that before you try.'

'How did he do it?'

Gavin looked to Shevaun. He knew she would be unlikely to sweeten the pill.

'A little number à la Virginia Woolf. Stones in pockets. Slip into river below weir.'

'And when?'

Dermot looked above his head and calculated.

'Thursday evening today. Funeral was Sunday. Must have been a week last Tuesday.'

'How much did Aidan tell you?' put in Shevaun, with a touch of irritation.

'Nothing detailed. I think he was a bit embarrassed. He may have suspected I knew and had preferred to ignore it. In that case his letter would have struck him as a breach of decorum.'

'Aidan's doing really well now. Directing commercials and with a feature film on the stocks.'

'I want to meet him.'

Dermot whistled softly.

'Major reconciliation scene. He and Colin hardly saw each other these last months.'

'Same goes for us,' added Shevaun. 'Mind you, I couldn't put up with Colin at the best of times.'

'Who else should I see?'

'Depends what you want to know.'

'Are you here on some kind of protracted wake?'

Dermot couldn't help smiling, and Gavin smiled too. Shevaun was beginning to wind down at last.

'Last time I saw Colin was four months ago, end of February. I went into Connolly's with a couple of friends and there he was, serving behind the bar.'

Gavin sat up.

'What became of the publishing job? He said there was a publishing job waiting for him.'

'Is that what he told you?'

Shevaun looked puzzled.

'You forget, dear friend, that we know nothing about how or why or where or when you two broke up. All we know is Colin is back in Dublin, hitting the bottle in a big way, and you just drop out of our lives.'

'Was he drinking that heavily in Glasgow?'

'From time to time. It came in bouts. Then he'd get back to writing and he seemed to forget about it. So you spoke to him in Connolly's?'

'I tried,' Shevaun muttered, 'as you might say, to engage him in conversation. The place was packed. He shouted one or two things back, then gave me a phone number on a piece of paper.'

There was a moment's silence.

'And when you phoned?'

Shevaun looked at Dermot, then back to Gavin.

'It was about a month later. A chap called Frank replied. American accent. Said Colin had left the week before. He'd gone off to Sligo.'

'Anyone else before Frank?'

'Not that we know of. But I told you, we hardly saw him.'

'You've still got the number?'

She nodded.

'I want to drive up there. Can I hire a car tomorrow?'

She looked at him as if he were mad.

'It'll cost the earth. We can get you a loan of Mike's. He always had a soft spot for you.'

'How many days have you got?'

Gavin smiled, as if admitting the craziness of the whole expedition.

'Three. I'm on duty Sunday night.'

'Then maybe we should turn in. You've got a lot on tomorrow.'

He overslept the following morning. The central heating had broken down and a damp chill settled on the eiderdown in the spare room. At a distance he vaguely followed the clatter of breakfast downstairs, Dermot's farewells as he set off for school, then the children's intermittent voices and a conclusive bang of the door as Shevaun took them out for a walk followed by the shopping. Hopping on the cold linoleum, Gavin wrapped an old dressing gown round him – as usual, he had come away without his pyjamas – and staggered pensively downstairs, scrunching his toes into the pile of the dusty carpet. Shevaun had left him half a grapefruit, cornflakes and milk on the kitchen table. The toaster was still switched on and beside it was a piece of paper with three phone numbers: Aidan, Frank and Michael.

He decided to wear a tie after all. It made him feel more on top of things. Gavin squinted at himself in the bathroom mirror, tightened the knot, centred it meticulously, then dusted the light dandruff off his shoulders. No one replied at Frank's number. At Michael's, a woman's voice came on the phone (had he gone straight?), was pleasant, and gave Gavin a faculty number. Now for Aidan.

'Hello. Aidan Sharp speaking.'

Gavin's lip quivered as if he were about to cry.

'Hello?'

'Aidan, Gavin here.'

'Good God! Are you phoning from Glasgow?'

'No, I'm in Dublin. Thanks for the letter. I got it on Wednesday night.'

'Was I right to send it? It struck me as a bit of a long shot.'

'Perfectly right, perfectly right. I want to talk to you.'

'You're in luck. I'm free for lunch today. There's an Italian place two blocks up from the post office on O'Connell Street. Pizzaiola they call it.'

'OK. What time?'

'Ten past one.'

'Ten past one it is, then.'

Gavin got there early and waited outside. He saw Aidan coming and recognized the languid, slightly loping gait and the quizzical smile. Blond hair with a gentle wave, the same narrow hips and stylish cut to the clothes. Just a touch tighter round the mouth. He kissed Gavin on the lips then led the way in. The lasagne was excellent.

'I still wonder whether I did the right thing.'

'Such scruples are out of character,' mused Gavin.

'Ah, but I like you. Always have done. Wish you could say the same of me.'

24

Gavin said nothing and drank some more wine.

'I thought you would come. In fact, I knew you would. But I'd still like to know just what you plan to do.'

'I don't really know myself. Who was Frank?'

Aidan raised an eyebrow.

'Rather unpleasant character. Got together with Colin early last autumn. Colin had to leave his lodgings before Christmas, so he moved in. Frank chucked him out in March.'

'I thought Colin had decided to go to Sligo.'

'No, that's not exactly true. He came round to my place. I put him up for a couple of days.'

'What sort of state was he in?'

'These will give you some idea.'

Aidan pulled out a bundle of jotters with larger sheets of paper wrapped round them. The sheets were the typescript of a radio programme. Colin's awkward, angular script careered across the unused side of each one.

'You carry them around with you?' asked Gavin.

Aidan laughed.

'I live just round the corner. You should remember. I had time to pop back and get them. You can return them to me some time over the next few days.'

Salad came, and escalopes, and then a sweet.

'He was writing better and better,' said Aidan, 'the better he got at destroying himself.'

'Sounds a bit romantic to me,' said Gavin.

'But it's true. He had it written into him like the end of a computer programme.'

'Nice way to absolve us all of responsibility.'

'That's something we can settle in private, each with his own conscience,' Aidan said, carefully and without hostility. He looked up again. 'Yours can be clear at any rate.'

'It's not my conscience I came about.' Gavin smiled wrily. 'I suppose I could always accuse myself of driving him away.'

There was a silence. I was right, thought Gavin. We really have nothing to say to one another. Aidan pulled a notebook from his pocket and began to scribble in it.

'The town is called Scarron and the place he worked was the Cross Hotel. Proprietor a certain Jack Hart. I've already told him you'd be coming. Mention my name. He'll fill you in on what happened. It's roughly a three hours' drive. Got a car?'

'I have a loan,' said Gavin, although he had not yet consulted Mike. 'Thanks, Aidan.'

'You'll report to me how you get on?'

It was half a question, half an instruction. Gavin reached for the bill but Aidan had already put his hand on it. Their glances met, tingling with a familiar aggressiveness.

'Why did you always like me?'

'Maybe I believed I knew what you would do, in most situations,' said Aidan, surprised at his own honesty.

An irritation he remembered from the past came over him when he got through to Mike at work. There were times when Shevaun's mothering verged perilously on interference. She had already been in touch. Yes, he was welcome to have the car and even keep it over the weekend if he wanted to. Unfortunately Mike had no time to see Gavin today. But if he called in at the lodge in Trinity he could pick up an envelope with the keys in it. The porter would show him to the car in the college car park.

Mike's kindness was such that Gavin nearly felt ashamed. He reflected that he should not have drunk wine at lunch. Being so far from Glasgow and workaday routines had led him to forget he might need all his wits about him. He stopped off in Bewley's for two black coffees before collecting the car. The memories the place revived were extremely painful to him. He had found it easier to forget those periods when things between himself and Colin were OK. Now he remembered how they had taken refuge here one afternoon, the first time Colin had brought him home, to muse over his family's awfulness and the peculiar obsessions of his mother. They had laughed uproariously and Gavin had thought, with a certainty that filled him with bitterness in retrospect, he is coming out of it now, he is moving away from them towards something more sane, less suffocating. He was wrong.

Finding his way around Dublin was as bewildering as it had been on his previous visits. It took him more than forty minutes to drive back to Dermot and Shevaun's. He was relieved to discover nobody at home. He left a note for Shevaun telling her he would be back in time for the evening meal next day, then threw the few things he needed for an overnight stay into a tattered holdall which poked out from underneath the bed he had slept in.

Once he had left the city behind, the dreary, flat perspectives of the central Irish plain made the journey appear endless in prospect. He realized how tired he was and, just to be safe, stopped several times in the hope he would doze off. It was impossible, but the pauses helped him keep his concentration. The signposting was as infuriating as ever. He could make little connection between the out of date road atlas Mike carried in the car and the route he was attempting to follow. Soon enough he left the major road behind and time and again had to stop at a crossroads and get out of the car to look at the old-fashioned signposts. Even then it was a puzzle to work out which direction he should take. Why did he find this journey so difficult? He wondered if fear of what he might face at its end made it an odyssey for him.

He reached Scarron in the early evening. It was south of Sligo, at some distance from the hills, in a stretch of bogland, a cross-roads town with ramshackle buildings lining either side of the street, like drunken soldiers unexpectedly summoned to parade. The hotel was set a little back from the road in a muddy court-yard. It had obviously seen better days. Behind it was a field and, at the end of the field, a stream, broad and shallow. The bridge over the stream stood near the crossroads and was pre-sumably the reason for Scarron's being there in the first place. How could Colin have managed to drown himself in such an insignificant stretch of water?

The interior of the hotel was what its exterior led one to expect. A fair number of locals had already gathered in the bar to the left of the reception area. The carpet was wearing thin and severely in need of a wash. Perhaps the odour that pervaded all three floors was due to it. Mr Hart was absent on business and not expected back until mid morning of the following day. Gavin panicked briefly. What was the point of stopping there if the person who could tell him about Colin's end was absent? How would he get through the evening and the night of waiting that lay ahead? He got a grip on himself soon enough, however, and checked in without divulging anything about the reason for his visit. He was forced to take a double room at a price that struck him as exorbitant. Luckily it was possible to pay by credit card and, on this basis, he ordered dinner in the dining room. His bedroom had one long, low window the ragged curtains did not fully cover over. The washhand basin was chipped and yellowing and, when he ran the hot water, the whole plumbing system set to cranking and chugging in order to cough up sufficient liquid for him to rinse his hands and face. The sheets were clean, though. They must have had good weather during the last few days, for the fabric smelt of sun and open air and had clearly been dried on the green behind the hotel. He could see the stream at an angle from his window. Already it exercised an odd pull upon him, as if it knew secrets about Colin he had only the vaguest hopes of recovering.

There were three other diners that evening, commercial sales-men from Dublin who, he gathered, met up here on a regular basis to relieve the loneliness of their repeated circuits. They eyed him suspiciously, as if fearful of having to make some token friendly gesture in his direction. He was only too glad to be left to his own devices. They got stuck into their beer and fish and chips, forgetting his presence soon enough. Gavin realized he was afraid to go to bed. He went into the bar after his meal and ordered a glass of wine. The request was met with astonishment. Eventually some sickly sweet Liebfraumilch arrived and he was able to hide himself away in a corner. He scrutinized the place repeatedly, imagining Colin at the bar, cleaning up once the drinkers had left, going to the front door and looking out on to the dreary street that offered the only possibility of escape. What had been going through his head? Gavin remembered the jotters. Maybe he could use them to read himself asleep.

Half an hour later he was in bed, having propped the single bedside lamp that worked at a teetering angle, so that it shed its light into his lap. Colin had used a black biro to write with. Gavin leafed through the pages: poems, diary entries, plans for short stories. There was no way he could get through it all that evening. The poems were excellent, even better than the ones Colin had been writing at the time they parted. He was moving towards stricter forms, sonnets with perfect syllable counts, unrhymed or assonating. Again and again he had managed a closing line with a startling, lapidary quality, as if everything that went before had

28

been a preparation for it, a structure it could rest upon so as to crown the whole with irresistible force.

Reluctantly, he began to scan the diary entries, in reverse order. The last was dated only two weeks earlier. Colin had killed himself not long after writing it. Gavin was able to conceive of suicide as an unpremeditated act of desperation. The jotters told a very different story. Colin found image after image to speak of his gradually hardening resolve. It was a seed sown inside him many years before, a foetus taking shape in his belly that would destroy him when it came to light. He even speculated about the father and mother of this deadly child, for he could not recognize it as his own and insisted that he carried it as a surrogate, that it was alien to him and that for this reason he would not survive its birth. He had written a quotation from a Russian poetess in big letters at the top of one page. 'For a year now,' it said, 'I have been trying death on like a garment.'

Gavin could not read any further. He put out the light and turned on to one side, touching his sex as if it could offer him protection from the dark, as if it carried an assurance of life, of his own ability to continue living amidst so much pain and darkness. There was no way he could have masturbated, although that might have comforted him. Now that Colin was dead he felt neither compassion nor exasperation but a kind of blinding fear. He almost believed the step Colin had taken invested him with a power that could be exercised from beyond the grave. What if his spirit were there in the room with Gavin, eyeing him from a corner, slipping along the walls or suspended from the ceiling? What did it feel towards him? Was Colin's spirit angry at Gavin for having failed to protect him? Protect him from what? Had Gavin really failed him? What were his responsibilities in this affair?

This was the point at which Gavin remembered the angel. He had had a conventionally Presbyterian upbringing. Angels had never been discussed at home or at Sunday school. But the church his family frequented every week had a pair of stained glass windows on the eastern wall and, when boredom with the sermon threatened to overwhelm him, Gavin used to gaze up at them and invent stories about the figures he could see there. There was St Andrew with his diagonal cross; a Glasgow merchant distributing beneficence to the poor; a personification of Charity, children thronging at her knees, her breasts enveloped chastely in a billowing fabric that barely allowed their shape to be discerned; a preaching Minister, perhaps one of the Covenanting heroes from the persecution days; and, inexplicably, crowning them all, one single angel with frizzy golden hair, a red hairband and wings tinged delicately pink.

Until Gavin was seven he had shared a bedroom with his older brother. Then they moved from their tenement flat to a larger house with its own entrance, a staircase in the hall and a garden to front and back. His parents expected him to be delighted at having a room for his own use. Instead he was forlorn. All through the first year he experienced great difficulty in getting to sleep, so used was he to his brother's snoring and to hearing that body's shifting through the night, the barely perceptible rustle of the sheet and blankets settling repeatedly around it. On his own, he felt immobilized by a silence only he could break. All his movements took on a momentous quality, as if they were challenges to the overarching darkness that risked provoking punishment.

The angel came to his rescue. He could not recall when the idea had first occurred to him. It might have been about four o'clock in the morning, for he remembered waking and being unable to get back to sleep. And he had decided to visualize the angel, standing at the foot of his bed, the wings no longer folded tranquilly behind its shoulders but vast, outstretched, like the tufted, moving banks of cloud so familiar to him from the skies of Glasgow. They wafted across him. He imagined he could feel their tickling passage right above his nose. The angel never spoke but it breathed as it gazed down upon him.

Its eyes had none of the piercing quality of human eyes. They did not bore through him or trouble him. In fact, they released a kind of energy that flowed into his body, starting somewhere just above his nose and trickling down in warm, leisurely eddies until it reached his fingertips and warmed his toes.

And now, in a dingy double bedroom of a provincial Irish hotel, in a place he would never have visited of his own choice, one he was at a loss to explain Colin's presence in, even more his death there, he turned to the angel for protection. It made

30

him laugh that he could visualize it so clearly. Not quite twenty years had passed. It had not aged. The wings were just as huge, the protection they provided just as trustworthy.

3

The magic worked so well that he was late for breakfast. As he passed by the reception area, the young man seated there told him Mr Hart had returned the night before, not long after twelve, much sooner than expected.

'What was it you wanted to discuss with him?'

'It's a personal matter, actually. Rather delicate. Can I see him after breakfast?'

Mr Hart was an Englishman with a blustering style that did not conceal an air of being marooned among incomprehensible natives, whose ways left him perplexed despite all his attempts to fathom them. As he was ushered into the office, Gavin found it easy to imagine a background for him. He was probably a stockbroker who had taken early retirement or been made redundant, had invested his funds in this outlandish place and was coming to the gradual, chill realization that he had walked into a tight corner from which there was no easy escape. He decided that Mrs Hart, if there had been one, had not accompanied her spouse on his mad venture. Had she died? Or deserted him? His unkempt shock of hair and shoddy jacket were eloquent of a lack of feminine attention. Gavin felt almost sorry for the man as soon as he mentioned Colin. His rotund, moon-like face clouded over.

'You've no idea of the commotion that poor fellow caused,' he said. 'My own discomfort has been the least of it. I've had a procession of people trailing all the way up here over the last ten days, not to mention the inquest. It's almost as if he had been a saint and they were looking for relics. What was your connection with him? You aren't Irish, if I'm not mistaken?'

His tone was suddenly suspicious. Did he have any inkling about Colin's sexual inclinations? Gavin wondered for a moment if he could be a clan member himself. That might explain Mrs

Hart's defection, although not his choice of exile. Any illicit sex that might be available in Scarron would undoubtedly be of the conventional variety. Gavin had prepared a careful answer for this question.

'I'm one of his Scottish cousins. Unfortunately none of the relatives over there managed to make it to the funeral. I'm kind of representing them. I was extremely upset when we got the news,' (Gavin's voice gave a treacherous dip at this point) 'so I decided to come over and see for myself where it happened.'

'Not quite two months, that's how long he spent here. I took him on in March. There isn't a lot to tell. All I know I passed on to that fancy fellow who arrived from Dublin, the one who works in films. Can't remember his name . . .'

'Aidan,' Gavin murmured.

'Yes, something like that. He mentioned you might be coming, but he said nothing about Scottish cousins. Anyway, the whole business has certainly cast a blight on my life. Not that I have any reason to feel guilty. The lad gave no indication to me of what was on his mind. And he was perfectly well treated by everybody here, make no mistake about that.'

'When did you notice he was missing?' Gavin asked.

'He should have been cleaning up the bar and getting it ready for opening at noon. Nobody realized anything odd was going on until a couple of customers wandered into the kitchen and asked why the bar door was still locked. I was away at the time myself. You see, I try to round out the earnings from here by doing deals in antiques from the older houses in the area. You'd be amazed at some of the things I've managed to find . . .'

'And did he do it that morning,' Gavin broke in, 'or the previous night?'

'I just don't know. I suppose nobody ever will. It never occurred to us to think of suicide, even when they found the body bobbing in the water next to the weir, late that afternoon.'

'How could it have been bobbing? I thought he put stones in his pockets!'

'Who told you that?'

'The people I stayed with the other night in Dublin,' answered Gavin, privately cursing Shevaun.

Mr Hart looked perplexed.

'The stream's so shallow,' persisted Gavin. 'How did he manage to drown in it?'

'All he had to do was walk down to the stretch above the weir. It's deep enough there. And the poor bugger couldn't swim.'

Of course, thought Gavin. How could I forget? Somehow this was much worse than the stones. They showed determination, while he could not get the idea out of his head that, once in the water, Colin had had second thoughts. The image of him floundering there, suddenly convinced that he wanted to live, was more painful than he could bear. That's you, he told himself. You're attributing your own will to live to him. He didn't have that. Death was what he wanted.

'We thought it was an accident,' Mr Hart went on, 'until we found the letter.'

'A letter? He left a letter?'

Mr Hart nodded and said nothing. In an odd way he enjoyed Gavin's suspense. Perhaps repeated telling of these circumstances offered a kind of consolation for the disturbance Colin had caused him.

'Who's got the letter?'

'His mother, I imagine.'

'Did you meet her?'

'Only spoke to her on the phone. She didn't come up with the others to collect the body. Sounded like an odd woman to me. But then she must be, to have had a son like that.'

Gavin wondered weakly if he was meant to contradict a statement that could hardly have been truer, even if it struck him as dishonouring Colin in a backhanded kind of way. Could his mother be blamed for it all?

'What was in the letter?'

'I'm afraid it's confidential. I read it and then passed it on to the family. If you're a cousin, no doubt you'll be seeing them in Dublin?'

The hotel proprietor was growing suspicious again.

'Oh yes, of course I will. The two branches of the family have been estranged for several years now. But this dreadful business is drawing us closer together.'

A dumb premonition swept through Gavin. He would be forced to contact Colin's mother after all. It was a horror of horrors he had deluded himself into believing he could avoid. But he needed to find out what that letter said.

'Look,' he said, 'I realize you have work to do. And you have been exceedingly kind already. But could you just accompany me to the spot he died in? It would mean a lot to me . . . and to the rest of the family in Scotland.'

Mr Hart looked at his watch and gave his grudging assent.

'It needn't take us long. It's only ten minutes' walk from here. Mind you, I won't hang around. If you want to pay your respects, to soak up the atmosphere, as it were, you're no doubt better doing that on your own.'

It was a beautiful spot, Gavin realized with gratitude, as he watched Mr Hart disappear along the towpath. The stream broadened out and deepened there and the water, motionless and chill as a slab of black marble, was overshadowed by alders and willows. The catkins had only just emerged. The foliage would be profuse in summer. The noise of the weir was not deafening, more a persistent, reassuring undertow to the silence that the pool was plunged in, an indication that, whatever it might swallow, life continued somewhere else. A broken-down wooden bench stood to one side where the path petered out. The ground rose slightly beyond it and a field gate was framed against the sky like a question mark. Gavin sat down, wondering what to do next. Noon was fast approaching. The sun burned the grey of the clouds to pure white as it found a chink to thrust its light through, and the brief ray caught the surface of the water, almost blinding him. It ought to have been an instant of huge grief. Instead he felt relieved, illuminated. Maybe Colin had done the right thing after all. His pain had found release. It was over. A part of his mind was saying, this is wrong, a tragedy has taken place here, while with another part he had a distinct image of taking Colin in his arms and hugging him as he told him: 'It's all right now. You're all right now.' Was it himself he was hugging? The part of him that grieved? Did any of this comfort get to Colin, wherever he was, whatever he was experiencing? Or had he come there merely for himself? I hold you, he thought, I'm holding you here, now, even though you wanted to escape. I hold you in my mind and in my heart. You are still there, you have not gone.

*

He got lost on the way back to Dublin. Not momentarily lost, or comically lost, the way his parents did when they returned to the motorway after a break for coffee, only to discover an hour later that they were driving back in the direction they had come from. Seriously lost. The dullness that had possessed him since finding Aidan's letter in the flat in Glasgow had lifted, giving place to something different, an elation that had a strain of alarm in it, for it was as if something was rising to the surface of him, a wave or an eruption, and he had no way of knowing what it would be like when it emerged. It did not lead him to drive dangerously, but it interfered sufficiently with his sense of orientation for him to take a series of wrong turnings.

Before leaving Scarron he had troubled Mr Hart once more. The proprietor was busy with accounts, so he refused to come himself, and instead asked the young man at reception to show Gavin the room Colin had slept in. It was on the ground floor next to the toilets and gave onto a sort of air vent which allowed a minimum of light to enter the working areas of the hotel. The kitchen ventilator was directly opposite, filling the bedroom with the scent of greasy cooking and troubling it with constant noise. The background of the water tipping over the weir was infinitely more soothing. Gavin did not pause for long. As he turned away he almost retched and had to fight back the impulse. In its own way, he reflected, that room was already a coffin. No wonder the chill water had appeared so welcoming.

He was abandoning all hope of finding his way back to Dublin when he realized how hungry he was. The flurry of emotion had made him forget any thought of lunch and it was close to six o'clock now. The country road he found himself on led round a bend and dipped to cross a bridge. There was an inn on the other side. The atmosphere could hardly have been more different from that of the Scarron Hotel. Crisply fried, breaded fish, with home-made chips and fresh salad, appeared with miraculous speed and it transpired that the only other guest in the dining-room, at that relatively early hour, was heading off to Dublin immediately afterwards. His pathfinding problems were resolved. Once Gavin's stomach was full, all sorts of different clarities came flooding in upon him. He kept his new acquaintance waiting while he called Dermot and Shevaun, to let them know he wouldn't be back in time to eat with them.

'Two messages for you,' said Shevaun. 'This phone hasn't been so busy in months.'

'Messages from who?'

'The first's from Aidan. He doesn't waste any time. Another conquest of yours, if you ask me, although you've never bothered to notice.'

Gavin spluttered. Why couldn't she get on with it, instead of messing around with speculations about a kind of love she didn't understand?

'Frank will be in Gregory's from nine o'clock this evening. He's expecting you.'

Gavin felt neither surprise nor indignation at Aidan's meddling. This made sense and his only concerns were practical. It was all part of his different mood now he had eaten.

'How am I going to recognize him?'

'Aidan's given him a thorough rundown. Wish I could have been a fly on the wall during that conversation! All you have to do is order a gin and tonic and look lost. The other message is from Colin's mother. No doubt you have Aidan to thank for it as well. She's enormously keen to see you. Says she has something to give you, a personal object that belonged to Colin. She'll meet you in Bewley's tomorrow, after morning Mass.'

Gavin was so stunned he fell silent. Shevaun charged on, unstoppable as ever.

'When did you say you were on duty on Sunday night?'

'Ten thirty.'

He did not have to think. The response was automatic.

'Have you asked yourself, dear friend, how you are going to get back for then? What on earth possessed you to come here by train?'

What indeed? He had no answer. It could have been a way of delaying the impact, or of giving himself time to think. All at once he panicked.

'I have to get back,' he said. 'It was hard enough getting three days' leave at no notice. I'll be lynched if I don't turn up on time.'

'Leave it with me,' said Shevaun. 'Your friends are more influential than you imagine. We'll get you to Bewley's tomorrow morning and back to Glasgow, to the front door of the hospital, even if it has to be on a broomstick.'

'That sounds like fun. The nurses would love it. Show us how genuine a feminist you are.'

His mood was definitely lighter. Shevaun snorted and hung up. In spite of the wrong turning he had taken, Gavin proved to have got much nearer Dublin than he had guessed. The man in front of him could hardly have been kinder. He even stopped beyond the traffic lights at the canal, once they had traversed the city's outer suburbs, to make sure Gavin knew what way he had to go. Gregory's was two minutes' walk from Trinity College but he did not mention the pub. It was not fear, only an instinctive discretion. At times he laughed at himself for the way he assumed people would take him for straight. His guide was in his early fifties, hair wavy and plentiful, mostly white. As they bid farewell, Gavin noticed he had attractive blue eyes and a finely shaped mouth above a dimpled chin. He felt sure, however, that his kindness had no hidden motive.

It took him nearly twenty minutes to find a parking place. By the time he left the car his heart was thumping. He looked at his watch: twenty past nine. He could not have said what it was that caused his agitation, fear of missing Frank or fear of confronting him. Gregory's was almost empty when he entered. It would not begin to fill up until well past eleven. He had rarely come there with Colin and disliked the place. Never a smoker, and with a professional interest in people's health, he found the spectacle of the clientèle in gay pubs both worrying and depressing. He could not conceive of himself picking a man up in one and taking him home. At times he felt this was a lack on his part, as if it made him less than fully gay. He ought to behave as everyone else seemed to behave and do the things they did. But the pressures to conform had never overcome his instinctive reluctance. If he fell for a man, it had to be in the light of day, and by chance, not by design.

He had no difficulty in recognizing Frank before Frank turned towards him. He was ready to dislike him and experienced a sense of relief when what he saw confirmed his expectations. Frank was balding, with dark, close-cropped hair, a walrus moustache streaked with grey large liquid eyes, and a vaguely Italian look about him. He was wearing black jeans, a dark T-shirt and a leather jacket and had a small but distinct pot-belly, rather like a baby-sized sombrero stuck on above his crotch. He was four or five inches shorter than Gavin. That made him more or less the same height as Colin. Their bodies must have fitted well together. It was a line of speculation Gavin preferred not to pursue.

'Sorry to be late,' he said, holding out his hand with awkward but resolute formality.

'Don't worry,' Frank said. 'I'm in here every Saturday, come rain, come shine, no matter whether I have a rendezvous or not.'

A scowl of irritation flitted across Gavin's face. He presumed the man enjoyed provoking him. It was hard to imagine Frank really believed they might end up going to bed together.

'We have a lot to talk about,' Frank went on.

I wonder if we have, thought Gavin, and said nothing.

'Want to take a seat?'

The American pointed to a corner opposite the bar, in semi-darkness, backed by old-fashioned panes of coloured glass, advertising a forgotten brand of tobacco. The head on his pint of Guinness left a white bib on Frank's moustache, like the froth a wave leaves behind as it recedes. He wiped it away and gave a sort of gasp of pleasure.

'You want me to tell you about Colin, right? Did you go to the funeral?'

Gavin shook his head.

'And you?'

'Me neither. All that family and religion business. Far too heavy.'

Gavin took a deep draught from his own pint. He needed alcohol. The car would be OK where he had left it and he could get a taxi back to Dermot and Shevaun's. He braced himself to ask the questions that concerned him. He was not keen to spend more time than he absolutely had to in Frank's company.

'How did you two meet?'

'In here,' Frank answered, with a broad smile, as if that explained everything, as if Gavin understood perfectly how these things worked and what they meant. Gavin realized with a shock that the next question he wanted to ask was, did you love him.

39

It could hardly have been less appropriate. He choked it back.

'How long have you been living in Dublin?'

'Fourteen years.'

Frank held Gavin's gaze insistently. If he would only stop trying to get off with me, or pretending that is what he is doing, thought Gavin, we could get down to business.

'And what brought you here?'

The polite questions, the sort you would ask at a party when confronted with someone who did not really interest you, formed on his lips without him thinking about them. And yet it was Colin he needed to know more about, not Frank. He was avoiding the issue.

'A lover. We met in New Jersey and I came overseas to be with him. He's still here now. We're both good friends. Colin and I could have been good friends if things had worked out differently. If he hadn't gone and done something so darned stupid.'

'How long were you together?' broke in Gavin.

'A couple of months. He moved in three days from the first time we slept together. He was pushed for a place to stay and I was happy for the company. At first, at any rate. He told me about you.'

'How much?'

'Enough.'

There was a silence. I'm not going to fall for that one, Gavin told himself. He had run out of questions.

'He had some kinky tastes, that guy,' Frank went on.

Gavin began to blush to the very roots of his hair. He reminded himself carefully that they were sitting in shadow, so that Frank could not see the effect his words were having. The American was not even looking at him now, but surveying the bar and the further corners of the room, checking out the new arrivals. Or perhaps he was merely giving Gavin time to loosen up, hoping to share who knew what lurid details. Gavin and Colin had never gone very far down that road. Colin possessed a delicately shaded French scarf made from remarkably strong fabric and from time to time he would ask Gavin to tie his wrists with it when they made love. It had never occurred to Gavin to wonder whether this was kinky or not. It was what Colin wanted and he enjoyed

40

it too. He liked the vulnerability, the sense of openness it brought, the paleness of Colin's exposed armpits with the tufts of golden hair in them as he stretched his arms above his head.

'I'm wondering how much he told you about them.'

Frank was looking straight at him now.

'I'm pretty strait-laced about these things, like most Scotsmen.'

For once, uncharacteristically, lying gave Gavin pleasure.

'Towards the end he wanted me to spank him. To punish him for something or other he had done. Or maybe just for who he was. I have one Italian parent and I got all that stuff about the Virgin Mary and so on when I was little. Not as heavily as they get it in this country, though. The way they beat their kids here is incredible. I was out of my depth with Colin. I'll try anything that's fun, that makes sex more exciting. But when we did that he got kind of scared and cold. Far, far away, as if I was beating him into a corner. It made me feel creepy.'

'What broke you up?'

Gavin wanted to stop him, wanted to get away as quickly as he could. His drink was nearly finished.

'Why did I kick him out, you mean?' Frank asked, and snickered. 'Why did you?'

'It didn't happen that way between us. It was Colin that walked out.'

'That's not what he told me.'

From the tone of Frank's voice, Gavin sensed he was telling the truth. Damn Colin! These fabrications made things so much more complicated. Reality was hard enough to get at without them interfering.

'He lost his job and started drinking heavily. I'd come home from work and find him flat out on the floor. He'd drained every bottle in the drinks cupboard.'

'Sounds like he got pretty desperate.'

'That's as may be. A partnership is one thing, running a nursing home is another. I have a life and a job to think of.'

Gavin was unsure whether to ask further questions or not. Perhaps he had learnt as much as he wished to about Colin's last relationship.

'Well,' he said, getting to his feet, 'I'd better be off.'

41

'It's barely ten o'clock. No time for another drink? Things are just starting to look interesting in here.'

'No. I drove back from the west today and I'm returning to Scotland tomorrow afternoon. I could do with an early night.'

Gavin paused. He knew thanks were in order but was afraid he would sound all too insincere.

'It was good of you to speak to me.'

Frank had already lost interest in him.

'Got the number of that Aidan guy? We only spoke on the phone but he sounded cute. Is he pretty? I'd like to give him a ring some day.'

'I haven't got it on me,' Gavin said, relieved not to be telling another lie. 'But you can find him in the phone book. Aidan Sommers. Oh-double-m.'

It was a secret revenge on Aidan. Let him sort this one out himself.

Gavin had hoped to leave Frank behind in the pub but, psychologically at least, that proved impossible. It took him ages to find a taxi that was free. When he got out at Dermot and Shevaun's there was a light on in an upstairs window, and another in the hall just through the door, but otherwise no sign of life. Like many people with small children, they evidently jumped at every opportunity for sleep that came their way. Gavin had left the holdall with his overnight stuff in the boot of Mike's car. His toilet bag was in it and he would be unable to brush his teeth tonight or to shave properly the next morning. And he had Colin's mother to deal with. He would have liked to soak in a long bath but was concerned about the noise he might make, so he threw his clothes off and got straight into bed instead.

The room was cold and he could not sleep. He started giving himself a hard time about all the things he had not asked Frank, then for being morbid in seeking out the details of Colin's final weeks. Why should it be any concern of his? The sensible thing would have been, once Colin walked out of the front door in Glasgow, to let him walk out of Gavin's life. And here he was, more than two years later, as heavily involved as he had ever been, and with a man who wasn't even there. Once Gavin did doze off, images of Frank kept drifting through his dreams, as he had seen him in the pub, then naked, with thick grey hair on his chest and a disturbingly pallid bum, bending over – yes, he was bending over Colin, who was lying on the floor face down, with vomit spattered around his head. Gavin woke up with a start. Two doors away the baby was crying. He could hear Dermot's voice soothing it, then calling in a stage whisper to Shevaun. They would be doing their best not to wake him. He got out of bed, pulled on his vest and underpants, and put his head around the door. Dermot was crossing the hall with the baby in his arms, now sobbing rhythmically. It would fall asleep again soon enough.

Gavin coughed and Dermot turned towards him.

'Welcome back,' he said. 'Sorry about Shona.'

'Don't worry,' said Gavin. 'Can I hold her?'

'Sure,' said Dermot. 'That means I can have a cigarette.'

The light was on in their bedroom and Shevaun was sitting up, her elbows on her knees, a pillow propped against the wall behind her. Gavin sat cross legged on the end of the bed. He was good with small children and he knew it. Sometimes he pretended he had a secret element, a magic crystal inside him, just next to his heart, and that when he held babies to it, they would automatically fall asleep. It often worked.

'Surprised you let him smoke in bed,' he said to Shevaun as Dermot lit up.

'That's the least of it,' she said.

It was odd. It sounded like a compliment, as if she was proud of him. Maybe she had reason to be.

'You look dreadful.'

Gavin said nothing, only nodded and held the baby closer. There was a creak from the doorway. The little boy was looking round questioningly and, having got the unspoken permission he was seeking, leapt up onto the bed and into his father's lap. Dermot put one hand on the boy's tummy and managed his cigarette with the other.

'Was it tough with Frank?' he asked.

'Don't think about it,' Shevaun interjected.

'Think about what?'

'About what they were like together. It doesn't help. It doesn't even matter. You'll only harm yourself.'

'She's right,' said Dermot.

'It's stupid,' Gavin said. 'But it really hurts.'

'It's not what you do that matters, it's who you do it with,' chanted Shevaun, as if it was a maxim she had picked up from the nuns at school.

Gavin looked at them. Had they always been entirely faithful to one another? What did they know about what he was going through? Could it be more than he thought?

'He was really tacky.'

'Colin must have been desperate.'

It occurred to Gavin that he would have liked to cry, in order to demonstrate something to them. Or else to himself. But he couldn't. There was nothing there. At any rate, not yet.

'We got you a flight,' said Shevaun, and the sides of her mouth curved upwards in a smile of triumph.

'You're booked on the three o'clock plane to Glasgow,' put in Dermot.

'How did you manage that?'

'Simple. A woman who spent four months in the shelter is working at the airport now. She owes me a favour or two. She was only too happy to juggle the books for us.'

'And payment?'

'You can sort that out when you get there. You've got a credit card?'

He nodded.

'Pity about the broomstick.'

Mike phoned after breakfast the next morning to check where he had left the car. Hearing his voice made Gavin perk up.

'It would be good to see you.'

'I'd like that too,' Mike said. 'Why don't I run you to the airport? I'll call by the house at one.'

Gavin left his case just inside the door. Shevaun drove him into town. She insisted she had business to see to at the shelter.

'Be on the pavement outside at half past noon,' she told him. 'Remember, we haven't got much time.'

Bewley's was surprisingly crowded for eleven o'clock on a Sunday morning. He wandered from floor to floor looking for Colin's mother, then gave up and went back downstairs to the

44

serving area. He was on the point of getting a tray for himself and finding a table to wait at when he spotted her advancing from the ladies' toilet. She had popped in to freshen herself up. He could tell as much from her heavily powdered cheeks and the strong whiff of scent as he kissed her close to the ear.

'Dear Gavin,' she effused, 'what a delight to see you. I was so unhappy that we seemed to have lost touch.'

Her very first words reminded him what a minefield being in her presence represented. She would feign everything, affection, comprehension, enlightened interest, provided no reference was ever made to her son's sexual tastes. What she required of Gavin was that he should support the lie about the years he had spent with Colin, the lie about who Colin had in fact been. His hand went to his Adam's apple, to the space beneath the knot in his tie, between the top button of his shirt and the skin on his neck. It felt like he was suffocating.

'It is so sad you had to miss the funeral,' she began, once they were seated.

I missed it because you made not the slightest effort to inform me, Gavin reflected.

'It was a wretched and yet a beautiful occasion,' she went on, slipping off her gloves and placing them on the table between them next to her missal. 'A mother whose son is a poet, however, must be prepared for the most frightful eventualities. And Colin was an *excellent* poet,' she concluded with emphasis, looking at Gavin for confirmation. He offered none.

'Dear Dr Sommers has spoken to me about the possibility of having them published. Would you support that idea, Gavin?'

Why is she asking me, he thought. What rights have I in the matter? And then he reflected, of course I have rights. But they are not literary. She doesn't acknowledge those. The sudden elevation of Aidan to doctoral status amused him. Colin's mother automatically attributed a generalized eminence to individuals she particularly approved of.

'It might make things easier for us,' he said. 'But it can't bring Colin back to life.'

'Let me tell you something,' she said confidentially, leaning towards him and playing with her teaspoon, staring into her coffee cup so that he got a full view of the top of her hat. 'I'm afraid it may sound a little unconventional. You won't be shocked, will you? Promise you won't be shocked.'

'I won't be shocked,' Gavin repeated in a tired sort of way.

'His pain is ended. Some people are better dead. My compassion for my youngest son is infinite and I am convinced that God's compassion will be no less. But he was a most unhappy and moody child whom no amount of love or tenderness could comfort. He was a burden to himself and to those who came in contact with him. I have no doubt he was a burden to you, Gavin. Colin chose his path and who were we to stop him?'

Her beady, chill eyes were staring hawklike at him. He was reminded of countless earlier occasions when he had marshalled his forces in fruitless attempts to combat her.

'I didn't get the chance.'

'And if you had, you think you would have succeeded?'

She smiled indulgently, as if such foolishness was unexpected but charming nonetheless. In a flash he saw just how insidious her manoeuvring was. She was telling him that she had been up to Colin's games, it was a secret they had shared, one that excluded Gavin, that he had been a victim to. In this way she could give herself the luxury of feeling sorry for him. It was almost as if Colin's suicide had been a plot hatched with his mother many years before.

'I would have stopped him.'

It felt like lying but Gavin was determined to say it anyway. He corrected himself.

'I *could* have stopped him.'

Mrs Harkins shook her head bemusedly and tutted. She had, in fact, scored yet another victory, by pushing him to the limits of what he could and could not say, of what she would allow him to say. He wanted to defy her but was uncertain how to. Perhaps he could have told her about her son's thighs, about the oddly-shaped mole in his right groin just next to the scrotum. She opened her handbag.

'I brought you a memento of Colin. It is the very least his family can do for such a dear, longstanding friend of his.'

Gavin dropped his coffee. The cup hit the floor with a crash, scattering the boiling dark brown liquid down his trousers. Mrs Harkins pushed her chair back and he leapt to his feet, grabbing a napkin. Suddenly a third figure was beside them. It was Aidan. Gavin would not have believed he could ever be so glad to see him. Aidan touched him on the shoulder, then turned to kiss Colin's mother with a show of warmth Gavin was convinced he did not feel. It gave Gavin time to recover his presence of mind, grab the French scarf from the table where she had left it and thrust it into his jacket pocket. Was there any way she could have known what that scarf meant to him? The idea that Colin might have told her was preposterous. And if not, what devilish instinct had led her to hit upon the very object that would constitute the greatest violation of their intimacy?

Colin's mother, who had risen to her feet to receive Aidan's kiss, picked up her gloves and missal from the table. Gavin's reaction was an infringement of her unspoken rules for their encounter. Nothing must disturb the glassy, brittle surface of courtesy and coping. Still too stunned to care about the social niceties, he darted one last question at her from his seat:

'The letter? What was in the letter?'

She made no secret of her displeasure now.

'The letter was a private family matter. It has been destroyed.'

'Destroyed?' Gavin was incredulous.

'I burnt it. It contained accusations and allegations which do no honour to my son's memory. But then, what can one expect a person to write who is in the frame of mind that precedes suicide?'

Gavin folded his arms and looked away. He knew his reaction was childish. At that particular moment he believed he would never again have any reason to treat with the woman. When his anger subsided she was gone and Aidan had taken her place opposite him.

'Pay no attention to her. She's a witch,' he said. 'I hope you didn't mind my butting in. I had an inkling you might need assistance.'

Gavin almost told him about the scarf. His right hand was in his pocket, holding it, caressing it. The feel of the fabric brought the image of Colin's wrists into his mind with exceptional lucidity. The moment passed.

'Did you read the jotters?' asked Aidan.

'Some of them. I couldn't bear to read them all.'

'And the poems?'

47

'I thought they were excellent. Are you really planning to have them published?'

'With your permission.'

Gavin felt a glow of pleasure he tried to conceal.

'Why is that important?'

'You are ... what's the word ... the survivor? The principal mourner?'

'Absent from the funeral.'

'Through no fault of your own.'

'Did you love Colin?'

The question slipped out, unannounced, all the more easily because of the things Gavin had not said, the other questions he had never put to Aidan.

'I wouldn't say I loved him, no. I was concerned about him. And I admired him in an odd kind of a way.'

Gavin studied Aidan's features with a sympathy he had not felt before. He suspected Shevaun was right. This man is attracted to something in me, he thought, without taking time to wonder what it might be. He himself discerned no corresponding qualities in Aidan.

'Aidan,' he said, 'you have been good to me.'

'Yes,' came the answer. 'I think I have.'

Mike was the last person Gavin spoke to before leaving Ireland. Dermot and Shevaun declined to come to the airport with them, waving goodbye from the front door of the house. Gavin was careful to leave the jotters on top of the chest of drawers in the hall. Shevaun undertook to get them back to Aidan later in the week. Mike looked younger and thinner in spite of the years that had passed.

'A woman answered when I phoned your flat,' Gavin said with a mischievous glint in his eye. 'Does that mean you're going straight?'

Mike had a hearty laugh.

'Not a bit. That was Diana. She's been living with me for three years now.'

'A marriage of convenience?'

'I had got to hate being on my own. Now she feels like part of the family. Not the most important member, though.'

'Who's that?'

'His name's Fintan.'

They had stopped at the traffic lights of a major junction. Mike reached into his breast pocket, pulled his wallet out, and let it fall open so that Gavin could see the photograph of a rather younger man, with what struck him as a very Irish face. Mike was an Englishman, from Nottingham originally. The sight of the photograph and his sense of Mike's happiness deflated the buoyancy that had possessed Gavin since he said goodbye to Aidan. Such plenitude for them, he thought, and for Colin the weir.

'He was still in the seminary when we met,' said Mike.

'That must have made things complicated.'

'Fintan was already getting them sorted out.'

'How old is he?'

'Twenty-four. That makes nine years between us.'

'A good space. I sometimes think a difference in age helps.'

'He works on a drugs project in north Dublin. That's where he is today. He has to man the unit every fourth weekend. Otherwise he'd be with us now.'

4

Gavin got a taxi into Glasgow from the airport at Abbotsinch. It dropped him outside the front door at Doune Quadrant. Each time he returned home he experienced a fresh rush of love for the place. The flat was in a row of fine Victorian tenements facing southwards over the river Kelvin, which ran through a deep gorge at this point. You could hear the water down below but all you could see was trees, both beyond the railings on this side, and concealing the BBC buildings on the opposite bank. Gavin paused to enjoy the sensation, while the taxi driver manoeuvred back and forth portentously, turning within that confined space. The departure of the taxi was a part of coming home and he wanted to savour it. The quadrant was a dead end so the vehicle had to leave the same way it had come in. The keys already in his hand, a pang struck Gavin without warning. What if Brian was not there? He had not phoned once during four days of absence. He had hardly spared a thought for Brian in all that time, although he had brought him a gift from Dublin airport. What right did he have to assume Brian would be waiting for him? He was more likely to be sitting fuming, alone in his own flat down in Partick. Yet Gavin could not bear the thought of walking through that door, bearing the load he bore with him from Ireland, and finding the place empty.

He breathed a sigh of huge relief when he reached the second-floor landing. The storm doors were folded right back. He could see, through the shaded Victorian glass, with its delicate tracery of vine tendrils and vases filled with flowers, that the lamp on the chest of drawers in the hall was switched on. Right inside the door stood Brian's cello case, like a miniature mummy, half open, its occupant having fled. He must have been practising in his favourite place, in the centre of the bay window in the

50

sitting-room, looking out across the valley. On a more humdrum evening Gavin would have been irritated to find the case there, blocking the entrance. Now he was so elated it was all he could do to master his emotion and cry out:

'Hello! I'm back!'

A subdued answer came from the kitchen. Brian would of course be sulking. He had good reason to, which was not always the case. Gavin dumped his luggage on the floor and slung his overcoat across the chair next to the bedroom door. Brian was washing up at the sink. Gavin gave a quick glance at the cooker. Food had been prepared. It was exactly what he needed and, at the same time, more, much more than he deserved. Brian did not turn round. His shoulders were silhouetted against the big window that the sink looked on to. Beyond it the ground rose steeply in shadow, with more trees.

'I'm really sorry,' Gavin stuttered awkwardly.

'Four days and not a word,' said Brian. 'Former lovers never lose their hold.'

Gavin had the mother and the father of a hard on. It didn't matter whether Brian was trying to hurt him or not. All he wanted was to make love and it looked as if that was the last thing he could hope for.

'Come here,' he said, opening his arms, his voice almost breaking as he spoke.

Brian turned and walked right up to him, without looking at him. His body was rigid but it relaxed in Gavin's arms and Gavin realized he was excited too. He could not think what to say. He was too busy recognizing his lover's smell, burying his face into his neck, his shoulder. This is what coming home means, he thought. Without a word, Brian took his hand and led him slowly to the bedroom. Gavin always felt like a small child when Brian did this, as if he wanted to show him a secret den or his favourite toy, a treasure nobody else must know about. Brian looked straight at him now and, with an odd, mischievous smile, pushed him over on to his back on the quilt. Gavin swung round and kicked his shoes off. In a trice Brian was lying next to him. He took Gavin's face in his hands and surveyed it quizzically.

'You've never stopped loving him, have you?' he murmured softly.

It was not a question, more a statement. An acknowledgement of the thing he had been trying to hurt Gavin with only a moment earlier.

Then something happened Gavin had not expected, like a wave that had been poised and frozen in his chest all through the last four days, and rose up now, into his head, his mouth, his eyes, his nostrils. It burst. He curled his body like a child's and wept convulsively into Brian's shirt, just beneath his left shoulder, holding onto him. He clutched Brian tightly, kneading the skin of his back with his hands, through both shirt and vest, hurting him as he did so, for Gavin was a strong man. Bit by bit the wave receded and he was able to lie back. Still he did not open his eyes. Brian rolled over on top of him, poised with his elbows on either side of Gavin's face, and started kissing him on the eyelids and the cheeks, tasting the salt tears as he did so, then on the lips at last. And, after a while, Gavin's lips opened.

'Who was at the door?' asked Kieran, when Mark rejoined him in the kitchen.

'Gavin,' answered Mark. 'I didn't catch the second name. Anyone I know?'

'Don't think so,' said Kieran. 'Is he alone?'

There were voices from the hall. They both fell silent.

'No, he's got his other half with him,' Kieran observed, answering his own question. 'I'd better go and say hello,' and he dried his hands on a dishcloth.

Mark noticed, with the habitual admiration he could not help feeling for Kieran, that he was wearing a stylish shirt and a splendidly refulgent tie, and had somehow managed to keep both spotless, no matter how absorbed in last-minute details of food preparation.

'Kieran, let me introduce Brian,' said Dougal.

They shook hands rather stiffly. Kieran had his own reasons for studying the newcomer's features closely. He already knew Gavin.

'Brian's feeling pretty wrecked,' said Gavin. 'I just collected him off the London shuttle.'

'We were wondering whether you would make it or not,' Kieran said.

'What's the news?' put in Dougal.

Brian shrugged.

'Not too good,' said Gavin. 'No improvement as yet.'

'He'll pull through,' Brian said, adding after a pause: 'Would it be all right if I unwind somewhere on my own for a bit? I don't think I can face a dinner table right away.'

'Of course,' said Dougal. 'I'll show you where the study is. Nobody will disturb you there. You can join the rest of us whenever you feel ready.'

'He's stunning,' Mark muttered to Kieran. 'What does Gavin do to get to sleep with that Adonis?'

He had been watching from the kitchen door and was rather piqued at not being introduced.

'He's just a thoroughly nice guy. A pediatrician.'

'Friend of Dougal's?'

'Yes. They were at university together. We bumped into him after a concert. He and Dougal started meeting for lunch.'

'And where was Brian? How come you'd never seen him?'

'He'd actually been playing in the orchestra that night. Front desk of the violoncellos. I suppose Gavin could have pointed him out to us if he and Dougal had recognized each other in time. I've been really curious to set eyes on him. I'm told he's very temperamental. A typical musician. Tough to live with.'

'With looks like that, he can afford to be.'

Dougal took Gavin into the sitting-room, supplied him with a glass of bubbly and went to give Kieran a hand in the kitchen. He felt rather more on top of things and equal to dealing with Mark. Alan was studying a framed photograph on the sitting-room mantelpiece. He took it down and turned to Gavin.

'This brings back memories,' he said.

'What kind of memories?' asked Gavin.

Gavin had an air of bourgeois solidity that made Alan think of his host the lawyer. Partly because he was recalling an incident that struck him as important, and partly out of devilment, he rose to the challenge. After all, he and Mark were on alien territory. Any chance to shock was worth exploiting.

5

'It reminds me of a photograph my mother kept above the fire at home,' he began. 'It wasn't a flat like this one. A third the size, if even that much. And nothing like so posh an area. I was brought up in Dundee and the family lived in a tenement just behind the Seagate. It's been demolished now, to make way for the 1970s shopping centre. There was a bunker in the kitchen. I can remember the coalmen trooping up the stairway one after the other when I was small, black with grime, their backs bent under the bags, and tipping them into the container with a rumbling that made me think a landslide was in progress.

'Every morning my mother would sweep out the previous night's ashes and make a fresh fire. It was a work of art, with bundled newspaper and twigs at the bottom supporting a careful edifice of coals. The few times I tried to do it for her it never worked. Around five o'clock in the afternoon my father would put a match to it, so as to have the room warm once tea was over and we came through to watch the television. The fireplace was spotlessly clean. Once a week my mother got down on her knees and scrubbed it, then wiped it dry and polished the metal surround until it gleamed. She kept a vase filled with cut flowers on a small table to one side. And the family photographs were carefully arranged on the mantelpiece.

'One of them held a particular fascination for me when I was a boy. Because of it, although that's not the only reason, I'm convinced I was already gay that far back, at the age of four or five. Nothing to do with arrested development. Or if it is, then mine's still arrested at that stage, whatever term the psychologists use to define it.

'The photograph showed a strikingly handsome man in naval uniform. I had no idea who had taken it or when. He was looking directly into the camera, smiling, or smirking might be a better word, with his arms folded. Definitely not on duty. It never occurred to me at the time to wonder who might be behind the lens, though I've thought a lot about that since. A lawn stretched into the distance. Odd, feathery trees rose into the sky with little white-robed figures scurrying to and fro beneath them. There was a smudge in one corner that could have been a cow, or a horse, or maybe even a rickshaw.

'India, Africa, China . . . ? I couldn't make up my mind where the snapshot had been taken. Something warned me not to ask my mother about it. Looking at it was like venturing into forbidden, tantalizing territory. I took care not to give it too much attention when other people were in the room. But when I was alone I could go up and peer at it, folding my hands and tilting my head so as to assume the posture of the man it showed. One day I was bold enough to lift it from its place of honour on the mantelpiece and carry it over to the window, hoping the daylight would reveal more details. Unfortunately the sun was reflected in the glass covering the photograph. No matter how carefully I shifted it backwards and forwards, the glare got in the way.

'All of a sudden the door was flung open and my mother bustled in, looking severe as she did most of the time, wearing an apron and a hairnet, her usual outfit when doing the housework. She sort of snorted, grabbed the photograph from my hands and put it back in its place on the mantelpiece. She gave me a shove and told me I must never touch any of the objects there. Each and every one was precious. If I dropped one and it broke, there would be hell to pay. She was trying to make out that she cared equally about all the photographs. I wasn't fooled. I knew that one was special.

'I left school at fourteen and started work with a builder in Dundee. Around that time I started doing toilets. You know, hanging around at the station or in the park, either inside or near the door, so you could see people approaching and get a good look at them as they went in. I take it you haven't done toilets . . .'

Gavin shook his head.

'. . . but that doesn't mean you have to look down your nose at people who do. Or so I hope. By the time I finished my apprenticeship, I was going down regularly to Edinburgh on Saturdays, with the pretext of a football match or clothes to buy. The geography was different there and the flora and fauna much more entertaining. There is a place they have demolished now we all used to call GHQ . . . General Headquarters. That's where I met the first man I had any kind of relationship with. It was thanks to him nagging and encouraging me I left the building trade and got the job that I'm in now.'

'What's that?' Gavin put in.

'An air steward,' said Alan, not without a touch of pride. 'Not bad after shifting bricks, eh? But back to the toilets. What made them so enthralling was the unpredictability. There was no way you could tell what was going to happen. They were packed at the most unlikely times, such as half way through a Sunday afternoon, or teatime on Saturdays, while on Friday nights and Saturday lunchtimes the place was like a desert. The anonymity frightened and excited me at one and the same time. Even though I haven't cottaged for years, I still get incredibly turned on when I set foot in a public urinal. Something about the smell, the sound of running water and the endless possibilities. Maybe turned on isn't the right term. It's more a kind of agitation close to panic.

'When I did them regularly, I tended to go for older men. Or maybe it was them that went for me. I felt safer with them, they gave me a kind of illusion of control. There were some who paid, some I was only too glad to go with and some who would nearly come to the point if you worked hard at it, then panic and rush off. I never had anyone attack me and never met a policeman. I suppose I can count myself lucky.

'How much of their faces you got to see depended on where precisely you did the business. One day, it was a Saturday in June, Scotland was playing Wales in the rugby finals out at Murrayfield. The city centre was swamped by groups of men carrying daffodils. A different kind of sport was on my mind. I scored more quickly than I had ever done, then left the toilet and went for a stroll to look at the shop windows. Within an hour or so I was ready for more and I went back. The guy I picked up this time was only a year or so younger than my parents. I'm the third child and my mother had me when she was twenty-two, so at the time I'm talking about she was in her early forties. A handsome man, gentler and less hurried than they usually are under those circumstances. He did a blow job on me then jerked off, cleaning up with a billowing white handkerchief. The detail has stuck in my mind. It seemed so bright in the half darkness of the cubicle. No kissing of course. That was the most forbidden thing of all, the one barrier you never crossed. Stupid, because it's the thing I like best, personally.

'He put his arms around me and asked some questions. It wasn't a prelude to more sex. I never thought he was going to invite me back or anything like that. I assumed he was married, the way most older guys who do the toilets are. He asked the questions as if the answers really mattered. Where I was born, what street I lived in, my father's job, how many children there were and so on. It made me suspicious. I interrupted and asked if he came from Dundee. Mind you, it was unlikely. I would have picked up a Dundee accent the moment he opened his mouth. Opened it to speak, that is. It turned out he came from Edinburgh, though he worked as a sailor and was based in London. He needed a context for me, he said. A frame to put around my picture. That way he could remember me when he was back at sea.

'His eagerness to talk made me suspicious. It was odd behaviour from a cottager. We still had to whisper, even though they hadn't started putting attendants in all the bigger toilets at that stage. Mind you, when they did, you could usually persuade them to turn a blind eye by slipping them a few quid. There must have been something about me that made an impression on him. I found out soon enough what it was. He zipped up his flies, gave me a pat on the back and left the cubicle. I poked my head around the door to watch him go. He stopped to wash his hands under the tap and, as he lifted his face, I saw it reflected in the mirror. It was the man in my mother's photograph, considerably older, but still recognizable.

'We didn't have a telephone then. There was no need for one. My parents were very isolated people, the only children of their parents. At least, that was as much as I knew at the time. The postie trudged up the stairwell every morning but he very rarely had anything for our box. Dad's pools or the parish newsletter for my Mum, that was about as far as it went. A letter of any kind was a major event. Normally my mother wouldn't open it till everyone was home. Then she got out her glasses and either read it aloud or gave us a summary, at the end of the meal.

'The week after the rugby cup final, not only a letter but a package arrived. I know because I saw it sitting on the sideboard in the hall when I came in. By that stage my brother and sister had left home. I had my parents to myself. They weren't the most cheerful company.

' "Not going to open the package?" my father said, when he had finished his pudding. "Where's it from?"

' "London."

' "Who do we know in London?"

' "Who do I know, you mean. It's addressed to me."

'My father refused to be provoked. The package contained a framed photograph, wrapped carefully in corrugated cardboard and bubble paper. As she took it out, a note slipped to the floor. Neither of them noticed it. I said nothing. My mother's expression was unchanged. The habitual frown on her brow intensified a little, if anything. But it could just have been the effort of examining the photograph without her glasses.

' "Who is it?" I asked.

'My father grunted. That was his usual response to questions he chose not to answer.

' "Long time since you've heard from him. So he's still at sea."

'I crouched on the floor, darted a hand under the table and retrieved the sheet of paper that had fallen.

' "From your dear brother Donald," I read out.

' "Give that here and don't be cheeky!" my mother shouted. I held it away from her grasp. I was taller than either of them and old enough to refuse to do what I was told.

' "I never knew you had a brother. I thought you were an only child."

'My father got out his pipe.

' "Getting a bit stuffy in here," he commented. "I'm going next door to light this at the fire."

'My mother rose to her feet and started tidying the dishes away.

'"Well, are you going to tell me or aren't you?"

'I was quite breathless, and trying to summon up courage to look at the photograph.

'"Don't add insolence to disobedience."

'"Your own mother will tell me if you don't."

'"That woman's not my mother. She's my granny."

'"So where's your mother then?"

'Leaving the dishes half washed, she sat down. It was a most unusual breach of routine. I realized I wouldn't need to push much harder. Now that my father had gone, she was perfectly willing to tell me. Maybe she even welcomed the opportunity to get it off her chest.

'"In Edinburgh. She got married to a medical student who became a GP. She doesn't want to remember the people or the place she came from."

'I was trying to get my mind round it all.

'"And where's your father? It wasn't Grandpa?"

'She made a derisive sputtering sound with her lips.

'"The story's twisted. But not that twisted. My mother went into service in Broughty Ferry when she was seventeen, in one of the big villas they built at the turn of the century for the jute mill owners. It was just before the war and there weren't many good openings for a girl from her background. She had an affair with the man of the house. You would think the mistress of the house would have noticed, but no. My mother told him she was pregnant. It didn't make any difference. He said they would deal with it when the time came. He was besotted with her. That changed when his wife found out. Like night and day. She was five months gone before the storm broke. They wanted her to have an abortion. Not in Dundee, it was too close at hand. They said if she went as far as Aberdeen it could be done safely, without anybody being the wiser."

'"And that was you?" I asked.

'She nodded and gave an odd smile. She never looked at me once, all the while she was telling that story. Her eyes were fixed on a knot in the wooden table, as if it was the knot that wanted the information rather than me.

'"They put up the money. She talked it through with Gran and they decided to keep the baby and the money as well. She had it, left for Edinburgh, and within a year was in the Wrens. She took up with the medical student and married him before he went off to Africa. Your Uncle Donald was born the following year."

'"Why have I never seen her?"

'My mother crowed sarcastically.

'"*You've* never seen her? I haven't seen her myself since I was born. She told Gran she would have to put it all behind her. She had a new life and she didn't want her fiancé or any of his family to know about me."

'"And Gran agreed?"

'"What else could she do? Her daughter had scant chance of finding a decent man anyway, coming from a slum in the centre of Dundee, without humping a bastard wain through the world into the bargain. Gran was delighted. And it made things simpler with me. She never had to share me with anybody."

'"So how did you find out?"

'"It was Donald. I've no idea how he got wind of it. He turned up at Gran's door one day and she burst into tears. She was so glad to see him she couldn't hold back what she knew. And that evening he came round here. Your Dad gave him short shrift."

'"Why?"

'"No point in bringing back a past that's painful. Reminding me of my shame."

'"What shame?"

'"Never heard of the blue line? The one they used to put on your birth certificate, when no one knew your father's name?"

'"They never told you what it was?"

'"Gran kept her word on that. It was a condition of the money being paid over. I don't even know what house I was born in. What makes you so interested in the photograph?"

'I had taken advantage of her absorption in the story to have a good look at a face I recognized, from the mirror in the toilets the preceding Saturday.

'"He's the sailor on the mantelpiece, isn't he? Where did you get it from?"

'"Same place as this one. It arrived through the post unasked."

'"Unwanted and unasked?"

'"You know what your Dad's like. He did it to protect me. He doesn't want me upset. That's why he gave the man such a cold reception. And he thought there was something odd about Donald. Mind you, he says that about you, too, at times. Something he couldn't pin down. Out of the ordinary. But he always gives in, in the end, if I go on at him long enough. It was me that pushed to have it on the mantelpiece. After all, he's a fine-looking man and as much family as I've got. Come to think of it, you've got his looks as well."'

Alan held the photograph in both hands, turning it to and fro, gazing into it intently as if, were he to persist long enough, it would show Uncle Donald in his sailor's uniform. But it stubbornly refused to change. It was a picture of a middle-aged wedding, showing Dougal's father with the woman he married after he left his first wife. Alan looked at Gavin directly with a wry smile on his lips.

'She was right, of course. And bloods draws blood. Isn't that what they say?'

6

Just as Alan ended his story Barry paused at the bottom of the stairs, adjusting his tie nervously. Indeed, the whole business of attending a dinner party made him so nervous he wondered why he bothered to turn up. It was the only engagement in his weekend. You would think that would have made it more attractive. And instead, as Barry's social life dwindled to the merest trickle, he found it increasingly hard to summon up sufficient enthusiasm even for the few items in his calendar. What made Dougal and Kieran keep on inviting him? No doubt it was because of old times. Because of Robert. Try as he might, he could not get away from Robert. He had not managed to renew his circle of friends since Robert's death. What was more, the ones he had retained from then continued to see him in his traditional role, as laughing stock and butt of Robert's merciless humour.

Barry had left his desk in the Scottish Office at five thirty as he did every weekday. A brisk walk homewards across the transversal arteries of Edinburgh's New Town, with panoramas of the sea and Fife he never bothered to look at, brought him to his thoroughly desirable first-floor apartment, not far from Stockbridge, within ten minutes' walk of Kieran and Dougal's. He ought to have been proud of the perfect order it was kept in. And to be honest, the neat and clerkish part of him rejoiced that all the knick-knacks were in their rightful places and that his cleaning lady had passed through leaving no trace of human interference, only an inhuman air of spotlessness and harmony.

Yet there were times when he longed to see evidence of a presence other than his own. A briefcase dumped inside the door. A pair of shoes halfway down the hall, or by the central heating radiator in the bedroom. An unwashed cup in the sink with tea-leaves in it, aromatic still. A voice to hail him, or even just a smell. A gurgling tap in the bathroom. Anything to relieve the monotony of his tidiness, his order, his good taste.

He had entered the invitation in his diary when it reached him a month before, with the generous advance notice customary, if not obligatory, in more sophisticated Edinburgh circles. A timely dinner invitation is not just a courtesy, however. It can be a trap. The most inventive liars find it hard to conjure up a previous engagement for the end of the following month. And if you do not lie quickly, you are skewered. Transfixed. Invited.

Lying awake in the early hours of Wednesday morning, in a way that was becoming more and more frequent with him, Barry had been thankful that he had this at least to look forward to, a brief spot of sociality preceding the bleakness of the weekend. At ten past six on Friday he slumped into his favourite green armchair, wondering why it mattered to have a favourite, since they were all his, and he could have spent an evening sampling each of them in turn, if he so wished. As he contemplated slipping off his gleaming, just a shade tight shoes, but decided not to, since the practice was untidy and it might become a habit, he realized that nothing would have been more welcome at that point than his own company, an oasis of untroubled solitude.

He would water his potted plants, survey the walls in each room to ensure none of the pictures was awry, go through the list of letters he had so long been planning to write, many of them answers to his Christmas mail, and prepare a dish of pasta for one person at around eight o'clock. From threatening, the silence of his home would become comforting, then numbing. It would embrace him with the uniformity of pristine white snow an exhausted traveller falls to his knees in, lulled by an illusion of warmth, when in reality he is progressively being frozen.

What he had to do instead was wash, shave his darkening chin again, select a shirt, dither about what to wear, formal or more casual, then pick one of his treasured collection of wines as a gift for his hosts, parting with it unwillingly, as always. Sharing a bottle of wine was becoming a rare occurrence in Barry's life. The most daunting task of all, however, was arriving and facing up to the other guests. That prospect was what brought him up sharp at the door. His index finger moved tentatively in the direction of the entryphone. He had just been struck by a delicious temptation not to press it, but to turn on his heels and go home, when a hand was placed on his shoulder.

It was Nicol, the farmer's son from Angus, the one who had started small in business and now owned a string of wine shops. He was carrying a bag, with what looked like four bottles in it. They would be a special vintage. Out of all the potential guests he could bring to mind, Nicol was the most congenial to Barry. He had never uttered an unkind word, even when a roomful of people were chiming in with Robert's wicked banter. And he retained a country roughness which marked him out in their circle, almost as much as Barry's English accent marked out him.

'Not going to ring?' asked Nicol.

'Where's Andrew?' Barry asked, as he pressed the buzzer.

'Buddying tonight. Can't come to dinner. But he might well join us later.'

We all have different ways of dealing with Robert's demise, thought Barry. Or of not dealing with it.

Rory and his Catalan were so late that the others were about to sit at table when they arrived. His years were beginning to tell on Rory. Though he cast himself as a libertine, he could not quite reciprocate Ramon's enthusiasm for sex. If the truth were to be told, he found himself regretting asking the young Catalan to come to dinner with him. He was a regular guest at Kieran and Dougal's, where he appreciated the excellent food and wine, but was irked to find himself again and again in a minority, at a table thronged with couples. Because even numbers were considered essential, he was regularly paired with another bachelor, and as often as not reacted with horror to the thought that he might have something in common with the man they had invited as a makeweight, that in his hosts' eyes they belonged to the same category.

Tonight, at least, he would arrive with a partner. But the said partner, some fifteen years the Scotsman's junior, arrived at Rory's door with a glint in his eyes that could only mean one thing. After all, he had been studying hard all week. It was understandable. Rory had the option of refusing. Instead, his vanity got the better of him. Even at forty-two, it reassured him to prove to himself that he could get it up for any man that wanted it. And Ramon was attractive, there could be no arguing about that.

Rory went about the lovemaking in a business-like fashion that did not exclude a certain tenderness but definitely allowed no intimacy. From the start he was aware that it would make them late for dinner. Only once they had both come and he glanced at the clock did he realize just how late. Ramon kept prolonging things, playing with Rory's body hair, then gradually but insistently provoking a second erection. The Scotsman had a movement of impatience. He hated it when things got complicated. Being incorrigibly late was a trait he disliked in himself. He preferred to keep it within reasonable limits.

'We have to go,' he said.

Firmly if affectionately, he pushed Ramon out of bed, then swung his own feet to the ground. There was not even time for a shower. If he had been entirely honest, he would have acknowledged a further reason for the awkwardness he felt in Ramon's company, a reason that led him to get involved in the first place, though he might well have denied it if confronted. Ramon reminded him of Jaume, in a way he found both precious and unnerving.

7

The one thing Rory would never forget about Jaume was his eyes. Not the surprise of coming upon a Catalan lover who had fair hair rather than dark, nor the golden glinting on his thighs, when he lay spreadeagled on the bed and waiting, nor even the laughter. That had been the most noticeably lovable thing about Jaume, bubbling forth unpredictably like water out of a Scottish bogland, there only when the rains were plentiful, constantly finding new paths for itself. People laughed for so many different reasons: to show that they were part of things, to cover their nervousness, to encourage others to appreciate a joke, or out of bitterness or scorn or raunchiness. Jaume's laugh was a statement about the nature of life, quite separate from any situation he might find himself in or any difficulty he might encounter and, for that very reason, absolutely trustworthy. It was beyond his own control, as if someone else were speaking through it. He could no more have turned it on than shrouded the sun in clouds or summoned up a hurricane.

But the thing Rory remembered was his eyes. Jaume was incorrigibly elusive. That was part of what drew people to him. Since entering puberty he had been sought after endlessly: first of all by older men, who beckoned to him on station platforms or rolled car windows down, and gave him their watches or a fistful of bills for the privilege of sucking him off. At university, girl students yearned for him. Without ever managing to delude themselves, they tried to believe he was the kind of husband their staid, bourgeois parents would have wished upon them, who would never ask for more than to go to the office each day in a neatly ironed shirt, a tie and tiepin, and to come home laden with disposable nappies. But they knew such beauty never could be vouchsafed them. They had no role in the tragedy it foreshadowed. A male student or two lusted after him from afar, taking up position carefully in the lecture theatre so as to observe the movements of Jaume's head and catch the fledgling down on his cheeks against the light. It may be hard to believe, but even in the mathematics class one or two were stopped in their tracks at the sight of him, as if he were the answer to an equation whose constituent terms they would never discover. He was presented to them, inexplicably perfect, beyond research or calculation.

When he got back from national service in Murcia and hit the bars in a big way, Jaume used to survey the clientele with the hauteur of an experienced housewife choosing oranges at the morning market, and finding that none of them is of sufficient quality to be worth taking home. He had to develop an ability to blot out the commotion he aroused, not even to register the smiles and nods and yearning glances. Otherwise the effort of deflecting or discouraging them would have worn him down utterly. So that a lot of the time Rory had the impression that Jaume, to put it in a nutshell, quite simply was not there.

That changed when they made love. Perhaps it was the only time it changed. If eyes could have been keys, or manhole covers, or wellheads with suspended buckets that would bring up who could tell what kind of water from the depths, then Jaume's eyes were such. The indefatigable fleeing, trafficking and teasing stopped. His gaze tracked Rory so intensely that he feared he might be swallowed up in it. Come further into me, it seemed to say. Come right inside me, come into my depths.

Rory told him on one occasion:

'I think I could make love just with your eyes.'

Jaume shut them and turned his head to one side as if he were embarrassed. Rory had never seen him in that state. And he did not even see it then, for Jaume managed successfully to conceal whatever was going on inside him. Rory felt he had violated a boundary nobody should ever step across. It made him guilty. Now, years on, it troubled him instead that Jaume had never been possessed. He had never managed to take every bit of him, ruthlessly, for just a moment. And everyone needed to be possessed, at least once in their lives.

A couple of years back, during the Festival, it had been in the

Traverse Theatre bar, at about half past one in the morning, when everyone was well on in their cups and he felt he was likely to get an honest answer, Rory had turned to Kieran and asked him point blank:

'Have you ever been possessed?'

'Repeatedly,' Kieran had answered. 'Thank God.'

It was a question he would not have dared to put to Jaume. They met as a result of a language class, one of the free classes which the school Rory was working for offered from time to time, in order to draw in fresh pupils. They were given two hours' tuition by a trainee teacher such as Rory and, if they chose, could subsequently enrol for a regular cycle of lessons at a reduced rate. The set-up itself was sufficient to make Rory extremely nervous, for he saw it as a test of his own ability, to be rated according to the number of students who signed on at the end of the class. What made him even more nervous was the way, time and again, his eyes were drawn to Jaume's.

Jaume sat at the back of the room, serene and composed, answering the few questions Rory put to him in an English that was grammatically perfect, despite the powerful Catalan twang in his accent. The fact that he made no mistakes came over as a challenge and, by daring to correct his pronunciation in one or two cases and insisting that Jaume repeat the words after him, Rory consciously accepted it. He could not decide whether he was pretending not to notice, or ensuring Jaume realized that he had noticed when, once the class was over, Jaume paused by the door of the room, nodding and smiling as the teacher sauntered past, then lingered in the vestibule, near to the main entrance of the school, while Rory led the handful of students who now wished to enrol into the office, and ensured they got the attention they required.

At the very last minute Rory experienced a mad desire to flee: to rush upstairs and hide in the deserted staff room, or else escape through the back door. But he steadied himself and went to meet his fate. Jaume lifted his head and smiled again, settling the strap of his bag across his shoulder, running the thumb of his right hand up and under it with a gesture that would become only too familiar, as a single golden curl slipped down onto his forehead.

They did not go to a gay bar that night but to a Galician restaurant just round the corner from the school, a favourite haunt of Jaume's. The conversation was of the most humdrum nature: Rory's school and family, the Scottish weather, his problems in finding a decent flat in Barcelona; the computing qualification Jaume had almost finished, his ambitions to go and study in the United States, the tiny hamlet near Lleida where his parents lived and to which he returned every other weekend. They could have been students on the same course, or supporters of the same football team, two young men drawn together by any one of a series of shared, banal enthusiasms or circumstances. And yet, again and again, Rory realized he was being offered a contract, and entered into it without a shade of hesitation. Yes, he said with his body and his eyes. Yes, I agree. We will.

Rory had no illusions. Jaume was doing the choosing and he, Rory, had been chosen. So far he had no clear idea for what. Not for one minute did he doubt that they were going to become lovers and that he was crossing a Rubicon in his life which would admit of no turning back. But the physical side was the least of what Jaume wanted from him. Now, at a distance of almost twenty years, the way he put it was that Jaume had required a witness. Not a spectator, Rory's part was far too active for that, and not merely in the sexual sense. A witness remembers and can testify, can leave a record. Maybe Rory was still struggling to find out how to do that.

Once the meal was ended Rory asked him home. It was his role, was what Jaume expected of him, and he fulfilled it loyally and with a certain solemnity. They hardly slept that night. There was no time for sleep. In the months that followed, his love for Jaume became so intimately blended with his love for Barcelona he found it impossible to disentangle them. It was a cramped yet sprawling, tawdry yet lovable city and one that he felt at home in after a remarkably short period of time. You would never have guessed it was built next to the sea, for Barcelona turns its back resolutely on the Mediterranean. Rory had travelled widely enough during his student days to be aware that the Catalan coastline at this point could not compare with those near Nice or Naples or Dubrovnik. During the winter there were days of brilliant sunshine when the light gave an unreal quality to the outlines of buildings and of trees, reminding him of the pop-up pictures in books he had loved as a child. But just as frequently the sky to the east was a featureless mass of grey clouds, reflected in the sullen surface of the water, like the sky north of his native city, and without the tantalizing promise of the hills of Fife.

He rented a flat on the top floor of a decaying tenement in the seedy area of old Barcelona, to the right of the Ramblas as you descend. It had been christened Chinatown by a local journalist who made a trip to San Francisco. Rory found it ironic that his neighbourhood should be named, not for itself, but after part of another city in a different continent. There was nothing Chinese about the Raval. Its streets formed a relentless, geometrical grid of buildings lacking any architectural distinction, thrown up in the city's industrial heyday to provide accommodation for workers flooding there from the countryside and from the rest of Spain. As he had a good sense of direction, Rory was able to experiment with a series of different routes leading through it to the top of the Ramblas, where the school he worked in was situated. He would never forget coming unexpectedly one morning upon a narrow alleyway thronged with prostitutes, tired, worn women in their forties and fifties, like overripe fruit the flies of pimps and lackadaisicals battened upon. If they were doing business at ten o'clock, presumably they must be able to find clients then, incredible as it seemed. The sight of such indefatigable industry sickened him and he wondered how he could ever have imagined there was anything glamorous about the brothels of Paris, Marseilles and Barcelona. Literature was one thing, the reality another. The Barcelona of Jean Genet was still there and could hardly have been more prepossessing in his day.

This was not the only edifying spectacle his neighbourhood supplied him with. More than once he did a double take on a garishly turned-out woman striding past, only to conclude that she was drag. The air of this slum quarter nibbled away at sexual identities, fraying and dismantling them, as if sexuality itself were an acid solution where more solid certainties dissolved.

Rory had known he was gay for as long as he could recall. Early memories included the shapely cavity at the back of the knee of a playmate, seen from an odd angle when he tumbled to the ground, at an age that could not have been much more than four. One Sunday a young trainee took the place of the middle-aged minister who regularly preached to their congregation. Rory hung spellbound on his every word, for the emotion the novice provoked was one of familiarity, of recognition. He was adolescent by this time, yet he expected unreasoningly that the sermon would reveal to him the secret purport of this feeling. At the Merchants' Company secondary school which he attended in Edinburgh he took part in the usual fumblings in toilets and cavortings in changing rooms, while carefully shunning the company of the one boy in his year whose effeminate mannerisms marked him out as different.

His name was Lawrence Simpson and he made a virtue of the campness he could not shake off, using a waspish tongue to defend himself. Even at this distance in time, shame overtook Rory when he remembered how he had joined with his peers in reviling the creature. *Mon semblable, mon frère*, he murmured to himself when he thought about him now. Not that Lawrence had come out of it badly. He had never been subjected to physical violence, only taunts and jibes. He had a job with the Royal Bank and earned a salary considerably higher than anything Rory could command as a journalist. Their paths occasionally crossed, in a restaurant in Leith, or at a concert during the festival, and they would exchange wary greetings, without risking questions about each other's life style.

Rory took his degree at an exclusively male college in Oxford. The absence of female companionship conferred a perilously heightened intensity on all friendships and enmities, and instinct warned Rory that such a hothouse atmosphere would be anything but favourable to the open avowal of his desires. He flirted briefly with a coterie of chapel-haunting queens from another college, situated at a safe distance from his own, but very quickly tired of their religious torments, the ecstasy with which they argued the rival charms of various choristers, and the kiss and confess pattern of their love lives. He dropped the contact within a matter of weeks.

He found out about his sexuality, about the actual meaning of the urges and transports he had so long been conscious of, in the

71

course of secret weekends sneaked in London. He would spend Saturday night in a cheap hostel when unable to procure bed-space by other, less orthodox means, though the approach was ill-suited to his temperament. By nature Rory was, or at any rate became, a chivalrous libertine, governed by an odd mixture of unrelenting sexual drive and sentiment. He liked to make the first move and take care of all practical arrangements. His ideal was to welcome a new man into his bed rather than to slip between a stranger's sheets. That made the effective passivity with which he accepted Jaume's tacit advances all the more surprising.

He spent little time in Edinburgh between entering fully into possession of his sexuality and leaving for Spain, though enough to savour the comically repressed delights of the Cobweb Disco and the Kenilworth Bar. Barcelona had the force of a revelation after such primness. If he had sought after images to explain the difference, Edinburgh would have been the corner shop in a country village, with goods of every kind crammed into a limited space, where the turnover of customers is so slow that the range of choice within each category is severely limited, and many articles remain upon the shelf long past their sell-by date. Barcelona, by contrast, resembled a row of highly specialized shops in the centre of a major city, each offering its own particular brand of goods.

Every gay bar in Barcelona catered to a specific clientele. Rory had sampled several of them before he met Jaume. Once they were together, he extended his repertoire immeasurably. In particular he remembered one Saturday evening when they began their travels, at the habitually late time of half past eleven, in a big barn of a place, intended for older men and those who desire older men. It was hard to make out individual features in the darkness that shrouded most of the premises, so Rory concentrated his attention on the dance floor. He was filled with delight when the conventional disco music stopped and the regulars lined up to dance what Jaume informed him was known as a *sevillana*. In actual fact, it was not entirely unlike Scottish country dancing, a sort of Mediterranean strip-the-willow where rigid posturing, reminiscent of farmyard roosters, and intricate writhing of the arms high above the head, like the sinuous movements of a sea anemone tugged by competing currents, replaced the sturdy vigour of the northern steps.

When they had had enough, he and Jaume called in at their favourite watering hole, a brightly lit and stylish bar that opened directly on to the street. It was a place where you could socialize or just go to be seen. The cruising that formed a constant undertow to the proceedings was sufficiently discreet not to interfere with urbane chatter or predictions about the outcome of the football match the following week. Rory was faithful to Jaume throughout those two years. It was the only monogamous period in his whole life. He had his hands full and could not have contemplated taking on a second lover, even if he had felt the need to. He found it impossible to imagine how he might desire another man. Yet it did not displease him to register the homage offered him by interested parties. At times he thought they could all have been lighthouses, sending beams up and down the bar, coded and terse messages that evoked a response when one beam intersected another. His own circled round again and again, aloof, impassive and indifferent.

Just before one o'clock, Jaume hauled him away and stopped a taxi. The place they ended up in was a basement bar on the other side of town. You paid a hefty sum for admission, which included your first drink. The atmosphere was so different they could almost have been in another country. Not a word of Catalan was to be heard. The clientèle was plebeian and uniformly Spanish-speaking: waiters, car mechanics, shop assistants, psychiatric nurses. A drag show was in progress. The painted backdrop depicted a street corner in Granada, or it could have been Seville. It was well enough done, with brilliantly coloured flowers in the window boxes and a church tower visible just beyond the corner. The *artistes* mimed convincingly to pre-recorded songs. There was even a passionate rendering of a sub-Lorca poem, filled with crescent moons of tragic augury, slaughtered lambs that bled profusely and dark horses galloping in frenzy through a desert of clattering stones.

Seen in retrospect, the two years after they met formed a single, undifferentiated span of time. Yet by the end of them he and Jaume were in very different places from those they had begun in. Somewhere early on in the second year of their relationship Jaume moved out of the barely furnished flat he had shared with four other students and got an attic all of his own in the Eixample, the distinctly grand bourgeois area planned by Cerdà in 1859, conceived as an addition to the city and now its modern centre. In an unspoken fashion Rory had expected that they would set up house together in due course of time. The possibility was never discussed. Anything that might make their relationship resemble a conventional union of the marital kind was anathema to Jaume. Again and again Rory speculated as to what Jaume's concept of a relationship might be. He never asked him. It was one of the many veils that hung between them and which Rory feared to disturb. With good reason, as it proved. In later years, once Jaume had settled permanently in the States and Rory was back in Edinburgh, and even after Jaume's death, Rory wondered what part his fear played in their interactions, and what it was that he had been afraid of. There were days when he would decide that he had feared exactly that which subsequently occurred, that his premonitions had been vindicated by the course events took. But on other days he railed at himself for not asking more questions, for not pinning Jaume down mentally as well as physically and shedding light on those dark corners. And then he would laugh bitterly and think, that is your old pattern emerging again, the knight in shining armour with an urge to save, deliver, purify. And anyone less capable than himself of saving another human being he could not conceive of.

He started the catalogue six months after discovering Jaume's first infidelity. Maybe that was the wrong word. It turned out to be one further manifestation of the code Jaume had been following from the start, one Rory had implicitly accepted on that distant evening and whose clauses were to be made clear to him in an extremely painful way. Jaume started a job just before Easter with an American multinational. He did not tell Rory that it was more or less inevitable he would be transferred to the States for longer and longer periods and might well be posted there for good. If it had been possible to force an explanation from him, Jaume would have claimed that he did not want to be unkind and that, by keeping Rory in the dark about this, as about so many details of his life, he saved him needless suffering. Rory had spent Christmas in Barcelona, alone as it transpired, for Jaume insisted that the day itself and the feast of St Stephen be dedicated to his family. The Scotsman was never introduced to them and set eyes upon them for the first time at Jaume's funeral. He did, however, succumb to pressure from his own family to the extent of planning a two-week holiday in Scotland over Easter.

He missed Jaume appallingly. Logically separation ought to have become easier the further their relationship proceeded. But Rory's emotions knew nothing of logic. The pain of separation was worsened because he proved unable to get hold of Jaume on the phone. It was a difficult enterprise in any case, even if Jaume had spent more time in his flat. The family phone was on a low table beneath a mirror by the front door so that any exchange of intimacies was excluded. When they went to Skye for a long weekend of incessant rain and healthy walking, the only possibility was a public phone box three miles down the road. Rory's parents officially knew nothing about the nature or the direction of his affections and he was keen not to arouse suspicion. The need to keep appearances as innocuous as possible restricted the times he was able to try phoning at. The one time he did start dialling at shortly after midnight his mother, ever vigilant, descended the stairs in her dressing gown and asked him what was the matter. Who could he be wanting to contact at such an uncivil hour? He invented a lame excuse about needing to speak to the director of his school and being unable to get through during the working day. She stood by him while he heard the Spanish tones ringing out in Jaume's bedroom. There was no answer.

Fondness rather than suspicion prompted him to return three days early. He had to pay a minimal surcharge at the travel agent for the change of date. The emotional relief it promised him meant he did not hesitate. He dumped his baggage at home, then got a taxi to the bottom of Jaume's stair and let himself in with the set of keys Jaume had given him as a security measure. Jaume was meticulous about all their arrangements. It did not cross Rory's mind, as he swung open the huge portal that gave on to the street, that he had never had occasion to use them in this way, that to do so without warning Jaume first might be unwise. As it was, he was hardly in the door, and moving through the dark towards the bedroom, thrilled with excitement at the thought of wakening and embracing his sleeping lover, when he heard voices and another key in the lock. The light went on and, from the other end of the hall, Rory saw two figures. The other man's arm was slung across Jaume's shoulder as he moved to kiss him. Jaume had already seen Rory and gone utterly silent. Afraid he was going to cry, Rory made a rush for the door, pushed them aside and thundered down the stairs. Nobody called after him.

Jaume penned a long and dignified letter, filled with lies, which reached Rory by post two mornings later. In choosing to believe it, Rory was following the dictates of a cultural code no less slavishly than Jaume had done by writing it. What Jaume's code was, Rory realized subsequently, when another Catalan friend, a straight man, gave him laughing advice on what he should do if caught being unfaithful.

'Lie,' he said, 'lie and then lie again. It's what they want to hear.'

He was thinking about women. Rory found the lies he longed for in the letter. It was perhaps the form of comfort he desired and certainly the only one Jaume was capable of giving him. A dear friend from his native village had arrived unexpectedly. Naturally they went out for a few drinks. Rory was foolish if he insisted on misinterpreting the physical demonstrations of affection that were inevitable between two men who had known each other since their first day at school. Running off in that fashion had not only been an insult to Jaume's probity, it had alarmed and puzzled the friend, and Jaume, who was not out to anyone at home, had had to devise complicated and, he feared, unconvincing excuses to account for the presence of a foreign man in his unlit flat just after midnight.

Rory apologized. The scene where he did so was, though he did not see it that way at the time, a re-enactment of their first night together, when he had accepted without conditions the unstated terms of a complex contract of Jaume's devising. Indeed, it was a part of the contract that he should not know the terms and that these should never be revealed to him in full. Jaume accepted his capitulation magnanimously and insisted that he and not Rory should treat them both to dinner at an expensive restaurant on Carrer Aribau, whose *bacallà* was reputed to be the tastiest and most delicate the city had to offer.

While both tried hard to pretend that nothing had happened, the debacle which took place that Easter marked a watershed in their relations. The running of Jaume's finances represented a mystery of Oriental proportions Rory would no more have dreamt of plumbing than he would have dreamt of reading the *Thousand and One Nights* from cover to cover in an uncut translation. Until now there had been a tacit understanding that Jaume's means were limited and that, when they went to the theatre or the cinema or spent a few days in a *pensió* in Sitges, Palafrugell or Estartit, Rory would pay. He did not do so all the time. The idea was that, had they divided expenses on an equal basis, Jaume would very quickly have run out of money and they would have been forced to sit at home, watching the television or listening to sentimental Spanish songs on scratchy records. When Jaume rented the attic in the Eixample, Rory asked some questions. He was fobbed off with a story about a great aunt in Lleida who had died, leaving unsuspected riches behind her, including this titbit which pertained to Jaume's mother. Jaume was looking after it temporarily, until arrangements could be made to sell it and recover much needed cash, which would go on his father's vineyard and his uncle's olive grove. Once he was on the American multinational's pay list, Jaume grew positively spendthrift and showered Rory with gifts: expensive ties, the best recordings of his favourite Catalan singer, a night in a box for an opera gala at the Gran Teatre del Liceu and even a massage at the hands of a practitioner Jaume had never mentioned before. They evidently knew each other well.

Rory felt displaced and insecure. The developments in their love life may have been an expression of this or of his suspicion (one he did not confess to himself for many months) that he was no longer, and perhaps had never been, Jaume's only or even his principal lover. Rory could not think of a time when he had not felt attracted to Jaume and had never failed to respond to even the subtlest of indications that sex would be welcome at a particular juncture. Now he discovered an insatiability and an inventiveness that amazed even himself. It was as if time was running out, as if Jaume was slipping from his grasp with the ineluctable quality of sand in a timeglass. What they did was never perverse. Rory loved sex too much for that. What he later read, and actively experimented with, in regard to fetishes and role-playing confused and perturbed him. If asked, he would have said that people who devised such diversions did not really like lovemaking, that they were a form of distraction, a turning aside from the scents and textures of their own physical selves. By the time unbearably hot and humid weather arrived in June, as it did with sickening predictability, he could have sworn there was not a nook or cranny of Jaume's body he had not wooed and explored. And yet he felt Jaume was less his than ever before.

Never unresponsive, Jaume actively welcomed these amatory athletics. If he had felt able to trust his own perceptions at this stage, Rory would have said Jaume was almost pleading with him, to be held, to be stopped. He had a dream about it one night and wrote it in his diary the next morning. He knew the dream was not original, but rather a remembering of a legend he had read a version of in a Greek book when at school. Just as he settled for journalism rather than fiction writing, so Rory wrily acknowledged that even the profoundest movements of his soul would make themselves known in borrowed, rather than invented images. He picked up a ball from the grass at his feet, one made of glass, the colour of the Edinburgh sky at eleven o'clock on a night in early July, luminous when you would expect it to be dark. As he held the ball, it started to smoke inside, changing in colour to flaming red. The heat of it burnt his palms. He held on nonetheless. It became molten and flowed from his grasp, as a liquid of blinding brightness. Just at the moment when he feared that he was holding nothing, he found himself gripping a salamander in his hands. It bit his fingertip and turned into a dove, a fish, a snake. And Rory held and held and held until he woke up, staring into the dark Catalan summer night, with a panic in his chest such as he had never before experienced.

The following day Jaume told him he was leaving for New York on the coming Sunday. What he said was that his company was sending him on a course for three months, at the end of which he would return to Barcelona, to introduce the new sales techniques he would by that time have learnt. Rory's misery stunned him into speechlessness. He had not the energy to protest or even ask for further details. He accompanied Jaume to the airport in a taxi and used his credit card to pay the excess charge on the ridiculous quantity of luggage his friend insisted on taking with him. Jaume claimed to have mislaid his own card temporarily.

Rory was aware that deep changes had taken place but was uncertain as to their nature. During the day and night (he did not sleep a wink) leading up to the departure a question so tormented him that it trembled on his lips, without him actually finding the courage to articulate it. Are we going to be faithful to one another? That was it. It sounded so pathetic he chastized himself for even framing it. Falling in love with Jaume had, in its way, meant putting his signature to a blank cheque. It was senseless to insist at this advanced stage on finding out what sum had been involved. Jaume left neither an address nor a phone number, though he did specify the date of his return. The company, he said, were going to put him up in a hotel when he got to New York. Once he had a definite place to stay he would communicate the details to Rory. There could of course be no question of intercontinental phone calls to his office. As far as his employers were concerned, Jaume had impeccable heterosexual credentials. That, at least, was his version of things.

8

On Saturday night Rory did a tour of the bars. He had spent every evening that week at home, not even stopping off after lessons to get a bite to eat in a fast food place on the Ramblas, as he so often did. The telephone was silent. Several things were brought home to him, not least his utter dependence on Jaume where human contact and a social life were concerned. The only call he received was a request for a private lesson. He accepted with alacrity. Any means of filling the gap he had been left with was a godsend. He could not make up his mind whether to change the sheets on the bed or not. Every time he got between them he was met with Jaume's smell. Were he to put fresh sheets on, he might get used to his lover's absence all the quicker. On the other hand, he was unwilling to imperil even the most intangible of triggers to his memory. If he woke up during the night, his nostrils were capable of deceiving him so that, for the briefest and most delicious of intervals, he assumed Jaume was still there, sleeping at his side.

He ended up in their preferred, stylish haunt and downed three beers in quick succession. A number of Jaume's friends came over to say hello and ask for news. Rory's morose responses rapidly froze their well-intentioned cordiality. He had not clarified before leaving the flat exactly what his purpose was. It was very uncharacteristic of Rory to have an agenda hidden from himself. Getting totally plastered was one possibility. Reviving memories of nights out with Jaume, and either alleviating or intensifying his loneliness in the process, was another. Again, he might have hoped that one of Jaume's friends would suggest a social activity for one of the next few days and, indeed, several of them tried to, without success. The one plan that did not cross his mind was to find another man. And yet that was what happened.

It irritated him at first, the way the guy in the black jacket kept catching his gaze. In the end Rory turned round and ordered a fourth beer, only to discover, when he raised his eyes, that the guy had changed position, moving to the opposite end of the bar so as to be directly in his line of vision. He thought of sticking out his tongue when they clocked each other afresh. Instead, the look on the guy's face totally disarmed him. He wants me, Rory realized. He wants what I can give. The pattern of more than two decades was set in that instant, as he prepared to make the acquaintance of the man who would occupy the second place in his catalogue. Rory was generous by nature, a considerate and unstinting lover who took a discreet pride in his prowess and largesse. The difficulty he had always experienced in turning down those who sought his ministrations, a difficulty his fascination for Jaume had succeeded in masking for not quite two years, led him to be somewhat indiscriminate later in life, but never in a destructive or even a humourless fashion. If he survived such promiscuity, it was because, with the exception of Toni, he utterly refused to screw a man who was not Jaume for eight years. By the time he had overcome this block, AIDS was a familiar hazard, so that Rory made religious use of condoms.

Toni was the man in the black jacket's name. When his eyes met Rory's for the umpteenth time that evening, he lifted his eyebrows and then looked as if he wanted to smile, but did not possess the necessary courage. He picked up his glass instead and buried his face in it to cover his embarrassment. His discomfort brought out Rory's fatherliness. Rory retreated from the bar to a freestanding pillar and, within a matter of minutes, Toni was leaning on the other side of it. He kept swivelling his head round on his neck to check Rory's glass and, when it was more or less empty, gestured towards it with his own, so precipitously he nearly dropped it crashing to the floor, as he offered to buy him another.

The blood was thundering in Rory's ears. He had an almost irresistible urge to reach down and caress the man in the black jacket's backside but retained enough presence of mind to stop himself from doing so. It would have been an unpardonable gaffe in such sophisticated, brightly lit surroundings. Toni would have looked well in an Italian Renaissance painting, as a bystander in one of those scenes where the members of a court happen incongruously on a miracle, a presentation in the temple or the burial of a saint, part of a procession of contemporary figures pushed right up against the front edge of the picture, as if the artist were uncertain which world they belonged to, the magical, sacred world of legendary events or the external, real one of the spectators beyond the frame.

When they got home Rory did not switch any of the lights on in the flat. Perhaps he preferred not to be reminded that the man at his side was not Jaume. Toni did not protest. He went obediently into the bedroom (it did not occur to Rory to wonder how he knew the way) and stood facing him with his back to the bed, at the ready, so that Rory was able to do exactly what he had been longing to do for more than an hour now. He put his hands to Toni's hips and grasped the bones on either side of his pelvis. He had a momentary sense of mad omnipotence, as if by flexing his muscles he could have shattered Toni's delicate form, with no more difficulty than if he had been a china vase. Instead he worked his thumbs up past the belt, under the shirt and into the skin of the hollows on either side. Toni obligingly slipped his jacket off. Rory was able to lift the shirt up over his head, turning it inside out, momentarily imprisoning Toni's arms and leaving his nipples defenceless, so he could bite at them one by one, confirming just how hard they were. When Rory fastened on his lips, Toni gave a grunt but continued to offer not the slightest resistance, sharpening the edge of anger there was in Rory's aggression. There was a sense in which he wanted Toni to stop him before it was too late, to tell him that what they were doing was wrong. Toni's unquestioning acquiescence made him the perfect object for Rory to direct his anger at, an erotic anger because Jaume was not there to be made love to.

He hurt Toni when he fucked him, unnecessarily, just at the beginning, out of hurry and despair and fury. Once inside, though, he gave him all the pleasure he could have asked for, Rory was sure about that. He felt bad about having hurt him when they did it again next morning, slowly and gently and with plenty of lubricant, by the light of day. Toni was tight and unaccustomed to being penetrated because it was he who had fucked Jaume and not the other way around. But the story is rushing ahead and, if it is not to be excessively confusing, or excessively incredible, must be recounted in the correct sequence. Rory fucked so hard that his dick was raw when he pulled it out. In later years he told himself he was lucky not to be dead thanks to a session like that. Fifteen years had passed in the interim but the virus must surely have been present in Barcelona in 1981. In a way he was grateful for his lack of awareness (though not as grateful as for not having been infected). Seen at a distance, such memories had a sweetness of their own in these times of grim responsibility, plague and plastic. Still, the main thing was to stay alive.

He and Toni lay next to one another like the figures of bishops on adjacent, sculpted tombs. Then Toni snuggled closer and put his head into the crook of Rory's arm. Rory reached over with his other arm and ruffled Toni's shock of hair. As he had hoped, it was springy and resistant to the touch as a tussock of heather on a Perthshire hilltop. It was a moment of peace and respite before what followed.

'I'll just go for a pee,' said Toni.

As he disappeared through the door into the unlit corridor a chill struck at Rory's heart. When Toni got back and lay down again he moved to one side.

'How did you know where to go?' he asked.

'I know everything about this flat,' Toni said. His voice quivered slightly, but there was an undertone of determination in it subsequent events were to bear out.

'What do you mean?'

'That poster on the wall is Polish. You bought it in a shop on Victoria Street in Edinburgh. That's the place you come from. There's an oil painting in the lounge in a gold frame. You brought it back with you two Christmases ago.' Toni was rushing now, stumbling over his words, yet without the slightest intention of allowing himself to be stopped. 'It shows your great-grandmother. She came from Nairn near Inverness. She kept a journal about your family which has been published. You have a copy of the second edition in the bookcase by your bed.'

He rolled over and almost fell to the floor as he began fumbling at the books, knocking them from the shelf in his rush to find the one he wanted.

'What is this?' shouted Rory, in a kind of snarling crescendo, as he reached for the light.

What he saw haunted him for many months thereafter. He did not reflect upon it at the time but, if he and Toni had not first made love, his reaction would have been very different. He would have thrust him from the flat there and then. He might well have chased him out of the front door, naked as he was, and thrown his clothes after him down the stairwell, without a second thought. But Rory was a chevalier at heart. He had held this man in his arms, taking from his lips and the rest of his body what he wanted, everything he needed in order to measure the full extent of the grief which was all that remained to him in place of Jaume. And as a consequence, no matter what awfulness was now to be revealed, Toni was henceforth under his protection. Furthermore, Toni was weeping, sobbing helplessly at the same time as he leafed through Rory's great-grandmother's book, looking for the passage Jaume so much loved, the one about the Gaelic-speaking servant and the songs she sang, the one he wanted to read out to Rory.

Rory was also a libertine, and the spectacle of Toni revealed to him by the bedside lamp was unutterably lovely. He was crouching next to the bed, his heels lifted just a little from the ground, his toes gripping the floor, the muscles in his calves and thighs full and tense, his buttocks hovering above his ankles, the jet black hair dusted across them gleaming where it caught the light. His face had the shape of a heraldic shield, tapering down towards the dimpled chin in two broad curves, the eyes and eyebrows delicately proportioned, the nose just a little smaller than you might have expected, pale with excitement and with fear. He found the passage he was looking for and began to read it in the most appalling English accent, so that Rory felt the urge to laugh. He was reading and weeping at the same time. Rory leapt to the floor in front of him and took the book away, laying it carefully on the bed. With the fingers of his other hand he tipped Toni's chin upwards, so that his dark eyes caught the light, made all the brighter by the tears in them, so different, so much deeper now than when encountered in the bar.

'It's got a lovely melody, that Gaelic song,' he murmured. 'Do you know how it goes?'

All he wanted was to quieten Toni, to soothe his fear. He began to hum the song under his breath, complete with leaps and snaps and odd, modal cadences, as he had learnt it from his grandmother. Surprise made Toni's jaw fall open. Nervousness, and the touch of fear he still felt, led him to move the tip of his tongue to and fro across his upper teeth. He was salivating. When the melody was finished, Rory leant towards him, kissing him, then pushed him gently backwards until he was flat on the floor, his legs spread wide, Rory on top of him. They made love again like that, rubbing against each other, softly and insistently, without a word or a sound except their breathing.

Grief and love were mixed in unfathomable proportions in the tangle of emotions that drew Rory to Toni, binding them to one another. They spent the whole of the following day and night together. During the day they made love again, then walked and ate and slept. There was more sex in the early evening. They put out the light about half past eight and both slept through the alarm the following morning. For the one and only time in all his teaching career, Rory was late for a class. Toni, who was a trainee graphic designer, made it to his office with five minutes to spare before the lunch break.

Nature, it is said, abhors a vacuum, and bereavement draws people closer together. It is as if the person who is lost served to keep those he was most intimate with at a distance from each other and, when they become conscious of the gap, they are irresistibly attracted, the way tissue will form over a wound. Need and love are redeployed. If Jaume himself were not physically dead, then at least the Jaume Rory had been in love with was. Or perhaps it would be more accurate to say that he had never existed.

Rory struggled to fathom Toni's motives in entering on a relationship with him, in part as a way of deferring the investigation of his own, but was unable to decide if he was functioning as a substitute for Jaume or whether, as Toni insisted, he had fallen in love with Rory at one remove. Surprise and even bemusement made his discovery of the extent and nature of Jaume's infidelities less painful than might otherwise have been the case. He and Toni did not broach the subject until they were out of the flat. They took an underground train and then walked up to the Parc Güell, where the banality of Sunday crowds and Japanese tourists made the oddness of their own connection easier to deal with.

'How long have you and Jaume been lovers?' he asked.

'About eight months,' Toni answered. 'Since before Christmas.'

'Where did you meet?'

Abashed, Toni looked to one side.

'In the sauna.'

'Was Jaume a regular?'

'Nine out of ten times I've been, he was there. But I haven't been for quite a while now.'

'Who else has he been having a relationship with?'

'Sebastián ... Alfonso ... David ...' Toni squinted at Rory from under half-shut eyelids, fearful of the kind of pain he might provoke. 'You really mean that you had no idea? Not about a single one of them? But you are the one he really loves. There can be no doubt of that.'

Rory felt a mixture of incredulity and exasperation. In a way it was what he wanted to hear, yet what difference could it make now?

'What makes you so sure?'

'Because of how he talked to me about you. That's why I fell in love with you.'

Toni had certainly been an exceptional listener. Rory made him play a game later on. He blindfolded Toni then watched as, naked, he went from room to room in the flat to get an object or point to a chair or a picture. Once or twice he slipped up and grew confused, as if Rory were putting him through a test he feared he might not pass. Confronted with such willing vulnerability, the same tenderness invaded Rory as over the Gaelic song. He placed a hand on Toni's shoulder and kissed him gently, rubbing his nose into the blindfold and watching from the corner of his eye as Toni's sex hardened and lifted, with the inevitability and trustworthiness of a flag climbing a flagpole on a feast day.

Jaume phoned on Wednesday night.

'Do you have an address to give me?'

'No, not yet. They still have to find me a place. I really hate

86

being in this hotel. It's too impersonal and I can't get to sleep because the air-conditioning makes such a racket.'

There was a pause. Rory waited with a touch of sadism for Jaume's next words. I know so much now you don't know I know, he thought.

'Are you all right? Lonely?'

'I'm doing not bad. Toni has been keeping me company.'

'Toni?'

Amused detachment. Rory admired Jaume's capacity to remain so unruffled.

'The graphic designer. You remember the one.'

Jaume's voice turned serious.

'Rory, you're not to believe a word he says. That man is loopy. He chased after me for weeks and weeks before I left and I didn't give him an inch. If I were to tell you the things he did you . . .'

Rory lowered the receiver gradually towards the phone. It rang again a minute later. He did not answer. As arranged, he met up with Toni the following evening for a meal. His motives in inviting him back afterwards were mixed. He probably would have wanted him there for the company and the comforting sex in any case but he also planned to check his testimony further. At first Toni refused then, when Rory pressurized him, entered into details of his lovemaking with Jaume he could not possibly have invented. At one and the same time Rory wished he had been able to catch him out and admired his basic probity. With an odd tweak of pain he reflected, this one really does love me. He laid down one inalterable condition for their relationship: he would not be faithful. When Rory said this, Toni's mouth formed into an odd shape, one he had not observed before, as if there was a wasp inside and it had stung him, but he was determined to give no proof of pain. Then he drew himself up, took a deep breath, and acquiesced.

Rory was systematic, even mathematical in his infidelities. He had a kind of rule that he would not make love to Toni more than three times in succession without having somebody else. The catalogue gave the whole process a symmetry and detachment that, he later realized, kept him from going mad. For each individual he entered the same details: name, date of birth, profession, telephone number when possible, how and where met, time elapsed between first contact and orgasm, what they had done together, sexual tastes (acted upon, expressed, or merely suspected) plus any other relevant information. When he left Barcelona to return to Scotland four years later, there were two hundred and fifteen entries. The twelve intervening years in Edinburgh brought the total to four hundred and seventy-three, of which one hundred and sixty-five had been clocked up while travelling. A further forty-two were foreign visitors to Scotland, met principally during the Festival, but also on ferry boats between the isles, on station platforms and, on one occasion, in a mountain rescue helicopter.

Jaume was persistent. Four letters arrived in quick succession, the envelopes tightly packed, Rory's address on them in the confident handwriting punctuated with flourishes he had so far only seen on rushed notes or in the flyleaves of books. He burnt them ceremoniously over an ashtray on the kitchen table. It gave him a feeling of liberation to reduce the lies they must contain to ashes. A friend was renting Jaume's flat in his absence. At least, so Rory had been told. He could not guess and did not care to find out what sort of a scenario these apparently reasonable arrangements might conceal. He took the precaution of calling round when he knew Nacho would be in, so as to return Jaume's keys and retrieve his own. Nacho knew nothing of what had happened and did not protest. Rory said he needed the keys to give to friends who would be visiting from Scotland.

In this way he avoided what he feared, finding Jaume sitting in the lounge one day upon returning home. Instead he waited for Rory at the entrance from the street, with a massive bunch of roses. Rory barely greeted him and brushed past, slamming the door shut behind him. When he got into the flat, the buzzer from below rang a few times, then fell silent. It puzzled him that Jaume did not try phoning. Maybe he felt the cards would be stacked against him if he were to rely on this medium for communicating. Two friends (not mutual friends – Rory realized they had none of those) were given the task, on separate occasions, of bearing verbal olive branches. Rory admitted them courteously, sat them down, and offered each a glass of vermouth. When they had delivered their messages, he gravely asked them why no one had told him what Jaume was really up to.

They reacted quite differently. Edgar sniggered and said you didn't tell on your friends, did you. And anyway, surely Rory must have twigged. It had been so manifest to everybody else. Lleonard looked mortified, put down his drink and did not touch it again for the rest of his visit. He had been deeply unhappy about Jaume's behaviour, he admitted. But you had to understand where he was coming from. After all, he was stunningly good-looking, and since the age of twelve had succeeded in bedding more or less whoever he wanted to, straight or gay, by merely beckoning. Was it perhaps unrealistic of Rory to expect that the leopard should change its spots in a relatively short space of time? His infidelities were not a sign that he did not love Rory. Quite the opposite, in fact. Lleonard's voice took on a different colouring as he proceeded.

'Jaume was afraid of how much you loved him,' he said. 'Having other men was his way of protecting himself.'

'And who protected me?' asked Rory.

'You're right,' Lleonard agreed, 'you're right. Forget him. I love him deeply but he will come to no good.'

Toni left Rory within a year. Rory was relieved when he announced his decision. He knew he was hurting Toni although he could no longer see any possibility of stopping himself.

'Don't imagine I don't love you just because I'm not making a fuss,' he said.

'I know you love me,' Toni murmured softly.

Toni was not good at being on his own. Within a month he had found another partner, an unsuitable one, who caused him such pain he had a minor breakdown. He spent ten days in hospital and stayed on medication for most of the following year. Rory visited him on each of the ten days and kept a watchful eye over him afterwards. Late the following spring Toni moved to a different company and his career took off dramatically. While they had been together he had loved to spend spare moments doodling on whatever came into his hands: the backs of envelopes, old school report sheets, extra photocopies Rory had not needed to use in class, and had brought back home to be used as scrap paper. Rory never threw any of them away.

'I always knew you would be famous one day,' he told him.

In the course of the next year Toni met the man he had been with since, a music critic who turned out to be Ramon's uncle. Rory and Ramon did not realize they had this connection in common until the dinner party reached the pudding course. Rory stayed in contact with a select few of Jaume's friends. Now that the cat was out of the bag, they were able to speak freely to him. It transpired that Jaume had spent little more than a week in the hotel before moving in with an older man, a merchant banker who doted on him and condoned his multifaceted love life. Gossip had it that it turned him on and that threesomes, and more, were the order of the day. Jaume spent two months back in Barcelona before returning to New York on a permanent basis. After settling in Scotland, Rory continued to holiday each year in Catalonia. He could have enquired whether his visits coincided with Jaume's but chose not to. One evening, in a garden restaurant in Sitges, with tables spread out in semi-darkness amidst potted orange trees, he caught that unmistakable laugh arriving from a distant corner. Without offering his companion an explanation, he asked the waiter to bring the bill, paid and left.

He was not surprised when news arrived that Jaume had pneumonia. In fact, he had seen it as simply a matter of time. A sufficient number of his acquaintances in Edinburgh were positive, already ill, or dead, for his thoughts to have winged their way to New York and the possible implications for Jaume. Rory would have welcomed a chance for them to make their peace. To go to New York on purpose seemed excessive. As it turned out, human error or sheer negligence prevented them from doing so in Barcelona. Jaume flew back, accompanied by his merchant banker, when he had barely four days left. They arrived discreetly, on a Thursday evening, and it took time for word to get around. Rory was staying with Toni and Josep on that particular visit. The heat in the city got too much for him and he went off on his own to a resort near Empùries, which boasted a lively gay beach. His plan was to spend the weekend there and return on Sunday. As it was, he hung on for another day. When he walked through the door at seven o'clock on Monday evening he found a distraught Toni sitting waiting for him. Jaume had died in a clinic in Sarrià at three o'clock that afternoon. He had been told

Rory was in Catalonia and had insisted they do everything they could to contact him.

'Why didn't you?' shouted Rory.

He never forgot the answer, and the circumstances linked to it. Toni had asked another friend, Florenci, to drive northwards and look for Rory. Florenci had picked a hitch-hiker up half an hour out of Barcelona. One thing led to another and he had abandoned the search in favour of an unexpected amatory weekend.

'I would never have found him anyway,' Florenci had told Toni.

Toni refused to let Rory confront the man.

'What point would there be in that now?' he asked.

Rory saw the body before the funeral. Ravaged by illness, it reminded him of pictures he had seen of the bog people in Northern Ireland, the ones Seamus Heaney had written a series of poems about. Wet conditions preserved their remains long beyond the natural span. Illness had deformed Jaume's before he reached thirty. His withered, leathery skin had the aspect of a shrunken gourd and its contents, too, seemed to have shrunk. There was no telling what had happened to that which had once animated it. It was difficult to imagine that this object had ever been human, far less beautiful. A confirmed atheist, Rory turned away without a tear.

Jaume's alternate weekends in Lleida with his family had of course been a pretence, as had the vineyard and the olive grove. His father was a prosperous industrialist from Sabadell, a satellite town of Barcelona, and his mother, who had means of her own, had bought the attic in the Eixample as a present for him on his graduation. Rory joined the line of mourners who shook hands with them after the ceremony. When he introduced himself, Jaume's father's features lit up briefly.

'Ah yes, the Scotsman,' he said. 'My son often spoke to us about you.'

9

Safely ensconced in a high armchair in the study, Brian heard the remaining guests arrive with a mixture of distaste and irritation, only pausing when the significantly different, rasping, virile timbre of Ramon's Catalan-inflected English struck his delicate musician's ear. He had not bothered to count. But he imagined there might be as many as ten men around the table, at least one of them a southerner. Coming from Glasgow rather than Edinburgh, he did not attach the importance other men at the dinner party did to accent as an indicator of nationality. Barry's voice was unusually high in pitch for such a tall man, but not unpleasant in its way. Brian felt a twinge of curiosity, quickly dispelled when he turned his attention to the book lying open in his lap.

Having checked whether he wanted a drink, Dougal had tactfully closed the study door behind him, leaving Brian to his own devices. Aeroplanes generally made him slightly sick. The shuttle from London that evening had been no exception. His first impulse was to collapse into a comfortable chair and close his eyes. The occasional noises that arrived from the front door, the hallway and the dining-room at its far end had a background of silence that he found immensely soothing. The study looked on to an inner set of gardens, bounded by a severe quadrangle of grimy Georgian tenements. No sound of traffic penetrated there. From where Brian was sitting, all you could see was the slope of the grey slate roof on the opposite side and a generous portion of sky, where the light of the June evening was waning but not quenched.

He turned his attention to the fireplace. The black, cast-iron surround sported delicate floral mouldings. Dougal had filled the grate with dried thistles and other stalks and sheaves, arranging them so beautifully no one could have contemplated striking a match and using them as the basis for a real fire. Brian switched on the lamp on a low table to his right. Three walls of the study were lined with bookshelves. Dougal had inherited the library from his great-uncle on his mother's side, a celebrated judge who never married and devoted much of his leisure time to assembling a collection of mainly eighteenth- and nineteenth-century volumes. The exquisite leather bindings not infrequently exceeded in value the pages they contained. Brian got to his feet and started to browse. He was not ready for the impressions he had gathered during the two previous days in London to crowd into his brain, demanding to be assimilated and made sense of. An outside stimulus would keep them at bay, at least until he went to bed.

The thought pulled him up short. He had nearly fought with Gavin in the car between the airport and the flat where he now found himself. Dougal had offered them a bed for the night. Gavin insisted it would be discourteous to refuse. He had had a tough week in the hospital. The last thing he wanted to do was to drive back through to the west after a night of socializing. What kind of a dinner party would it be if he was not able to drink?

'I can drive,' Brian had said. 'It's just that after being away I want my own bed. And I was never keen on meeting this crowd of people anyway. You know I find strangers a trial. Haven't I been through enough during this trip to London?'

Gavin grunted. Silence fell. Nothing had been agreed. It was unlike Brian to lose an argument. And yet he caught himself assuming he would sleep in the guest room tonight. What kind of a sign was that? He had not taken to Dougal. He looked as if he came from a prosperous, unquestioning Edinburgh background, too like his own unquestioned one in Glasgow. And the decoration of the flat was insufferably pretentious. Kieran, on the other hand, intrigued him. Intrigued him and attracted him, he admitted that. In a sense he wished Kieran would seek him out in his retreat, would come through the door and start a conversation. It would be so much easier than having to study him amidst the uproar and high spirits of an increasingly drunken party.

The book he had chosen, as far as he could tell, was a collection of Oriental tales from the Victorian period. The title page gave very little away. There was no indication of the translator's name, or of what language the originals were written in. It had fallen open at an illustration that immediately caught his attention. It was an engraving done with consummate skill, lines of elusive finesse accumulating and separating to constitute all the elements of a picture which, he presumed, represented an episode from the story on the opposite page.

There was an encampment in the foreground and, huddled around it, a group of men in exotic clothing. They might have been gipsies or robbers but had more the air of businessmen or merchants, in spite of their elaborate furs and teetering, cylindrical hats. To their right was a tent with the shape of an upturned fruit bowl. Brian surmised there would be a framework of carefully trimmed branches underneath, the bark smoothed in the course of many journeys of careful handling and use, so that it shone as if polished. Over them the travellers would spread tapestries and carpets. Even in that twilight the fabrics glowed with the reflection of the campfire. To the left horses were tethered, their shapes little more than a darkening of the shadows where they stood.

To the rear, against the sky, something different was happening. A cliff rose sheer above a river, so sheer that only the thinnest of fringes of grass at the top of it hinted at the plain which lay beyond. A young man clothed in a diaphanous white robe had leapt that very minute from the height. Had the illustrator delayed only a little longer, he would have disappeared from view, drowned or dashed to pieces on the rocks at the river's edge. As it was, a segment of sky was interposed between his feet and the ground. He was lifted into the air rather like Christ, in a picture of the Resurrection Brian vaguely remembered, so possessed by the force which reft him from the tomb that he subsisted in a state of levitation, hovering above three sleeping soldiers, a white banner with a red cross upon it fluttering in his hand. Brian's eyes moved to the facing page.

Dashkur rushed headlong through the marketplace like a mad creature. Skirting the stalls where the confectioners displayed their wares, he knocked several jars of pickled fruit and a tray of spices to the ground, without noticing. When the edge of his cloak caught on a corner of the saddlemaker's counter, he pulled it free with such violence that he dislodged the whole structure. The contents started an irresistible slide towards the ground in a slow, ponderous avalanche of gleaming leather and tinkling, clattering harnesses.

'Leflef!' he cried. 'Leflef, my beloved! Can you truly have deserted me?'

He had been calling that dearest (to him) of names for so long, and was so short of breath from running, that the words could barely be made out, amidst the hubbub of buying and selling which surrounded him. All that emerged from his lips was a subdued complaint, like the murmur of a child which cannot find its mother, and contemplates the vastness of the empty world as if it were a great puzzle, when all hope of tracing the key has been lost.

He scampered onwards, immune to the curses and imprecations hurled at his disappearing shoulders, again and again jogging an elbow, or treading on the hem of a saffron-coloured garment, causing the owner to cry out in irritation. So distraught was he that he collided head-on with a merchant, who could not have been more enraged if he had received a deliberate buffet on the cheek. The man's friend Gulrak, a swordmaker, made a comical mockery of pursuing the culprit, brandishing a keen Damascus blade, to the merriment of everyone standing nearby. The torrent of oaths which issued from his mouth would have brought a blush to the cheeks of the sauciest brothel owner in Baghdad. But Dashkur was already too far off to catch a single syllable.

He sped on like the desert wind, indifferent to whose eyes it blinds with sand, or to the groans and creakings of the palm trees, in an oasis it has briefly shaken with its turbulence. The day was drawing to a close. Night prepared to cast its swift blue cloak over the firmament, one stars glinted in like jewels, sewn to form careful signifying patterns: blessed constellations travellers can use to guide them on their way, once sky and steppe can no longer be distinguished from each other.

The marketplace was at his back. From unseen balconies where servants fanned their mistresses, untiring and impassive as the cow which flicks its tail to ward off flies, women's voices rose in plaintive song. Now he panted along alleyways that twisted and turned, erratic threads of dust, pitted with ruts and dried-out puddles. The low mud walls to right and left shielded gardens from the eager gaze of passers-by. Beyond them lay groves of orange and lemon trees, their leaves still glinting with the stolen light of day, the twilight silence in which they were submerged broken only by the plopping and plashing of fish, in ponds whose surfaces had reflected bright fruit a moment before.

The tradesmen and their families who sought refuge there from the heat of the afternoon had withdrawn indoors to pray and eat. Before long servants would spread pallets of intricately woven straw beneath the branches, and their masters join them in the fragrant darkness. Once the tree frogs had set up a chorus of incessant croaking, they would summon sleep to descend upon them from the stars, bringing its cargo of dreams, perilous fantasies and premonitions.

There was little hope that sleep might cool Dashkur's aching forehead that night. Losing first one sandal, then the other, he scurried on, indifferent to the sharp-edged stones that cut into his soles, and to the mud that caked his ankles and his heels, slowing his progress as he passed the garden of the Grand Vizier. Significantly higher than those of its neighbours, the walls were decorated with the crudely stencilled faces of demons and capricious spirits, whose task it was to ward intruders off. Just a week before, Dashkur had delighted the company assembled there by singing and playing on the rebeck. As was expected of him and was fitting, he had extolled the maze planted by the Grand Vizier's uncle many years ago, so intricate the Crown Prince wandered in it for a day and a night, before at last conceding defeat and blowing on his horn, upon which signal the Grand Vizier sent a favourite dwarf inside to rescue him. Next Dashkur improvized a satire on the avarice of Shisnal, whose seven daughters wasted their youth away in a garden on the other side of the city. They were said to be more ravishing than the moon reflected in a rain pool on the steppe, yet the flower of their beauty was condemned to languish unplucked, because their widowed father refused to relinquish the most infinitesimal part of his riches as a dowry for even one of them.

As what he had seen in the first light of dawn were not enough, the news he received on the afternoon of that terrible day had caused Dashkur to break his rebeck across his knee, and swear an oath that his fingers would never grasp a bow again, until he either regained his beloved's affections, or wreaked a terrible vengeance for the wound he had received. He then fell into an exhausted sleep. When he awoke, the pain was so great he cried out that a worm, having taken up its residence in his gut, was gnawing at his intestines, so determinedly that nothing but a wraith would be left of him once it had its fill. Death alone could offer him relief. Ignoring the frantic protests of his mother and his sisters, and without a thought for the absent father who loved him so dearly, or the brothers who would have given their lives to defend his honour, he ran out of the courtyard of their house, intent on reaching the cliff of Araxas and hurling himself from its top into the waters of the river Senn.

It was a solace to leave the echo of human voices, and the last trace of human habitation behind him. Like a lone yacht setting sail upon the ocean, with no prospect of a roadstead, or of any ending to its voyage except shipwreck, he let the great steppe close around him on all sides. The soft grass was unspeakably welcome to his tread. In front, the thin sliver of a new moon rose above the vanished horizon, spilling her light onto the green expanse, like milk leaked from a broken vessel, teasing him, indicating a constantly shifting path on which he could ascend, beyond the idle concerns of ordinary men and women, to a higher world, where love and hurt were only memories.

And then he tripped.

The impact was so sudden and unexpected he had no time to fling his hands out to defend himself, and his forehead hit the ground with a force that stunned him. He did not realize he had been weeping all the time he ran. Now, with his face thrust deep into the grass, he noticed tears still streaming from his eyes, though that earth was so fertile and all-encompassing it had no need of watering from Dashkur. An impulse of anger and curiosity made him wonder what had caused him to fall. Sitting up on his haunches, snuffling still, he rummaged around until his fingers grasped the offending object. It was a sloughed-off snake skin. As he lifted it, a voice spoke to him from the darkness at his side.

'Be not afraid,' it whispered. 'You find yourself, poor mortal, in the presence of the serpent goddess, Wu.'

Appalled to be confronted by a divinity, Dashkur instinctively assumed a posture of adoration. He brought his knees tightly together and bent his back right over, so that his forehead touched the ground.

'Raise your head, o mortal,' the voice continued. 'Gaze upon me. I have not assumed a form so brilliant human eyes cannot behold it, nor one so ugly it will inspire disgust in you.'

The words she uttered had a hissing, lisping quality, like the sound of water scattered over burning stones in the bathhouse, when the air has become so hot men can no longer breathe, or like the wave that advances, then retreats on the shore of an inland sea, when a galley with many rowers has passed where the bed is deepest. The thirst of the pebbles at the edge is briefly slaked, before the hot sun parches them once more. Fearfully, cautiously, Dashkur raised his head. Before him the form of a woman shimmered through the darkness, indistinct, a luminous green. She was squatting on her heels the way peasant women did. An ample scarf shrouded her head, so that the face was in shadow. He blinked. When he opened his eyes again, though the outline was unchanged, he found himself peering into a pit of phosphorescent green snakes that moved incessantly, wreathing and coiling like the troubled surface of a boiling liquid. It made him dizzy to look upon them.

'O divine one,' he said, his voice quivering with terror, 'have mercy on a mortal who has come upon you unexpectedly, and whose last intent it was to show you discourtesy or cause you injury. And yet such is my misery that the most terrible death you could inflict upon me as punishment would be a welcome deliverance.'

The voice laughed. In its laughter the hot stones sizzled more fiercely still. The wave hitting the water's edge raised the pebbles and set them clattering against each other, like a skeleton's teeth.

'Do not speak of pain or punishment,' it said. 'The fantasy of an immortal one who has been slighted is endlessly fertile in devising torments. Even to hear of them would extinguish the life within you in the twinkling of an eye. Fear not!' it commanded, for Dashkur had begun to whimper and moan in terror. 'Fear not! I intend no harm to you. Indeed, frail creature, I am in your debt, and my sole concern will be to repay the service you have done me.

'Have you not heard how, in the dawning of time, I crept to the highest crag of the mountain Al Siddan, in the distant Caucasus? I coiled and uncoiled my lithe form without growing tired, slithering towards ever loftier regions, though it meant I had to leave all possibility of concealment far behind me. The thought of the nest of Keradem, prince of eagles, and of the delicious eggs concealed there, drew me to the pinnacle of the world. Scarcely had I battened upon that delicate hoard, piercing their casing with my tongue and sucking the exquisite juices from within consuming no fewer than five creatures that had not yet assumed solid form, still barely perceptible filaments in a divine solution, than the father of the brood returned. Inflamed with vengefulness, he seized me in his claws, dashing me repeatedly against the cliff face in a frenzy of destruction. When he saw that I could not be broken, he let me fall, but not before pronouncing the curse which weighs upon me even today.

'Alone of all the brood of serpents, it is not given to me, their monarch, to slough off my ancient skin when, at the turn of a hundred years, its grows too slack, and I begin to putrefy within it. I need the help of another living creature, if I am to escape. What is more, I cannot seek to procure that help, for it must be given me unwittingly. And know, Dashkur, son of Sherepnan, that it has fallen to you, at the end of this millennium, to free me from the narrow house I was imprisoned in. Speak now! What boon do you crave of me as recompense?'

'To die! To die!' wailed Dashkur. 'That is the only boon I crave! My life is worth nothing to me, and I desire nonentity alone, since I have lost the love of Leflef, the most skilled instrument maker in Birjand!'

'Do not be foolish!' warned the voice.

The immortal one was losing patience. The hissing of her syllables recalled the noise a blade makes, when it cleaves the air in the hands of a master warrior, who will soon be lopping off wrists and heads and ankles, for it is as cutting as it is delicate. On the one occasion when, rather than set his body convulsing with an infusion of deadly venom, she had offered a mortal her munificence, it irked her to be told he had no use for it. Dashkur covered his face with his hands. Squinting through the slits between his fingers, he saw that the air contained within Wu's outline now resembled a pool a heavy stone has been dropped into, so that myriad small fry dart in all directions through the limpid water, in a chaos of distorted, slanting strokes, like the wild script of a mad calligrapher.

The fishes' movements grew more calm.

'Ask me three questions,' she told him, 'and I will answer you the truth, such as is given only to immortal ones to know.'

'Where is Leflef?' Dashkur said. The question was so pressing for him he did not need to take thought in order to formulate it. Again the laughter came.

'Do you not hear? Can you not feel the ground trembling to the drumming of his horse's hooves, although he is so many leagues from us already? The beast's mane is ruffled by the wind of its own passage, even on this stillest of nights. He is galloping towards Tabriz, and the court of Al Hujan the Caliph.'

'And who is at his side?' asked Dashkur. 'Is it Ka, the Caliph's eldest son?'

'It is,' the goddess answered. 'The love between them is still young and, while he does not turn to look at him, the mind of Leflef is filled with the beauty of the man riding at his side, that skin no less golden than the sands which border the Caspian Sea, the chest burnished like a cuirass of bronze beaten out smooth, with not a fleck of dust or tarnish on it, the shoulders rising from the collar bone to support the neck, as the trunk of a young sapling rises from the ground, in perfect suppleness.'

The cry Dashkur uttered would have melted the heart of any woman or man who heard it. Not so with Wu. Her serpent eyes, with their unmoving lids, saw far beyond the span of his short life. The pain of his loving was, for her, as transient as the shadow a beetle casts upon the clay, before it burrows back into the darkness of the earth again. She waited. Dashkur hardly dared to ask his final question. It wrung itself from his lips against his will.

'And shall I enjoy once more the love of Leflef, in all my mortal days on earth?'

'No, never more. And yet all shall be well, and all manner of thing shall be well. And now, since such is your desire, and since the exultation of rebirth is so great in me that nothing exceeds my powers beneath the moon tonight, I shall sweep you to the cliff of Araxas with my own strength, and hurl you from its top into the waters of the Senn. You shall not find death at the end of your flight, but a rebirth as deserved and involuntary as the one you have conferred on me.'

Who can say if chance led Shiram to raise his eyes from the campfire, just as the light of the new moon caught Dashkur's garments, palely fluttering on their airborne journey? Or did the goddess Wu cause him to do so? The hour when the carpet sellers usually bedded down was long since past. The melancholy which so often sets in, after an important undertaking has been completed, made them reluctant to break up their circle and court capricious sleep, each on his own. In any case, the rumbling of the river in the background, cutting a deeper channel for itself and speeding along impatiently as it curved beneath the cliff of Araxas, looked set to banish any hope of rest.

The wandering life which Shiram's father led belied his wealth. One of the richest merchants from Tbilisi to Teheran, he had not abandoned the simplicity of his accustomed ways, or the bluntness with which he preferred to express himself. Squatting down next to his son, he puffed contentedly at a clay pipe, whose tip alternately turned incandescent, then faded, as the movement of a glowworm's wings reveal, then hide its radiance, on a night in May. This was their traditional stopping place on the first night out from Birjand. Every single carpet they brought with them had been sold. The conversation ranged from banter and inconsequential matters to exaggerated, long drawn-out accounts of the negotiations that had been successfully concluded, in the shadowy booth on the market place they rented every year. Relieved of their cargo, the men were heavily laden with gold and silver. A firearm was positioned, cocked and ready, on the ground at the feet of each one of them. Their last port of call in the city had been the powder merchant's store. As they strove to entertain one another and banish the oppression that had descended upon them, their ears were also straining to catch the echo of a footfall, or a horse's hoof, which might give warning of an imminent attack.

Shiram had been longing for the new moon to rise above the cliff top. Its rays would illuminate the shadows that surrounded them, diminishing the likelihood of their being surprised. The first watch of the night was to be his. No hint of drowsiness weighed upon his eyelids. He was so startled by what he saw that he jumped to his feet, though it did not betoken any danger.

'A man!' he shouted. 'Either it is a bird unknown to me, or a man has thrown himself from the cliff of Araxas!'

The distant flutter as of a standard, unfurled and glimmering in the moonlight, had already vanished.

'Let him alone,' his father murmured, taking the pipe from between his lips. 'If he seeks death in the waters of the river, why should we rob him of a peace he so ardently desires?'

'This is the first night of the new moon,' answered Shiram, laughter in his voice, 'a night of gifts. I want to see what the moon has brought me, no matter whether it be man or bird!'

The words were barely uttered when he mounted his horse. Circling round the campfire once, he set off at a gallop towards the river's edge. His two favourite companions followed close behind. They were relieved to find a pretext for dispelling the gloom that had assailed them by the campfire. The moon had fully surmounted the cliff, and shed its light on all sides. Shiram reined his mount in at the river bank. The currents here were powerful and unpredictable. A man and his horse risked being swept away without warning. A luminous bundle darted on the surface of the water, sank, then bobbed again.

'Quick!' Shiram called. 'Cut across to the other side of the bend! The current will thrust it towards the bank!'

Having surmounted the bend, the river broadened out and quietened. Nearest them, the shore was composed of an ample beach of shingle. Beneath their horses' hooves, the pebbles clattered and the shallow water sputtered. Shiram's prediction was right. Before it could sink for a third time, the bundle was propelled towards them. He dismounted and waded out to rescue it. As the men lifted Dashkur from the river, the current teased the last corner of his clothing from between his legs, leaving him naked in their arms.

'A youth,' one of them said, 'on the verge of manhood. Only the finest of down darkens his cheeks.'

'We must get the water out of him,' said Shiram.

They laid him on the grass and massaged his chest. The eyes did not open. His lips parted again and again, as if vomiting. Nothing but water issued forth. Shiram bent close.

'He is alive,' he pronounced. 'I can feel his breathing on my face. Let us take him to the tents.'

10

Dougal's watercress soup encountered general approval. He sat at the head of the table, nearest to the door which gave on to the hall and then the kitchen. Gavin was to his right. Alan took the place next to Gavin. They had continued chatting to each other, once the story of the photograph was finished. Kieran sat next to Alan, with Mark facing him on the other side. While nothing had been said, a safe distance had successfully been established between the latter pair and Dougal, as if by an instinctive agreement. Rory sat on Dougal's left, an empty place separating him from Mark. It was the place Brian would have taken if he had been going to eat with them. Neither Kieran nor Dougal cleared away the cutlery, the underplate and soup plate from it. No one knew at what point Brian would choose to join the other guests. There was also a likelihood of Nicol's partner Andrew arriving in the course of the evening, perhaps even before they had risen from the table. Nicol sat at the opposite end from Dougal, with Ramon on his right and Barry on his left. Invariably nervous when amidst a large group of people, Barry had kept close to Nicol from the time they came upstairs, regarding him as his safest ally in a threatening situation. Rory took care not to sit next to Ramon. He did not want anyone to get the impression that they were a couple. It would have damaged both his *amour propre* and his reputation. He did not envisage keeping up with the Catalan for much longer.

Several of the guests had brought their bubbly with them from the sitting-room. Given that the fish course was imminent, the bottles of white were opened and they filled their glasses. The tongues even of the more recalcitrant among them were loosened as a result. After some cheerful banter about Rory and Ramon, to which the journalist responded in monosyllables, the conversation turned to first nights and one-night stands.

When Dougal disappeared into the kitchen with the first load of soup plates, Kieran took the opportunity of a moment's silence to catch everyone's attention. Mark had slipped away from the table to the toilet, so that he was absent during the first part of Kieran's tale. Nevertheless Alan who, despite his devil-may-care exterior, could not suppress a twinge of jealousy when they were in Kieran's company, pricked up his ears, eager to glean any details he had not yet heard about Mark's previous relationship.

'The night I am thinking about,' began Kieran, 'belongs to the time when things between Mark and me were coming badly unstuck. We kept getting back together for a week, or ten days, then Mark would disappear again. The next I heard he was having a passionate fling with someone he had picked up at the disco. A different guy each time, of course. It felt like they were sandpapering me inside, the way people do when they have stripped the paper off a wall, before they paint it.'

The note of bitterness in his voice surprised everyone. They were all intent on his words. Dougal could be heard loading the dishwasher in the kitchen. He had not come back for the second load of plates. Kieran took a deep breath.

'Thing is, though, walls don't hurt. When I closed my eyes, I imagined I could see blood leaching out inside me, seeping down towards the floor. I used to dream about it. What made it worse was I was struggling at my job. The previous April I got a distinction for my thesis. Halfway through August I started teaching in a secondary school. It wasn't what I wanted to do. I fell into it through a kind of inertia. Then a lecturer at college disappeared overnight. I got a phone call asking me to step into his shoes. They couldn't offer me a contract right away, they said, but that would sort itself out by Christmas. They were desperate.

'The new head of department, who had just taken up his post, had acted as the external for my thesis. It was right down his street. He'd evidently taken a shine to me. Pity it didn't last!' Kieran laughed. 'Anyway, it was too good an opportunity to miss. Problems with discipline were making life at school a misery. Going back to college struck me as a godsend and it was. The education authority were not exactly chuffed when I announced I was leaving with minimum notice. The headmaster had me into his office, gave me a dressing down and told me that, as far as he was concerned, I could depart the following day. That's what I did. I bid farewell for good to secondary education.

'Life in college, however, proved a lot tougher than I expected. These days we have special ways of looking after new arrivals on the staff. They get a mentor, their teaching and marking is supervised, and so forth. When I began, you either swam or sank. Everything you did was surrounded by an eerie silence. It could have meant you were so embarrassingly bad nobody dared raise the matter, or else that you were getting along fine, and there was no call to interfere. I backed the latter option, though I had no hard evidence either way.

'I would have peculiar, nightmarish days when I expected to feel a hand on my forearm, then a voice would say: "We're on to you, son. We know you're an impostor. The game is up. You're going to be exposed." On two separate occasions, I woke around five o'clock, and lay in bed waiting for the alarm to ring, trying to gather sufficient courage to phone in and tell them I had had enough. I couldn't face the prospect of striding down those corridors, and pontificating to large groups of students, when I barely knew as much as they did on the subject.

'At any rate, that's how it felt. But you have a sudden burst of energy around half past seven and it all seems feasible again. The most useful piece of advice I got was from an older woman colleague who is a chain smoker. She took early retirement this year, presumably because the new health regulations mean she can't get a puff anywhere in the building. "When a student starts giving you a hard time in a tutorial," she told me, "and you're not sure how to squash him, just look him very hard in the eye and say: 'Are you *sure*?' It hasn't failed me yet." If the difficulty at school was getting the kids to shut up, at college you practically had to prise their mouths open to get them to say anything. So I never had to put her tactic to the test. Still, I felt better for having it up my sleeve.

'I muddled through until exam time at the end of second term. The first two batches of scripts were manageable. It only took me about twice as long as I'd calculated to mark them. The day after I finished them, one hundred and twenty first-year scripts were plumped down on my desk. I panicked. It was a Tuesday afternoon. I made a pile of twenty-five and waded through them. Doubts tormented me. Was the 65 I was about to give really so much better than the 63 I had awarded to a question four papers earlier? There was nothing for it but to go back and read that question again. The longer I spent over it, the harder it became to make my mind up. My confidence collapsed. I got the tippex out so I could alter the marks, but in the time it took to dry, I forgot what the new mark I wanted to give had been.'

By this time Mark was back at the table and seated opposite Kieran, listening as closely as the rest. Kieran did not go into the details of the conversation he was about to mention.

'I had had a particularly acrimonious phone call from guess who the previous night. I couldn't get it out of my mind. Easter was only ten days away. Darkness was falling outside. I glanced at my watch. It was half past seven. All at once it dawned on me that I was expected at the head of department's house for dinner that evening. He was still living with his wife and children, in a ground-floor conversion with a garden on the south side of Edinburgh. I grabbed a tie from the top drawer in my desk. You see, I got into the habit of keeping one or two there. If you're feeling nervous about facing people, a tie will always help. Students are anything but radical. They're much more likely to take you seriously if you dress formally. And I needed all the assistance I could give myself that evening. I went into the staff toilets, where there was a mirror, to sort the knot out. Then, on an afterthought, I stuffed about fifty scripts into a Safeway's plastic bag. I didn't have to come into college the next day and maybe, if I had another go at them at home, they wouldn't be quite so daunting.

'I cannot tell you how awful the dinner party was. I was the only person on the right side of forty. What's more, I was the only one not in a couple. They talked about hanging squabbles in the Kelvingrove Gallery through in Glasgow, and about who was up for chairs in Oxford, Kent and Bristol. I couldn't think of anything to say. The more time went by without me opening my mouth, the more unlikely it became that I ever would. The head of department tried to feed me lines. He looked at me pleadingly. I suspect he was wanting to show me off. Or maybe there was a job going in one of the institutions these people came from, and he was setting me up for an interview. All I could think about was a phrase from the phone conversation with Mark.'

Kieran raised his eyes and looked directly at Mark.

'You all know what a wicked tongue he's got. Not as bad as Robert's, mind you. But bad enough. Probably I would laugh it off today. Then I found it devastating. For a day or two, at least. So I decided the only way to save a disastrous evening was to go to the pub and find a man for the night.

'I got to my feet and excused myself before coffee arrived. The head of department came with me, and helped me get my coat on. He was resigned by this stage, as if he realized it was all too much for me to handle. Naturally I hadn't said a thing about my private life. I wasn't out to anyone at work then. You couldn't afford to be, on a temporary contract. At least, that's how I saw it at the time. I was halfway down the garden path when he called me back. In his hand was the plastic bag with the scripts.

' "Careful! Mustn't forget these!" he said, wagging his finger. He added a few choice words about the appalling things that would happen to me if I were to misplace even one of them. I could feel my face going deep red. He was confirming my basic sense of incompetence, you see. I took them from him, more or less ran to the main road, and waved at the first taxi which passed by. Luckily it was free. I was far from the centre of town. I didn't tell the driver my precise destination. I felt too wary to do that. Instead I gave the names of the two streets that meet nearest to it. He probably knew where I was headed the minute I got in, before I could open my mouth!

'Walking into the pub was just like coming home. Never have I found that distinctive blend of beer fumes, cigarette smoke and cheap scent so welcoming. Before I reached the bar, I clocked the guy I left with in the end. He was taller than me, lanky, with close-cropped red hair and dreamy blue eyes. He came from the Pans, Prestonpans, and he had an East Lothian accent you could have cut with a knife. I found it seductive. That was the state I was reduced to. I laid into the wine heavily at the dinner party. After two pints in the pub I would have been anyone's. I'm glad I got him sorted out before I was too much the worse for drink.

I think that even pimples would have turned me on that evening.

'It's odd, isn't it? I don't know if it has occurred to other people. Maybe it's not true for them. Every time I've had a one-night stand it's been about somebody else. It's never mattered that much who I went home with, because it was all directed at another person, either a consolation for not being with them, or a form of revenge. That could be why my one-night stands have invariably been disastrous. It's when you miss your partner most you come closest to betraying them. You don't really feel that awful gap unless you're used to having somebody around.

'Anyway, back to the redhead. He was training as a signalman with British Rail. All he wanted to do was talk endlessly about his job. He'd just finished a week-long course. Soon he was explaining the structure of the major Scottish junctions to me. He had the names of the different signalling systems by heart. I was relieved. It made getting off with each other so much easier. I concentrated on keeping my balance and not falling over. He told me he spent a lot of time in the evenings sorting out his uniform. He was inordinately proud of it. He had to get a special brand of button polish that they sell in just one shop in Edinburgh. I should have scented trouble at that stage. But I had barely escaped the rigours of a formal dinner party. I was delighted that everything was going according to plan. I knocked the beer back and let his words flow over me. Rather than listening to what he was saying, I was studying his lips and wondering what it would be like to kiss them. They kept looming at me. Perhaps I was keeling over already, I can't tell. When we got up to go, I tripped on the steps leading to the pavement outside. He grabbed hold of me to keep me upright.

'We had reached the kerb when he turned to me and asked: "Weren't you carrying a bag when you came in?" The scripts! He was more sober than I was and insisted on going back and getting them himself. The effect of the cold air outside was to dampen my spirits. But after he had been so helpful about the scripts, I'd have felt a heel if I'd pulled out. So when he reappeared, I let him put his arm around my shoulder and stop a taxi.

'He lived two flights up a close in Stockbridge. The toilet was to your left as you came in, the sitting-room to your right, at the end of a long, narrow corridor, the kitchen off it, and the bedroom to your left. An enormous train set took up the whole of the sitting-room. It was spectacular. There was a station as you came in through the door, complete with ticket windows, buffet, left luggage office and four platforms. To one side the landscape rose in a range of hills, so the trains could pop in and out of tunnels as they sped on their way around the board. At the far end was the sea coast, with a beach. The train line ran close by it. There were deck chairs, with miniature holidaymakers sitting in them, and an ice cream van drawn up rather oddly at the water's edge, as if it had just driven out of the sea. A group of holidaymakers were connected to the electricity supply, so that they waved their arms each time a train went past. The man from Prestonpans was especially proud of this piece of inspiration. On the right was a goods yard with gantries, three signal boxes, a shed for washing and painting running stock, and a canteen for the rail-waymen, which featured a green billiard board with brightly coloured balls scattered across it.

'It may have been the drunken state I was in. I found the whole thing spellbinding. He fiddled with the controls, and two trains began skeltering round at a breathtaking pace. You would have sworn they were going to crash into each other. He had it arranged so they entered the same hill from opposite sides. A tragic accident in the tunnel seemed inevitable. And instead they came out unscathed, travelling in a quite different direction from the one you had expected.

'I was squatting down so as to see it at eye level. He ruffled my hair, then lifted me gently under the shoulders, from behind, unbuttoned my shirt, and started stroking my chest and my stomach. I turned my head around. He was just tall enough for us to kiss in that position. It was romantic but rather awkward. Next he took my hand and led me into the bedroom. He hadn't switched the train set off. What followed happened against a background of trains, rattling past the beach, whizzing in and out of tunnels and veering round the corners of the board. I didn't know what to expect and was past caring anyway. He knelt down, unzipped my flies and started giving me a blow job. I had the hard-on to end all hard-ons. Partly it was the trains, partly feeling we were little boys again, in a world where there was no danger the grown-ups might find out what we had got up to.

' "Don't move," he said, and opened the doors of his wardrobe. I looked around the room. One wall was completely hidden by posters of steam trains. Detailed plans of track layout covered another. When he turned back to face me, he was holding a British Rail signalman's hat and a whistle. He popped the hat on to my head and stuffed the whistle into my mouth. It was all such a hoot I couldn't stop laughing.

' "You blow, I blow," he said, with a bewitching grin.

'Maybe you've never asked yourselves whether it's possible to have an orgasm and blow a whistle at the same time. Let me assure you that it is, from personal experience. Though what was happening at crotch level rather cramped my style as far as directing trains was concerned. Sounds such as I produced have not been heard on a station platform in Scotland for many years. When he was finished, all of a sudden I felt really awkward. That's happened to me more than once after coming, when I've been having sex with a man I hardly know, in strange surroundings. You know what they say. *Omne animal* . . .

'The signalman said nothing. He still had all his clothes on. He wiped his lips, turned away, started rummaging in the bottom of the wardrobe, and dragged out a big holdall. I had no idea what was coming now. Curiosity and trepidation, that's what I felt. As well as an enormous tiredness. And all the while there was the din of the trains, performing their mad gyrations through in the next room. I chose the coward's way out. I took my chance while his back was turned, zipped my flies up, made a mad rush for the door, and thundered downstairs, into the night air on Raeburn Place.

'When I awoke the following morning, I had three thoughts one after the other. First, that this was the worst hangover I had had since graduating. Second, that I had to spend the day correcting scripts, and was in no fit state to do so. And third, that the scripts were where I had left them, in a Safeway's plastic bag, on the floor of the sitting-room, underneath a giant train set in the Stockbridge flat.'

'Kieran,' said Dougal from the doorway, 'can you come and help me serve the fish course, please? The plates are in the oven.'

'Oops,' said Kieran. 'I've been neglecting my duties as host.'

The guests at the dinner party never did find out what happened to the scripts. Rory was no longer listening. His attention had wandered far off, at an earlier stage in Kieran's narrative. Talk of one-night stands had set him thinking of a night, or rather of three nights, some years before, and of the man he spent them with.

11

As he moved his hands across it, Angus's skin made Rory think of glistening snow. Not the snow of a mountainside, that stings the touch with its coldness. Living, breathing snow, glowing rose-coloured or white, here and there with a shimmer of pale blue. His bed had never held anything so perfect as that skin. Afraid to go further, he paused, fearful too definite a pressure might lead it to dissolve beneath his fingers.

The name, of course, was not Angus. That was all Rory knew. 'Everything I say to you will be a lie,' he had announced, standing there in his socks on the other side of the bed, glaring in a mixture of defiance and seductiveness before he pulled them off and got in. At once the detective in Rory was aroused, alert to every modulation of the Anglicized, distinctly Edinburgh accent. Imagining a school, a family, a home. Privilege. Angus might lie when he spoke. But would his body be able to lie? The rising of the hip, where the pelvis bone emerged, like the ridge of a hill emerging from the silky greenness of the lower slopes? The uplands of his chest, with the nipples standing jewel-hard and intense, the hairs around them so golden they almost disappeared into the luminosity of his skin? Could they lie?

'Angus,' Rory said slowly, trying not to smile, testing whether the man would respond, whether the name produced an automatic reaction.

The blue eyes did not flicker even for a moment. If Angus were indeed intent on constructing a barrier of lies, he did so with absolute seriousness, as though his livelihood depended upon it. Not once, in the course of all that long night's lovemaking, did he laugh or even smile. That he should retain such vigilance, reaching orgasm and subsiding out of it without ever truly relaxing, without breaking his intensity of concentration for a fragment of a second, was what Rory found most achingly seductive of all.

He had never seen him in the pub before. Indeed, for all that the cynic within protested and berated him, Rory felt sure he was one of the first men, if not the first, to explore that body thoroughly, now and again a little more roughly than might have been justifiable, yet without evoking a protest, or even an acknowledgement that he was taking liberties without asking permission first.

It was a surprisingly speedy accord. That militated against Angus's being entirely inexperienced, for long years of practice had taught Rory that the uninitiated could be infuriatingly tentative. It could take upwards of forty minutes, even an hour, to get a man who had entered the pub for the first time to return a glance, never mind engage in conversation, to alert him to the possibility of leaving with someone he had not set eyes on before that night. Whereas Angus had met his gaze coolly and dispassionately, parrying Rory's feeble attempts at dialogue with an indifference that verged on rudeness. When Rory gulped the last of his beer down, before he could propose buying another round, Angus had said quite simply:

'Shall we go, then?'

What ensnared him was the gradual, then at last total concession of physical intimacy as the night progressed, while at the same time the youth kept his mind at an unflinching distance. The eyes were indecipherable. Rory had got him just in time. It was a beauty that would not last. His flesh had the doughy quality Rory found irresistible in younger Scottish men, like white bread that has not quite been baked through. Very quickly it would cease to shimmer and turn flabby, hanging from the bone in a manner that deformed the underlying structure, rather than emphasizing its every symmetry, as happened now. It was indeed like snow, Rory thought, and would not survive the passing of winter. If snow was a flowering of beauty, then winter was its summer. He had no inkling how to penetrate that cloak of beauty so as to unveil the mysteries it hid.

When he came (allowing Rory to nudge him towards climax, like one dinghy nudging another into harbour, the allowing always going before each thrust, so that Rory had no sense of possessing or taking control, rather of a constant and fruitless pursuit) Rory held him as if he were a child. Angus's body went rigid for a matter of seconds, then quivered in a paroxysm that could as easily have been of pain as of pleasure. The head was turned away, towards a corner of the ceiling, as if some detail of the stucco work offered the solution to an enigma which pre-occupied Angus more deeply, at this instant in time, than any feature of the man he had on top of him. When Rory came in his turn, the younger man lay unmoving, observing him with a blend of curiosity and detachment, even a strain of pity, alternately frightening and insulting.

Rory was tempted to murmur, 'Don't watch me,' to deny the other, if he could, a revelation that had been so consummately denied him.

'You're cold,' he said afterwards, a note of pleading in his voice, as well as admiration.

'It's not a well-heated flat,' said Angus, pulling the downie up to cover both their nakednesses. Rory was not sure whether he had misunderstood or if Angus was only pretending to mis-understand him. It felt safer not to ask.

'I'm not your first man?'

The game they were playing was far from light-hearted. While realizing it would be hopelessly ambitious to imagine he could learn, so early on, the nature of the stakes, Rory at least wanted to find out about the rules. He was uncertain, for example, whether asking questions such as this was a proof of weakness or of strength.

'Would you like to be my first man?'

Rory had his hand between the man's legs, underneath the covers, touching the place between his asshole and his scrotum, noting the different quality of the skin that clothed the genitals. He found Angus's assurance breathtaking, this ability to concede so much and so little at the same time. He could have squeezed his balls, or tickled them. Instead, he cupped them in his hand, treasuring the warmth they gave. That, at least, Angus could not withhold. His head rested on joined hands. The hair in his armpits was golden too. Rory considered resisting the temptation to kiss that exposed place, then gave in.

'There's a chest of drawers like that one in my parents' home,' said Angus. 'Where did you get it from?'

He was surveying everything in the room, carefully itemizing all the furniture.

'Am I supposed to conclude that there is no chest of drawers, or that you don't have any parents?'

'Oh, I wouldn't lie about that. Only about important things.'

'And parents aren't important?'

Angus looked at him in surprise.

'What makes you ask that?'

'How old are you?'

'Twenty . . . four.'

There was a perceptible interval between the words.

'And you?'

'Thirty-eight,' said Rory, quick as a flash.

He had deluded himself, briefly, that being able to reveal everything put him in a position of strength. In fact it felt like falling into a trap.

'And if I were to start lying too?'

'Be my guest,' said Angus, unperturbed.

His sex was thickening again beneath Rory's light stroking. He looked at Rory with something like a question in his eyes and, as Rory bent to kiss him, lifted his head ever so slightly from the pillow. I am learning the code, thought Rory. I am able to guess what is expected of me.

After the second time Angus got out of bed. Staying put was not something Rory would normally have done. Family instincts of hospitality, if nothing else, would have prevented him. Out-manoeuvred, he chose a semblance of rudeness as his defence, watching from beneath the patterned downie cover as Angus put first one leg, then the other through his spotlessly white underpants. He had a pang of regret when the torso disappeared inside a singlet. With a confidence which was so astonishingly uniform it could have been a mask for insecurity, but was more probably the effect of money and education, Angus swung the wardrobe door open, as if he had always known there would be a mirror on its inner face he could use to adjust his tie, and the collar of his jacket.

'And if I were to pursue you?' he asked.

'Don't,' said Angus.

He had his raincoat on now.

'How do you know I'm not a policeman? I could have eyes all over Edinburgh.'

'I know you're not,' said Angus, bending to kiss him goodbye.

'Will I see you again?'

'What makes you think I know the answer to that question?'

And he was gone. Rory found it hard to credit the finality with which the front door closed, the familiar sound produced by unfamiliar hands. He looked around the room, asking himself if he could have imagined it all. But there was a distinct depression in the pillow to his left. As he lay back, the light from the bedside lamp, slanting across the pillowcase, set a single blonde hair glinting, oscillating in a breeze imperceptible to anything more weighty. Rory caught at it. It did not try to escape his grasp. It was just long enough for him to wind around two fingers. Angus. Not even a name was left to him.

They met again much sooner than Rory expected. He had spent the afternoon in Glasgow, trying to get copy for an article about a rumpus among members of the Labour group that ruled the city council. The train he planned to return on was cancelled. He practically had to fight to get on the next one, which was so crammed with fractious, tired commuters he was forced to stand for the whole journey through to Edinburgh. Looking down the carriage, he could glimpse the heads of the passengers who had their backs to him. In one of them, the shade of the blond hair and the distinctive wave in it, he recognized, or thought he did, with a shudder of excitement, Angus. He considered struggling to the doors, so as to be among the first to descend. That way he could hurry through the crowd on platform 14, get some headway, turn round and confront him, if his supposition proved to be right.

But something in the idea repelled him. Perhaps it offended his pride, or he understood that the very act of reaching out would for ever banish any possibility of making love with Angus again, of finding out more about him. Ten minutes later, in the basement of the Marks & Spencer's store on Princes Street, sorting through the chicken cuts, in various different sauces, packaged for lonely diners, he grazed the elbow of the person next to him. It was Angus.

The meeting was an accident on Rory's part. Was it that way for the other man? His demeanour could not have been more different than on their previous encounter. His voice had a low burr of barely suppressed excitement. He hardly took his eyes off Rory. They had a foolish conversation about prepared vegetables and microwave ovens. Rory kept waiting for Angus to end it, and when he did not, decided it was up to him to act.

'Shall we go to the payout?' he asked.

'I have to get a couple more things. Why don't you come with me?'

The raincoat was the same. Immaculately polished, expensive footwear, of a rich red like a raw steak, freshly cut. Angus carried a metal basket in one hand, his briefcase in the other. Rory wished he had X-ray vision, so as to penetrate the stylishly battered leather and inspect the contents. A pensions adviser? There was too much energy about the man for that. A young doctor? He needed to look more exhausted. And he lacked the self-sufficient air that is characteristic of interns, however inexperienced they may be, as if they had to learn to simulate from the start of their careers a knowledge they only gradually acquire. A lawyer? His tie, Rory decided, was not a lawyer's tie. It had an Escher-like design, with salamanders biting one another's tails, against a background that looked like a cluster of Aztec pyramids.

'The flat's not far away,' Angus observed, joining him on the other side of the checkout.

Piqued, Rory was on the point of correcting him ('my flat'). In fact he was too relieved, at having the situation so painlessly and effortlessly resolved, to quibble. Angus served him that evening. There was no other way to put it. He was at Rory's disposition, as a faithful and impeccably perverse valet might have been at his master's, in one of those eighteenth-century picaresque novels Rory sometimes took as the basis for his fantasies. During a protracted spell of pleasure, curtailed only by the necessities of safe sex, standing at the edge of the bed, Rory studied Angus on his knees in front of him. The nape of his neck, as the head moved back and forth or swung from side to side, so as to rub the erect penis against his cheeks, possessed the steadfastness of a tree

118

trunk, along with the suppleness of an eel. The lamp next to the bed evoked constantly changing reflexes from the thick blond hair. Rory decided that the man he had glimpsed on the train was not Angus. He knew the back of that head now. He would never be mistaken about it again.

It was an old, top-floor flat on a sharply descending street in the New Town. The kitchen was paved with Caithness flagstones. Rory took the precaution of closing the window shutters, which creaked and were in need of paint. In socks and underpants alone, they busied themselves preparing a meal, snipping open plastic packages and shaking the last drops, with their opaque sediment, from the recesses of a bottle of olive oil. They said very little. The crunching of the pepper mill, as Angus drove it round, startled them both. He moved deftly and efficiently from cooker to fridge, so much so Rory concluded he was in the habit of cooking every evening, perhaps not only for himself. He looked from Angus's body, with that familiar chill glow, the nipples still so erect he could have sworn they cast a tiny shadow, to his own, older, worn and more experienced, the abundant hair that clothed his chest and stomach dappled now with grey. He longed to press one to the other. But the mute dance, the ritual they were engaged in, had a fixity he chose not to disrupt.

Angus dried while he washed up. When Rory finished mopping the sink, he had vanished. He found him burrowing into the bed again, reflective, and experienced an odd twinge of displeasure. His territory was being invaded. He had a piece to write. He did not, after all, want his guest to spend the night with him. Perhaps he was not as totally at this man's mercy as he had imagined.

'Mind if I smoke?' he asked, getting in next to him.

'Not at all. I'll have one too.'

It was suspicious. Rory could have sworn that he was not a smoker.

'I was thinking about something that happened while I was at school.'

'Why?'

'I don't know. The atmosphere of this place. The furniture, the curtains. It breathes an air of twenty years ago. Have you lived here for long?'

'More or less since I came back from Spain. The stuff comes from an aunt's house outside Elgin. She died and left it all to me.'

'Lucky boy. Was there lots of money?'

'Enough to buy this place.'

Angus stubbed his cigarette out only half-consumed.

'Where did you go to school?' asked Rory.

'Glenalmond.'

What coolness, Rory thought. How does he know I didn't go there? How can he lie so tranquilly? And at the same time, he was taking notes, already calculating what could be checked and how. The husband of a cousin was a master at Glenalmond, had been for over ten years, and might be able to supply the necessary confirmation. A confirmation that Angus was lying. That, at any rate, was what Rory surmised. He had been pumping friends and relations for so long, in the course of his work as a journalist, that he had lost any sense of shame about exploiting contacts in this way.

'I'm remembering a man who taught me there. A man who died.'

'That's sad,' said Rory.

It sounded callous and insufficient even to him. But then, he did not know whether he was dealing with a real death or a fictitious one.

'He was my first . . . man.'

'Not your first love?' put in Rory, quick as a flash.

'Why bring love into it? What do you know about love? Do you confuse this with love?' said Angus.

His voice was veined with genuine anger. Maybe Rory was intended to listen only, not to interrupt. All of a sudden he felt ashamed, cowed and exposed. Did he already feel love for this man? Could that, in some obscure way, be a crime? Or was the wrong thing that there was no love whatsoever between them?

'I loved him,' Angus went on. 'After my mother, he was the first person I really loved. She didn't want me to be sent away to school. It was my father and my uncle who insisted. She managed to postpone the departure until I was eleven. Although I had turned sixteen that summer, I still pined for her. It could have been because the summer holidays were so close, I don't

120

know. May and June were the hardest months. Any constraint becomes unbearable when it is just about to end, rather than halfway through, which is what you might expect. Her letters came quicker and quicker that year. I always sensed she was unhappy with my father. They were moving towards a definite break throughout the spring. She never broached the topic with me. It was our nanny who confessed it all.'

'You had a nanny,' Rory said, 'when you were sixteen.'

'Oh, she had been kept busy looking after my younger sisters. There were four of them. And once they were all at school, the poor creature had no desire to leave us, even though a distant relative had bequeathed her a draughty flat in Carnoustie. She preferred to stay with us, and we agreed.'

'Living in an attic of the family mansion. Preserving memories and photographs. With a view of the distant sea.'

'How did you guess?' said Angus. 'It's in the East Neuk of Fife. My mother lives there now. Nanny is long since dead. I never got to take him there.'

He paused. Rory was still aware of an undertow of exasperation. He was determined not to give Angus an easy ride. How well he handles my interruptions, he was thinking. The man has no sense of irony. It is unworthy of him. His body has an edge that his mind lacks. And yet, somewhere in all this fabrication, a core of truth must lie.

'To take who?'

'Damian was his name. Damian Smythe. An Oxford graduate. He came to teach us classics. He arrived at Christmas and by the beginning of the summer he was dead. I'll never forget the first lesson he gave us. It was a whiff of a different world. He spoke for more than half an hour about romantic homosexuality among the ancients. The word had never been mentioned in our presence. And then he went on and on about a writer called Henry Gibson . . .'

Rory racked his brains, but could find no connection for the name, no Scottish author or historian who fitted.

'. . . and of course it was Henrik Ibsen he meant, you know, the Norwegian playwright, the one who was so important for Joyce.'

Rory nodded, and decided that Angus did not work in the arts sector. No one with that kind of job would take such trouble to demonstrate his cultural credentials.

'Then somehow he worked George Eliot in. The most rational woman in the Victorian age, he called her. Yet she screamed the house down the night her lover died. That was another unmentionable term.'

'Two in one lesson,' observed Rory.

'He wore a cravat.'

'And he seduced you.'

'Maybe it was me that seduced him. I wrote him an English composition. It was a signal. And he got it. It was full of purple passages I would blush to read today. A cry for help which provoked a response. He had a red sports car.'

'He must have had a lot of money.'

'He was like you. An inheritance arrived shortly before he graduated. Not enough to buy a flat. He blew it all on a fast car. And we spent the month of June roaring up and down the roads of Strathearn, scattering terrified pheasants, traumatizing the wives of retired colonels who were doddering along at the wheels of blue Mercedes. All we killed was the occasional hedgehog and a stray cat.'

'You're lucky you didn't hit a tree.'

'Not while I was with him. He did that on his own.'

Although he did not believe a word of it, there was something about the story that brought Rory up short. He wondered if simulated or imagined grief could demand the same respect as the real thing.

'We made the connection via Catullus. Small as the Latin class was, people still couldn't agree about the texts they wanted to prepare for A-level. Damian loved Catullus. I could tell he did, though he hated open displays of emotion. He looked round the class in a detached sort of way, as if it didn't matter, saying he found it hard to believe absolutely nobody was interested in such a splendid poet. His eyes lingered on me, and he said: "What about you . . ."'

He stopped in mid-sentence, a look of alarm on his face.

'Angus,' Rory supplied obligingly. 'What about you, Angus?'

'Angus and Damian. I know it sounds odd. It sounded odd to me even then. We were beautiful together. He was as beautiful

122

at that age as I am now. There were six years between us. We arranged to meet in the garden late the following afternoon, so as to begin construing the Latin poems. After half an hour we took a walk in the woods, past the cane thicket down by the stream. I leant my back against an oak tree. He put his hands on the trunk, on either side of me, and kissed me on the lips.'

'Did it stop there?'

'He fucked me. Later, in the car.'

'That isn't easy.'

'Oh, we did it in the fields as well. The barley was ripening.'

'Must have been scratchy.'

The notion of penetrating Angus had not occurred to Rory. He found it obscurely frightening. It would have been like penetrating snow, as if his sex could have got frozen, however welcoming that softness might initially appear to be.

'It hurt the first times. It never entered my head we might do that. He was very insistent and I didn't want to refuse him. It's an odd thing, being penetrated by a man who dies. As if he carries on being inside you. There are moments when I imagine I can still feel him there.'

Rory was out of his depth.

'I must say I prefer sex with the living.'

Angus sniggered.

'Do I sound crazy? At times I do. It's odd the things that come into my head.'

He turned on his elbow and planted a kiss on Rory's lips, with characteristic aplomb. Any illusion that barriers were being lowered was immediately dispelled.

'I'll have to be going.'

Perversely, Rory now wanted him to linger on.

'Where did they bury him?'

'In the village churchyard, not far from the school. There was nowhere else to take him. Both his parents were dead. The inheritance came from his last close relative. They summoned me to identify the body.'

'That was strange.'

'Maybe identification is the wrong way to put it. He carried a photograph of me with him. He survived the accident for a few hours. When they were taking him to hospital he kept saying my name. It could have provoked the most dreadful scandal. But of course the headmaster hushed it up, what with me being under age and all that.'

'Wasn't there more than one Angus at the school?'

'Stop interrupting me. When I got there he was dead already. I shall never forget how beautiful his head was, with a trail of dried blood from his mouth and down his chin. I bent down and kissed it, you know. I kissed the blood even though it was dry.'

The picture stuck in Rory's mind. The funny thing was, he had in fact attended a boarding school only a little less prestigious than the one in Angus's account. Involutarily, he gave Damian Smythe the features of a master he had had a crush on, not a classics master, but the one who taught them woodwork. He was considerably older than Angus claimed Damian had been, and lived close to the school with a wife and two children. In the days that followed their second meeting, Rory could not free himself of the image of Angus bending over Damian, whose head was reclined on a spotlessly white hospital pillowcase, at an angle that had already become rigid, with that red blemish, glinting slightly in the electric light, disfiguring both lip and chin.

It was at the time when a group of men and women from different bodies in Scotland, including certain political parties, the trade unions and the churches, were in the process of concluding their discussions on a blueprint for a devolved parliament. Committed to outright independence, the nationalists had refused to take part. Their intransigence irritated Rory. He voted SNP in every election that found him in the country. It was a gut reaction more than anything else. Coming from the prosperous area east of Inverness, from a family of business people and doctors, he regarded industrial Scotland with an instinctive distrust which affected his attitude to the Labour party, its elected representatives and their rhetoric. His interests were moving increasingly towards political journalism, and what he learnt of the working of local government administration in the central belt did nothing but confirm the prejudice he had inherited.

Rightly or wrongly, he perceived the Conservative party, on a national level, as anti-Scottish in a not always covert manner. An unmarried uncle had written short stories in the Doric dialect, which encountered a considerable degree of success when published in a local newspaper. Rory had a powerful sense of himself as someone with Scottish roots in both the north-east and the Highlands. And therefore, though the pronouncements of its politicians often struck him as ill-considered or muddled, he continued to support the nationalist party unwaveringly.

This meant he was the natural person for the newspaper to send to a draughty school hall in Granton, early one evening, when the devolution proposals were put forward to the press. Spokespeople from both the Conservative party and the SNP would be present, though neither had been involved in the deliberations of the group. Rory sat next to two colleagues both of whom he liked, Alasdair Sim from the *Herald* and Joe Lumsden, who wrote on Scottish subjects for the *Independent*. Disappointing though the turnout was, Rory could not suppress a degree of excitement at the occasion and the conclusions the group had reached, which included a recommendation that at least half of those sitting in the new parliament should be women. He scribbled furiously, hardly lifting his head until the nationalist spokesman was announced.

It was Angus. Later, when Rory wondered how they had failed to come across each other in the course of his work, he learnt that the person designated had fallen sick a day or two before. Angus was drafted in to replace him. It was his first important assignment, and he saw it as a major chance to shine. Rory's reaction was unexpected. He wanted to hide, to duck down behind the row of chairs in front, or bury his face in the shoulders of the man next to him, as if it were he who had to conceal something, as if he were the one whose presence was a breach of tact, the violation of an agreement. The certainty that he was blushing prevented him exchanging the usual comments with either of the men beside him, or even looking at them. He could not make out a word of what Angus was saying. He was waiting for the inevitable to happen. And since the numbers in the hall were so low, it soon did.

Angus caught sight of him and stopped in mid-sentence. His jaw fell open. He was reading from a battered wooden lectern, his notes in front of him, his hands gripping either side of it. Instead of pulling himself together and forging ahead, he looked around the hall, as if he expected someone there to come to his assistance, to find a way of rescuing him. As he stood there, gaping, Rory's feelings changed from embarrassment and an obscure guilt to anger and contempt. Angus cleared his throat and said in low, almost inaudible tones, so different from the ones he had set out in:

'I'm sorry. I'm feeling unwell. I'm going to have to stop.'

He picked up his papers and left the platform.

In the pub afterwards, the journalists were at a loss to account for the SNP spokesman's fiasco.

'I've never seen the chap before,' said Joe. 'Do either of you know him?'

'He's one of the up and coming new cadres,' said Alasdair. 'David Reid, from Bathgate. In spite of his performance today, he's likely to go far. He's just got engaged to the chief executive's daughter.'

He mentioned a high-ranking official whose name frequently figured in the headlines.

'Nothing like marrying into the organization!' said Joe. 'He doesn't sound like he was born in Bathgate.'

'He manicures his image carefully, that one. As ambitious as they come. It makes it all the more surprising that he should run aground the way he did. After all, it was hardly an intimidating occasion. The hall was half empty. There was no danger of him being challenged or drawn into a discussion. All he had to do was outline the party's position and sit down again.'

'I can't think what got into him,' said Rory, lifting his pint.

He was looking morose, but then that was his habitual mask when dealing with the outside world.

'You'd almost think he'd been to a public school,' said Joe.

'Aye, but he doesn't take it that far,' said Alasdair. 'It would be counterproductive for a nationalist to sound too English. He mustn't lose the common touch. Competent and educated but still with the people, that's the ethos he needs to embody.'

'Bathgate's hardly the most beautiful place in central Scotland,' put in Rory, unsure whether he just felt the need to say something, or was fishing for more information.

'It used to be very Orange, didn't it?' said Joe. 'Will he have managed to shake off his religious prejudices, I wonder.'

'Indeed,' said Alasdair. 'Suspicion of those hasn't done his party much good in the past. I wonder if he's like the other chaps I know from Bathgate, though.'

He smiled, ordered another round, and continued.

'It's my theory that Bathgate mothers have a special technique. Or else there's something uncanny in the air of the place. Two close friends of mine were brought up there. They're both in their late thirties now. Every Sunday, come rain, come shine, they abandon family, girlfriends, the lot, and drive home to have lunch with their mothers.'

'Sandy Grieve even takes his to church beforehand,' added Joe.

'I don't think Angus is like that,' said Rory. 'He kind of breaks the mould.'

'David, you mean,' said Joe. 'It's unusual for you to get a name wrong, Rory! Why should he be different? Do you know something that you aren't telling us?'

'Oh, just going on tonight's performance,' said Rory.

'Let's hope it doesn't do him serious harm,' said Joe. 'His bosses won't be pleased.'

'Yes, but you're allowed to slip up once or twice. They don't have so many bright young men they can afford to squander them. And none as good-looking as that guy,' added Alasdair.

'Indeed. There's something almost feminine about the care he takes of himself,' concluded Joe.

'Marriage should put paid to that,' said Alasdair.

Rory was tucked up in bed by eleven, hurrying to reach the end of an old, dog-eared paperback detective novel, when the door-bell rang. He had decided not to answer but it rang again, more insistently. Pulling on his dressing gown, he tiptoed to the front door of the flat, without putting the light on, and peered through the spyhole.

It was Angus. He let him in.

'Not a usual time for callers,' observed Rory.

'Under the circumstances . . .' Angus said, panting still, though he had had time to catch his breath while waiting on the landing.

'It may have bothered you,' said Rory coldly. 'Why should it bother me? David, is it?'

'Keep calling me Angus. It'll make things simpler.'

He had taken off his raincoat. He made his way into the bedroom and threw it onto the bed. He was shaking and found it
difficult to be still.

'Things are perfectly simple. You were lying, you were found
out and it's over.'

'You're not going to leak this to the papers, are you? For God's
sake, don't do anything so hasty! If only I'd known you were a
journalist . . .'

'You'd never have spoken to me? What do you take me for?
What makes you sure that people care? You're engaged to a party
official's daughter and, at the same time, you pick up men, go
home with them, and spin a web of lies because it entertains you.
Do you think that's newsworthy?'

'Isn't it?' asked Angus lamely.

'It's been done before. Mind you, if you were a cabinet
minister . . .'

'Give me time.'

There was a pause. Angus reached over and fingered the lapels
on Rory's dressing gown. He was too nervous for a more direct
approach. Rory pulled them together and tied the cord firmly
around his waist.

'Is that all?'

'But there's so much to talk about!'

'What do you mean? It's insignificant and it stinks.'

'Ah-hah! You're angry! Now you're going to preach a sermon
to me.'

'You think because I'm gay and don't lie about it, because I
take you home and into my bed and ask no questions, because
I listen to your crazy stories almost as if I believed them, that I
don't have any morals?'

'Let me hear them, then. They're sure to be unusual.'

'They certainly prevent me having anything more to do with
you.'

Angus's face fell. He was genuinely surprised.

'But why? Do I disgust you? Have I stopped being attractive
because I stumbled halfway through a speech and couldn't get
my nerve back? You're angry, angry and hurt, that's all. There's
no need for you to react this way. Look, I can stay over tonight.
I don't have to go back home.'

'You mean your fiancée isn't waiting for you? Don't you sleep with her? Or is there a clause in party regulations about virgin brides?'

'You know everything, then.'

'No doubt you've taken her home to Bathgate, to meet the family.'

Angus sat down on the edge of the bed, disconcerted but determined to fight.

'What's immoral about my behaviour? Why is it worse than yours? I don't have any other choice.'

'A shotgun wedding.'

'What would you do if you were me? Act the openly gay politician, turning up at rallies and election meetings with the boyfriend of the moment? Is that what you expect?'

'I can name at least one man who doesn't hide it. And he's been promised a portfolio in the next government.'

'If they get in,' said Angus, in a jeering tone. 'Down in London. Not here in Scotland. What sort of a world do you think we live in? An out gay man on the SNP executive! Whoever that is, I can tell you, it won't be me!'

'You're such a cynic!' said Rory, so angry he was almost shouting. 'If you're in with the nationalists, it ought to be out of some sort of principle. Instead you make a lie the basis of it all.'

'I'm not a liar. I'm a realist.'

'A liar *and* a realist.'

'Give me a drink.'

Rory was less eager to get rid of him by this stage. Not that he had changed his mind about continuing. It would be more judicious, he decided, to prolong the conversation until he himself got the chance to calm down. And so, ever the gentleman, he relented, and led Angus through to the front room. Angus had never set foot in it. It made him gasp, it was so huge. The aunt whose money Rory had used to buy the flat had been a painter of some repute. Partly out of fondness for her, partly because he was told it would be a reliable investment, he hung on to the canvases she still possessed at the time of her death. One stood next to a window, on her old easel. It showed an interior giving onto a garden, in bright, French colours, and made an odd impression against the jet black of the Edinburgh night beyond the astragals. Rory poured two malts and crouched down by the gas fire, clicking at the switch till it ignited.

'This isn't what I expected at all,' said Angus.

Rory said nothing. The first mouthful of whisky made his throat feel like a deliciously warm chimney, into which smoke is ascending from an aromatic fire of turf and peats.

'I thought you would blackmail me. You know, insist I kept coming back, or you would spill the beans about me.'

'Would that have turned you on? Pretending you were forced to do it? And instead you're not coming back ever again. This is your last visit.'

'Back to the moral high ground. What gives you the right?'

'Does your fiancée know? Or even suspect?'

'Ruth? It would never enter her mind. She's away from Edinburgh half the time, anyway. A business lawyer, a high-flier. That's why I can be with you tonight.'

'Does she know she's sharing you?'

'What kind of language is that? How many people have I been sharing you with? I bet you don't know the meaning of monogamy! Have you ever been faithful to anyone in your life?'

Rory merely smirked and took another sip of malt.

'I don't want to end up like you, do you understand?' Angus went on. 'Because you're sad. Sad and alone. Here you are, rattling around in this huge flat like the last biscuit left in the tin. When it gets too much for you, you trot down to the pub and see what's going. You're not bad for your age, I'll give you that. But what will you do when you are forty-eight? Fifty-eight? Seventy? I want a life. A home and a wife and children. And respectability. My own place in society. People below me, people who look up to me and listen to what I say.'

Rory spoke slowly and deliberately, in a fashion that did not conceal the passion behind his words.

'I cannot tell you the number of men I have slept with. You wouldn't believe me if I did. And yet I have been honest with every one of them. I have never cheated, or promised what I could not give, or pretended to be anything other than the thing I am. And I am not ashamed of it. I'd be lying if I said I find it easy. I hear the sniggers behind my back at work, people nudging each other or passing remarks, just a touch too obviously, so I can't fail to notice, though I behave as if I don't. I can imagine the kind of things they say about me, half of them true, the other half invented. There are assignments they won't send me on, because it might all come out, because they're worried that my "tendencies" might affect my judgement. That's how I know nothing is given to me, nothing is handed to me on a plate. I have to earn it all. It's not great. But it's a life.'

Angus got to his feet.

'Pathetic, that's what I call it. It wouldn't suit me one bit.'

'So she knows nothing at all.'

'Look,' said Angus, hands in his pockets, assuming a belligerent stance, 'don't imagine I enjoy this. Making love with her is something that has to be gone through with. It's part of the bargain. You . . .' He stopped, wondering why he was saying this, what led him to be so frank, then shook his head and continued. 'You're not what I would call good-looking. But there's something there, something about you. I can't put it into words. It's what draws me to you. As for Ruth, in time there'll be children. Then, afterwards, it will be easier.'

'You mean, you can't be asked to breed for ever?'

'One thing is certain. There won't be any other women.'

'No, you wouldn't be attracted by that. And the other men?'

Rory waited at the door while Angus went into the bedroom to get his raincoat.

'Goodbye, David.'

'Angus,' came the soft answer. 'Let's keep it Angus, just the way things were.'

12

Rory could not tell whether the bitter taste in his mouth came from his fish or from the nocturnal scene he was remembering. He looked more closely at his plate and realized it was a caper, which had burst in his mouth like a tiny bomb of foreign sharpness. He had refused the *sauce aurore*, finding its delicate pink shade contrived and suspect, in favour of the alternative dressing, a mixture of black olives, parsley, anchovies and capers, finely chopped and glistening under a sheen of fragrant oil. He lifted some of the mixture on the blade of his knife and spread it across the white, flaky fish before bringing another forkful to his mouth.

The talk was still about first nights.

'*The List*,' Alan was saying, 'that's where you get the real weirdos.'

'What do you mean?' asked Ramon.

'The classifieds,' said Mark. 'You know the kind of thing. *Reasonable looks, straight-looking, good sense of humour, seeks similar for fun and maybe something more.*'

'It's the first thing in *The List* people turn to. At least, in my experience,' said Kieran.

'I've never replied to any of those,' put in Barry.

'But you read them,' Kieran said.

'Come off it!' Alan scoffed. 'I'd swear there isn't a single person round this table who hasn't answered a personal ad at one stage or another. When they didn't go the whole hog and concoct one of their own, that is.'

'You're in a better position if you put your own one in,' Nicol observed. 'That way you get to choose.'

'Yes,' said Alan, 'you can sift your way through the whole lot of them till you get to the real nutcases.'

By nature, Nicol was a man of few words. It was unusual for

him to intervene in the conversation in this way. At the mention of *The List*, his face had broken into a broad smile. Dougal happened to be watching and, with a quizzical raising of his eyebrows from the other end of the dinner table, encouraged him to tell more. But there was no way Nicol would have considered enouncing the phrase that had come into his head, or explaining the memories which it evoked. *And, to complete the picture, I have an extremely hairy body.* He almost laughed out loud just hearing it in his mind.

Nicol was what they call a big long drink of water, six foot three inches tall, a country boy, the son of farming folk in Angus, and had never thought of himself as handsome. Fifteen years spent in the capital had taught him to make a watertight distinction between the dialect he used at home and the careful English which was now his everyday means of communication. Still, if a former schoolmate, or a friend of the family, from Forfar or the surroundings, happened to be in Edinburgh for a graduation, a wedding, or simply a mammoth shopping spree (they called it 'retail therapy'), he would slip back into Scots, without noticing, when they met up for a drink at the end of the day. It would not have crossed their minds that he might be gay. They had specific rules for defining and dealing with effeminate men in their own society and Nicol did not fit these. Yet it struck Nicol as inevitable that, thanks to an unwary phrase, or a gesture, or the way his eyes lingered on some youth standing at the bar, he would give the game away and be branded irrevocably.

When he explained how terrified he was, Kieran suggested maybe this was what he really wanted, for them to find out in spite of him, so that there could be an end to all the concealment. Seeing the logic of the observation, Nicol nodded. But it did nothing to lessen the anguish he felt the next time the same situation presented itself.

He was generally contented with his life. He could have asked for nothing more to crown it than the chance to take Andrew home, to sit around the table with his father, his brother, his sister-in-law and the grandchildren, and for everything to be acknowledged and accepted. Andrew had declared his willingness to come on more than one occasion, and was perfectly ready to go along with whatever kind of playacting Nicol judged appropriate. But Nicol was an absolutist and would have none of it. It had to be all or nothing and, for the moment, it was nothing.

Until the middle of his twenties the dominant emotion in his life was shame: shame at his own background, and shame about the thing he knew he was. With the wiser eyes of thirty-seven, he perceived, in the bookishness which already set him apart from his brother and his school companions when he was barely seven, the expression of another difference, one he could not have put words to at that stage.

His mother noticed it. The year before he started secondary school, when they were in the kitchen alone, washing up after a meal, she said to him, as if she were joking, but with an edge to her voice he recognized, and which told him she was deadly serious:

'You're not going to grow up into one of those jessie boys, now, are you?'

Remembering the scene in English, he chuckled ruefully. He could no longer imagine how she would have put it in Scots. At the time, her warning both frightened him and struck him as unfair. He had spent three exhausting hours in the barn with his father and the vet the night before, struggling to deliver a calf that had taken up the wrong position in the womb. The vet had advised abandoning their efforts, but Nicol's father was adamant and, when they brought the creature out alive, turned to his son with such jubilation he thought he was going to hug him. A show of emotion of that kind would have constituted too enormous a breach of Scottish decorum. All his father did was slap him across the back and tell him it was time for bed. He was not invited to sit up by the fire with the two grown men, drinking whisky and painstakingly reliving every detail of the birth.

There were nine years between Nicol and his elder brother Frank, who was unable to help them out that night as he was busy courting. The year Nicol sat his Highers was also the year Frank got married and moved into the cottage next to the farm with his wife. Their younger son's academic success aroused perplexity in both parents, as if he had blasted off without warning into space. The further he went, the more difficult they found

134

it to distinguish his whereabouts, or what sort of a destination the trajectory might lead to. He came to envy the grunting familiarity with which they treated Frank, and even the coarse jokes he and his wife were subjected to, in the first weeks of their marriage.

Nicol knew that, under normal circumstances, he ought to have been the best man. He never forgot the stinging sense of injustice that filled him when a cousin from Alyth was chosen in his place. The cousin got to lead the bridesmaid on to the dance floor, when everybody knew Nicol was an exceptionally good dancer, almost as renowned for that as for his skill at football.

An urge towards self-frustration was blighting several areas of his life. He resolved not to get up from his seat all night, but lacked the stubbornness to stick to his decision. The wedding party was still going strong at four o'clock the next morning. It would have been unthinkable for Nicol to leave before it ended. As it was, his schoolfriend Anna, the one he sat next to in most classes and exchanged history notes with, broke etiquette by coming over and dragging him off for a Canadian barn dance. After that he found it hard to sit down at all.

He did not doubt now, when he looked back, that a lot of romping and messing about must have gone on among his contemporaries, both during the intervals between classes at school and in the countryside around the farm when school was over. Nicol never got involved. That was ironic. If he had been straight, he would not have shirked group masturbation sessions, or the crude horseplay of dominance and submission boys engage in once puberty has arrived, and they can vaunt a resilient erection. The fact that he was gay made the very idea terrifying. The horseplay would have meant something to him it could not mean to anybody else. The extra meaning risked exposing him. An almost religious primness, which led more than one relative to ask his mother when he was planning to become a minister, was the self-protective barrier he chose.

Nicol enjoyed dancing and enjoyed watching a good dancer. As he accompanied first Anna, then a series of other lasses round the floor, he judiciously appraised the moves of the adjacent couples, naturally paying more attention to the men than to the women. His eyes kept being drawn to a farmer from outside

Montrose, a strikingly handsome man in his early forties whose eldest son was two years below Nicol at school. His hair grew thick and wavy right from the top of his forehead and was turning grey early, without getting any less luxuriant. Elegant and sturdy, his movements had an effortless precision that took Nicol's breath away. What also took his breath away was the fact that his homage was not lost on the farmer. Nicol blushed, missed the beat and stood on the foot of the girl he was dancing with. Apologizing profusely, he excused himself and, to cover his confusion, disappeared out of the tent for a pee.

Rain had fallen earlier that evening. The smells out of doors had an exceptional acuteness. Nicol paused at the door of the tent, breathing the chill air into his lungs and listening to the wind, as it tormented the sycamore trees beyond the barn. He often imagined that the noise the leaves made was a language, protesting, defiant and cajoling by turns, depending on the mood the trees were in, and the fierceness of the gusts that tore at them. He was bathed in sweat, as if he had just emerged from a hot swimming pool. It was a relief to have a moment to unwind, far from prying eyes and social duties and niceties. As he strode into the bushes to relieve himself, he heard steps following. Nothing unusual about that. Peeing into the ferns was something he had enjoyed doing since he was a small boy. There was no point in male guests tramping across the yard to use the toilet in the house, and bringing all that sharn in on their shoes.

The other man stopped just short of him. The only sound they added to the night was of liquid hitting the undergrowth in a steaming jet. Then the man spoke a word or two about the dancing and the quality of the band. Nicol realized he had known, no, hoped the man behind would be the farmer. He paused to shake his sex dry. As he did so, the man drew closer, lifted an arm and gripped the nape of Nicol's neck in his hand. It was an appraising, comforting, reassuring gesture, something he might have done to an animal he admired or was especially fond of. A shiver went through the whole of Nicol's frame. Still grasping his neck, the farmer moved closer and kissed him on the lips.

It was more than he could bear. What made it so disturbing was the familiarity of everything about the man: his smell, the way he moved his body, the fact that Nicol knew his wife, his

136

mother and all four of his children, and was acquainted with details of their family life, as well as all the fanciful embroideries country gossip added. It was as if the earth he had trodden on since taking his first steps had risen up to embrace him. He pulled free and ran panting back into the tent.

The first face he distinguished, luckily enough, was Anna's.

'For God's sake, Nicol, what has happened? You look as if you've seen a ghost!'

She took his arm and led him to an empty table at one side. Of course there was no way that he could tell her. She sat there for nearly half an hour, holding his hand under the tablecloth, taking gulps of beer and exchanging banter with the groups of young folk that came over. They thought she was getting off with him. Instead she was defending him. When Nicol at last found the courage to look up, the farmer was speaking to the local policeman. Then his wife approached and leant upon his shoulder, ready to go. As they left, he searched for Nicol with his eyes and, when he saw him, raised his hand, waved and smiled. Nicol sat frozen, unable to respond.

He took Honours History at Edinburgh University. His parents came to the graduation ceremony. Apart from that, they treated him as they had always done. Occasionally his mother would grumble about the quantity of books he had accumulated in his bedroom. They gathered dust, she said, and she had enough work on her hands as it was. She noticed the physical cluttering, but had not an inkling of the mental acrobatics her son was going through. There was no thought of setting aside a quiet time and place for him to read. Nor were any concessions made when examination time approached. As always, he was expected to take his share in the work of the farm, alongside his father and brother. Indeed, he felt he had to atone for his intellectual accomplishments by demonstrating that he continued to be their equal in bodily strength. Years later, his mother frowned at the word 'finals', as if she had never heard it before, when it came up in conversation with a family friend from Dundee, whose daughter was showing alarming signs of stress as the fateful day loomed nearer. His mother took it for granted that Nicol would manage the tasks he faced at university, while assuming the additional burden of relieving his parents of the need even to ask about them. In a way he was grateful for the arrangement. It fitted in with the multilayered apartheid he saw for many years as his sole prospect of surviving.

He abandoned football when he was on the point of being selected to play for the university. It was because of the changing rooms. Try as he might, he could not keep his eyes off the bodies of his fellow players. Showering was a nightmare. Nicol was physically well-endowed, and twice he got a hard-on that sent him rushing for his towel the moment he emerged from the comforting jet of water. He railed at himself for being a peeping Tom, an incipient member of the dirty raincoat brigade. If it had been put to him that the sight of his own limbs provoked a similar turbulence in not a few of his companions, he would have been incredulous. This was the period when he resolved that nobody must ever learn the truth of what he was. From time to time he would mournfully replay a deathbed scene in which he breathed his last amid general grief, still clutching his secret tightly to him. It was the only happy ending he could imagine for his life.

He behaved like a typically Scottish student in that Anglicized environment. Discussion at tutorials was dominated by stridently confident men and women from down south, public school types who had not quite made it to Oxford or Cambridge. They had a consequent edge of insecurity Nicol could have used as a lever, had they not belonged to a culture too alien to his own for him to notice it. For the people he had grown up among, to draw attention to yourself, to make a display of your abilities, was a betrayal of community values that risked bringing ostracism as a punishment. And to contradict a teacher, or any figure of authority, however foolish and fatuous the comments they might make, was inconceivable. They were servants to the community who drew their worth from the trust placed in them. To challenge them would have been to question the wisdom of that trust.

One day the tutor grew impatient with the line of argument being developed by a woman in the class.

'I'm sorry,' he broke in, 'but your reasoning is fundamentally flawed.'

'I think your reasoning is fundamentally flawed,' she shot back at him.

Nicol was mortified. He made a pact with himself never to open his mouth in a tutorial unless absolutely forced to, while at the same time studying with a frenzy that produced essay marks among the best in his year. That brought its own kind of nemesis. Anything that made him conspicuous endangered the security of his façade. The way to stay safe was to escape notice. When he got into the Honours class, he deliberately toned down his work. His marks became more mediocre, and he emerged with an unremarkable second-class degree.

The only time he betrayed himself was when asleep. If his daytime activities and waking thoughts had been enough to go by, he would have passed for a normal adult, with a rather low sexual drive, the kind who would find marriage or partnership just too much trouble for the benefits it offered. And instead, the more rigid his surveillance between waking and going to bed, the more garish were the imaginings that filled his dreams. A dream of this kind was the final straw that led him to abandon football, much to the irritation of his trainer. A player who had caught his eye in the showers appeared to him that night, in a position for which he had no words. Nothing else happened in the dream. The emotion that filled Nicol at the sight was sufficient to appal him.

There were times when it got more than he could bear. He glanced ever so furtively, when passing by the general noticeboard, at announcements of the meetings of the University Lesbian and Gay Society. From chitchat he gathered the names and locations of the city's best known pubs and cruising spots, the places where the queers went, as his flatmates put it. That was another reason for doing nothing. He shared a tenement flat in Tollcross with a lad from Dundee and another from Kirriemuir, in an easy intimacy, composed of evenings in front of the video and weekend piss-ups. It was automatic and natural for them to ask where he had been on any night he did not spend with them. Their circle of acquaintance was so small they could easily check the accuracy of his story.

Nicol never got properly drunk. He was too afraid of what he might let slip. One night in the fortnight preceding his final exams, when the stress of preparation was making his generalized misery more acute, he took a handful of coins, left the house, and called Gay Switchboard from a public phone box. He had memorized the number from a notice several weeks before. He had to call three separate times before he found the courage to speak.

'How can I know?' he asked.

'I suppose the only way to find out is to try,' came the answer.

The voice proposed befriending him, which would have meant arranging a meeting with two switchboard workers, at a time and place to be chosen by Nicol. The prospect was far too scary. He ended the call by gently lowering the receiver, in the course of one of his own increasingly protracted silences.

Nicol wore a cloak of loneliness all through his early years in Edinburgh. He could have sworn the city itself was swathed in it as in the *haars*, sea mists rising from the Firth of Forth which can give the place a wintry feel, even in August, when there is brilliant sunshine only ten miles away. On days like those, the austerity of the city's architecture, its church towers caked in a grime the atmosphere was thankfully now free of, and the hard-bitten faces of its working people, who lack the swagger and rich humour of similar folk in Glasgow, struck him as manifestations of a curse that burdened him and it. A curse of isolation, frustration and sadness.

Anna stayed on a further year at school. Her Highers had been less brilliant than Nicol's and, never confident about her academic abilities, she chose to repeat two of them and add a third. Though they were not in the same classes, they met regularly for lunch and coffee. She had none of Nicol's difficulties in integrating. In Forfar she had held aloof from boys. In Edinburgh she had a string of partners before meeting Scott, the one she eventually married. They all found her friendship with Nicol odd, due to its faithfulness and its intensity. He ought to have been a rival. In a sense he was, where intimacy and time spent together were concerned. The fact that he never tried to get off with Anna disturbed their self-esteem. They took it for a sign something was wrong with her, something inferior, which could reflect on them.

For her part, Anna observed Nicol's slow petrification with alarm. She had her own suspicions as to the cause of his unhappiness, but would not have dared to put them to him. Something had to give way or else, in the end, he would. She resolved to step in and prevent that happening if necessary.

Anna was instrumental in introducing Nicol to Jill, and it was thanks to Jill that Nicol met Andrew. It all happened very quickly, in the weeks immediately after finals. Nicol and Anna had an unspoken agreement by which, at least once a month, they went to a disco on a Friday night, and danced themselves into complete exhaustion. Scott objected strongly to these desertions. But there was no way he could persuade Anna not to go.

'What's that guy's attraction?' he asked her. 'He doesn't fancy you. If he did, you would know by now. And yet he has some kind of a hold on you.'

For this particular outing they went to Mambo's. The music was South American. Jill knew Anna from a women's reading group they both attended. She came from Aberdeen, and had a French mother who had divorced her father several years before. Her father had a management post in the oil industry. Whether to atone to his daughter for his manifold betrayals of her mother, or out of natural generosity, he bought her a large flat when she came to Edinburgh. She shared it with another woman and two men, giving notorious parties where gin and vodka flowed unstintingly, and dope was available for anyone who wished to smoke it. She dressed with continental stylishness, sporting expensive foulards and a cigarette holder. It was her secret ambition to be a latterday Dorothy Parker. The limited materials Edinburgh offered for such a lifestyle were a source of constant chagrin to her. She did her best to surround herself with attractive and witty men. Consequently, her parties were mixed, in the sense that both straight and gay people attended them. Lesbians, however, kept a low profile. There were limits to even Jill's nonconformism.

That evening she had come to the disco with a group of gay men, which included Andrew. Jill fell for Nicol and Nicol fell for Andrew, in a matter of minutes, long enough to be introduced and to size each other up. Jill took it that any man dancing with Anna must be straight. She had this in common with the folk

141

Nicol had left behind in Forfar, that she assumed exotic flowers would not flourish in the soil of Angus. While she enjoyed Anna's company, Jill could not stand Scott. Though she was pleased to see her with a different man, she found it hard to believe Anna capable of two-timing, and she was right. The path was clear for her to add Nicol to her list.

She came over and asked them to join her group. Nicol had eyes only for Andrew. He was the tallest of the four men with Jill, though not quite as tall as Nicol. He danced with a splendid economy of movement. Again and again, Nicol's gaze was drawn to the gentle swinging of his pelvis, and the way it made the whole of his body undulate. His head moved neither to the right nor to the left, while his arms rotated slowly, as if hypnotized by the rhythm of the music. For Nicol it was not unlike being in the changing rooms, except that nothing here was surreptitious or clandestine. They had come to dance. Andrew was offering the spectacle of his dancing to whoever wanted to watch.

The next time he met Anna for lunch, by some strange coincidence Jill was there too. He got invited to a party the following Saturday, ten days after his last exam, and accepted without hesitation. It was on the tip of his tongue to ask if Andrew would be there. That would have given the game away. If Jill found out about him too soon, his chances of getting to know Andrew would vanish into thin air.

The week of the party he started his summer job. He had been sending out applications for long term employment at the rate of three or four each week. The results were disappointing. Only about one in ten produced a reply: polite, curt refusals, repeating the same phrases over and over, till he felt nauseated. He got a single interview, with a London company, after which he heard nothing more. His parents did not raise the question of his coming home. As far as he could tell, they were as much in the dark about his future as himself. When he told his mother later that summer that he was selling wine to earn his keep, her reaction implied that, to her, this was a perfectly acceptable sequel to studying for a university degree. At least he was under no pressure to achieve.

The shop was managed by a certain Mr Carruthers, who quickly took a liking to him. Nicol was strong and willing, lifted with ease loads that set the others groaning, and could be trusted to tot up the takings accurately and meticulously, at the close of business in the evening. The other employees were so keen to get away they often abandoned the figures after three wrong calculations, leaving Mr Carruthers to sort out the mess when he arrived next morning. Nicol had excellent French, and was sharp enough to acquire a reading knowledge of Italian, within the limits imposed by the wine trade, in a matter of weeks. This allowed Mr Carruthers to indulge in some exploratory buying, which paid off handsomely. The branch gained a reputation for its selection of French whites, and of reds from northern Italy.

About the middle of Nicol's first week there, Andrew wandered into the shop, in the company of a male friend with an earring and a blond rinse. He did not appear to recognize Nicol. This could have been typical Edinburgh discretion. As he handed over two bottles rolled up in brown paper, Nicol took the plunge:

'You're friends of Jill's, aren't you?'

A shadow of suspicion crossed Andrew's face and then it brightened.

'You were in Mambo's the other week. With that girl from Angus, what's her name . . .'

'Anna,' Nicol supplied. Then, after another gulp of breath, he went on: 'Live near here then?'

'Just round the corner. But I'll be working in Glasgow from next Monday.'

'Does that mean you're moving through?'

'No, I'm going to commute. It's a three months' posting. A traineeship at the BBC.'

Nicol was evidently supposed to be impressed. He did not need information of this kind to focus his thoughts on Andrew, who was already moving away to join his friend, hovering impatiently by the Californian shelves.

'Coming to the party at the weekend?'

'Yes. See you there,' Andrew called from the door.

Instead of going directly home after work, as was his habit, Nicol called in at the pub next door for a pint. The top two buttons of Andrew's shirt had been undone and he could not stop thinking about the long, sleek dark hairs they revealed, mingling with the lower part of Andrew's beard, so that the pale skin of his neck was almost completely hidden. When he emerged it was still light. He turned the corner to gaze down the short street of Victorian tenements, with the primary school at the far end, wondering which flat Andrew slept in, and if anyone slept with him. Most Edinburgh façades of the period are austere and featureless. These ones were supplied with generous bay windows. Nobody had drawn the curtains. The glow of lamplight from within was comforting, even enticing.

Anna phoned him on the morning of the party. The edge in her voice told him something was wrong. She wanted to talk to him urgently. He was due in at the shop at noon. They agreed to meet at a quarter to eleven.

'I'm pregnant,' she told him, and burst into tears.

He had never seen her so distressed. Without thinking, he pushed his chair back, gradually lifted her to her feet and held her. The coffee bar was relatively empty. A couple of people raised their heads, then courteously pretended not to notice. As an embrace, it could hardly have been more chaste, yet the comfort dispensed was none the less effective for that.

Nicol rang Mr Carruthers to tell him he might be anything up to an hour late. Anna needed to talk. What she had to say could have been squeezed into ten minutes. She went over the same ground repeatedly. It reminded him of what the farmyard cats did before bedding down. They would get up and walk around, then settle, then do it all again, until they felt entirely comfortable about the place that they had chosen. This was the first time he and Anna had spoken about sex. All the ins and outs of contraception flashed past Nicol in dizzying succession. The doctor had advised her to come off the pill because of a reaction she was having and she had done so without telling Scott.

'Why not?'

'It's not the kind of thing we talk about,' she said in a pleading sort of way.

'But what did you imagine was going to happen?' Nicol asked.

She had avoided making love for ten days because she did not like the idea of asking him to use a condom. In the end they had an argument, not directly about that, though Nicol suspected it might have been the underlying cause. After they made up, one thing led to another. He hadn't forced her, Nicol mustn't think

144

that. She had wanted it as much as he had. It was a kind of baptism of fire for Nicol. He realized he had disregarded Scott, just like Anna's other boyfriends, as a distraction that would pass, while his friendship with her was destined to outlast all such involvements. It had not occurred to him to think of her having sex, or what complications might ensue. Least of all had he expected her to get into a mess she could not handle, and come to him. For help? He had no idea what kind of help he could offer, except to show he felt as alarmed as she did. Her body looked different to him, when he thought of another body taking shape inside it.

'How can you be sure?'

'I did a test this morning. Maybe I'll get an abortion.'

No sooner were the words out than he realized he hated the idea. His next thought was, what do my feelings matter? The mention of abortion brought more tears. Anna admitted that what really troubled her was the prospect of getting married. Scott had proposed to her already, more than once. She had not known what answer to give. Both Scott and Anna rose in Nicol's estimation as a result. He was glad Scott was serious enough to ask, and pleased that his closest friend had not rushed headlong at the chance.

'It's such a trap,' she wept. 'I'm far too young.'

He enjoyed the party hugely, partly because he got properly drunk. He found that gin and tonic, not his usual tipple, went down remarkably well. Jill had friends working for her in the kitchen. The details of food preparation brought her out in a rash, she claimed. She would provide the cash, even do the shopping, provided others did the cooking. Nicol rolled his sleeves up and pitched in. It felt not unlike being in the back room at the wine store, and it gave him a sense of being part of things.

When everything was ready, they took the various dishes through to the front room. Andrew had arrived. He was on his own, which struck Nicol as a positive sign. He sniffed at the bean chilli Nicol was carrying and said how good it looked. Not as good as you do, thought Nicol. Andrew was wearing an Indian shirt of printed cotton. He had had his hair and beard trimmed that morning. He let it slip that his birthday fell early the next week. There was a round of congratulations. People started forcing drinks on him. Always willing to humour the company, he downed them manfully. Nicol noticed that he was swaying slightly as the evening wore on. He himself moved from group to group, conscious of the need to avoid Jill without actually being discourteous. He was both looking forward to and dreading the start of dancing. Luckily people did not dance in couples. There was a general hopping, shaking and gyrating in the dining-room. He was close to laughing at the styles of some of the guests. Jill came through to look for him. She was smoking dope with a laid-back group in the kitchen and wanted him to join in.

'But I've never smoked marijuana,' he said in alarm.

'Not something you cultivate down on the farm?' she asked, taking his arm and pulling him along after her.

Within five minutes he was sitting on the floor, his back to the cooker and Jill's head in his lap. He actually found the conversation quite interesting, though he kept silent. Partly it was the gin, partly wondering what to do about Andrew. It was up to him to make a move. Andrew did not even know he was interested. And if Andrew was not? The sweet smell of the dope tickled his nostrils. If he were not careful, Jill would start getting amorous. At that moment, one of the gay guys put his head round the door.

'Where is our hostess? Totally spaced out as per usual?'

'It's my party and I can do what I like. Luckily I don't feel like crying.'

'We're off to the disco. No offence but the dancing here is just crap.'

'Darling, if I expected fidelity I would have different friends.'

She lifted a languid hand to bid them farewell. Nicol got to his feet.

'Just going to the loo,' he lied.

His heart was pounding. The front door was open. Three men were already outside on the landing, another two were putting their coats on. As Nicol hesitated, Andrew emerged from the bedroom, tottering, then straightened himself up. He looked at Nicol and gave a drunken smile.

'You coming too?' he asked.

Nicol had no illusions about the significance of the frontier he

146

crossed just then. He was thankful not to be doing it in a more public fashion. None of the other guests was in the hall. In physical terms it could hardly have been simpler. The implications took longer to unfold. He grabbed his jacket and gave Andrew his shoulder to lean on. They walked out of the flat and downstairs. When they reached the pavement outside, Andrew gave a shudder, rushed to the gutter and vomited.

'Somebody had better take him home,' a gay guy volunteered.

'I will,' said Nicol quietly. 'Where does he live?'

The question was disingenuous only in part. He knew the street but not the number. They got a taxi, which Nicol paid for. He had to put his hand into Andrew's trouser pocket to find the key, while supporting his weight with the other arm. Andrew was still feeling sick and dazed. When they got in, and Nicol switched the hall light on, the man Andrew had come into the wine shop with put his head round one of the bedroom doors. He gave a grin and pointed to the room next to his.

'Stick him in there,' he said, and disappeared.

As soon as Nicol got him onto the bed, Andrew rolled over and fell asleep. Nicol asked himself what happened now. He deserved some kind of reward, though he could not have said what it was he expected. One thing was certain, there was no going back. Even if keeping Jill and her friends in the dark had been an option, he would have chosen not to. So powerful was the wave of optimism sweeping through him he decided to stay. He kicked his shoes off, loosened his belt and got on to the bed. Lying flat on his back, he stretched his arm out so that Andrew's head could rest upon it. He was tremendously excited. Andrew turned over in his sleep and nestled more closely into Nicol. As he did so, something happened between Nicol's legs. In a wave of agony and shame Nicol realized he was coming.

13

There was no way he could stop it now. A damp patch appeared on his beige corduroys. Getting up to clean it, or to strip off, would have meant wakening Andrew. Nicol was too happy lying close to him to risk doing that.

The next thing he knew, the curtains were flung open with a metallic rasping. His eyes went to the clock. Ten past six. A figure stood by the window. It was Andrew. He had just had a shower. The scent of bath gel filled the room. He was wearing nothing but a pair of underpants. Nicol had never seen anyone so hairy. He could have been an orang-utan. It fascinated and repelled him at the same time.

Andrew saw the stain on Nicol's trousers.

'You filthy bastard,' he said quietly. 'Get out of here. Go wank off somewhere else.'

Nicol pulled himself up onto his elbows.

'Don't get things wrong,' he said. 'I just . . .'

'It doesn't matter what you just,' Andrew broke in.

To his astonishment, Nicol saw that he was close to tears. They were both frightened, in different ways and of different things.

'Get out of here. You know where the front door is. Pronto.'

He felt a touch of anger and thought, if it's a question of strength there is no question who will win. His next thought was, I'm in love with this man, no matter how much body hair he has or what he thinks of me. Things could hardly have turned out worse than this, and his hopes had been so high.

He got reports that Jill had been entertaining groups of friends with tales of the country bumpkin who ravished Andrew. It was the most lurid coming-out story she had heard in a long time, she claimed. She had no objections to men getting off with each other. But to take an ill friend home, then have sex with him while he was semi-conscious was not just kinky, it was sick. Presumably this was the version of events Andrew had given her. He called Anna the next day, aching to pour out the details of what had happened. There had been no need to find words at the party. All he had to do was let his body take him where it wanted to go. The words he needed to tell Anna about the past, about the things he felt for Andrew and the consequences they had led to, did not exist for him as yet. And she was hardly in a position to offer consolation.

'We're going to get married,' she told him. 'I'll keep the baby.'

'Is it what you want?'

'It's what I choose. I don't know if that's the same thing.'

Anna was going to abandon her university course and stay at home to look after the child. When he put the receiver down, Nicol wondered for an odd moment whether similar disasters had befallen them. If life had set a trap for her, it had excluded him, banishing him from a land he had never quite managed to set foot in. She had been banished in a parallel fashion, from the things she wished to accomplish, the future she hoped to have.

The marriage took place in a registry office at the end of July. Nicol asked Anna why she had decided against a church ceremony. She smiled.

'Because then I would have had to choose a bridesmaid. At a registry office there are only witnesses. That way I can have you.'

Nicol left for Luxembourg two days later, to take up the one job offer he had received since graduating. On the eve of his departure he allowed himself to do something that had been on his mind since the disastrous night with Andrew. He had been afraid to give in to the temptation, because he was not sure where it might lead. Now that he knew he would be out of the country within twenty-four hours, it felt safe to go to Waverley Station first thing in the morning, and wait for Andrew to get on the Glasgow train. It did not cross Nicol's mind to try and speak to him. He knew which platform the train would leave from and, if he took up a position on the Victorian walkway high above, felt certain he would catch a glimpse of him. It was a secret way of saying goodbye. He waited until half past nine to see a familiar figure, wearing a tie and a jacket, and carrying a purple knapsack, hurry on to the train. It had been the right thing to do. He left the station feeling distinctly better, and went to finish his preparations for the journey.

The next three years were spent translating documents at a very generous salary, most of which he was able to bank in Scotland. Each day he would work through a certain number of tapes in French, producing a similar number recorded in his own voice in English. His colleagues complained that the job was repetitive and undemanding. Nicol loved its utter predictability. When he got home at the end of the day, he had plenty of mental energy left. He read and re-read two books he had brought from Angus, Lewis Grassic Gibbon's trilogy of farm and city life, and a selection of poems by Violet Jacob. He did not think the literary quality of the poems very high. But the dialect they used, and the scenes and emotions they described, kept his sense of home alive, in alien surroundings.

He loved one in particular, a dialogue between an Angus man in London and the wind arriving from the north. The exile asks it for news of the places it has seen and, tantalizingly, each answer moves closer to home, beginning with the tides of the Forth just north of Edinburgh, then moving across Fife and the Tay estuary until Angus is reached. At that point the exile breaks in and asks the wind to be silent, for he cannot bear to hear the places he longs for so ardently being named. Nicol had a tape of the song, set to music by a folk singer and with a new title. Sometimes, when he was sitting translating, the music would go through his head, without distracting him from what he was doing.

He read voraciously in French. History to start with, then screeds of fiction. During the second year he read Proust from start to finish, in the original, with impatience and fascination, and a sense of betrayal when the last volume reached its close. He became so engrossed he carried whichever volume he happened to be reading on the tram with him to work, and sat with it in the inner courtyard where the staff had lunch. His colleagues christened him 'the bookworm'. He laughed and took no offence.

The level of alcohol consumption, among the languid expatriates in the social circles he had access to, alarmed him. He turned down invitations to cocktail parties whenever he could, judging that reading was a safer palliative for homesickness and one that would be easier to set aside, if need be, when the right time came. However, he became passionate about wines. He befriended a supplier in the old part of the city, and built up a discreet selection of vintage bottles, which came home to Scotland with him. He delved into the literature of French wines, reaching a point where it came more naturally to him to describe the bouquet of a bottle in that language than in either of his own. An appropriate vocabulary must exist in English, but he did not know it. As for Scots, it was a tongue in which wine-drinking had no place.

In May of his third year in Luxembourg news reached him that his mother was dying. He arranged for three weeks' unpaid leave and caught a plane to London. She died on the day after his arrival. His father behaved as if he had received a blow to the gut he would never recover from. He found it hard to remain standing for any length of time. When seated, he would clutch his belly with both hands, as if to catch hold of the pain he felt, so as either to knead it into something different, or wrench it out and gain relief. Nicol's brother wept so noisily and theatrically everyone lost patience with him. Nicol himself had an inexplicable sense of liberation.

Female neighbours invaded the house, taking charge of cooking and cleaning. His mother was laid in her coffin in the front sitting-room, to be inspected by a procession of relatives and acquaintances. The place had not been so busy since the day she married. She had not been an especially happy woman. His father doted on her, and would not have asked for more than to enjoy her companionship until the day he died. Once she had agreed to marry him, it was as if he reached a plateau of unquestioning contentment. Nicol's mother always hankered after something different, something she never put into words, whose nature neither he nor she would ever learn now. It struck him that her experience might not be very different from Anna's. Or maybe he was projecting his intimacy with Anna on to a woman he had never known well.

The incessant visiting gave him a sense of suffocation. He got into his brother's car and drove eastwards, in the direction of Montrose. The town lies at the upper end of a thin tongue of land, separating the basin named after it, rich in birds and plants, from the open sea. Nicol left the car on the verge of a country road and began walking along the water's edge. Before he knew it, he was within sight of the House of Dun, where Violet Jacob had been born. The circumstances of her life had taken her far from home, just like Nicol. She had married an Irish cavalry officer, spending her adult years in India, then the Welsh marches, before returning to Angus as a widow, by which time the house was no longer in the family. The song he loved kept going through his head.

When he got back into the car, he drove northwards on to the Cairn o' Mount road, which leads over a pass into Aberdeenshire, and climbed on foot to the twin Pictish forts that guard it. Truly, he thought, this is the most beautiful place in the world. The view from the summit embraced Montrose, the North Sea, the inland basin, the fertile farmlands of Angus and, dim to the west, the foothills of the Grampians. He would come home.

By the time the will was read, he was staying in Edinburgh. He had to come back specially to hear it. His father and brother did their best to convince him to join them on the farm. Their arguments had a tempting quality that frightened him. He had decided to come home, not only to Scotland, but to himself, although he did not know how to make either process a success. If, as well as being gay, he was going to live a gay lifestyle, the farm was hardly the right setting. To live there would be to bury himself beyond all hope of discovery by his own kind.

His mother possessed property in her own right and distributed it with scrupulous fairness. The expression on his brother's face, when it became clear that he and his wife and children would inherit only half, and not two thirds or all of her estate, filled Nicol with anger and a kind of exultation. She had known, at some unspoken level, how things would be, and was determined to share her gifts out equally. Perhaps she sensed how difficult a path awaited her younger son and wanted to offer him all the material support she could. For half an hour or so, it looked as if Frank might contest the will. Their father's view prevailed. It was agreed that they would sell their mother's property, and divide the proceeds according to her wishes.

Nicol had two and a half weeks of leave remaining. He was in no hurry to get back to Luxemburg. He had an exciting feeling that things were going to change, that he was going to take steps, although he did not yet know which. The first thing he did was to arrange lunch with Anna.

The night before, tired of watching television in the secluded guest house he had chosen, he walked up towards Princes Street, ordering some white wine in a pub on Rose Street. He was raising the glass to his lips when he heard himself hailed from the other side of the bar. It was Mr Carruthers. The meeting could not have been more fortunate. Mr Carruthers was about to open a winery in Leith. All the preparations had been made. The launch was scheduled to take place in five days' time. He asked polite questions about Nicol's job in Luxembourg. Nicol realized the answers were falling on deaf ears and stopped.

'You wouldn't be free to give me a hand with opening the shop, now, would you?' asked Mr Carruthers.

The assistant he was relying upon had let him down. He was at a loss for a replacement. Advertising was a lengthy business, he said, and you never knew who you might end up with. Nicol was a good worker and there would be plenty for him to do. In fact, he could name the wage he wanted.

Now it was Nicol's turn to hesitate. Then, in a great flurry, he said it all. He was coming home from Luxembourg in three months' time, once he had served out his notice. He had money to invest, the sum inherited from his mother plus what he had laid aside while working abroad. Would Mr Carruthers consider letting him in on the business? They could arrange a meeting with a lawyer, now or when Nicol returned, to iron out the details about investing and sharing the profits. For a split second, Nicol thought he was going to refuse. But Mr Carruthers rubbed his hands together and gave a crow of jubilation. Nicol named the figure he had at his disposal. They shook hands and agreed to enter into partnership.

Anna left her little girl in Scott's mother's care, so as to give Nicol all of her attention. As it was, not until after lunch, when they were strolling along Princes Street in an unfocused sort of way, and lingered in front of a huge plate glass window to look at the shoes inside through their reflected images, did he blurt it out:

'I'm gay, Anna. And I've decided to do something about it.'

The next minute her arms were round his neck. She gave him such an energetic hug he nearly choked.

'What's all this?' he asked, laughing.

'I'm so pleased. Because now you are going to be happy.'

I wish I could be that confident, thought Nicol.

The revelation justified their calling in at a coffee shop and devoting what remained of the afternoon to strategies. Nicol had entered a gay club in Luxembourg, only to emerge again within fifteen minutes. Silence had fallen immediately. The regular clients surveyed him with hostility. He had a few phrases in the local dialect at his command, but in that setting all confidence deserted him. There was no way he could have embarked on a conversation. He used this experience to justify a refusal to visit any of the gay pubs in Edinburgh. He did not tell Anna that he feared running straight into Andrew if he did.

Anna told him he should put an advertisement in the personal column of *The List*. Nicol posed several objections. He was going back to Luxembourg at the end of the month, and would not return to Scotland until September. Would there be time to meet and assess the person who replied, if he was lucky enough to get a reply? And what address could he use?

'Use mine,' said Anna.

'What will Scott think of that?'

'Nothing, if I don't tell him. Don't expect to meet the love of your life right away, though. Just see how far you want to take it with whoever turns up. Build up some experience. After all, you have to make up for all the learning I was able to do before I was twenty.'

They met again to finalize a text. Nicol brought a copy of *The List* and they pored over the columns, puzzling out the acronyms before settling for something simple: *Attractive gay man, 25, tall, cleanshaven, lives in Edinburgh, inexperienced, seeks similar for friendship and possible relationship.*

'You're getting as much fun out of this as I am,' he told Anna.

'Do I get to open the replies?' she asked.

'No. But you get to see them once I have.'

The days spent working with Mr Carruthers, once the advertisement had been placed, were the happiest Nicol could remember in a long time. Indeed, he asked himself if he had known

154

this kind of happiness before. It was odd, seeing that no major change had taken place as yet. He was still returning to Luxembourg, to the same grim, lonely life as before. Then where did the joy come from? Maybe what mattered was that he was different now himself. And that meant the world he lived in had to change.

Both he and Anna bought *The List* on the morning the advertisement appeared. He phoned her every other day, until the replies came. There were five. They arrived in a single large envelope.

My name is Steve, the first one read. *I suppose I am a quiet guy really and I enjoy staying at home with a few cans of beer and watching the sport on TV. My friends tell me I am attractive and when I am not feeling too lazy I go and work out at the gym so my body is in pretty good shape. Oh and I also like playing badminton. I have been unemployed for two years but I still hope I can get a job somewhere before too long. In the meantime it would be nice to have somebody to share the long days with (and the nights). Get in touch if you want to meet up.* He gave a phone number.

The second came as a bit of a surprise. *There is nothing in your advertisement to suggest that you are into panty fun,* it said. *But I am an eternal optimist and experience tells me that the most ordinary-looking guys can turn out to have very kinky tastes. My collection of frilly underwear needs to be seen to be believed. I would relish the chance to try some of it on you, particularly if you have a hairy bum. You have no idea how entertaining it can be and you might look very good in my gear. I would especially like to persuade you to wear a kilt on top. Delicate lingerie goes so well with our national dress. I am considerably older than you. I would not expect you to do anything more than engage in a spot of harmless underwear modelling as and when it suits.* Name and address and phone number came with this one.

The third was written hurriedly on a sheet torn from a pad with punched holes, for use in a loose-leaf folder. *Thank God for advertisements in* The List, it said. *I live in a small town just across the Firth of Forth, and nobody knows that I am gay. I have no idea what to do about it. It would be Hell for me if my family or my friends were to find out. I even have a girlfriend because that is the only way to survive. I am pleased you live in Edinburgh. In the big cities you can be anonymous. I can't promise you very much. I have never had*

the chance to try so I don't know what I like and what I don't. And a
relationship is more than I could handle at present. But if you want to
meet for a drink, on a strictly friendship basis, that would be nice. If
you feel like experimenting between the sheets, that would help me too.
A phone number followed, with the words *Be discreet!* next to it,
doubly underlined.

I am 22. I am passive and I like sucking and being fucked, the fourth
began. *If you have a big knob and would like to try me, get in touch*
and we can have good times together. There was a phone number
and a photograph. The guy had a likeable face. Nicol found it
hard to reconcile the letter with the image.

The fifth reply was the longest. *I have never answered a classified*
ad before, it said, *and I am afraid you will think that, if I do, I must*
be desperate. Or rather, maybe I think that! But then, logically, if you
wrote it in the first place, you are in the same situation. So I suppose
I am desperate. Not that things are going badly for me on the surface.
I'm employed by the BBC and I like my job. I have enough money and
am pretty good-looking – I think! I'm out at work and I have my own
flat. So what is missing in my life? It's hard to say. Actually, it would
be good to get the chance to find out. It might be you! And then again,
it might not. People come and people go, there are plenty of parties and
places to visit at the weekends. I have nice holidays and come back
sun-tanned and my tan lasts longer than it does on most of the friends
I go away with. I suppose it would be easier if I could put my finger
on one thing and say it was that that bothered me. Time to stop rattling
on. I understand that in this context it's normal to explain something
about what you like in bed. Well, just about everything. Plus a few
things I haven't had the chance to try. But if I write this, it might
frighten you off, since you say you're inexperienced. No, that's not
true, I find it difficult to put my likes and dislikes down on paper. It's
not experience of the body that matters, my friend, it is experience of
the heart! And that doesn't come cheap or easy. Anyway, I'm just over
six feet tall, dark hair, moustache and beard, twelve stone in weight,
knob in decent proportion to the rest of me (in case that's an issue).
Oh and, to complete the picture, I have an extremely hairy body. It
bothers some people and me, too, at times. But that's how my mother
made me and there isn't much I can do about it. I've known guys to
be totally turned off by it. Others think it's marvellous. I'd like to find
someone who didn't make a fuss. After all, it's me. I don't want to give

you my address, just in case you are a nutcase or a crank. But I'd take a chance on meeting you. What about outside the Filmhouse next Thursday night, about half past seven? I'll be carrying a bunch of pink carnations so you know who I am. If we like the look of each other, we can go for a drink. If not, we'll pass like ships in the night and . . . on to the next one.

The letter was signed *Andrew*. Nicol put it down on the bedside cabinet and took a deep breath. His heart was thumping. He actually felt cornered. Here he was, trying to open up new avenues for himself, brought right back to square one. And if the letter was not from Andrew? There were too many coincidences for it not to be.

He was sorry about the others. He didn't think he could cope with panty fun, or with the guy who sent the photograph, but the other two sounded OK. And now Andrew had arrived on the scene, they didn't have a chance. How was he going to explain about that infamous night? Should he apologize? Was it not likely that, the minute Andrew set eyes on him, he'd scarper? If only he could write beforehand and give his version of events! His thoughts went round and round. The end result was hopelessness. There was nothing to do but stand in the place indicated, at the time Andrew had chosen, prepared to meet his fate.

That was what Nicol did. Andrew failed to appear. Or else (and he decided this explanation was more likely) he had glimpsed Nicol from the other side of the street, put two and two together, and gone home. Anna asked him what he was worrying about. One down and at least two to go! He did not even attempt to explain. Getting Andrew's letter, seeing Andrew's handwriting, had taken him back more than three years, to the morning when he stood on the raised walkway in Waverley Station. It would have been better to have stopped loving Andrew. But he still did. As long as that was the case, he could be satisfied with no one else.

A sixth letter arrived after his departure. Anna forwarded it to him in Luxembourg. *I'm really sorry,* it began. *I feel I'm a jerk for putting anyone through a thing like that. It's never happened to me to be stood up in a public place but it's one of my nightmares. I had even bought the carnations that morning, because I was afraid I wouldn't find any if I left it till the last minute. And it's funny, I had a dream about you the night before. I'd never have thought I was so romantic! You were walking alongside a stretch of water with a country house beyond it, and hills in the background. Curlews were calling. It reminded me of a guy from Angus I once knew, who turned out to be a shit. The reason I didn't come is blindingly simple, and courtesy of British Rail. I had to stay on later than usual at work in Glasgow. The train got stopped by a signal failure outside Falkirk. We staggered into Waverley at eight o'clock. I got a taxi up to the Filmhouse and stood in front of it with my carnations for half an hour. But of course you had gone. I knew you would have. It's my fault. All I had to do was trust you a bit more and give a phone number or an address. Anyway, if you want to try again, my details follow. We could make it on a day I don't go through to Glasgow. Or maybe you're so pissed off you can't be bothered. Then again, you probably got loads of replies, and are already in the arms of the man of your dreams. A pity, since I actually did dream about you. Once at least.*

Nicol thought a lot about his answer. *Andrew,* it began, *I was really angry with you that night in front of the theatre. Can you imagine, first, the nerve it takes to put an ad in the classifieds? And then, to stand there for more than half an hour, gradually realizing nobody is going to come? For what it's worth, I got five replies to my ad and, because of the kind of guy I am, chose to reply to only one. You'll have noticed from the stamp I'm not in Edinburgh any longer. That's because I have to serve out three months' notice here before I can come back. I was so discouraged by what happened with you, I decided not to take the others any further. Can I believe what you say in your letter? Or are you setting me up for another disappointment? If you really want to meet me, you're going to have to wait a while. I wonder how many other men you'll have had inside that time. As I said in my ad, I am inexperienced, and I don't want to get my heart broken by somebody who isn't serious about relationships. So I'm not sure where that leaves us. I may be misjudging you and that would be a pity. But haven't you yourself misjudged people in the past? And were you ready to give them the benefit of the doubt?*

Andrew answered by return. *It's funny what you say about misjudging. Three years have gone by since a guy brought me home from a party. He wasn't supposed to be gay and, as far as I know, has not come out since then. I think it's senseless for a gay man to fall for a straight one. And yet I spent the whole of that party hoping he was*

158

going to make up to me. Instead he sat in the kitchen cuddling the girl whose flat it was. He wasn't even going out with her. I suspect he was simply looking for a shag for the night. I was so uptight I drank far too much. We were on the point of leaving for the disco when this guy appeared in the hall, with an odd expression on his face. You know what it's like when you're so pissed nothing seems to matter any more. Or maybe you don't. Anyway, I dared him to come along, and then collapsed at the bottom of the stairs. The next thing I know, I wake up in bed, with this guy next to me and come all over his trousers. The straight had got his gay experience, without even letting me know! I should have shouted at him. Instead I nearly burst into tears. It felt like I had been raped. And for all that, I've never stopped thinking about him.

Nicol's impatience got the upper hand. He went to book a plane ticket. *If you want another chance,* he wrote, *meet me outside the wine shop on the corner of your street, this Saturday at one o'clock.* He had no idea how many of his own rules he was breaking all at once: a rule about being careful with money, another about thinking things through before taking action, a third about not trusting where trust might not be justified. Andrew arrived on the stroke of one, with a bunch of pink carnations.

'I knew it would be you,' he said quietly. 'Let's try again.'

They had a pub lunch first, eating almost in silence, then went back to the flat.

'Where's your flatmate?' Nicol asked. He felt extremely awkward.

'He moved out last summer. I'm on my own. Come through.'

They lay down on the bed.

'I came without intending to that night. I couldn't stop myself.'

'Don't stop yourself now,' Andrew said and began unbuttoning Nicol's shirt.

They slept afterwards. When Andrew awoke, Nicol was observing him intently, taking in every detail.

'You *do* have an extremely hairy body,' he said. 'I've never seen one like it.'

'Hold me,' Andrew said. 'It's what I want.'

'I can do that,' said Nicol. 'I can give you what you want.'

14

'Now I know what kept you so long at the market,' said Shiram's father.

The tent in which Dashkur lay sleeping resembled a flower-seller's booth. No expense had been spared. There were yellow and purple irises, gladioli both russet and orange, and a veritable sea of tulips, their colours ranging from a blue verging on black to a pink as delicate as the first hint of dawn, a pale intimation of coming day, that gathers along the horizon like sediment in a bottle of clear, precious liquid. The interior of the tent could have been a meadow in bloom, though no meadow known to man would have spontaneously brought forth blossoms of such splendour and sophistication. The pots containing them were some of brass, others of terracotta. Others still had been fired and painted in rich, mathematical designs that swam before the eyes. Here and there a bee hovered above a flower, rubbing its furry legs against the stamen, so drunk from the pollen it had to steady itself and check its orientation before moving on. The pots were placed on stools at different heights and angles. Between them and behind them Shiram had strewn, not carpets, for none of those remained, but samples of work and unfinished fragments.

'What is the purpose of it all?'

Three days had passed since they left Araxas. The youth fished from the river had not opened his eyes. Attempts to prize his mouth open and administer him thin gruel, or a paste of legumes flavoured with nuts, proved fruitless. It had been Shiram's idea to rub the gum of the rhenous tree, which they carried with them for bruises and aches, into his chest, down his sides and along his groin. He claimed that it would keep the youth warm, and that his body would absorb the virtues of the plant even though no sustenance entered his mouth.

160

Now they had reached Sallat. The town nestles in a wooded valley. Secret springs bubble to the surface of the slopes all around it. The water is so chill and fresh that the townsfolk have no cause to grumble, even on the most stifling of summer days. They grow all manner of fruits, vegetables and tubers, but the glory of their market, the fame of which sets strangers seeking the place for days on end, until at last, if lucky, they come upon the hidden paths, is constituted by its flowers. When they stopped off there on their way to Birjand, the carpet sellers allowed the Imam to buy three prayer rugs at a knock-down price. Commercially it was a senseless move. But it was important to retain the good will of the people of Sallat, who could offer them comfort, society and rest from the empty steppes which stretched on either side. As long as they remained in the place, their untiring vigilance could be relaxed, for there was no danger here of being set upon by brigands.

The return of the carpet sellers was eagerly awaited in Sallat. Experience indicated that a part, at least, of their takings in Birjand would be spent on food and drink and gifts to carry home. Shiram, however, had that morning squandered five times what they would normally disburse in the course of two days' sojourn.

'Take him, if you are in love with him,' said his father. 'Have him as your catamite. He threw his life away when he leapt from the cliff. By right it falls to whoever rescued him. There cannot be a question of payment to his parents, or to his owner, if he was in thrall.'

'He does not have the look of one who laboured,' said Shiram, lifting the left forearm so that his father could see the hand. 'There is no trace of cuts or callouses. The youth comes of a prosperous family. And he is too old to be a catamite. There are already the beginnings of a beard upon his chin.'

'It is well said of the people of Birjand that they are passionate and strong-willed,' his father resumed. 'If one of them takes an idea in his head, nothing will deter him from carrying it through to completion, be it the construction of a palace, or a journey, or a suicide. They worship gods whose names have been forgotten in other places. When the envoys of Baghdad swept all before them, bringing word of the prophet and his doings to the most

161

isolated corner of this land, in Birjand nobody paid the slightest attention. At times I think the people of that city act from a spirit of pure contradiction. Had the envoys been persecuted elsewhere, the men and women of Birjand would have welcomed them and made them kings.'

'He is going to waken today,' murmured Shiram. 'I am sure of it. His breathing has grown gentler. When the flap at the door of the tent shifts in the wind, and the light of day enters more brightly, his eyelids tremble. His spirit is impatient to behold the world again.'

'The light of day penetrates this tent only as a pale glimmer among shadows. Take him into the sun and he will awaken at once.'

'Or burn. The returning spirit must not be overawed with too much brilliance. And yet it must be duly welcomed. That is why I have surrounded him with flowers. After his fall, the shock of the water and, most of all, the despair which drove him to leap from such a height, we have to tempt him back into the land of men and women. His first thought must be of the beauty of living, transitory things, of all the glory that he risked leaving behind.'

'You are unjust when you speak in such a fashion of the people of Birjand. Is that not where we ply our richest trade? They are such lovers of fine craftsmanship that there is no point in bringing any but the choicest of our wares to sell them. The prices they will pay are so generous this one journey every year would suffice for our livelihood.'

'I cannot understand why you wish to treat the youth with such delicacy. If he is to be your bed companion, then he should learn to obey you. He should not only consent to your every desire, but strive to guess in advance what you may want from him. You have laid him out like the body of a saint upon a catafalque!'

The father placed his arm across his son's shoulder. Shiram was sitting cross-legged on a stool. Standing at his side, the father's head in its white turban bobbed at the height of his son's cheek.

'You are the third of my five sons,' he said. 'One by one, the other four have married and abandoned me. Weary of the hardships of this wandering life, they preferred to grow fat sitting at a hearth next to their wives and servants. I have been blessed

162

with ten grandchildren, whom I burden with presents and with money each time I return home. I chose the wives myself, haggling over the dowry and instructing them, with your mother's help, in the duties and the privileges of their station. Have you never asked yourself why I did not propose a wife for you? Do you think I have not noticed how, when we sit and sip coffee at the road's edge on a busy crossing, your eyes seek out, not the young women their veils conceal and reveal, but the youths who stride by, or ride past on horseback? How many times a pair of eyes has met your gaze, and I have expected you to rise up and leave me, returning that evening or the morning after, your limbs still aching from the exercise of love!'

The old man's eyes flashed as he warmed to his theme.

'You must not continue to sleep alone, my son! To enter a solitary bed at dusk and leave it with the dawning! It is not natural, or good, or what the gods prescribe for mortals! I could not care a rotten fig what kind of pleasures you seek, or with whom. But you must learn the joys of the flesh! Think of the riches that are stored up for you. Alone of all your brothers, you have neither wife, nor children, nor household to maintain. You have laboured with me longer and more diligently than any of the others. It is therefore just that the greatest reward should be yours. And when the new moon brings you such a gift, instead of embracing it, you treat it like a holy thing that cannot be touched! The youth is beautiful, more beautiful than any I have seen since this beard turned completely white! Take him as your own.'

In answer, Shiram leant forward and lifted Dashkur's right forearm. The fingers of the hand were firmly clenched, but not so tightly that his father could not make out what they held. The old man gasped and took a step back, making the double sign of warding with his fingers.

'Wu!' he cried. 'A skin of Wu! The youth is under her protection!'

'Indeed,' nodded Shiram. 'Yet even if it were not so, I could not possess him against his will. When I bent over his dark form on the grass, and felt the living breath upon my cheek, I gave my love to him. That is how it is and will be for all time. Go now, Father, for he is awakening.'

Dashkur's head moved from side to side. The shadow of a

smile flitted across his lips. He lifted his arms above his head, stretching them as if he were shaking a covering from on top of him. The fingers of his right hand did not release their treasure. Then he grunted and opened his eyes.

'What was your dream of?' asked Shiram.

'How do you know I had a dream?'

'It passed over your face before you wakened.'

'I was walking with my sister Nal, along the banks of the stream of Birjand where it emerges from the willow grove, before it passes by the workshops of the dyers, and their discharges set it exploding with colours, so brilliant that the eyes cannot look upon them for long.'

'And what were you speaking of?'

'Of love. I no longer remember what she said.'

Dashkur's eyes widened in alarm. He winced as if he had received a blow.

'Who are you? Why am I here? Am I dead?'

'No, you are alive. This is a tent. I am Shiram, son of Wek the carpet seller. And if you listen, you will hear, not far away, the singing of the women of Sallat, as they wash their blankets at the well.'

'But I wanted to die! You have no right to keep me here!'

'It was not I. What have you in your hand?'

Slowly, Dashkur raised his head from the pillow and looked at the snake skin.

'It was the goddess Wu who saved you,' said Shiram.

'And why are there so many flowers around me?'

'I brought them here to welcome you into the world.'

Dashkur showed no sign of surprise or gratitude. He was calmer now.

'What pain was it that made you desire death? It must have been very great.'

'If you are indeed the son of Wek, then I have heard of you. You and your companions visit Birjand once a year, arriving with the autumn equinox. Ever since I was a child I have wondered why you choose that period. If you were to come only a little earlier, you could be in the city for the Fair of Vanities.'

'I have wondered that too. But the time was established before I was born.'

'So you have never seen the Fair of Vanities?'

'No, I have not.'

'Ah, then you have not lived. There are no funnier or more joyous days in any city from Baghdad to Samarkand. Every morning the Crown Prince rides from the north gate to the south on a farting cushion that is as noisy as a trumpet. A band of shawms and serpents does a circuit of the streets. Behind them come small children, in groups of four and five, performing the dance of the swallows. That is to ensure the birds a safe journey on their way home. If the dance is successful, the children will extract a promise from the swallows to return the following year to precisely the same nests they used to shelter their young the previous spring. And because the mother of the Crown Prince selects only the most skilful and gracious of the children for the dancing, they have never failed to gain the promise yet.

'The Grand Vizier must dress as a buffoon. Every time he comes upon a group of more than three people, whether men or women, he has to tell them a funny story they have never heard before. If he fails, he must give each of them a coin of purest gold. At noon each day, the court dignitaries and the council of eleven proceed from the palace gates to the great fountain, hopping, turning cartwheels, or walking on their hands. For the duration of the Fair the fountain is sweetened with herbs and rose petals. They are met there by ten women, bearing baskets of lemons. The dignitaries and the councillors take the lemons from them, draw water from the fountain, and serve all who wish the freshest lemonade until the third hour after noon. Then they may return to the palace, in the same manner as they came.'

'I had not heard about the lemonade,' said Shiram.

'And what about the insults auction? Newly devised insults are knocked down to the highest bidder. Anyone who wishes to can take part, as bidder or as seller. The bidders are admitted four at a time. If you have an insult to sell, you whisper it in the ear of the auctioneer, who whispers it in turn to each of the bidders. They have sworn in advance not to divulge it if they fail to buy. And then, until the following year, only the winning bidder has the right to use it. Adran, the wife of the Chief Clockmaker, bought an insult there that made the Grand Vizier's wife faint when she used it on her.'

'Can you remember what it was?' asked Shiram.

'I would consider it beneath me to pronounce such words,' said Dashkur, 'even if I had paid a small fortune for them.'

'I heard there was a kissing auction, too,' said Shiram.

'No, that is not true. There is a kissing contest. That is very different and more beautiful. In the courtyard of the temple of Aktir stand two wow-wow trees. No one can recall who planted them or when. They are old but, as they grow extremely slowly, they are still no higher than the courtyard walls. The leaves of their topmost branches are reflected in the windows on the temple's second floor. You cannot tell which trunk the leaves belong to, for the branches are so intertwined the two trees could be one.'

'And they are the image of faithful lovers.'

'That is right,' said Dashkur. 'For that reason the kissing contest is held in their shade. It is said that kissing is a skill learnt by experience. A kiss is the harmonious accord of the spirits of the two involved, just as a bow touching two strings can draw a pleasing chord from them.'

'When you speak of bows and strings, your face darkens. Does that mean the pain you spoke of is connected with music?'

'It does indeed. I did not wish to take part in the contest, although to do so is considered a great honour. Shildar, the daughter of Laneth, had been selected as one of the ten competitors. She needed to find a partner. I have played with her since before I began to speak. She begged me to come. She was afraid to kiss in full view of the judges and said she would be comforted by the touch of lips whose first words she had heard. That was where Leflef saw me.'

'Was he a judge, or a competitor?'

'Neither. He was too old. He was one of the musicians accompanying the feast. I did not notice him. He told me afterwards that that was where he set his heart on me. The kiss may last no longer than the chime of a small bell takes to fade. The bell chimes ten times, then the judges pronounce their verdict. Leflef said he could not chase the thought of my lips from his head from that day on.'

'And did you and Shildar win the contest?'

'We did. We wore the garlands they gave us for the remainder

166

of the Fair. Leflef began to send gifts to my father's house. Roses, a flute, and then a leather jerkin. Each gift was accompanied by a set of verses by the Court Poet, urging me to yield myself to him. My father was discontented and said that it was wrong of the man to importune me in this way. But we agreed that I should go and speak to him in his own house. When I visited him, I intended to persuade him to stop pestering me. He received me without ceremony, as if it had been predestined that I should come, and steered the conversation onto things of every day, so that I had no chance to deliver the speech I had prepared. He led me to his workshop and let me inspect the instruments he had there, including the rebecks. I lifted them to gauge their weight, plucked at the strings to test their resonance and practised drawing different bows across each one. He was unwilling to let me try the finest one, saying it had been commissioned by a wealthy Armenian. It was made from cherry wood, with a dark varnish that glowed even in the halflight of the workshop. Yet when he saw how much I desired it, he bent over me and whispered in my ear that that would be his gift to me, if I agreed to share his bed.'

'So it was avarice that led you to give in?'

'I cannot tell you how much I longed to play that instrument. He told me he had thought of me constantly while working on it and that it was only right it should go to me, rather than to the man who had ordered it. Afterwards I came to doubt the truth of what he said. Avarice, perhaps, and vanity. And inexperience. For many months I believed I did not love him. Only when I lost him did I understand how wrong I had been. Before our first night together I was afraid. Then I realized I had no need to be.'

'Was he a gentle lover?'

'I think now he was very clumsy. After the passion of the first encounters he grew reticent, and sparing of caresses. He did not want me with him more than one or two nights each week. He pleaded tiredness, saying that if I were at his side he would not sleep, and that if he was to work properly the following day, he needed rest. Almost every evening, though, I would eat at his home and play and sing before his guests. The Court Poet was a regular visitor, the third son of the Grand Vizier too. Shisnal the miser came as well. They spoke of precious fabrics and tapestries, of painted chests and jewellery and goldsmiths. They were supposed to be friends, but when I listened to them, they sounded more like competitors, or like schoolboys getting ready to engage in a race. Once the meal was over, I would leave with Leflef's other guests.

'I did not return the key he had given me for those first nights. It opens a small postern in his courtyard, and allowed me to enter and leave the house passing by the fishpond, so that his concierge need not be disturbed. I grew bored and frustrated. Maybe the pleasure I had experienced in his bed changed my appearance, I cannot tell, but I began to receive compliments and propositions from many quarters. I was given discreetly to understand that the Crown Prince himself would welcome a visit from me, especially were I to bring my rebeck and play to him before the lovemaking.'

'Did you accept the invitation?' asked Shiram.

'No,' said Dashkur. 'Is it possible that you can have visited Birjand every year, without hearing that the Crown Prince is famed for his ugliness? His palms sweat and his body is ill-smelling. His front teeth stick so far out that he cannot close his lips properly, and his speech is indistinct and graceless. The gossip is he has to pay for lovers. That is considered shameful in Birjand for a man of his age.

'Before the Fair of Vanities this year, I quarrelled with Leflef and swore I would never share his bed again. During the days of the fair I had five different lovers, one after the other. At the end of the Fair, I continued with the fifth. When I returned home that fateful morning, in the hour before dawn, my mother upbraided me in tears. I cried too, and realized Leflef was the one I truly loved. My infidelities had been a way of punishing him. All I wanted was to lie in his arms again. Without even thinking of my bed, I left the house and used the postern key to enter his garden. He was sleeping in the open, by the fishpond, underneath the lemon trees, for the night had been hot and oppressive. I called to him, and he awakened. It was then I saw that he was not alone.

'Though everybody seemed to know, nobody had told me that Ka, son of the Caliph of Tabriz, was now Leflef's bedmate. Ka had come to Birjand on an embassy from his father, which he carefully planned to coincide with the Fair, and stayed on afterwards.'

'How did they meet?'

'I do not know.'

'And what did Leflef say to you?'

'Something foolish. My favourite bow had snapped some weeks before the Fair. He made me another, and it was delivered to me after we had quarrelled. He asked whether I was satisfied with it.'

'And Ka?'

'He did not speak a word. I could feel his eyes boring into me, from the shadow of the lemons. I dropped the key and ran. When I got home, I fell into the deepest of sleeps. By the afternoon, word had spread through the city that Leflef had departed with Ka for Tabriz, without bidding farewell to any of his friends or relatives, or giving any indication when he would return. I set off running as fast as I could towards the cliff of Araxas.'

'And now what will you do?'

'Since it seems I cannot die, I will go to Tabriz and try to win him back.'

'Can I come with you?'

Shiram's voice had quavered. He was blushing to the roots of his hair.

'What makes you want to do that? I do not love you, and I have nothing to give you.'

'Do you know the road to that city? How far have you travelled in your life?'

'Never so far that I could not see the towers of Birjand on the horizon.'

'Then you will need a guide.'

'And you will give me clothes, and sandals? And what am I to do with this?'

Dashkur stretched forth the palm of his right hand, on it the sloughed-off sacred snake skin.

'We shall put it in a leather pouch. You can carry it hanging on a cord around your neck. That way you will never be without the protection of the goddess.'

'But if we arrive in Tabriz together, people will think that we are lovers. They will say that I have found another, just as Leflef found Ka. If that gets to his ears, I shall lose all hope of winning him back.'

'Then we shall say I am your servant. I shall wear humble garments and obey you. And we shall ride to Tabriz on one horse.'

15

'Of course Robert,' said Alan, 'went further than anybody else, where the classifieds are concerned.'

'What makes you say that?' asked Gavin.

The lemon sorbet and salads had been cleared away and they were on to the main course. A pork joint in its rich, fruity sauce adorned each plate, steaming fragrantly in the light of the candles, which burnt more brightly now that ten o'clock was past, and the day had finally begun to fade.

'He put an ad in and swore he'd bed every man who responded.'

'And did he?'

Kieran laughed.

'I remember all that. We were living in the same flat, in Drummond Place, at the time. I'm sure he got round most of them.'

'He claimed there were twenty-five replies,' said Mark.

'That might have been too much, even for Robert,' put in Rory.

'Do you remember the golf clubs?' Kieran asked Mark. 'That was the funniest "do not disturb" sign I have ever seen.'

'I don't get it,' said Ramon, with a frown.

'During the month after the ad,' said Mark, 'I came round several times to visit Kieran, and found a bag of golf clubs lying just inside the door of the flat. It meant that Robert had one of his lovers in.'

'That one was married with kids and worked in local government,' said Kieran.

'Didn't he come from Duddingston or somewhere really posh like that?' Mark asked. 'If I remember rightly, he was an elder of the kirk as well.'

'Yes,' said Kieran. 'Once they'd had it off, he'd describe the kirk session meetings to Robert and agonize over the troubles he was having with his teenage son. He also admitted to fancying the minister.'

'And the clubs?' asked Ramon, still waiting for a satisfactory explanation.

'The excuse he gave his wife,' said Mark, 'was that he was playing golf. It was the easiest way to get time on his own. When you come down to it, it was all healthy exercise of one kind or another. Naturally he had to take the clubs along. And leave them somewhere.'

'So they ended up just inside our front door,' concluded Kieran.

'Don't worry. He took his balls in with him,' leered Mark.

'Wasn't there a bit of a moral dilemma there? I mean, sleeping with a married man who is deceiving his wife?' asked Gavin.

'When they were handing morals round,' said Mark, 'Robert got passed by. I don't know how it happened. It was an oversight. His share must have gone to someone else.'

'Then there was the guy,' said Kieran, 'who worked in the box office at the Royal Lyceum. Robert was still getting free tickets for the theatre on the strength of that night a year before he died.'

'And did he tell you about his graduation dinner?' Alan asked. 'The family went to an expensive hotel in Gullane for lunch. One of the waiters gave Robert the glad eye. A redhead from Port Seton. Robert polished off his main course, left the table, disappeared into the gents and got a blow job.'

'Still wearing his M.A. gown,' chuckled Kieran.

'Apparently it was a real turn-on for the waiter,' added Alan. 'Then they buttoned up their flies and pulled the chain. Robert returned to his place and the waiter served the sweets.'

'What did he die of?' Ramon asked.

He immediately regretted the question, which he realized was quite unnecessary. For some reason, everyone looked at Barry.

'Must have been AIDS,' said Gavin.

'How do you know?' Alan asked.

'I can tell from the expression on your faces.'

'Was he working at the Institute then?' put in Dougal, trying to bring the conversation back to lighter themes.

'When do you mean?'

'When you were living in the same flat,' Dougal told Kieran, 'along with God knows how many other queens.'

'It was a big flat. There were seven of you, weren't there?' Mark asked.

'Yes indeed. All of us gay,' said Kieran, yielding to a wave of nostalgia. 'We certainly had fun.'

'I loved the story about the supermarket,' Alan said.

'What was that?' asked Nicol.

'You tell it,' Alan said to Kieran.

'It goes a long way back. If it ever happened, that is. Before I even met him, Robert was working on the checkouts at a super-market in Canonmills. One day he noticed an old woman with an oddly shaped knitted hat halfway down the queue. Her turn had almost arrived when she fainted. Simply keeled over.'

'So what did he do?'

'He got up and went round and tried to revive her. She appeared to have lost consciousness, as if she had gone into a coma. They got alarmed and appealed over the public address system for a doctor to come to that particular checkout, if by chance there was one in the supermarket at the time.'

'And what was the matter?'

'The doctor felt her pulse, patted her cheeks, looked round at them and said: "You're not going to believe this. She's suffering from hypothermia." Then it occurred to someone to take the hat off. She had a packet of fish fingers frozen to her head.'

'It's a good story,' said Nicol, 'whether it actually happened or not.'

'I suppose any kind of shoplifting has attendant risks,' said Dougal.

'But what is the Institute?' asked Ramon, who was listening intently, determined to miss nothing. He did not find the last story funny and was disappointed at the turn the conversation had taken after Dougal's interruption.

'If you ask me, the place never existed,' Barry interposed. 'It was just a figment of Robert's imagination.'

'Why do you always try and make him out to be better than he was?' Alan said aggressively. 'There was nothing wrong with what he did. Morals or no morals, he had fun.' He was on the point of adding, 'More than can be said for you,' but stopped himself in time.

'The Institute,' said Rory, 'if Robert was to be believed, was a

173

sort of brothel cum orgy house, on Danube Street, where the straight brothels used to be. They may be there still, for all I know. For months on end gay Edinburgh could talk about nothing else. It occupied a whole town house – the basement and three floors above. Robert worked at the bar for the better part of a year. He claimed to have done other things as well.'

'It was the job he held down longest, when you think of it,' put in Kieran. 'Until he got work in the travel agent's. He was nothing if not plausible. He could talk himself into any kind of employment. Then he would get bored and either give up, or do something so outrageous they had to sack him.'

'Remember the time he took rope in and tied his boss to her chair, because she had been annoying him? That way he said he could get on with his work in peace,' said Mark. 'I don't know why she didn't take him to court. She actually took it as a joke. I bumped into her at the cinema one night, after Robert died. That was the first time she mentioned it. He even waylaid the woman with the trolley in the corridor, brought a cup of coffee in and held it to his boss's lips so she could sip at it. Then about eleven o'clock, she managed to get one hand free and manoeuvre her chair over to the phone. People came up from downstairs and untied her. Robert got his books that afternoon.'

'What kept him on at the travel agent's was the cheap air tickets,' said Alan.

'Otherwise he'd never have gone over to the States,' said Kieran. 'You know how hopeless he was at saving money.'

'That was what did for him, if you ask me,' said Rory.

'You mean he got the virus there?'

'Seems logical.'

'I spoke to him about it before going,' said Kieran. 'To be honest, I went on and on at him about it.'

'"Cling film from head to foot." Wasn't that the way he put it?' asked Mark.

'Maybe he forgot to cover the important part,' said Nicol.

'Mind you, he could easily have picked it up in Edinburgh, even then,' Dougal observed. 'There was no need to go so far.'

'I hope the things he said about the Institute were true,' said Kieran. 'They're so colourful. Did he tell you about the Catholic priest?'

'The one who had a host tattooed on his dick, so he could say he was giving Robert the sacrament?' Mark came in.

'That's not original!' cried Nicol. 'I know where he got that from! It's in a book by Jean Genet called *The Thief's Journal*. He pinched it!'

'I don't know which I find harder to believe,' said Dougal. 'That a priest would get his dick tattooed, or that Robert could have read Jean Genet.'

'The bar was in the basement. Not that I've ever been there,' said Rory, with an expressive wiggling of his eyebrows, that encouraged his listeners to think that he was lying. 'I'm going entirely on hearsay. The reception was on the ground floor, with the orgy room to one side. There were private rooms on the first floor and on the top floor, under the roof, what they called the Star Chamber.'

'What on earth was that?' asked Gavin.

'It's really odd the way you all claim not to have been there,' put in Ramon, 'when everyone seems to know so much about the place.'

No one paid any attention to him.

'The room where you could get your fantasies acted out,' said Kieran. 'According to Robert, he could earn more from a night in there than in two weeks behind the bar.'

'Marshall Clements the advocate, the one who died in the spring, was a regular customer,' said Alan. 'He wanted to be stripped down to his underpants and then spanked with a hairbrush. Robert had to keep telling him he was a naughty boy and he would answer yes, yes, he really deserved to be treated that way. He would beg Robert to spank him on the bare skin but Robert had to refuse to take the underpants off.'

'That's real sadism, isn't it?' said Kieran. 'When they ask you to make them suffer and you refuse.'

'Each time they did it people were invited up from downstairs to act as an audience,' said Mark. 'Marshall insisted that it had to be public.'

'Why are kinky folk all so distinguished?' asked Nicol. 'Is there a special gene that makes them high achievers?'

'Queens in high places, that's what it's called,' Mark put in.

'You know the Chinese proverb,' said Dougal. 'The further up

175

the tree a monkey is, the more of its backside you get to see.'

'They're rich, so you hear all about their fantasies,' said Rory. 'They can actually pay to have them acted out. All the poor can do is think about theirs.'

'There was a judge too, wasn't there?' prompted Kieran.

'He came with his full regalia,' said Alan. 'They placed a big wooden table in front of him so he could deliver sentence, wearing his wig, banging a hammer as he spoke. And all the time he had to be sitting on Robert's dick.'

'You wonder how he kept it up,' said Gavin.

'You wonder how he thought up all those stories,' Barry interjected.

'Lots of public figures went,' said Mark. 'He had stories about Wilfred Hartmann too. You know, the guy whose obituary was in the paper yesterday.'

'The music professor?' Gavin asked. 'Brian was taught by him.'

'I wrote that obituary,' Rory said. 'But I never came across any indication he was gay. Mind you, he was never the same after the Italian business.'

'What do you mean?'

'He disappeared without telling anyone, and turned up halfway down a country road somewhere in Tuscany. They had to ship him back. He was retired discreetly a month or so afterwards.'

16

A peasant found him not long after dawn, crumpled on the ground beneath an olive tree. Back in Scotland, the daily newspapers reported that the occupant of the Henderson chair, in the Faculty of Music of the University of Edinburgh, had been taken poorly while on holiday in Tuscany. He was supposed to have officiated at the ceremony for the awarding of honorary degrees that very day. There was no serious cause for concern, they assured their readers. Prematurely, it turned out.

Wilfred was not ill, merely asleep. The flies of his trousers were undone and one hand rested on his ageing, wrinkled sex. He had had a wank after bedding down the previous night. His breath smelt strongly of whisky. The peasant, who was an observant character, though luckily a man of few words, noticed an empty hip flask lying on the other side of the tree trunk. It was a detail that did not get into the papers.

Wilfred had hurled it away after drinking his last mouthful. He had wanked thinking of Laszlo in far-off Vienna, all those years ago, before his first symphony met with such huge success and was performed in concert halls all round the world, and before he came northwards to Scotland, trailing clouds of rather faded and ambivalent glory. Driven to exasperation by his arrogant conservatism, his London colleagues, thanks to a carefully planned and executed series of bureaucratic manoeuvres, succeeded in propelling him towards the Edinburgh chair. Harmless obscurity in a distant northern province was, they felt, what he deserved. They could not have predicted such a sudden, ignominious end to his career.

He was retired discreetly from the university, the autumn after his return from Italy. By the terms of his contract, he could have continued teaching until his seventieth birthday. Mention of compulsory retirement would have raised a scandal. The official version was that he had suffered a physical collapse during the summer. While his mental faculties were in no way impaired, early retirement would allow him to recuperate completely, as well as providing extra leisure time. He could yet again attempt to rediscover the buried talent that had fired his great symphony, petering out inexplicably so soon afterwards. The settlement was generous. Moreover, forty-two years after its inception, he still received sufficient royalties from that one work to keep him in the style to which he had grown accustomed.

The royalties also funded his worsening drink problem. Throughout that winter Wilfred could be found, usually in an advanced state of inebriation, in one or other of the pubs in Thistle Street which boasted an especially late licence. On one occasion, when it proved beyond his powers to insert his key into the main door of the Dundas Street close he lived in, he stumbled uphill and spent the night with the dossers, on the steps leading down into Waverley Station.

By that stage his wife was no longer living with him. Wilfred's disintegration had reached a point where she lost both interest and hope. She was trying to make a new life for herself with their daughter.

It was a source of much embarrassment to the Faculty of Music that such an eminent former member of staff could not be invited back to present prizes, open a concert or sign a begging letter to graduates. The scandal looming over him, mooted in the letter he received that fateful day, never broke, though towards the end he became a garrulous drunkard and, had any of his cronies shown sufficient perspicacity, or even interest, it would have been a simple matter to glean from him, over yet another pint, the details of the terrible affair which led him to seek out Caspar Brandt, in the hills north of Lucca. Mark received a garbled version of the facts, rather against his will, late one Friday evening.

Wilfred never found out who had written the letter. After she died, it crossed his mind it might have been his wife. But by that stage she could not be challenged. It lay waiting for him on the desk one Tuesday morning. Normally his secretary opened all the mail, even those envelopes marked "confidential". The odd look of this one held her back. Each individual letter had been cut painstakingly from newsprint. Wilfred's name and designation straggled from left to right, as when a child strives to make a straight line but cannot quite succeed.

I have suspected for years you did not write it, said the letter. *Now I am in possession of the proof. Whatever glories you accumulated by passing it off as your own, they are as nothing to the shame you will face once I expose you.* There was more, in the same mildly demented tone. The symphony itself was never specifically mentioned. Wilfred knew immediately which work of his was intended.

His reaction surprised him. He could not credit the reality of the letter. In his twenties and thirties he had dreamt repeatedly, even obsessively, of such an eventuality. As he approached middle age, it receded into the background, so that he rarely spared a thought for the circumstances surrounding the genesis of his masterpiece. Many people believed they were acquainted with the process of its writing. But the full picture, he felt sure, was vouchsafed to him alone. This uniqueness should have rendered him invulnerable. He had believed he was safe for ever. Now his security was shattered, in a fashion he struggled to comprehend.

He wandered over to his office window and studied the puffy, grey Edinburgh sky. Everything looked perfectly normal. The spinster who always walked her dogs at this time in the morning was walking them just as he had anticipated. A traffic warden worked his way lugubriously from car to car, checking the status of the parking meters. As Wilfred watched, he pulled a notebook from his pocket and began writing. All these events belonged to an order of things which he recognized and trusted. The letter did not. Yet when he turned back to the desk, it still lay there. The lid of the grand piano was open. A green felt cloth covered the keys, protecting them from dust. On one side of the lectern stood a black and white photograph of Wilfred, shaking hands with a celebrated conductor, after a recent 'revival' of the symphony before a Berlin audience. Both the 'in' and 'out' trays on his desk were neatly ordered, their contents of the habitual, comfortingly small dimensions.

As he gazed, blackest panic screamed within him. A whirl-pool suddenly took hold of the room. These precious objects, each of which spoke of his eminent position and how he had attained and maintained it, were swept around in a whirligig so savage nothing but flotsam and jetsam would remain in a matter of minutes. He clutched at the standard lamp so violently he nearly knocked it over. Then, with a movement he could generally restrain until close upon lunchtime and which, he noted with dismay, was losing its ability to reassure him, he bent down over the drinks cabinet and poured himself a stiff whisky.

Somehow he got through to five o'clock, present in body alone at meetings he had to chair and ought to have steered to a disci-plined conclusion, rather than allowing them to peter out in anec-dotes and ill-concealed bickering. He could not have said where his thoughts were. He slipped out of the faculty front door like a criminal, barely saluting the janitor, and hailed a taxi. As it drew to a halt in Abercromby Place, a set of lighted windows told him Lyuba was at home.

His mistress had aged, if anything, even faster than Wilfred. He enjoyed systematically betraying his spouse. Lyuba's presence in Edinburgh was all the deadlier a weapon because Millie, Wil-fred's second wife, did everything she could to deny it. Their marital exchanges, when he arrived home at eleven, having failed yet again to inform her he would not be returning for an evening meal, or when she discovered halfway through Saturday morning that he had arranged a whole series of activities for the weekend, which did not include her, were of a Pinteresque banality and desolation. At times he was tempted to hit her for not challenging him, not protesting.

The time when his wife had interested him sexually was so far gone it might never have been. Lyuba's body, too, had begun, ever so slightly, to disgust him, rather as his own did, at odd moments. White pubic hairs were inevitable, if regrettable in a man. In a woman, they were an abomination.Yet there were precious things that tied him to her. Erotic memories of this and other liaisons. They had pooled the latter in the past, in London, and evoked them still from time to time. When he was younger, he found it enormously exciting to hear her speak of other men in certain tones. It fuelled his desire. The lack of competitors, in more recent years, mortified it.

The blow he received on this particular evening was doubly painful for being so unexpected. He knew he had urged her to seek another lover or lovers. He could remember doing so barely a week before. She had found one now.

'Stuart Dow,' he repeated, trying to conceal how crestfallen he was. 'Not what I would have expected. And is he good?'

'What do you mean?'

'I mean, in bed.'

He was trying the old strategy, which had made these secondary affairs a part of their relationship, bringing them, as it were, within Wilfred's jurisdiction.

'Wilfred, you worry me at times. I have always found your sexual curiosity about other men peculiar, disturbing even. Have you ever asked yourself what it means?'

'I don't know what you're getting at.'

'What would a psychiatrist make of it? Not that it matters now, anyway. I am tired of those games. And Stuart will arrive in just over an hour, so we have little time.'

'You mean that I don't get to meet him?'

'I don't think he would relish that.'

'And what about me? About my feelings?'

Lyuba lit a cigarette. Her hand trembled as she replaced the heavy cut glass lighter on the coffee table. She was managing to retain control of the situation, but with an effort.

'Edinburgh is not London, Wilfred. Anonymity is impossible here. Social life in this city is like a maze, where each path appearing to lead outwards brings one forcibly back to the centre. And the code ... the code is different, at least amongst circles such as ours. A man as relentlessly unfaithful to his wife as you have been cannot be popular. Especially when his wife is known to everybody, and the woman he is supposed to be betraying her with is, too.'

Lyuba paused. She realized the 'supposed to' was a provocation, and waited to see if Wilfred would respond. He might have done, if the letter he received that morning had not absorbed all his available energies. He had come with the intention of unburdening himself, of telling Lyuba everything. Now he had to adjust to the changed circumstances and decide whether it was worth telling her anything at all.

'I know you think I moved up here to be with you,' Lyuba went on, 'and in part that is true. But things were coming to an end for me in London in any case. Do you know that I considered returning home to the new Russia?' She laughed. 'Not like Brodsky or Ashkenazy, I am too conscious of my relative insignificance to dream of that. You never thought I might have alternatives, did you? And I chose not to discuss them with you. Now I have got used to Scotland. I know I can live well here, in comfort and in peace. I am contented. I could never afford a flat of this size in London, or in such a street. And I have friends who, if at times they bore me, are as faithful as any I ever had.'

'An advocate,' murmured Wilfred, still thinking about Dow.

'And a widower,' Lyuba specified.

'What do you expect me to do with Millie? Murder her?'

In the silence which followed, Wilfred was aware of the burring of a taxi engine just below the window. He looked at Lyuba. No reaction. It was too soon to be her new lover.

'What did you come to tell me?' she asked. 'Is something special troubling you? Or had you grown tired of all this too?'

'I'm going away for a few days,' Wilfred heard himself say.

He avoided her gaze. He could not have lied to Lyuba. It filled him with dismay to be concealing such an important event as the letter's arrival. That marked an ending more definitely than any tears or shouting could have done.

'To Italy. To Lucca. Or the countryside near Lucca.'

'Have you no duties at the university?'

'I'm cancelling them.'

'Oh.'

She did not ask the reason, and stubbed out her cigarette.

'I'd better go, then.'

They said nothing more as she saw him to the door. It felt strange to be going home so early. Millie met him in the hallway, a smile of surprise and pleasure on her face. She had already eaten but she fed him patiently. She had a shrewd idea where he was coming from, and wondered if his unusual mood portended hopeful news for her. Wilfred, for his part, was nervous. One mainstay of his life had slipped away. He could not quite credit

182

Millie's steadfastness. It was logical that she, too, should disappear, in this new state of things.

His mind was working furiously fast. On the one hand, he was contemplating the course of action he had fixed upon, almost involuntarily, while sitting in Lyuba's lounge. On the other, he struggled to keep at bay the flood of memories assailing him, from the time when he was twenty-two and in Vienna, with Laszlo scribbling furiously next door.

'I'm going away tomorrow,' he said, breaking the silence.

Millie, having just poured him a second glass of chilled white wine, replaced the bottle in the fridge. She suppressed the question which rose to her lips ('Am I coming, too?') and asked, instead:

'Have you booked your ticket?'

'That'll be no problem. My secretary can do it before lunchtime. I'll fly to Pisa. Or Lucca, if the Pisa flights are full.'

Eager to give the impression that he was in control of things, Wilfred forgot that Lucca has no airport of its own.

'A meeting? Or a conference?'

'I'm calling on Caspar Brandt.'

'Oh.'

Wilfred was telling Millie all he could of what he had been unable to share with Lyuba. The reason for his journey, however, must remain a secret. Keen to gauge how much further she could go, without eliciting the usual dismissive comment from her husband, after which he would rise from the table without a word, and disappear into his study, she prompted him:

'The one from the competition?'

'Yes. A pity he didn't win the prize. It'd make him happier to see me.'

'Does he know you're coming?'

'Not yet.'

Millie paused. She had forgotten nothing of what Wilfred told her, in the early days, when they had shared their respective pasts, as mature lovers are wont, even obliged, to do. The highly edited version of Wilfred's she received then was present to her in every detail.

'You and he go back a long time.'

'To Vienna, yes.'

183

'Of course, he has never had a success like yours.'

'But he has continued writing. He has been writing consistently for over twenty years now. They think highly of him on the continent.'

Millie cringed mentally, in anticipation of a blow that did not fall. She knew where this sort of discussion led. Wilfred would attribute his failure as a creative artist to her failure as his muse, and to the failure of their loveless, hopeless marriage. To have the conversation take that tack would be more than she could bear.

'But not in this country. We know better.'

'That is partly due to me.'

'I'm sure you're right about his music.'

'And I am not,' Wilfred said tartly.

Their exchange had returned to well trodden paths. It was customary for him to snub her in this way, and for her to subside into silence as a result. Sharing a bed can be like sleeping alone, worse still than sleeping alone, when estrangement has taken hold. Husband and wife lay awake at different times, then, briefly, at the same, each pretending not to notice the other's wakefulness, lest the acknowledgement should force upon them an intimacy they shunned for different reasons. Millie did not wish to be hurt again. The reek of alcohol on her husband's breath was dismally familiar.

Wilfred, for his part, knew something had changed, though he could not have explained what. He brushed aside his deputy's protests, when he announced his departure the following morning. By the time his plane landed in Pisa, the swift Mediterranean darkness, such a contrast to the aching, infinitely protracted Scottish summer twilights, had already fallen. There was no point in trying to reach Caspar that night. He checked into a hotel.

The further upwards in price range one goes, the more anonymous hotel rooms become. The cheapest give an unmistakable sense of the country, even the town where one is staying, albeit only by the intricacies of their plumbing. Wilfred's room was sufficiently expensive to be indistinguishable from similar ones he had slept in in New York, Berlin, St Petersburg and London. The windows looked on to a busy thoroughfare. While double

184

glazing shut out most of the noise, passing vehicles set distorted rectangles of light veering round the walls. The hum of the air-conditioning punctuated his dreams. He awoke once convinced he could smell escaping gas, and had to reassure himself that there were no gas appliances in his room, or even on this floor of the hotel.

Laszlo was returning. He acknowledged that with a growing sense of fear. He awoke from one dream convinced Laszlo had written the infamous letter. He sought to recover the rational certainty, intermittently vanished, that the Hungarian was long since dead, more than forty years in the grave. He might have been a potholer who has slipped down into a lightless cavern, and gropes for a cord he knows must dangle somewhere, which will allow his companions to drag him back into the daylight.

He paid with his credit card and asked for a receipt. He did not reflect, in his confused state, that he could hardly expect the departmental budget to cover this particular trip. When he demanded a taxi to Lucca, the receptionist gulped, and managed to persuade him to take a train, there being more or less a half-hourly service on the branch line between the towns. He did not spare a glance for the rather depressing riverside in Pisa, or for the miracle of Our Lady of the Thorns, the toy-sized church perched at the Arno's edge, as if built of green and white marzipan, its survival inexplicable beneath that already torrid mid-morning sun. Nor did he enter inside Lucca's walls. He had, however, realized that the second driver was as unlikely to accept plastic as the first, so instructed him to pause outside a bank, emerging with a sheaf of notes in that infuriatingly overstated currency, all pointless zeros nobody had the good sense to abolish.

It took well over an hour to locate Caspar's retreat. Wilfred would not have known the address, had his secretary not carefully filed all the correspondence relating to the prize competition where Caspar had, largely due to Wilfred's intervention, won second rather than first place and, as a result, neither money nor performance sponsorship. They proceeded from the highway to a secondary road, then to a dirt track, the driver pausing at house after house to enquire about the composer's whereabouts. When at last they arrived, the red tiles of the roof, encrusted with lichen of a comfortable brown, could be glimpsed on their left, beyond a grove of olives teetering down the slope. The taxi driver declined to negotiate the steep path carrying Wilfred's case, or even to wait and see if there was anyone at home. Wilfred hardly registered the sum he was told to produce, or the driver's surprise that his passenger did indeed carry such a sizeable amount of cash upon his person. The man had been preparing for an altercation. His taxi roared off up the hillside, its wheels grating in the dry dust of the ruts, leaving Wilfred amidst sporadic birdsong and the baked aroma of wild herbs in the sun.

An adolescent came to the door. He had a shock of jet black hair and looked as if the unexpected ringing of the doorbell had forced him out of bed. Wilfred's English meant nothing to him. A voice from within, which Wilfred recognized, called in Italian. All he caught was the boy's name: Lucio. Then Caspar's face appeared in the dimness behind his shoulders.

More than two decades had elapsed since their last meeting. Wilfred had seen photographs of his former fellow student, half-Polish, half-German, in the intervening period. Nevertheless, he unconsciously expected the man still to be in his twenties, with the youthful vulnerability and seriousness that had characterized him, when they saw each other nearly every other day. The changes time had wrought filled him with indignation.

For Caspar, Wilfred's visit was no less unexpected than an embassy from outer space. The wildest speculations filled his head. Perhaps he had come to apologize for the competition outcome, or to tell him that, because of an irregularity in procedure, the result had been annulled, so that Caspar had a second chance of winning. He told Lucio to bring the suitcase indoors. As Wilfred removed his coat and Caspar's eyes got used to the light, he realized something was seriously wrong. Wilfred's disintegration had already begun and was proceeding at an alarming rate.

'Can I get you some food? Do you want a drink of water? Or something stronger?'

'Actually,' Wilfred murmured, 'I'd like to lie down. Is there a place where I can sleep?'

When he came to, it was early afternoon. The machine-like scratching of cicadas beyond the window was so deafening they could have been inside his room. He heard a murmur of voices below and peered out. A table had been laid in the pergola outside the kitchen door. A place was set for him.

The meal could hardly have been simpler. A steaming bowl of pasta with olives, uncooked, chopped tomatoes, crumbly white cheese and plentiful basil, then a salad so coarse and tasty Wilfred concluded it must come from the garden. The borage flowers run through it gave it odd dashes of purple. The red wine came in mineral water bottles but was none the less welcome for that. The three men ate in silence, then the youngest rose to clear the table.

'This is my son, Lucio,' Caspar said.

'Your son?'

'Not by my first wife, the one you knew. She died many years ago. Lucio's mother is Italian. She is visiting relatives in Livorno. She'll be back tomorrow. Coffee? Or more wine?'

Wilfred plumped for wine. They retreated to a pair of wicker-work armchairs in the shade of the vine trellis. Lucio took his place silently in the background.

'The reason for my visit . . .' he began, then stopped. 'You must be wondering what brought me here. It was a letter.'

Caspar nodded and said nothing.

'A letter about my first symphony. I thought you might have written it.'

'Me? What kind of letter?'

'An anonymous letter. A poison pen letter. I think that is what you call it.'

Caspar half rose from his seat.

'And you have come here to accuse me?'

'No, no, I apologize, please. Now we are here I can see how ridiculous my suspicions were.'

'What reason would I have for doing that?' Caspar asked, paying no heed. A flash of illumination crossed his face, and he began to laugh. 'Ah, now I see. Because of the competition. You think because I failed to win the competition, and you were on the jury, I would take revenge in this form.'

'Forget what I said. Let me put it this way. I need to know who wrote that letter. And you are the only person I can think of who might help me.'

187

'Why?'

'Because you were there at the time. A witness.'

'At what time? I just don't understand.'

Wilfred glanced at Lucio's unmoving features in the shadow. It felt inappropriate to be talking of all this in front of the boy. Yet it would have been presumptuous, even in his eyes, to ask Caspar to despatch his son elsewhere.

'When it was written. At the time Laszlo died.'

Two tears rolled down Wilfred's cheeks. He poured himself another glass of wine. Despite the shock of the insult he had received, Caspar could not help feeling a touch of compassion for the man. He had envied Wilfred for so many years, had engaged in so many silent, bitter monologues about his success and the recognition he had achieved. And here he was, come to Caspar's retreat in the hills north of Lucca, to find a witness for the terrible defeat his life was turning into.

'What is the connection? Between Laszlo's death and your symphony, that is? Apart from them happening at roughly the same time?'

'You mean you never suspected?'

'Suspected what?'

It struck Wilfred as incredible that the truth of the matter should elude the grasp of someone who had observed it all so closely. He changed tack.

'Laszlo was an invert.'

'A what? Oh, homosexual? Is that your word for it? How very nineteen-fifties.' Caspar shrugged his shoulders. 'Doesn't surprise me. Is that connected with his suicide?'

'Your guess is as good as mine.'

Wilfred could lie, when he chose to, with splendid aplomb.

'Just being different is hardly sufficient reason. I know plenty of well-adjusted "inverts", as you call them. I presumed it was because he had failed his exams. His money ran out, there was no way he could stay on at the conservatory, and he wanted to avoid going back to Hungary at any cost.'

Torn between the duplicity practised during many years and an overwhelming desire to speak the truth, Wilfred merely nodded.

'You were kind to him. You took him in and paid for the flat.

But I thought you had moved out before he killed himself.'

Wilfred felt close to despair. Here, where he had imagined everything was already known, and could therefore, mystically, be resolved, he beat his head against a wall of incomprehension that refused to yield. Suddenly it did.

'You were lovers?'

'Yes. He wrote the symphony.'

'What?'

Caspar's voice rose in such a crescendo that a bird, which had been nestling in the foliage above their heads, was startled and flew off, with a flapping of wings that echoed uncannily in the hot silence. Still Lucio did not move, his eyes fixed on Wilfred's face. Caspar's brain was working overtime.

'That's what was in the letter?'

'Yes.'

'And is it true?'

'I told you that it was.'

Caspar was filled with elation. It was not only glee at Wilfred's predicament. He was an ardent student of human nature. What Wilfred confessed opened up a completely new perspective on a sequence of events that had been buried, solid and resolved, in the distant past. Now everything was changed.

'That's incredible!' he said. 'Do you mean you have built your entire career on a lie? On an imposture?'

Then, curious for more detail:

'But are you a lover of women or of men? You married Eva shortly after Laszlo died. We all assumed it was the shock of losing him that made your mind up for you.'

'It was an aberration. A friendship that went wrong. To think of it repels me now.'

Frankness was too new a strategy for Wilfred to stick to it for long. His confession would be a patchwork of truth and falsehood.

'I realized the mistake I was making before it was too late. For me, that is.'

'You abandoned him and so he killed himself.'

'He had threatened to do it more than once. I didn't believe him. Even if I had, there was no way I could have stayed.'

Drink did not affect Wilfred's diction. He enunciated each

189

word distinctly, with a weight of authority that grew more ponderous the further he wandered from the truth.

'What made you realize it was wrong for you?'

'A thing we did. A sexual thing. It disgusted me, alerted me to the path that I was following. It took every ounce of strength I had to break free.'

Wilfred never felt a stronger repulsion for Laszlo than when he knew Laszlo desired him. At the beginning he had managed to pretend that all he sought was physical release. Eva, whom he had decided some time before would be his wife, came from a stolid Catholic family. Physical intimacy outside the marriage bed was unthinkable. What Wilfred looked on as his romps with Laszlo were a way of cleaning himself, of siphoning lust off so that it would not sully Eva's purity. Or so he imagined. He could not bear to think that the changes he observed in Laszlo, his languor, the way he spread his legs open, a fleeting expression in his eyes, found their counterpart in changes he himself was undergoing. Laszlo came to bear the double weight of two desires. Small wonder that it crushed him. Wilfred's hope was that, when Laszlo perished, the lust that drew them together would die too.

'He didn't have that strength. Poor fellow,' commented Caspar.

'After I moved out, I continued paying the rent. The man was destitute. I would go back from time to time. But the intervals between my visits got longer and longer. I couldn't bear the scenes he made.'

'And when he died, you found the symphony among his papers?'

'Yes.'

'Did it require a lot of work?'

'Not much.'

This was the truth.

'So you do not even have the satisfaction of co-authorship.'

Wilfred shook his head. Lucio rose and whispered into his father's ear.

'Look,' said Caspar, a little awkwardly, 'we normally sleep after lunch. And I always work from five till eight. Could we resume our discussion over dinner? In any case, I'd like some time to take in what you've told me.'

*

Wilfred lay fully dressed on his bed, sweating in the heat, his eyes open and staring wide. He had taunted Laszlo over the suicide.

'Go on then, do it,' he had said. 'Don't think you can keep me here by threatening me.'

It gave him an enormous sense of power to imagine that his words could push Laszlo over the edge. The balance of a life lay in his hands. The break had not been clean. Wilfred kept hold of a key when he moved out. After all, he had paid the rent until the end of the following month. It was his right to do so. He found it harder to relinquish Laszlo's body than he expected. His visits followed the same pattern. He would arrive at an unpredictable hour of the day, climbing the stair in a Viennese tenement as huge and featureless as a barracks, past the toilet on each landing till he reached the last floor but one. Laszlo would be working or asleep, they would have sex, he would play Wilfred the latest passages of the symphony on an upright piano, Wilfred would get up to go, and there would be a scene.

He tiptoed downstairs to the kitchen. Caspar and Lucio were still asleep. As he had hoped, a bottle of wine, the third to be opened during lunch, stood by the sink, still nearly full. He was in need of further comforting. He took a glass, filled it, went back upstairs, and placed the bottle on the cabinet next to his bed.

On the last occasion they spoke to one another, Laszlo had begged Wilfred to leave him money. He had nothing to buy food with. He had not been working at his score that time. He claimed that the symphony was near completion. He was afraid to put the finishing touches to it, he said. What else was there for him to live for? Wilfred found him slumped on the bed, staring at the doorway when he entered the room. He had to shake himself free in order to get out of the flat after nightfall, once they had had sex. At last the situation had begun to frighten him.

'You disgust me,' he shouted, 'do you know that? You disgust me!'

He let a week go by before returning. He had never stayed away so many days. When he let himself in, the smell of gas alerted him to what had happened. He felt no surprise. No emotion at all, other than an overwhelming sensation of peace, even of triumph. The odd thing was, Laszlo was entirely naked. The image returned overpoweringly to him as he lay there on a strange, uncomfortably lumpy bed in the hills above Lucca: the kitchen, Laszlo's kneeling form before the oven and the eerie pallor of his buttocks, buttocks Wilfred knew so well, in the halflight from the inner courtyard. He did the things he had seen people do in American films – stuffed a handkerchief over his nose, threw the windows open wide, and pulled Laszlo's body out and onto the floor. There was a stillness to that moment that made him wish it could have lasted for ever.

Now, in the hills above Lucca, with everything so exceptionally present to him, he admitted what he had done, though it was as impossible as ever to find an acceptable reason. He had gone to the other end of the flat, where the smell of gas was weakest, to the bedroom, and masturbated into the untidy bed Laszlo had abandoned. It was an orgasm of triumph, for that life had come to depend, he imagined, entirely on him, and its conclusion was an affirmation of his power. Bit by bit, ruthlessly, he had withdrawn himself from Laszlo, who had not survived. And the symphony?

Before descending four flights of stairs to inform the porter, before they went out together to call the police (for Russian troops were stationed in Vienna in those days, and telephones were few and far between) Wilfred meticulously gathered together the drafts, the scattered notes and fragments, as well as the final copy Laszlo had barely finished, and crammed them into the briefcase which he carried. He hid it in the stairhead toilet, behind the WC. He knew from experience that the occupants of the other flats on the landing, with whom it was shared, would not return until the evening.

The symphony, he realized, had been the ultimate abomination. Wilfred had come to Vienna to study composition and conducting. His composition exercises were lifeless and academic, a mere working out of rules and imitated patterns, with minimal invention of his own. Laszlo, by contrast, who could never make a class on time, who slept in on the morning of his examinations or got drunk the night before, wrote with a fluidity that filled Wilfred with envy. The Hungarian claimed that all the work had been done before he put pen to paper, which was, for him, merely a question of transcription. The long afternoons he spent staring at the ceiling, smoking vacantly in the kitchen, or in a cheap café, when he managed to get dressed and leave the building, were when in fact he did his composition.

It had been a torment for Wilfred to realize that a creature he both loved and despised, so fragile and dependent an unkind word or gesture could drive him to despair, possessed a faculty he was denied. Laszlo's death had put an end to that injustice. As the Italian light grew gentler, and the outlines of the shadows in his bedroom fuzzier while, beyond the window and beneath the pergola, Lucio impatiently flipped over the pages of his latest comic book, eager to reach the end, it came to Wilfred that his animosity towards Caspar had the same basis.

He had to get away. If he did not, then Caspar would die as Laszlo had died. It would be Wilfred's fault again. The envy that had consumed him throughout all these years, which the success of his stolen symphony had done nothing to diminish, was of murderous dimensions. The quantity of wine he had drunk brought Wilfred close to delirium. He could not bear the idea of Caspar, under that same roof, patiently honing music that, if it won him little renown in his lifetime would, Wilfred was certain, earn him fame and gratitude when he was dead.

He staggered to his feet, tottered downstairs and, in his stupefied condition, grabbed the unbelievably heavy coat he had brought with him. Lucio, standing by a fig tree now, at the far end of the garden, wearing an unravelling straw hat and selecting the ripest fruit for the dinner table, looked up and caught sight of their strange guest, as he laboured uphill, then disappeared over the horizon. He would tell his father about it when they had their evening meal. It was not worth distracting him from his work for such a trifle.

17

'You all sit here,' Barry thought, 'talking about Robert as if he belonged to you, as if your words could sum him up and say exactly what he was. Nobody turns to me to ask me what I think. And the truth is, I know things about him none of you will ever know. It hasn't even occurred to you I might have slept with him.'

Barry made his first appearance in the pub Robert and his friends used as their local, three months after being posted to the Scottish Office up in Edinburgh. He knew what he was looking for, or thought he did. He had found it already, a couple of times, in London. A one-night stand, a temporary release, after which nothing really appeared to have changed. There was no connection between the hopes he nurtured and the place he ended up in or, to be more precise, what ended up in his bed.

He argued with himself that, if all he had in prospect was a repeat of what he had already experienced, there was no point in continuing to bring men home. He expected them to make him feel different about himself. About his ungainliness, the lack of proportion in his body, his ugly hands, his flabby stomach, his difficulty with small talk, or with any kind of interchange among strangers. The hope was that he would be transformed. But being gay, as far as he could tell, was a game of snakes and ladders, where his throw again and again landed him on a ladder that brought him back to his starting point with a thump. In London, one man came more or less immediately, waited dutifully, with ill-concealed impatience, for Barry to reciprocate, then got out of bed, washed himself and disappeared back into the night. The other stayed for breakfast and was distinctly put out that Barry had only muesli, not fresh orange juice, to offer him, and that the coffee was instant. He had sweated profusely into the sheets, leaving a smell behind which Barry found distasteful, so that the first thing he did, on getting home after work the following day, was stuff them into the washing machine and make up a fresh bed. He had hardly shut his eyes the previous night and turned in, exhausted, at nine o'clock. He was definitely meant to sleep alone, he decided.

Despite the scant fruits it produced, and his reluctance to engage in it, Barry returned to the chase in Edinburgh. It was harder there. The anonymity of London meant that, in the four pubs he visited between resolving that he had to be proactive and moving north, he had at least possessed the attractions of a new face. It was just possible that people considered him exotic when he first hit the scene in Scotland. Within a matter of weeks, however, they stopped even noticing him, while he himself soon identified a range of familiar faces, in the dreary certainty that nothing would transpire with any single one of them. Such was his lack of confidence he assumed that each of the pub's denizens, with the sole exception of himself, always found exactly the partner he wanted, dedicating Friday and Saturday nights to passionate sexual activity which left no emotional scars or wants behind it. It did not occur to him that they were equally alone and friendless, or that he might have constituted what they sought for, if only he and they had managed to overcome barriers of timidity and self-frustration and make a move.

On Friday, and often enough on Saturday too, Barry spent the hours from ten to midnight propped against the bar, drinking his statutory two pints, then leaving with a resolute outer pretence that this was what he had expected, even planned, rather than a further debacle. Nobody needed to tell him things would not hot up till well after midnight. His regular, spinsterish ways, however, meant that at weekends the alarm went off just one hour later than on weekdays. There were clothes to be ironed and carpets to be hoovered, his salary not yet being sufficiently high for him to contemplate employing a home help. And an unflinching schedule was all he had to hold on to, in the midst of such loneliness.

Robert did not deign him with as much as a glance. He would watch them, Robert and his friends, meeting up by arrangement, arriving in pairs or threes, very rarely singly, from a play or a film, or coming together by what looked like accident, but with a naturalness, an inevitability, that brought a lump to his throat. They inhabited a promised land, an America he longed to set out for. But he had lost the map and had no idea what route might lead him to them, allowing him to set foot at last on those Blessed Isles.

There could be no doubt that Robert was the master of ceremonies and that the others, some of whom he later learnt to know as Kieran, Alan, Mark, Rory and Andrew, expected, even demanded to be entertained by him. Robert had an inexhaustible flow of patter. When he paused at a theatrically calculated moment, an outburst of general laughter invariably followed. Maybe he was telling them about the woman friend who, presumably fancying him, had, when well on in drink, summoned up the courage to ask if he was gay.

'I'm saying nothing,' he had answered, 'darling. But I'll tell you one thing. I love frocks!' Or else he was repeating the well worn story of his first fuck, which he insisted had taken place upstairs, in the bedroom he and his brother shared, while directly below his parents were watching *Coronation Street* on the television, in the sitting-room of their council house.

Having sex, he claimed, was like drinking a glass of water, nothing more nor less. And all that mattered was to find fresh water as often as you could. When he moved or spoke, Robert was animated by a seductive ambivalence that endowed him with both grace and deadliness. His vicious wit was of a species certain men, not all of them gay, choose to define as feminine, with a misogyny only matched by Robert's own. He was effeminate and virile at one and the same time, attractive in a conventional way provided he kept still. His handsomeness was such he could easily have modelled tweed jackets for an expensive magazine, staring into the middle distance, with the comfortable complacency of a junior businessman who has just completed a successful deal, or of the grouse hunter who, a moment later, will grasp his firearm and tread the moors. Robert had indeed taken part in grouse hunting, one August in his late teens, though as a beater rather than a shooter. He insisted that he had found his way into the landowner's bed, and referred to the man forever afterwards as Mrs McChatterley when he told the story.

Barry watched the group from a distance, with the keenest interest. He imagined he could gauge the personality of each of its members from the movement of their bodies and their facial expressions, the positions they assumed with respect to one another, the frequency with which they ordered a drink and what they chose. It never crossed his mind, even in his wildest dreams, that one day he could be a part of it, although the role he assumed as favoured butt of Robert's humour was eminently predictable. Nor did he think that he would reach a stage where, having the option of joining them by doing nothing more than turning up in the pub, he would at times choose not to, because the solitude of his own home was more enticing, or because Robert was no longer of their number.

Barry never forgot the date. He remembered not only that it was a Saturday in July, but that it was the twenty-seventh. He could even see before him, now, at five years' distance, the cushion fabrics he had sorted through, and the one he eventually decided on, with Robert's help. It was most unusual for him to enter the pub at four o'clock in the afternoon. He would not have done so if he had not got into such a state of indecision about the fabric. He was additionally nervous because of the dinner invitation looming. He was in line for promotion, and the meal that evening was an unofficial hurdle on the road to greater influence and a considerably higher salary. He had not gone to the pub on Friday so as to get as much rest as possible before the unwanted exposure to conventional society. Calling in at the pub was a way of consoling himself for having to renounce his habitual weekend drink.

It was a sunny afternoon. The doors of the pub stood open. Light flowed in from the street through the upper half of the windows. The panes in the lower half were coloured green and blue, and the sheen they gave the interior made it look like an aquarium. It was practically empty but still smoky. Barry had got his drink and taken a first sip when he caught sight of Robert. Astoundingly, he was alone, rather morose, and undisguisedly pleased to see Barry. Within ten minutes it had been agreed they would return to the shop together, so that Robert could help Barry make up his mind about the fabric.

Once it had been ordered and paid for, he invited Barry home for coffee. It was not his first time in Robert's flat. On previous occasions a whole claque of friends had been there, a group Barry could safely camouflage himself among, slipping away when the talk got too smutty, or the hour too late for him to stay on comfortably.

Even at this distance, Barry could not think of that afternoon without emotion. He had Robert to himself. He was the sole focus of Robert's attention. The man could not have been kinder or more considerate. He brewed fine Dutch coffee, sat Barry on the sofa, and asked him about everything he wished to talk about: his interior decoration, his colleagues at work, his childhood in Sussex and his university years in London. Barry lost all sense of time, melting in the sun of Robert's kindness. Robert gave no sign of being concerned that Barry might draw back when led into the bedroom, or quail before the revelation of Robert's body as he undressed. The assumption he would yield unquestioningly made things easier for Barry. His consent was not an issue.

Robert worked out regularly, even obsessively, at the gym. His trunk tapered becomingly towards the waist and his lower chest and thighs were surprisingly hairy. Barry barely glimpsed the glory of his sex before Robert began undressing him in turn. He had never asked himself what Robert might be like as a lover, his imagination had never gone that far. If he had done, he would have predicted brusqueness, egotism, even violence, not the tender, almost motherly solicitude with which the man removed his clothes, caressed the nape of his neck with one hand, his groin and then his sex with the other, pressed his lips against Barry's and, without hurry or insistence, let him feel the whole force of that tongue inside his mouth, unashamed and probing.

Barry had attended a prestigious boarding school as a day boy. It was one seed of the feeling of inferiority which burgeoned so amply later in life, making him a confused, uncertain adult. He did not always come home at four o'clock. When activities were planned for later in the day, he was expected to stay on, so that the two groups of pupils, boarders and day boys, could follow an identical curriculum, within the limits of the possible.

On Tuesday and Thursday they had physical education in the gym, from half past six till eight o'clock. If Barry did not dread the classes, positively relishing them, this was not because of any

198

physical prowess on his part. He had no ball sense and totally lacked the spirit of aggression essential to success in competitive sports. He worshipped the gym teacher, a family man nearing fifty who, incongruously, smoked. In his presence, Barry felt utterly safe. At that man's behest he could have achieved anything. Scaling the wall bars in record time to clutch the rope swung deftly to him, he would have sailed across to the opposite side of the gymnasium, vaulting a couple of bucks in the process, for good measure. He never got the chance to demonstrate the extent of his adoration. The master hardly noticed his existence. The moment Barry loved most of all was when, on winter evenings, at their head, the man paused by the open door of the gymnasium and, moving his hands easily across the bank of switches, flooded with light a space that had been shrouded in darkness a moment before.

That was what Robert did with Barry's body. Each touch of his fingers, of the palms of his hands, drenched it in brilliance, illuminating it with a light more powerful than that of the summer afternoon, beyond the curtained window. He brought another Barry into being, one Barry had never been conscious of, even as a remote possibility. Barry did not know of Titian's picture in the National Gallery where, in a morning light that marks a new age for mankind, a Magdalene whose relationship with Christ has always been veined with sinful ambivalence, identifies him in his gardener's disguise. She begs to be allowed to touch his risen body, only to meet with a refusal: *Noli me tangere.* Robert had little in common with Mary Magdalene, or Barry with a Christ recently emerged from the tomb. Yet he experienced a kind of resurrection, a rising from the dead. And he was filled with such a sense of power, of invulnerability, that when Robert gently turned him onto his stomach, moistening his anus with a jelly that was almost, but not quite, as cold as ice, and which heightened pleasantly the slightest sensation, then penetrated him, Barry did not protest, or think of condoms. He conceded everything he could, regretting only that he had no more to give. Had he possessed five rectums, every one would have been Robert's.

They showered afterwards, separately, and Barry washed the opaque mixture of sperm and lubricant from his anus with a sense of wonder. He had never expected to find himself doing anything like this. He duly appeared at the dinner party, immaculately groomed and with his characteristic air of premature middle age, but pregnant with a revelation that kept him glowing throughout the evening and surprised his senior colleagues pleasantly. He got the promotion and hired a home help.

The peasant whose scrofula has been healed by a king's miraculous touch does not expect to feel that touch again. He and Robert made no subsequent reference to what had happened. It never occurred to Barry to expect a repetition. The problem was that Robert, as well as his own, might have laid a different seed in Barry's body. He was taken into hospital for the first time late that autumn.

Barry could not bring himself to speak about his worries. He witnessed the tremendous fuss Andrew, who had counted Robert among his lovers many years ago, before getting together with Nicol, made, and the relief when his test brought a negative result, and wondered how many of the group were in a similar position. From an incautious remark, he understood that Mark had tested too. He had a shrewd suspicion that Kieran followed suit. As far as he could gauge, the fears of both had proved unjustified. There was no sign of the changes in demeanour or behaviour he would have expected a positive result to bring.

Did Barry condemn himself without a trial? Did he assume that he would prove unfortunate, in this affair as in so many others, and that he alone had received a gift from Robert which the others had been spared? No one he knew had had sex with Robert at such a recent date, and without any protection. His mood swung from calm resignation, a sense almost of vindication, of the destiny he predicted for himself manifesting at last in its full awfulness, to moments of utter panic. A skin rash in his groin proved, according to his GP, to be the result of sweat aggravated by stress. When it took him well over a month to shake off an influenza virus, the GP prescribed rest and a new hobby. When Barry complained of sweating overnight, he suggested aspirins for the fever, or lighter bedclothes. Asked if anything in particular was causing him anxiety, he said no. It was a burden he preferred to shoulder singly.

Tonight, at the dinner party, he felt it slipping from him.

Brought up an Anglican, he had not set foot in a church since leaving school. He refused to contemplate the possibility that the individual personality might persist in some form after death. And in spite of that, he was acutely aware of Robert's presence, in and around them. It might just be that this was the first time, as far as he could remember, a group of people who knew Robert had reminisced so consciously and freely. But he knew the superstition according to which, if a ghost returns, specific action must be taken to set it at rest. Barry had no inkling what that action might be. He turned his attention to the conversation once more.

'Guess what the busiest time of the year was at the Institute,' Mark was saying.

'I can see this coming,' said Kieran.

'Go on. Guess.'

'The Festival,' said Nicol. 'It had to be the Festival.'

'No.'

'New Year then.'

'Wrong again.'

'During the General Assembly of the Church of Scotland,' Rory said. 'Am I right?'

Mark nodded.

'All those sex-starved clergymen from manses in the Highlands, or from rain-lashed council estates on hillsides in Strathclyde, where their every movement could be seen. Unleashed on the capital for a week. Free of wives, children, mothers-in-law. On the rampage with their fantasies.'

'You'd think they'd go to straight brothels,' Gavin said.

'We don't know what the straight ones got up to,' said Mark. 'Robert insisted that one year they organized a ring-dance of ministers in the orgy room. Round and round and round. Wearing nothing but their dog-collars, each of them holding onto the penis of the man next to him. One of them was seventy-three but it didn't appear to make any difference. He was just as energetic as the rest.'

Nicol burst out laughing.

'What a marvellous idea,' he said. 'I only wish I could believe it.'

'There were photographs,' said Alan.

201

'And where are they now?'

'Disappeared.'

'Robert kept a dog-collar on the mantelpiece in his room at Drummond Place,' said Kieran. 'I can vouch for that. He said it was a souvenir. It had been signed.'

'Did you read what the Episcopalian Bishop of Edinburgh has been saying? About starting to ordain gay priests?' asked Nicol.

'Makes you wonder where the guy's been living for the past twenty years,' said Alan. 'It's like Tennant's saying they're going to start brewing beer.'

'If Scottish congregations only knew,' said Kieran, 'how many of their clergymen leave another man in bed when they get up to come to church on a Sunday morning.'

'Whether you want to believe it or not, the place existed,' put in Dougal.

'How do you know?'

'Because of all the fuss when it closed down. Keith Williamson engaged my firm to act for him.'

'You're not breaching professional confidence here, are you?' Gavin asked.

'It was public knowledge at the time. And the rest of what I know didn't come to me at work. I only do conveyancing. The criminal department is quite separate.'

'Wasn't there a Royal involved?' asked Mark.

'So they said.'

'Bored with Balmoral.'

'There were supposed to have been photographs, too. Purely for entertainment and private use. Not a word of blackmail. But someone got the wind up and the police moved in. Things looked really black for Keith for a few weeks.'

'And he got off?'

'The establishment closed down overnight. Charges were never brought.'

'Any idea why?' asked Gavin.

'Presumably they were afraid it would all come out if they took him to court. He may have threatened them. I wouldn't put it past him.'

'And where is he now?'

'Managing a hotel in central London. Or so I'm told,' said Dougal.

'He's opened a new place just down the road from Princess Di's old house,' Rory said.

'How do you know?' Kieran asked.

'I keep in touch with him. We met for a drink the last time I was down there.'

'As a client, or a friend?'

Rory just smirked.

'Anyone for more pork?' asked Dougal.

'Aren't you going to open the wine I brought?' Nicol intervened. 'It's a burgundy from the early eighties. Last four bottles in the shop.'

'We could have a toast,' said Alan.

'Who to?'

'To Robert, obviously.'

Glasses were filled and they drank a toast, seated, in silence, without clinking glasses. The atmosphere became subdued.

'What now?' asked Mark.

'Another toast?'

'Who to this time? We'll never agree.'

'We've probably all got different things in our heads,' Gavin observed. 'Or different people.'

'Don't let's make it too formal. Or too artificial,' Kieran said.

'I know,' said Rory. 'We can have a communal toast.'

'What do you mean?'

'We stand up, raise our glasses, and everyone says what he wants to drink to. Then we clink glasses and down them all at once.'

There was general agreement. They stood up.

'Who begins?' asked Gavin.

'Let Ramon begin,' said Mark, 'as our European representative.'

'I drink,' said Ramon, 'to the demon on the Night of Sant Antoni.'

'I drink,' said Mark, 'to the first time I saw the Pet Shop Boys play live.'

'I drink,' said Barry, 'to a Saturday afternoon in late July, 1991. No matter what the consequences.'

'I am grateful,' said Dougal. 'I don't know who to, but I certainly know what for. I am grateful, and I drink to that.'

'I drink,' said Rory, 'to all the ones who never made it to this table. The ones who killed themselves, the ones who got married, the ones who were so cowed and frightened they never had any kind of sex life at all. To the ones who are still in the closet,' he went on, for he had drunk a lot already, and drink always made him eloquent and sentimental, 'gathering enough courage to come out, and to each of us, for having made it this far, with all our trials and all our joys . . .'

'To the Dutchman,' said Alan, whom drink made indiscreet, 'I was having sex with in the toilet on my last transatlantic flight, when we hit a patch of air turbulence and I was sure we wouldn't come out alive. It was some of the best sex I ever had. And to my fellow steward Jamie, who sussed where I was and covered for me.'

'I drink,' said Gavin, 'to my children. Not the children of my body, for I have none of those. The children I have cared for, every one of them that passed through my hands in the hospital. Most of all to those who died. The little ones that didn't make it. They are more truly mine than any of the healthy children could ever be.'

'Children,' Nicol said, musingly. 'I drink to Isobel Anna Cunningham, my god-daughter.'

'Ellen McLaverty, Balcarres Road, Drumchapel,' Kieran said.

18

'It isnae Marion at all, it's Mark!' Kieran's mother shouted and burst into tears.

She was sitting at the kitchen table in the flat in Montague Street, a flat she had never visited before and had never been meant to visit. The inconceivable had taken place. She had made the journey from Glasgow across to Edinburgh on her own initiative, without warning Kieran, without asking him for encouragement or help, driven by sheer worry and curiosity. And now she knew.

One of their flatmates had let her in. What else could he have been expected to do? It had been Paul, still clogged and drowsy with sleep, getting ready to go out and sign on for his social security benefit. Opening the front door, he was confronted by a Glasgow woman in her early fifties, still attractive, nervous, clutching her handbag, trying to summon up enough courage to ring the doorbell, perhaps with a premonition of what she might discover once she entered.

'Is my son Kieran home?' she asked. The strange face and unfamiliar surroundings gave her voice a shade of aggression it rarely possessed.

Paul was no fool. He had the room next door to Kieran and Mark's. If they were driven mad at times by his penchant for playing high-energy music in the small hours of the morning, he had the privilege of eavesdropping, whether he wanted to or not, on the increasingly acrimonious scenes that broke out between them. He knew nothing about Kieran's mother. He had not even bothered to ascertain whether either or both of Kieran's parents were still alive. Finding Ellen McLaverty on the doorstep, he merely pointed in the direction of the kitchen, with its heaped-up dirty plates, overflowing ashtrays and grimy tablecloth, then buttoning his jerkin tightly, for it was a horribly cold February day, clattered off down the communal stairway. It occurred to him that Kieran could have sent a call for help to the other side of central Scotland. But Ellen did not have the air of an expected guest. Trouble was brewing. Paul resolved to stay clear.

Partly out of habit, and partly because she knew she was trespassing, Ellen took off her coat and cardigan, laid them carefully on a chair which she pushed back under the table, made space for her handbag on the dresser and set to cleaning up. She preferred to believe that she had come out of concern for her offspring, who had been having a dreadful time with that girl he was always complaining about, the one who treated him so heartlessly and kept going off with other men. It had crossed her mind that they might be living together. She had even wondered if Marion would answer the door. Before she rang she had been preparing herself mentally for such an eventuality on the landing outside.

She had not expected to find Kieran in. If what he told her could be trusted, he went off to the library about half past nine every day to work on his thesis, which was due to be submitted at the end of the year. Why then had she carefully planned her arrival for the middle of the morning?

Because he was concealing something from her which she needed to know. Given her own past, Ellen was hardly in a position to entertain moral prejudices about her son living with his girlfriend. Instinct warned her that something different, more insidious and terrible than anything she could possibly conceive of, had got her only child entangled in its net. She did not doubt that he would extricate himself in time. She was, however, growing impatient, angered by the extent of his distress every time he made the trip across to Glasgow to visit her. He would sort out whatever mess he had got himself into all the quicker with his mother's help.

For her part, she could not understand why this Marion woman came back to him again and again if she didn't really want him. It would have made more sense for her to dump him once and for all. Kieran's role was clearer. It was a hard for a man to tell a woman where she could go, no matter how badly she behaved. And it was always hard to act decisively if you were the one less loved. His mother had no reluctance in that area. She positively warmed to the task. Would she be allowed to take it on?

By the time Kieran got home for a late lunch, several things had happened.

Ellen came upon an almost total lack of cleaning materials. Leaving the front door on the latch, and jamming the main door to the stairway with a brick she found conveniently close by, she slipped out to the Pakistani shop on the corner for bleach and washing-up liquid, scrubbing pads, sponge pads and a fresh dishcloth. By midday she had the kitchen more or less as she would have wanted it. She even cleaned the window panes on the inside. The outside was a more demanding job. She would need her son's help with that.

She made herself a cup of tea, sat at the table and had a solitary, but none the less tranquillizing cigarette. Every single one of the married women whose homes she cleaned on a twice-weekly basis objected strongly to her lighting up while on the premises. She went into the back garden if the urge to smoke came upon her strongly. Never again would she drop the stubs onto the lawn as she had done on that first day, with bitter consequences. Nowadays she slipped the evidence into a used envelope which she would dump in the wastepaper basket at the bus stop where she got her transport home.

She lit a second cigarette, drew the smoke deep into her lungs and asked herself: What next? She did not put the answer into words. Leaving her cigarette burning in the ashtray, she got up and opened first one, then another of the doors off the hall.

It was obvious that a girl lived in the first room. It was long and narrow and had a window at the far end. The flat was at one corner of a rectangle of tenements and the window was wedged into the angle. If you looked out you could see into the rooms of the flat at the same level on the street round the corner. Ellen thanked her stars she had managed to escape from Spring-burn to a council estate. There nobody could spy on you unless they trespassed into your garden. And then you could send them packing with a few choice words! A single bed stood against one wall and a wardrobe against the other, leaving barely sufficient room to squeeze through to the dressing-table with adjustable side mirrors which was pushed up against the window.

The girl had made herself up in a rush before going to work that morning. A couple of bottles had rolled over on their sides, her jar of foundation cream was lying open, and the brush she used to powder her cheeks had not been put back in its proper place. With an enjoyable sense of transgression, Ellen sniffed at one perfume, then sprayed ever so little of another onto her right wrist and held it up to her nose. The girl had good taste. The perfumes were more expensive than anything she would have dared to buy for herself. She tried to think what kind of a job she might be in. Perhaps their priorities were different. It could be as simple as that. If she earned enough money to acquire quality scent without thinking twice about it, it was hard to imagine why she continued to live in such a cold, cramped room. The bed had been tossed half-heartedly into order and a pair of black tights abandoned on top of it. Ellen fondled the fabric, checked the brand and then moved on.

She was preparing to turn the handle on the next door, gently, in case the occupant might still be asleep, when a suspicion struck her like a thunderbolt. The room she had inspected could be Marion's. Nothing Kieran had said justified this conclusion. But then, she was proceeding on the basis that he had been less than forthright with her. The only doubt in her mind was how much he had kept secret. Retracing her steps, she slid the top drawer of the dressing-table open and found what she needed at once – a driving licence in the name of Jennifer Smeaton. She gave a sigh of relief and congratulated herself on her audacity. There were even three of a roll of four photographs, the kind you get at a booth in the railway station for passports or transport cards. The girl in them looked nothing like Kieran's description of Marion. She had a likeable smile that made her mouth curl up at either side. Ellen did not think she would like Marion's smile. Marion's hair was short and dark, this girl's long and fair. Kieran had also said that Marion's ears stuck out at either side of her head. Ellen found it hard to understand how that could be attractive in a girl.

As she proceeded in the investigation, her intentions became clearer to her. In her heart she knew Kieran was lying. That justified an unannounced visit and a little spot of innocent detective work. There were so many ways you could look at the situation. As far as she was concerned, he was sorely in need of her intervention, however strongly he might have rejected the suggestion if consulted first.

The second room was obsessively tidy. Not content with pulling the bed straight, its occupant had mitred the corners, plumped up the pillows and smoothed the cover carefully, moving from the centre out to the sides. Ellen assessed his work with expert eyes and approved. She assumed a man must live there because the dominant theme in the room was football. A poster of the current St Mirren eleven was pinned to the back of the door. If you were lying in bed, your eyes would naturally be drawn to it. A football strip in St Mirren colours hung on the wall above the bed. It reminded her oddly of how her aunts in Antrim used religious images to decorate their cottage. Ellen tiptoed in. This man hoovered his carpet. It was a task none of the people he shared with could find time for. She lifted the catch on the cupboard and opened it. His shirts were ironed and neatly arranged on hangers. He had used lavender to scent the inner compartment. Everything was folded: underpants, vests, towels. Even the socks were meticulously paired and laid out flat on the appointed shelf to form a pattern. Ellen was impressed. If only this could have been Kieran's room! But then, there was not a book in sight. Since her son had left his job, gone back to college and taken his Highers, he had been living in a solution of books. That was one reason why he wore such dowdy clothes. All his money went on other things.

Two doors remained unopened. Ellen steeled herself, took a deep breath and entered the first. Compared with the rooms she had inspected so far, this one gave an overwhelming impression of colour. The double bed (she gulped) was almost hidden by the biggest downie she had ever seen. The cover had stripes in all the hues of the rainbow, running in different directions, interrupting and intersecting each other like the pattern of crazy paving down a garden path. It made her feel dizzy just to look at it. You could never get that kind of downie to lie straight. It reminded her of the surface of a loch when the wind is getting up: choppy, unpredictable and uncontrollable. Changing the cover must be a major undertaking.

She went right in and shut the door behind her. She would

have described the room as busy rather than untidy. It was the biggest bedroom in the house, she noted with pleasure, soon quashed by the reflection that, if it was Kieran's, he did not stay in it alone. Something troubled her and, as she looked around, it hardened to an inner certainty. There was no trace of a woman in the room. With a decisiveness that surprised her, she strode across to the wardrobe and swung the door open. On one side were ties and underwear, a suit, short trousers and a scarf, all of which she recognized as Kieran's. She had not seen any of the clothes on the other side before. Now she noticed the posters on the wall. David Bowie was not necessarily compromising. There was a bill for a Derek Jarman season at the Filmhouse. The name meant nothing to her. Next to it was a picture of two young men, viewed from the back, just beyond the tideline on the edge of a beach. They were very suntanned, you could see that because all they were wearing was shorts. One had his arm around the other's neck. It gave her a queer sensation to look at them.

There were two armchairs and only one desk. It was where Kieran studied. She could tell from the titles of the books on the shelf above. The postcards confirmed her growing, terrible suspicion. There was a marble statue of a man with no clothes on at all, standing and looking into the distance as if he were waiting for a bus. What sort of a country could he come from, where people stood at bus stops stark naked and got statues made of them? Beside him was a youth who looked Italian, wearing a sort of crumpled smock open at the neck. A pity he had chosen a fabric that didn't iron well. She couldn't understand anybody posing for their portrait and not putting their best clothes on. You couldn't see what he was wearing further down, because he was staggering beneath an enormous basket of fruit: red apples, purple figs and burnished grapes, all with an uncanny, waxen sheen. Presumably real fruit went off too quickly and the painter had used artificial props. Another postcard showed a dying warrior, draped across his shield, clad in a wolfskin so that the head and open jaws served as a cap. He had a pinched face that struck her as Irish. He was obviously about to breathe his last but, if you looked at him from another angle, he could have been waiting for something totally different to happen, lying expectant on a couch.

She shut her mind to the thought. It was useless. The closer she got to the answer she was seeking, the more unscrupulous she became. She got to her knees and rummaged under the bed, pulling out a stack of magazines. No further confirmation was needed. They were not violently pornographic but featured page after page of youngish men with fetching smiles and hardly any clothes on, in a range of inviting positions. No two members were exactly alike. All of them were in evidence, in varying states of erection, beneath the fabric or peeping out between unbuttoned flies. Ellen put the magazines back where she had found them and sat on the bed.

'Holy Mother of God!' she heard herself say.

A pain had taken shape next to her heart that was as cutting as if they had left a pair of scissors inside her after an operation. That was what had happened to her cousin Andy when he went into hospital two years ago. He had recounted the incident in enormous detail, without saying a word about the acute pain it caused him.

What was she going to do? Her first impulse was to check that no trace was left of her visit, slip away back to Glasgow and breathe no word of what had happened to Kieran. Then she remembered Paul had let her in. It would be impossible to pretend she had not been in the flat. If only Bessie McAlinden were still alive, Ellen could have phoned her on the spot. Bessie had acted as a substitute mother to her for many years. Ellen was convinced she could have offered useful advice, even now when they were faced with the unthinkable.

Not only was it unthinkable, it was unspeakable as well. Where would she find the words to say it? Deirdre McFall was another possibility. Since remarrying, however, she had thoughts only for her new man and the semi-detached house in Bearsden they had moved into. Ellen was no fool. Given Deirdre's recent change of status, unattached friends, if not an embarrassment, were at the least elements difficult to integrate into a transformed life. An unwary confession might lead to her being dropped entirely. Ellen intended to hang on to all the friends she had, even if concealing her son's life style were the price she had to pay.

She started going over Kieran's last visit in her mind, remembering what he had told her then. That made her angry and the anger gave her an illusion of bravery. She needed to be brave if she was to begin to deal with what she had discovered.

'I've not the faintest idea where to turn, Mum,' he had said, once he had recounted his latest falling out with Marion and finished crying.

'Chuck her, son. There are plenty more fish in the sea.'

'It's not as simple as that. She loves me, I know it. The problem is she hasn't realized yet. There's no way I'm going to chuck her.'

'How did you meet each other? What are her parents like? Does she come from a nice family?'

'It happened after a party,' Kieran had answered vaguely.

'What sort of a party? Whose party? Would you not be better meeting someone through your work?'

'I've explained to you, Mum. My work is very lonely. Sitting in a library taking notes, then writing them up at home. You don't meet anyone that way.'

'And what's it like when you're together? Do you feel happy? Could you see yourself marrying her?'

'I've no thought of getting married for a long time yet, Mum. I'm far too young.'

'You're thirty-one, son. That doesn't sound young to me. Sounds more like you're in danger of missing the boat.'

'When we're together,' mused Kieran, who was still thinking about her last question, 'I feel complete. Like there's a bit of me I keep forgetting about, one that nobody else sees. When I'm with Marion, I get in touch with it again. I feel things for her I've never felt for anyone else. Companionship is part of it but there's much more. It's as if being together is how things were always meant to be. It's as straightforward as that. Only it doesn't last.'

'You do what you want, son, but mind and don't get her pregnant. Especially if you two aren't getting along that well.'

'Oh, there's no danger of that,' he said, with a certainty she found odd even then. 'That's the last of my worries. And it's not true we don't get along. She has a lot of growing up to do, that's all.'

She was sitting on the bed as she went over the conversation in her head. She spotted a photograph of Kieran, in a plastic frame from Boots, on the low cabinet beside her. Written across the top was: 'For Mark, with love from Kieran'. Behind it stood a smaller photograph of the two of them. Mark was not quite as tall as Kieran. He had short, dark hair and ears that stuck out. To be honest, she had been surprised when he supplied that detail about a girl. It wasn't that a girl's ears can't stick out as much as a boy's. But normally you don't talk about it. Mark, Marion. It all fitted together.

Kieran spent most of the week that followed digesting what had happened. He was at a loss to explain what led him to return home for lunch on that day of all days. There were times when he believed in telepathy. His mother's face had presented itself repeatedly to his mind in the course of the morning and he had started worrying whether something awful could have happened to her. Normally he had soup and a roll at a takeaway shop near to the library and did not make his way home till after six. If he had followed the usual pattern, Mark would have got there first and discovered Ellen before he did. What a disaster that would have been! His work in the library was proceeding slowly, as often happened. Generally he had enough fortitude to struggle on until he reached a smoother patch. You couldn't expect the research to go well every day. On that fateful morning he yielded to temptation, stacked his things up neatly, abandoned his seat and called in at the supermarket on the way home.

At least emptying the plastic bags gave him something to do while his mother sobbed at the kitchen table. He put the perishables in the fridge and checked through the cartons of milk and yogurt that were already there, throwing the ones that were past their expiry date into the rubbish bin. Many things were being jettisoned today, lies and illusions as well as dairy products. As he grew calmer, Kieran realized how furious he was. He wished the cartons had been milkbottles. If only he could have shattered them dramatically against the wall. That would have diverted attention from the issues in hand and might even have raised his mother's spirits. He knew from past experience that she was not averse to a touch of drama. Taking a deep breath, he filled the electric kettle and plugged it in. He would make a cup of tea.

'Want a bite of lunch, Mum?' he asked.

All he got for an answer was a fresh outburst of sobbing. He should really have taken her in his arms but she was being so unreasonable he lost all patience with her. Sitting down, he took her hands in his, pulling them to either side so as to see straight into her tear-stained face.

'So what about Wattie Thompson?'

'What do you mean?'

She went very quiet all of a sudden.

'You know exactly what I mean. Wattie Thompson the janitor. The one who did your hair on Saturday afternoons when I was at school. What's all this rubbish about being shocked? You haven't got a moral leg to stand on!'

Ellen felt better. She had been expecting an apology, Kieran down on his knees, condemning himself and what he was and did, then a promise to leave the flat that very minute and come home and live with her in Drumchapel. His reaction was totally unexpected. To be honest, if another solution could be found, she would rather he stayed on in Edinburgh. Her problem was one of etiquette. She had no inkling of what to do in these circumstances. What are you supposed to say to a son who takes it up the backside? That was what being homosexual meant to her. The logical deduction that, if some liked having it done, others must like doing it, otherwise all of them were up the creek, never crossed her mind. And there was no way she could have interrogated Kieran as to his sexual preferences. He might easily have been one of those who find penetration both painful and distasteful.

Her assumptions about what he did in bed remained unchallenged and she sipped her tea suspiciously. The brown liquid he poured into her cup acquired an anomalous, untrustworthy aspect. Ellen had relied so far on a rudimentary rule book, much of it the result of Bessie McAlinden's counsels, which told her what behaviour was appropriate to the various situations she might confront in life. This one had been left out. She would be forced to improvise, and that was something she had little talent for.

19

She had brought Kieran up in a single end in Springburn, a one-room tenement flat with a shared toilet on the stair outside. Not until he was twelve did they move to Drumchapel, to a home in a block of four which had its own garden, a hall, a sitting-room and kitchenette communicating by a hatch, two bedrooms, a combined toilet and bathroom, and reliable plumbing. Gone were the days when the outside pipes would freeze and she and her son had to trudge across the street and fill buckets at the sinks of obliging neighbours. The move had put a stop to her relations with Wattie Thompson. Maybe that had been for the best. He was the janitor at the combined primary and secondary schools two blocks away from where they lived. The younger children had stern instructions not to mix with the older ones but it wasn't easy to keep them apart, in spite of the railings separating the two playgrounds.

When Kieran started school, a nun was headmistress of the primary section. Ellen never took to Sister Mary of Jesus. She suspected it was a remark of Sister Mary's that had given rise to the whole bullying episode. Kieran was hauled up in front of her along with Alan Tait. His father had the ironmonger's shop on Saracen St. Those were the years before they knocked half the tenements down and removed nearly everyone to freshly built estates on the edge of the city. The physical conditions they lived in improved beyond measure, but the new streets were bleak and unfriendly, perched on windswept hillsides. Gone was the old communal warmth which had made life in those near slums, more than bearable, worthy of celebration. By the time Kieran was born the famous locomotive factory had closed down. Ellen could still remember the undertone of excitement that pervaded the streets of Springburn when a locomotive had been completed, and they were preparing to transport it down to the city centre. Great bales of straw would be piled up at the street corners, in case there should be a collision while manoeuvring. The streets themselves were glinting and slippery with oil, to make the business of shifting the locomotive easier.

She did not know Mr Tait well, as she rarely had reason to go into an ironmonger's shop. He was reputed to be a careful businessman with a thriving trade. No doubt this explained the very different treatment Sister Mary of Jesus meted out to Alan and to Kieran. They had been talking through the railings to a group of lads from the secondary school. The headmistress merely ruffled Alan's hair and told him to speak to his Daddy about the affair when he got home. She turned to Kieran and, in the other boy's hearing, said:

'Of course you never had a Daddy. And given the mother you find yourself with, it's hardly surprising you've started getting boys from better homes into trouble.'

Ellen did not believe Sister Mary could know much about the circumstances of Kieran's birth. But she would know that his mother was not a regular attender at Sunday mass in the parish church. And she would have seen that, whenever a form had to be completed, the name at the top was 'Miss' and not 'Mrs' McLaverty. So she had no illusions that Kieran was anything other than a child of sin. That was what Ellen's own parents had said when she broke the news that she was pregnant to them. The headmistress's words went over Kieran's head, literally and figuratively. He realized nonetheless that his mother was being attacked and kicked the nun in the shins for her pains. That did little to mend matters. He was made to sit alone in a corner of the classroom for the rest of the day. Thanks to Alan, word got round that Kieran never had a father. Taunts led to fights. By the end of the week he was being subjected to ostracism and bullying on a systematic basis.

He said nothing about it to his mother until he came home with a bleeding nose, for which he could invent no explanation other than the true one. She gave him two flavours of ice cream instead of one with his trifle at tea time and brought him his cocoa in bed, signs of special tenderness which were extremely welcome. He cried when he told her about the treatment he was being given. As he drank his cocoa down, she sat at the end of the bed, lit a cigarette and said:

'Know what you have to do, son?'

Kieran shook his head woefully.

'Get one of the older lads to protect you. Put yourself on his side. Tell him you need his help and you'll be loyal to him for ever afterwards, if he sticks up for you.'

Kieran didn't think twice who to ask. And it worked. He had had his eye on Lawrence Mitchell since the previous spring. Lawrence was about to graduate to the secondary school. Soon he would be on the other side of those railings. The thought gave Kieran pain. Lawrence was special to him in a way he was unable to describe, often calling to him when going past with a group of older friends. He never said anything significant, merely:

'How're you doing, wee man?' or 'Good day the day, wee man?'

Kieran would smile and return the friendly wave.

He waited till the day Billy Cunningham attacked. Swagger as he might, Billy did not frighten Kieran, who tried out a new technique. He gripped Billy round the neck as fiercely as he was able, then forced the head down and thrust his knee several times into Billy's face. It worked splendidly. Within two minutes Billy was weeping and pleading to be released. This minor, yet significant, victory put Kieran in a better position, psychologically speaking, to enlist Lawrence's help. He did not look too angry at being distracted from the five-a-side football match he was engaged in. They moved to one side, next to the railings between the two playgrounds, and Kieran explained everything: what Sister Mary of Jesus had said, how Alan had put it about, and the unfair way he was being treated as a result. He could deal easily enough with Billy Cunningham. Bigger boys were more of a problem. He was thoroughly fed up and wanted things to return to normal.

'Just leave it to me, wee man,' said Lawrence.

Before the end of the lunch break he had spoken to Billy and a couple of other ringleaders. While nothing was said to Kieran, the atmosphere changed perceptibly. Three or four boys, former friends who had made themselves scarce during the bullying, re-established cordial relations. Soon the playground became safe for him. He no longer sat through classes with his eyes on the clock, dreading the moment when the pupils would be released and the hounding could start.

That was not all. Kieran got to walk home with Lawrence and his friends. If Kieran was late, he only had to tell Ellen he had been talking to his new friend, the older one who protected him. She nodded approvingly and took his food from the oven, where she had left it to keep warm. Shrivelled peas were a small price to pay for Lawrence's company. He led Kieran along his favourite stretches of the canal, showing him the best vantage points to inspect passing trains from. He smoked a cigarette so Kieran could see how it was done. They discussed geography, which was Kieran's pet subject at the time. He could reel off the capitals of all the countries in Europe at a speed that made Lawrence's mouth drop open.

Lawrence had a brother at home who was 'slow'. That was the word he always used, not handicapped or backward, merely 'slow'. For some reason he especially loved this brother and was convinced he could communicate with him in a fashion denied to every other member of the family. He would expound at length the thoughts that went through his brother's head, what it was like for him to have difficulty in moving, to wet himself and have to be taken to the toilet, to watch his brothers and sisters growing and flourishing and know that he would have none of the blessings they hoped for in life: a job, a home and children.

In intimate moments, his voice trembling with excitement, Lawrence told Kieran about his plans for the future. He wanted to go to Australia. A brother of his mother's had emigrated the minute he finished school. Now he was married and had a farm and three sons west of Brisbane. He sent a batch of photographs back every year at Christmas. Lawrence's family made a ritual of poring over them, month after month, until the new batch arrived and the old ones could be put away. Lawrence had to put off emigrating, he told Kieran with a touch of sadness, due to his other ambition. He was going to become a doctor and invent the pill which would cure his brother. After all, there was a pill for every known illness. It made sense there should be a pill for this one too.

'I'm determined to find it,' Lawrence told him. 'But I have to learn about all the other diseases and practise on real people, before they'll allow me to try anything new.'

'How long might it take?' asked Kieran.

'Could be as much as ten years,' said Lawrence, at the same time absolutely serious and enjoying the impression he was making on the younger boy.

'And will you emigrate to Australia before you find the pill or afterwards?'

'Before,' he said. 'A man has better chances in a new place.'

Kieran did not have an exclusive claim on his new friend's leisure time. He could count on them spending the hour after school in each other's company. And if Lawrence tipped him the word at morning mass, on the rare occasions when Kieran and Ellen attended, they would meet up on Sunday afternoon. Lawrence's movements on weekday evenings and Saturdays remained a mystery.

One Sunday, when he had not been to mass and was missing Lawrence more than usual, Kieran decided to take a chance and look for him where they had met the week before, in an overgrown hollow between the railway cutting and a row of smoke-blackened tenements. It was May. The rich vegetation made it easy to hide from prying eyes and indulge in whatever brand of mischief appeared most enticing. Inching closer through the bushes, Kieran heard several voices murmuring. One of them was Lawrence's. He dropped on to his belly and slid along the grass till he could see into the hollow. Although Lawrence had his back to him, Kieran spotted the beloved head and shoulders right away. The others were engrossed in contemplating an object Lawrence was holding in his hand. Someone cuffed Kieran across the ear. He rolled over with a cry. The lookout had discovered him.

'We've got a spy!' he shouted.

'It's only me! It's only me!' cried Kieran.

His own voice sounded shrill and high-pitched after the other boy's, erratically guttural, in the process of breaking. The lookout grabbed him by the ear and led him into the centre of the circle. The others paid no attention. Afraid to miss something important, the lookout released his hold and squatted down next to the rest. Kieran followed suit.

Lawrence had his penis in his hand. It was a remarkable organ and Kieran did not forget the sight in a hurry. Lawrence held it like a captured animal, with an air of wonderment and discovery, stroking it with a rhythm that apparently gave it pleasure, for it grew and grew as they watched. Several of the other boys already had their hands in their trousers, imitating Lawrence and checking the results. Needless to say, no other member was produced for comparison. Lawrence had not acknowledged Kieran's arrival. Now he looked across and murmured:

'Go on. You can touch it if you want to.'

It was a remarkable honour. Anybody present would have given an arm and a leg to be the first to examine Lawrence's sex. Instead he, the youngest, the intruder, had been chosen. He stretched out his hand. The thing was warm and hard. As he grasped it, it gave a kind of quiver, of recognition maybe, like a horse that knows its rider and is eager to gallop off now everything is in order. He gripped it more firmly and looked into Lawrence's face. The eyes were closed, the head tipped back ever so slightly. The lips were parted. The words 'I love you' flashed across Kieran's mind. It was enough. He let go. Fair was fair. The others had to have their turn.

During the week that followed there was a new quality in Lawrence's attitude to him: a kind of impatience. They stopped off after school as usual to talk about this and that, but it was as if Lawrence had other business on his mind which he hesitated to put into words. Kieran did not mention Sunday's experiment, powerfully as it loomed in his memory. Just before falling asleep, he could evoke a warm and secure feeling by recalling the sensation of gripping his friend's penis. He pretended he had it there next to him under the bedclothes. But the impression was fading. He needed to refresh his memory before too long. It would have been excessively bold to propose a repeat performance. As things turned out he did not need to.

'Are you doing anything on Saturday afternoon?' Lawrence asked after classes on Friday.

'No,' Kieran said, lying without hesitation. The truth was, Saturday afternoons were a special time in the week. It would not be easy for him to arrange to be free.

'Can you meet me at the jannie's shed behind the school, then?

After dinner?' said Lawrence. 'Nobody else, mind, just the two of us?'

There was a tension in the last question which Lawrence tried to shake off by laughing and giving Kieran a mock punch. Why did he bother to lay down this condition? Kieran was too avid of Lawrence's company to bring anyone else along if it could possibly be avoided.

The problem was that every Saturday he had lunch with Bessie McAlinden and spent the rest of the afternoon in her flat. Ellen insisted on having her hair done then. It did not occur to Kieran to object that other people's mothers found fortnightly or three-weekly visits sufficient, that they hardly had enough ready cash for such luxuries, and that her hair, as often as not, looked exactly the same when she returned as when she had gone out. If any-thing, it was generally a bit untidier. Ellen's visits to the hair-dresser were part of the order of things and not susceptible to argument or discussion. Evidently they cheered her up, if the mood she unfailingly returned in was anything to go by.

That made the sacrifice of spending an afternoon in Bessie's company more worthwhile. Card games and television were ruled out. Bessie found useful things for him to do: polishing the silver, helping her roll up a skein of wool, dusting the skirting board or rearranging the belongings stored on top of a cupboard, as often as not boxes containing ancient hats of wondrous colour and design. Kieran would not have minded trying them on. He did not put the idea to Bessie.

On the Saturday in question, he helped her clear away, wash and dry the dishes, then announced, with his heart in his mouth, that he had to go out.

'What do you mean, go out?'

'I've things to do,' said Kieran.

He walked to the front door, opened it, stepped over the threshold and closed it firmly behind him. He half expected Bessie to run after him. She was too astonished by his quiet aplomb to offer the slightest challenge. Kieran had had his eye on the clock all the time they were eating. The meal had pro-ceeded with agonizing slowness. Afraid he might miss Lawrence, he sprinted down the stairs and out into the street. The janitor's shed was behind the secondary school, on the other side of the

221

fateful railings. Both playgrounds were left open for the local children to use outside school hours. For Lawrence to arrange a meeting beyond the boundary was in itself an indication that something unusual was afoot. Luckily none of the boys who were knocking a ball around in a desultory fashion tried to stop him. Once he was round the corner of the building he slowed to a trot. He could already see Lawrence waiting by the shed.

As he approached, Lawrence lifted his finger to his lips with a grin.

'Wattie's humping somebody,' he whispered into Kieran's ear. 'Come and take a look.'

Kieran had heard the word 'humping' before. He knew the right context in which to use it and the reactions it could be relied upon to produce. But he had only the vaguest conception of what it might mean anatomically. All manner of objects were kept in Wattie's shed: a roller for the lawns and borders, shears, a rake, oil drums, brushes and mops, and tarpaulins of assorted shapes and sizes. Wattie had cleared a space in the centre of the floor and spread one of the latter out. Two bodies were moving on top of it, one straddling the other so that you saw the back of the head of the person on top and the face of the person underneath. It was his mother.

She wore a peculiar expression he did not forget in a hurry, a frown of concentration that reminded him of the time he had got lice in his hair and she had combed through it painstakingly for nearly an hour to remove the eggs, or how she looked when she cut his fingernails for him. She was engaged in a delicate operation that required her full attention but had no obvious connection with personal hygiene or with keeping smart. There was something different here, an extra element Kieran struggled to define. Oddly she was not looking at Wattie, who was on top of her, but instead at a point on the ceiling of the shed. He would have loved to ask her what her expression meant. While he was not disturbed, or even greatly surprised by the spectacle revealed to him, he instinctively knew he would refrain from raising the matter with Ellen at a later date, and from identifying her to his friend now.

Lawrence was already pulling at his shoulder. He raised his finger to his lips another time and led the way to the railway cutting. He was unusually silent. Kieran trotted on behind, wondering what further novelties the afternoon held in store. It made him angry to think of the excitement he had missed. Did this kind of thing always go on while he was spending the hours after lunch with Bessie? When they were well into the cover of the thicket, Lawrence guided Kieran gently round in front of him and indicated that he should bend over, supporting his weight on a low branch. Kieran was wearing short trousers. Lawrence did not lower them. Instead, Kieran felt something rub against the inside of his bare leg. At first he assumed it must be a stick but it was warm and quivering as well as hard. With a rush of pleasure he understood and gripped the thing between his legs. Lawrence thrust for barely a few seconds, tightly and comfortably, before he came. Kieran was nonplussed to see a rich-smelling liquid rather like glue spurt out and onto the leaves in front of him.

That was how it was between them from then on. They never kissed or hugged and Lawrence made no attempt to penetrate him. Perhaps he did not know this was a possibility. Kieran would have liked to take the thing in his hands. As they never spoke about what happened, it was hard to propose any kind of variation. The main source of his pleasure lay in the physical intimacy and the chance to oblige his friend and protector. Lawrence apparently experienced an enormous sense of relief each time they did it. Kieran wondered why they did not repeat the process more frequently. He would have been more than willing. It never happened more than twice in the same week. Their meetings continued until Kieran and Ellen moved to Drumchapel, by which time Kieran was approaching puberty and more and more aware of a swelling in his own groin, when Lawrence stood behind him.

On one occasion only Lawrence undertook the considerable journey to Drumchapel by public transport to seek him out. It was a Sunday evening. Ellen raised no objection when the two sauntered off for a stroll. Kieran was concerned Lawrence might recognize her from the scene in the shed but nothing was said. Things were more difficult this time because they had to hunt for a safe place and trees were few and far between on the new estate. Moreover, Kieran was growing quickly and it was hard for him to grip Lawrence's penis at the right angle between his legs. Lawrence did not move away once he had come as was his habit. He felt between Kieran's legs to ascertain the corresponding swelling.

'What do you think about homosexuality?' he said.

There was an edge to his voice Kieran had not noted before and which he did not like. The word was a long one and Lawrence pronounced it without hesitation. He had come upon it in a book about medicine for teenagers and had been practising it under his breath for several days.

'What's that?' asked Kieran.

'It's what we've just been doing,' answered Lawrence. 'Some people say it's wrong.'

Kieran was flabbergasted.

'How could it possibly be wrong?'

He never spoke to Lawrence again.

'Who told you about me and Wattie Thompson?' Ellen asked. 'It can't have been Bessie. She never found out about it, God rest her soul. It must have been that busybody Anne McCafferty. What were you doing discussing my affairs with her?'

'It doesn't matter how I got to know. You were young at the time and you must have needed a man. I don't think what you did was wrong. But I won't have you arriving here now and telling me what I can do and what I can't.'

Ellen was relieved. All at once, and in a most unexpected fashion, she found herself relieved of two burdens. She no longer had to moralize with Kieran, a role she had never been comfortable with and had failed wretchedly at on the few occasions she attempted it. And there was no longer any need to keep silent about a richly passionate episode of her past, which she had often yearned to discuss with him. Her fears that it might prompt a rejection if she did so were unfounded. He had known about it all along so obviously there was no cause for concern. Kieran took her to John Lewis's that afternoon and bought her a range of kitchen gadgets he could ill afford. An inner voice warned him that it was conscience money. Ellen's undisguised delight meant he could cheerfully ignore it. The department store is close to the main bus station and he hoped Ellen would go directly home to Glasgow. She announced, however, with a bravery he could only respect, that she wanted to meet 'Marion'. Kieran gave a start and the twinkle in her eye told him she had been joking. The meeting was not a success. Mark had difficulty in concealing his impatience. Ellen rose awkwardly from the kitchen table when he arrived home and shook his hand coldly, then informed her son that she was ready to be accompanied to the bus station. They walked the streets in silence. Kieran feared that if he said something it might shatter the fragile understanding they had established. As she got on the bus, Ellen shook her head and looked at him with meaning.

'If it's a man you want and not a woman, son, there's nothing I can say or do. Except tell you to get yourself a better one. That lad's not right for you at all.'

20

Kieran waited until he and Dougal were ten months into their relationship before taking him through to Glasgow to meet his mother. It was a turning point for Dougal. The particular spiritual illumination he arrived at on that day was forever linked in his memory with a headline in one of the scandal magazines Ellen kept stacked up in the toilet of her home, to occupy her mind while she was sitting there: 'My knickers started to bubble'. When the words caught his eye, he was so preoccupied with other thoughts, and so alarmed at the environment he found himself in, that he pursued his curiosity no further. He regretted it after-wards, when it was too late. And on their next visit to Drum-chapel that issue had disappeared. Had there been a special quality to the material the item of lingerie was made of that led it to seethe and suppurate on contact with the skin? Was the woman who had uttered the phrase prone to such an intensity of sexual excitement that the heat she experienced was trans-mitted to her underwear? Or had it been little more than a manu-facturing defect that meant it was impossible to iron them?

They were invited through for tea at five o'clock on Saturday. Dougal presumed this meant an evening meal although he was not sure and did not dare to ask. Kieran insisted on driving his own ramshackle car. At first Dougal could not understand why. Generally he refused to travel round in it. The roof was pitted with large blotches of rust that might have been the bulletholes left after a mafia attack on an Italian magistrate. When they got to Drumchapel the reasons became amply clear. It was important for Dougal to have a car of a certain standard because of the people he worked with and the chance he might bump into or be seen by clients. A cheap or rundown car would be evidence that business was going badly, which had never, so far, been the case and which, even if it were, had to be kept religiously secret. Parked outside Ellen's house, his BMW would have been an invitation to vandalism. And bringing it would have constituted a real failure in taste on both their parts. He realized that.

Kieran had more or less moved in with him by this stage. It was an imperceptible process and they did not discuss the implications until Christmas time, when Dougal had gained enough confidence to raise the subject of Kieran selling up his own flat so that they could pool their resources. Before that time he periodically panicked, not because anything specific was going wrong. Had there been real difficulties, regular quarrels or a single, glaring incompatibility, he might have felt less scared, for he would have had a lever he could use when needed to, in order to prise the two of them apart. Having his lover around on a permanent basis meant venturing into uncharted territory and it simply made him very scared. Kieran's friends started phoning him at Dougal's place so that it became natural for Kieran to pick up the phone if he were closest to it. And in due time, he picked up the phone and found Dougal's mother at the other end. It was a piece of good fortune that this occurred on a Saturday afternoon and that, in any case, she stayed in the same city. Otherwise she might have arrived for the weekend and Dougal would have faced the choice of either having Kieran clear out or acknowledging everything, double bed and all.

The panic came at the oddest moments and persisted long after they had comfortably settled in together, though it assailed him with a lesser frequency. When they were finishing their evening meal and Kieran had stopped babbling away happily about the undercurrents of envy and competition at work, or about who was said to be getting off with whom or his latest ideas for their next holiday, and silence had fallen, Dougal would suddenly think: I have nothing to say. I am running out of things to tell him. There is no way I can respond and he is going to notice and then (the thought did not continue in words, but this was its drift) he will come so close that he will see beyond any barrier I have managed to erect, and he will see . . . Nothing? Dougal was not sure. At such moments he did not know what was there or what it felt about Kieran or what he felt about it. They had different bedtime habits. By eleven o'clock Kieran was bleary-eyed and would turn in. The bed was flanked by expensive but discreet antique cabinets. These bore lamps with gloriously fulsome bulbous China bases and shades that had the magnolia colour of disgracefully rich ice cream. After some initial hassle it was agreed that he would leave the lamp on Dougal's side lit, so that Dougal could read for a bit when he had finished watching television, and was ready for sleep.

The panic had a different quality then. It was to do with the security of Kieran's sleeping. I could do anything now, Dougal thought. I could hit him, or run away, or decide to leave him, or withdraw into that cold, cold place I lived in for so many years. He doesn't realize how dangerous this closeness is. Look how he turns over and I can see a damp spot on the pillow where he has dribbled slightly, and the skin of the high curve of his ears glows as if it were a light source of its own.

One night he must have sat for more than an hour like that, just allowing the thoughts to go through his mind, knowing all the time that he would not have hurt a hair of this man's head, would not even have wanted to brush roughly against his body while they slept or to graze the skin of his ankle with an uncut toenail. He cried that time, very quietly. There was utter silence in the street outside except for the wind ruffling the trees. In the end he put the light out, wondering how he would get through the next day at work now it was so late and he would get so little sleep. He put both his arms round Kieran and, without waking, Kieran turned and turned, with the litheness of a squirrel, or like a child scrabbling and scrabbling against its bedclothes, until at last it can lie comfortable. Dougal held him until he was calm.

Ellen cooked liver and onions for tea. Dougal hated liver. It was the one kind of meat that made him want to retch. She had used cheap fat and the smell hit his nostrils as soon as she opened the door. It was all much, much worse than he had anticipated. There were tasteless framed prints from Woolworth's on the walls, little girls in straw hats smothered in flowers and sheaves of ripe corn, barges on Dutch canals and a horrendous caricature Ellen had squandered her holiday money to have done on the seafront at Lanzarote. Pottery ducks described a dutiful arc above the mantelpiece. There were china fruit baskets and a thistle decanter, antimacassars on the furniture and a fireside rug that clashed appallingly with the already garish carpet in the sitting-room. They ate there. Ellen had turned down the television but it was Kieran who switched it off, with no apparent signs of embarrassment or awkwardness. The soup she gave them was tinned. From the start of the meal she pressed buttered white sliced bread on both of them, and filled the teacups standing ready at their places.

Kieran and Ellen talked incessantly, breaking in upon one another or supplying details and even finishing each other's sentences in their eagerness to terminate one area of discussion and get onto the next one. A couple of times Kieran rubbed his knee against Dougal's under the table but he was incapable of responding, too horrified by what he saw around him and by his own reaction. A voice inside him said it was impossible. They were too different from one another. There was no way he, Dougal, could incorporate this woman and her world into his life. She had placed her packet of cigarettes and her lighter to her right on the table and he surmised she was only waiting for the main course to be finished to light up. What would come next? Bread and butter pudding? Lemon meringue pie? How would the sequence of abominations continue?

The greatest abomination, he knew it, was his own refusal. Yet it was stronger than himself. And as he refused to be part of this, he watched in impotence everything he shared with Kieran, everything Kieran meant to him, slipping from his grasp.

'Excuse me,' he muttered, and got up to leave the table. They hardly seemed to notice, so engrossed were they in their discussion. Dougal locked the bathroom door with a sigh of relief, undid his belt, dropped his trousers and sat down. It did not strike him then, but he was returning to what had been the only safe place in his own home, when his parents were shouting at each other. Nobody noticed how much time he spent in the lavatory, though his mother did once enquire absentmindedly about piles. He used to take books in with him to read and sometimes he would merely retreat there when he had no need to use it at all, because he knew he would not be disturbed. He always carefully flushed the toilet before leaving. It was the most innocent of deceptions.

The downstairs bathroom at home had a mock Tudor-style window of rippled glass giving onto the garden. You could observe the swaying of the bushes outside and the different effects the light made as it penetrated them and struck the window, at various times of the day. To the left as you sat there, above the central heating radiator, was a copy of an Italian Renaissance painting. Much later on, after he had left home and was on the way to becoming a partner in his firm, he saw the original in a museum in Venice and understood it was a Presentation of the Virgin. A flight of steps occupied the centre of the picture. There was a curved arch beneath them where a beggar lurked. A little girl was climbing the steps, utterly alone, towards a patriarch in flowing robes and a turban. When he was a child he had often wondered what she was doing and if she would ever make it. She looked tired and frightened. Maybe it would be better if the patriarch never enfolded her in his arms, if she were to sprout wings and soar off to a different destination, a different story that was part of another religion.

In Ellen's toilet an electric heater took the place of the radiator. There was a shelf above it and, on the shelf, not one but two pink toilet rolls, each encased in a sort of crocheted body stocking she had no doubt made herself. Considerable care had gone into the making. The toilet roll covers were supposed to imitate hats. They were pink except for a dark blue band at the bottom, just above the brim. At one point the band burgeoned into a bouquet of flowers in the same dark blue colour. It must have required considerable skill to bring that off. From the toilet rolls, his eyes went to the scandal magazine and the headline. That was when he started to laugh. He laughed so much he was afraid that they might hear him. What made him laugh was his own situation, in darkest Drumchapel, on the cludgie with his trousers down and so, so afraid, but afraid of what? Of himself? He had come here following the man he loved and now the man he loved was chattering away oblivious, in one house with the two people most precious to him in the world, Dougal had no doubt about that. And what had he, Dougal, to be afraid of? He could cope. He got up and cleaned himself, pulled the chain, washed his hands, unsnibbed the door and went back into the sitting-room.

He was too excited by the thing he had discovered to realize, when he sat down again, that both Kieran and Ellen were looking at him with concern, or that, seeing his expression, their worries lightened. Nor did he notice the effort they subsequently made to include him in their conversation, because he himself felt he had lots to say, about his job and his own mother's problems, and the fact that no, his father was not dead, but lived with another woman only a few streets away from the family home in the same part of Edinburgh, and that was why his mother drank so much and he insisted on spending time with her at weekends, whenever humanly possible.

About nine o'clock Ellen got the whisky out. Kieran didn't drink as he was driving home. Dougal joined her in two glasses. When they said goodbye, he bent over her, placed a hand on each of her thin shoulders and let her kiss him on the cheek.

It was early November and a filthy night. The journey between Glasgow and Edinburgh is not motorway until the latter part. Even on the brightest of summer evenings, the countryside is dull and unattractive. That night they had to keep the windscreen wipers going all the time. Beyond their car, the world was a screen of blackness, traversed only by headlights, streetlamps, and the gleam of both, or of illuminated signs, on the sopping wet surface of the roads. They talked for a bit and then fell silent. Dougal put his right hand on Kieran's knee. As they left the city and headed out past Easterhouse he moved it up his thigh, but not too close to the crotch, because he was driving and it would be foolish to get him excited. The revelation in the cludgie brought him a calm he had not experienced before and which he was confident he could recover intermittently. The confidence was about what he had seen, that he could not only accept it and live with it but that, in the course of time, he could learn to love it.

It did not occur to him to wonder what Kieran's thoughts were. Instead, aware of a need to establish contact between them, he asked the question that was on his mind.

'You never speak about your father. What was he like? Is he still alive?'

'It's a peculiar story. I never met my father. I don't even know his name. My mum was brought up in Coatbridge, in a very strictly Catholic family. I don't think she even spoke to a Protestant until she moved to Glasgow, except for hurling insults at each other when they went past the school playground. There are five children in the family. All of them are still alive, although I don't see much of them. Three girls and two boys. She is the last but one. After she left school she got a job in the Co-op. Their dad had been made redundant and it was really important that the younger ones should bring money into the home as soon as they possibly could. When things were better they went to Rothesay for their annual holidays during the Glasgow Fair. You know, that's the second half of July, immediately after the Edinburgh one. The time of the year when it rains most heavily in Scotland!

'Anyway, after two years in the Co-op without a holiday she was really fed up. So she arranged to work in a tea shop in Luss, during her summer break. It was a way of solving several problems at once. She could get away from Coatbridge for a bit, keep her job on at the Co-op, make a bit of money to bring home, and see another part of Scotland. Have you ever been to Luss?'

'Oh, yes,' said Dougal.

The question might have been intended to check whether he was listening. There was no need. He was intent on every word. What puzzled him, the warning signal, was Kieran's eerie lightness of tone. When he was a teenager, he had gone more than once with his parents to spend the weekend in a hotel on Loch Fyne, at St Catherine's, where the road loops round the loch head before descending towards Inverary. Luss had been a convenient place to stop for lunch during the long drive out from Edinburgh.

'Well, she went there with two other girls she'd been at school with. It was a combined tea shop and restaurant, open until eight o'clock at night serving high teas and fish suppers. They stayed on afterwards to clear up and wash the dishes, because everything started up again the next morning at nine. The three of them shared a room in a cottage on the other side of the main road, beyond the hotel. So on the way home they passed the hotel bar. One of the other girls got into the habit of stopping off for a nightcap. The men there used to chat her up and she really enjoyed getting the attention. What's more, they weren't just locals or hunting, shooting and fishing people up from the south. Younger lads would come in who were hiking on the hills and staying at the youth hostel. And this girl would tell my mum and the other friend what a marvellous time she'd had.

'My mum was seventeen, I think, and she'd never been inside a pub. I know it sounds incredible but it was true. Her dad was a teetotaller who spent his nights at home and there was a kind of horror of drink in the family. So she only went into the hotel bar once, during her four weeks in Luss. And that once was enough.'

There was a silence. Dougal's instinct told him to say nothing, just to wait.

'They met three boys from the youth hostel, students from Glasgow University. My mum thinks they might have been medical students but she doesn't really remember. When the bar closed at ten o'clock, one of the girls went home. My mother and the other one went up the brae with two of the students. She doesn't remember exactly what happened, except that it was a lovely night, dark under the trees and in the bushes. She must have been very innocent. She never even asked his name. When she got back to Glasgow, she started feeling sick in the mornings. One time it was so bad she couldn't face going into work. And they realized she was pregnant.'

A long pause followed. All that could be heard was the swish, swish of the windscreen wipers and the sustained groaning of the small car's engine as it braced the long climb towards Harthill. This part of the motorway had overhead lighting. The beams swept across the bonnet and, briefly, the dashboard with the regularity of waves breaking on sand. Dougal's hand was still on Kieran's thigh. He turned to look at him and saw the tears pouring down his cheeks.

'We'd better stop,' he said. 'You can't drive if you're crying. There's a service station just ahead. Pull in there.'

'The only motorway service station in Scotland,' said Kieran. His voice was steady. 'What a country.'

He put the indicator on and it clicked and flashed as he slowed the car. Dougal had a sudden sense of injustice.

'It's not the only one. What about Kinross, on the way from Edinburgh up to Perth?'

'Oh, but that doesn't count. You have to come off the motorway to go to that one.'

In many ways it was an apology for a service station. There

were facilities on one side only so that half the clients had to trudge across the motorway on a long covered walkway. Luckily they were on the nearest side. Kieran forked right, still decelerating, and pulled into the car park, slotting the car neatly between a Volkswagen and a minibus that had just arrived. Dougal pulled a handkerchief from his pocket. He always carried one, carefully ironed. They had that baked smell hot irons leave behind them, one Kieran was familiar with, for he frequently had to borrow them, though not for tears.

'Dry your eyes,' said Dougal, 'and we'll go and have a coffee.'

It sounded brusque, but he was watching a bevy of football supporters descending from the minibus, shouting and laughing and slamming the doors. Irvine Welsh types, he thought. So many different Scotlands. Seeing them put him on guard. Kieran was oblivious. One of the guys peered through the windscreen insolently at them. He might be asking himself questions. Dougal wondered how safe it was to stop.

'I'd like to take you in my arms,' he said. 'But it'll have to wait till we get home.'

'Let's go,' said Kieran. 'I've finished adjusting my make-up.'

It was odd, the kind of closeness Dougal felt as they trudged through the drizzle to the coffee shop. The way he kept near to Kieran expressed so many things, concern, protectiveness, even fear, and yet it had to be done in such a way as to give no one who might see them the slightest suspicion they were anything more than friends. The football supporters were in front of them. He carefully slowed his pace. Kieran was absorbed in his own thoughts.

'Did you ever see the film *Cinema Paradiso*?' he asked.

'No. Why?'

'It's maybe not an especially good film. Far too sentimental. But there's one splendid scene in it. It's about a small boy growing up in a remote village in Sicily and how he becomes enamoured of the cinema. He gets to help the projectionist in the parish picture hall and the older man acts as his mentor. The boy learns all about mounting the reels, switching from one to the other, how to take care of them and wind them backwards and forwards and so on. There is a fire in the hall one night and the old man loses his sight. But that's not the bit I mean. The whole film is structured as a flashback. It begins in Rome and the boy is a successful filmmaker, sophisticated, one of those unbelievably handsome mature Italian men, in his forties maybe, not quite overweight but getting there, hair slightly greying. And, you see, he thinks back to how it all started.

'He's just got the news that the old man has died. And two reels of film have arrived. It was a parish outfit they operated in and the parish priest insisted that everything had to be rigidly censored. So the old man spent a lot of time going over the films beforehand and cutting out all the love scenes. Not that there was anything outrageous, quite the contrary. What he had to excise were the bits where they kissed. And when the hero of the film opens the reels, he finds a present. It's all the censored sections, kiss upon kiss upon kiss. And at the end he sits alone in a projection room and watches all the bits he couldn't see when he was a boy.'

They had got their coffees and were sitting by the glass wall of the coffee shop. Dougal could hardly have been more tense. On the one hand he was listening to Kieran, wondering if he was OK or if he was going to break down again. On the other he was observing the football supporters, only two tables away. They were rowdy and noisy but now and again two of them turned to look in his direction. Dougal wondered if their suspicions had been aroused and if they were going to say anything. Suddenly he realized Kieran's silence required a question and gave him his full attention.

'And why does that come into your mind?'

'Because of where we are now. There's nothing I'd like more than for you to take me in your arms. We can't do that because we are two men. If we were a man and a woman it would be different. Have you ever thought how many times that has happened? Of all those farewells? In international airports, in railway stations, at bus stops? Not just between two men, but between women as well? Of all those kisses that couldn't be given, the tears they couldn't shed, the way they wanted to hug and had to hold it back? If there is any justice in the world' – (God, thought Dougal, he's going to cry again, and what am I going to do, how am I going to get him home and past these people) – 'then all those scenes are stored up on film, somewhere, and one day,' (he gulped, but carried on) 'one day, in a huge cinema, they'll be projected onto the screen, and we can watch them. And not just us. Everybody will be there, the straights as well. And they'll cheer and cheer and cheer and we will never have to hide ourselves again.'

Something had been happening inside Dougal. It was like a horse at a show trial, circling and circling, coming up to the hurdle and shying away, then coming up and trying again. He said it.

'I love you more than I have words for.'

It was out of him. Kieran had his coffee mug right up at his lips, ready to sip. He was looking away, out through the glass at the cars hurtling eastwards. Now he turned his gaze to Dougal but he did not say anything. Dougal realized he had been expecting something to happen, either a reaction from Kieran or for the motorway cafe to collapse in smithereens around them after what he had said. Instead all that happened was that Kieran scrunched his eyebrows together, blew at his coffee and took another sip. As if there was nothing surprising about Dougal's words. As if they had been the most normal thing in the world.

Dougal fucked him for the first time that same night. He had such a hard-on for the remaining miles to Edinburgh it nearly hurt. And he didn't want to let Kieran see. He was still enough of a Puritan to believe that love, tenderness and intense sexual aggression belonged in different boxes and couldn't be combined. At any rate, it wasn't something he could rationalize with words, even if he could experience it and discover that it made sense. Until then he had worked on the basis that the moments when you felt love and the moments when you wanted sex so much you nearly burst were separate. During his twenties and his early thirties, he had had sex with an embarrassingly large number of people, often in truly outlandish circumstances. There was no way he would have wanted to feel love for any of them.

Kieran raised the issue of penetration two months into the relationship. Dougal shied away from it. It was not that he feared he would be unable to perform. It was more a question of coming to terms with Kieran's desire, a request that was so undisguised and unproblematic. What sort of person wanted that? Dougal had never felt the need, although on the few occasions when he

236

had penetrated others he had gained intense enjoyment from it. He was a man and doing that constituted no obstacle to his manliness. But Kieran was a man too. How could he want something so different? It was almost as if to penetrate him would have been to dishonour him, and Dougal loved him too consciously for that. Kieran had not pushed the question. If he was philosophical enough to resign himself to the fact that this might never be part of his lovemaking with Dougal, he was also sufficiently optimistic to trust that things would work out in the end, and probably in a fashion he could neither anticipate nor contemplate.

When they got back that night it was barely eleven o'clock. Dougal more or less pushed him onto the bed and started undressing him, touching him without any preamble at all sorts of places in his body, in a way that said, I can do this to you, I have the right to do this to you, you are mine and this is how it is between us. In a way that Kieran found hugely exciting. When they were both naked and Dougal said 'I want to be inside you', Kieran took it as the kind of thing you often said when making love, something that was in your head and the thought of which made the sensations more intense, so he said nothing in reply and only kissed him more passionately.

'No,' said Dougal, lifting his head, so that Kieran, who was flat on his back, could not reach his lips. 'I mean it. I want to be inside you. I want to fuck you.'

He stretched his hand out and put the light on. They could see each other's eyes.

'Why now?' asked Kieran, puzzled and a little irritated. It was going so well he saw no point in interrupting now. He could feel his hard-on lessening.

'I don't know. It just seems like the right time.'

'But we haven't any condoms.'

'We can go and get some.'

'Are you crazy? It must be nearly midnight.'

'There'll be a chemist's open. I can take the car.'

Dougal had already leapt up and started pulling his clothes on. He picked up his watch from the bedside table, checked the time and wound it up. God, he's serious, thought Kieran, and his mood changed.

'I'll come with you.'

He had his shirt on now and kissed Dougal on the lips.

'We'll need some lubricant,' he said. 'It's been some time.'

It was half a joke. Dougal said nothing. They circled for nearly half an hour before finding the chemist's which was on night duty. It was close to the university, not far from the flat where Kieran used to live with Mark. He knew the people who ran it. They were a Pakistani family. A startlingly handsome man had worked there for as long as Kieran could remember. Now his wife and his children, who must be between eight and ten years old, were often to be seen there. When they came through the door, the place was empty and the father was behind the counter. Dougal fell silent.

'A packet of condoms,' Kieran said, finding it difficult not to burst out laughing. It was so comical, the way Dougal's determination had dissolved into embarrassment at the crucial juncture. He was sure the chemist recognized him. They had been in the habit of chatting to one another, about nothing in particular, in the days when he was a regular customer. 'Extra strong ones. And a tube of KY jelly.'

'How much will that be?' Dougal asked, in a strained voice, as he accepted the packet.

The Pakistani man looked from one to the other. His face broke into a broad smile.

'Don't worry,' he said, in the same strong Asian accent. 'This one's on me.'

21

'Have you ever considered,' Mark asked Ramon, as he cut through a layer of crumbly meringue, the colour of pale syrup, with his spoon, then scooped some, with a plentiful helping of raspberries and whipped cream, into his mouth, 'the concept of sexual geography?'

There were three desserts in all: the fruit pavlova, a plum *clafoutis*, and Italian almond biscuits to be dipped in *vin santo* before you ate them. The biscuits came from a renowned Italian grocer's at the top of Leith Walk. They were so hard that you felt you might risk breaking a tooth, if you tried to bite into them before soaking them in wine. Kieran and Dougal had brought the wine back from their last holiday in Tuscany. It was richly sweet and rather cloying and made Kieran think of communion wine. He had tasted some when training as an altarboy. They caught him out, and his prospects of appearing in public in a black cassock and embroidered surplice evaporated permanently.

The last words had been rather indistinct because Mark's mouth was full. Ramon caught them clearly enough.

'I'm not sure what you mean,' he answered warily.

The drink was going to Mark's head, not yet sufficiently to dull his thinking processes.

'You know those photographs you get in tourist brochures, of a city monument by night? The camera requires a long exposure and all the cars that pass by leave the trail of their headlights on the image, as if they were tramrails, or the wires that trolleybuses use?'

Ramon nodded.

'Snails leave marks like that. I've noticed it on the pavements here, after dark. You would think somebody had unravelled a thin, grey cassette tape on the flagstones, but it's just their moisture drying out.'

'Well, look around this table! What would it be like if there were lines like that connecting everyone who has had sex together? You'd need three colours, of course: people who've had sex, those who are having it right now, and those who are going to have it at some point in the future.'

He subsided into thoughtfulness.

'What about the ones who aren't here?' asked Ramon, with Robert in mind.

'The image gets too complicated,' Mark rejoined. 'You wouldn't be able to see the monument any longer, for all the lines.'

'Who is Isobel Anna Cunningham?' Barry asked Nicol. 'I never knew you had a god-daughter.'

Isobel was the last of Anna and Scott's three daughters. Unplanned and, initially at least, unwanted. Anna and Nicol gradually lost sight of each other had. Anna was, she admitted to herself, rather jealous of Andrew, and Scott could hardly have coped with meeting the two men as couple to couple. They bought a house in Dalgety Bay, over the road bridge, on the other side of the Firth of Forth from the city. If it had been in Edinburgh, Scott's parents might just have helped with looking after the children. Dalgety Bay was that bit farther away and Anna had to cope alone.

She struggled to resign herself to a life of domestic chores, saying goodbye to Daddy in the morning and welcoming him home at night, on the basis that it could not possibly last for ever. Contact with Nicol was limited to cards at Christmas time and on their birthdays. Thanks to the Angus grapevine, her mother in Forfar seemed to know more of his doings than Anna ever did though, naturally, certain aspects of his personal life were a closed book to the people back at home.

She managed to avoid directing the anger which periodically overwhelmed her at the restrictions on her life against her children. As for her relationship with Scott, she had no terms of comparison by which to evaluate it. There were days when she loathed him profoundly for what they had become. It was unfair to blame him, she knew it. And he knew the way she felt. She could tell when he flinched at an unusually sharp word and avoided brushing against her or even looking at her directly. His eyes would glaze over as if he were protecting himself and he became abnormally, even aggressively affectionate with their daughters. Either he was seeking compensation for the warmth she could not give him at such times, or provocatively showering on them the affection he could not communicate to her.

The possibility of a nursery school place for the younger child was a glimmer of promise on the horizon. They were waiting to hear if she had got it when, entirely by chance, they bumped into Nicol and Andrew out shopping one Saturday afternoon in Edinburgh. The two men appeared to be doing more or less the same thing as Scott and Anna. They were carrying curtain rails and hooks, an ironing board and a new downie cover. The crucial difference was they had no little girls in tow. It had been a tiring expedition and Anna's mood was not of the brightest. She introduced her daughters, Scott met Andrew, then she paused, wondering what else to say.

'We'll be in touch, then.'

That was all. Scott drove home, she felt, even more cautiously than usual. The little girls disappeared upstairs to play and Anna made a cup of tea.

'I hadn't seen Nicol since the wedding,' Scott said, with an air of wonder.

'You didn't know he was a poof?'

'Anna!' He sounded genuinely shocked. 'That's your word. Not mine.'

'You always said there was something odd about him.'

'I was jealous of all the time you spent with him. As simple as that.'

In bed that night, she wondered why she had used a term she herself hated. Had she hoped to provoke Scott into the intolerant reaction she half-expected, and which would have condemned him in her eyes? Or was her intention to pre-empt it, by assuming the bigot's role before he could? She took the accidental meeting as a signal. On Wednesday that week Scott had a half-day off. She arranged to see Nicol in a café on the High Street. Scott could look after the little girl. She would take the train through so as

241

to leave him with the car. The conversation between old friends did not proceed smoothly.

'Why are you suspicious of me?' she asked.

'Suspicious? I'm not suspicious!'

'Yes, you are.'

He stopped to think.

'I took it that our ways had parted. You had your life, I had mine. What are we meant to talk about? My holiday plans with Andrew?'

'Are you afraid I'd blurt things out to the people at home?'

'No, Anna, it's not that. I wouldn't know how to talk to you about certain subjects.'

'What makes my relationship so different from yours?'

'You're married, Anna. That's something I'll never be.'

'Isn't what you and Andrew have a kind of marriage?'

'Of course it isn't. How can you say that? We're two men, and you're a man and a woman. It's not the same. Why are you being so aggressive?'

'Am I being aggressive? Because I'm unhappy, I suppose.'

'Anna, I don't want you to complain to me about you and Scott. Don't use me for that. It's not fair.'

'Why not? Aren't you my friend?'

'I'm not sure any more. I sometimes wonder if people who are married know how to have friends.'

'Who's sounding angry now?'

'It looks to me as if you've got it all. An attractive husband. A bungalow and a garden. Two lovely children. Visits from the in-laws, family Christmases in Edinburgh or Angus . . .'

'What more could anyone want?'

'. . . and you're unhappy?'

'Are you any happier?'

'Yes, I am. I just envy you the luxury of normality. Nothing more than that. Not needing to think. Not having to ask any questions. Some day I'll feel that being the way I am is a privilege. I haven't got that far yet.'

'Are you telling me you'd rather be heterosexual?'

Nicol relaxed all of a sudden. His voice became quite different.

'It's been a tough week, Anna. Andrew took the test.'

'What test?'

'See what I mean? An HIV test. A friend of ours died last month. A man he'd been with. Oh, years ago. But he couldn't stop worrying about it.'

'And . . .'

'It was negative. He's OK. But it's been horrible.'

Anna was completely out of her depth. They really did inhabit different worlds. She tried to imagine how she would feel if confronted with a woman Scott had been involved with, then gave up. As far as she knew, she had been his first and only lover. Mind you, she had never asked him. Maybe she should. It was something she assumed, and suddenly the assumption struck her as odd.

Nicol looked relieved now he had told her. He offered to get another coffee. Anna, for her part, felt hopeless. The gap was impossible to bridge. There were so many things she had wanted to tell him about, to get his advice about. Things, she reflected guiltily, it would be more natural to discuss with her husband. She preferred to share them with a friend. The prospect of being free during the day. Getting a job. Finishing her degree. The options were limitless.

'No. I'd better be off now,' she lied, drearily, got up, and said goodbye.

Five weeks later, Nicol happened to pop into John Lewis's during his lunch hour. The following weekend would be the anniversary of his and Andrew's first meeting, at that disastrous party. One of the ways he was planning to mark it was by getting new sheets for the bed. A simple enough gesture. But a change of colour, downie and all, struck him as significant. He was on the third floor, hesitating between different shades of yellow, when he caught sight, out of the corner of his eye, of a figure he recognized. A woman was wandering past the specimens of curtain fabric. She was odd and familiar at one and the same time. Familiar because it was Anna. Odd because she was wearing a striped nightie, white and pale green.

Turning fully round, he blinked to make sure he was not hallucinating. She moved slowly, as if floating, down the passageway. Here and there a face looked up but no one said anything or tried to stop her. Before he could think, Nicol was at the end of the passageway. He opened his arms as she came towards him. She had bare feet.

'Anna!' he said. 'What are you doing?'

'I decided not to,' she announced. 'I came away.'

'Away from where?'

She did not answer, looking past his shoulder. Then, in the most ordinary fashion imaginable:

'Can we have a sandwich? I'm hungry.'

He took her arm and led her into the eatery, on the top floor in the St James' Centre extension. Beyond the glass roof there is only sky. To the right, Calton Hill and, beneath it, slate roofs descending towards Leith in a cascade. Beyond, the waters of the firth with here and there a ship, seeming becalmed and, to the north, Fife. The way she was dressed, she fitted that backdrop well. She could have been a denizen of the sky, an angel descended to make an announcement he still did not understand. Once he had joined her, Nicol noticed he somehow became, in the eyes of bystanders, responsible for her, so that the looks of disapproval and alarm were directed at him, rather than at the woman everybody took for his wife.

He thanked his stars he had stopped at the cash machine. Anna was enormously hungry and ordered three rounds of sandwiches with wholemeal bread, a bowl of soup, a slice of toffee cheesecake and a coffee to round it all off. Carrying the tray, he steered her to the point where there were fewest people, a raised area to one side that looks on to the roof of the Catholic cathedral.

She devoured the sandwiches. Nicol thought about making conversation and decided not to.

'Should I phone Scott?' he hazarded.

Her eyes flashed in alarm.

'No,' she said. 'Not yet, at any rate. He'll be delighted.'

'Because . . .'

Nicol knew there must be an explanation but preferred to be as indirect as possible.

'It nearly made me laugh, he was so funny about it. When he was trying to convince me, I mean. "What if it were another Einstein?" he said. "Or if it discovers a cure for cancer?" But I wouldn't listen to him.'

'And "it" . . .' prompted Nicol, though he had already guessed.

244

She tapped her stomach. There was no visible protuberance.

'The baby,' she said. 'Now we'll find out.'

The soup had cooled to the lukewarm temperature she preferred and she tucked into it with gusto. Nicol ought to have been getting back to the shop. He decided not to check his watch. Nothing terrible would happen if he turned up late. The early afternoons were not a busy time.

'Motherhood doesn't come naturally to me,' Anna volunteered. 'It just came upon me. Fell on top of me, rather, like a landslide. You'd be as good at it as I am, I could swear. All of a sudden it is there or they are there and they never go away, never stop wanting things, till they exhaust you, and even then they don't stop.'

She had tipped a little of the coffee she was sipping on to her nightie without noticing. The liquid stained into a slim, messy blob that would be hard to wash out.

'I try to be good to them, though. Honestly I do.'

Nicol pointed at her stomach with his index finger.

'How many months . . .'

'Weeks, only weeks. Five. So it'll be born in February next year.'

'What made you change your mind?'

'I checked in this morning. Scott ran me there. He wanted to come back and collect me but I told him I could get a taxi. It's just too complicated with the little ones, ferrying them back and forth. Katie gets ill in the car. To tell you the truth, I liked the idea of being on my own. I wasn't sure how I would feel afterwards, especially when I saw him. I've blamed him for so many things and now it seems unjust.'

'He's a nice man,' said Nicol. The words were banal but he meant them.

'He was for keeping it. I suppose there was a touch of humour in the things he said. But when I wouldn't budge he stopped insisting.'

'And why didn't you . . . ?'

'Oh, there was some hitch at the hospital. A doctor had fallen ill or hadn't turned up or something. They showed me into a single room and left me there. I took my clothes off and got into bed. It felt like the right thing to do. And I sort of lost track of time. And then, all of a sudden, I had to escape. So I got my nightie on and started walking.'

'And no one stopped you?'

'A man spoke to me halfway up Leith Walk. He wasn't drunk or begging or anything. Just concerned. I ignored him and walked on.'

'And John Lewis's?'

'Where else would I come? This café is my favourite place in Edinburgh. I thought I might buy something, to celebrate. Then I realized I'd forgotten my purse.'

'We can buy something now,' said Nicol, who was also beginning to feel they had reason to celebrate.

'Have you got money?'

'I've got my plastic.'

A doubt crossed his mind.

'You don't want me to take you back?'

'Good God, no. I never want to see the inside of that place again.'

'And Scott?'

'He can wait. He's not expecting to see me until sixish. After all, he's getting a big enough present today.'

Nicol had been struggling to remember a word.

'Philo ... philo ... philoprogenitive,' he said, all in a rush.

'What on earth does that mean?'

'It's a word I've always liked. It means men who love children. Especially their own. Or maybe just their own, I can't remember. Where do you want to go?'

'Let's start at the kitchenware department in the basement. I want to look at the Le Creuset pots. And I've been meaning to buy a stainless steel colander for ages. The plastic one we have at home is getting tatty ...'

Nicol never made it back to the shop that afternoon. He was the boss and could do that kind of thing, although he hated setting staff a bad example. He stopped worrying about Anna's nightie. Laden with parcels, they went to Monsoon and got her a new raincoat. People did turn round to look at the pair of them on the way there. But the whole thing had taken on a carnival aspect and he stared cheekily back.

Anna refused to let him drive her home. He was doubly

relieved. Andrew had the car that day and getting hold of it could have been complicated. At the very least, they would have had to rendezvous in the city centre. And he did not want to share the day with Andrew. Better if it was just the two of them. Facing Scott was a prospect he did not relish, either. So he loaded Anna and her parcels into a taxi and gave the driver twenty-five pounds. The man had already entered into the spirit of the thing. His face lit up when he realized he had landed such a lengthy fare.

Scott phoned not long before bedtime.

'Everyone's asleep,' he whispered. 'I got them off to bed at last.'

A silence.

'I'm so grateful to you for this afternoon.'

Another silence, more protracted. Gradually Nicol realized that the man at the other end of the phone was crying, almost but not quite inaudibly. After what he and Andrew had gone through not long before, he felt surprisingly comfortable with tears. He waited, patiently, until the moment passed.

'You'll be the godfather, won't you?' Scott said at last. 'We'd both like that.'

22

Shiram proposed stopping for the night in a hamlet two hours' riding south of Tabriz. Dashkur, however, grew increasingly agitated the moment he glimpsed the city's outline, on gently rising ground in the far distance. Although they had been travelling for four full days, he insisted it would be dangerous to delay any longer, and begged Shiram to push on till the gates. It was a gamble. Had they arrived only a few minutes after sunset, it would have been impossible to gain entrance. As it was, admission proved surprisingly easy. So many travellers had entered Tabriz in the course of the day that the guards were exhausted and indifferent. They waved the pair on, barely taking in their names or the story they had invented to justify their visit.

The streets of the city were thronged. Excited voices babbled in different tongues. They passed by a dyer's workshop. Shiram's courteous enquiry elicited a curt answer from the foreman. Tomorrow there was to be a wedding feast in the palace of the Caliph and he had not yet finished dyeing certain hangings which had been specially commanded. As they turned away, Shiram leading their horse by the reins, for it was impossible to ride through the dense mass of passers-by, the dyer called after them, almost apologetically, that he would risk his head if he failed to produce the order in time.

They were both grimy and thirsty and stopped at the first tavern that they saw.

'You will be lucky to find a pallet or even a corner to sleep in tonight,' the proprietor affirmed, plumping a carafe of dark red wine down on the table they were sitting at. 'Every chink of space that could accommodate a visitor to Tabriz has been filled.'

'What is the feast?' Dashkur asked one of a group of men next to them. 'Who is to be married tomorrow?'

Their neighbours had already debated the topic exhaustively and, having run out of comments of their own, were eager to involve strangers in the discussion, to see what further juices it might yield.

'Ka, the eldest son of our Caliph Al-Hujan, is to be married,' was the answer.

'Has he not recently returned from Birjand?' Dashkur asked, mastering his emotions with difficulty.

'Yes indeed,' replied his interlocutor, with a laugh, 'and he returned with intentions very different from his father's. The Caliph took advantage of his absence to conclude the negotiations for a marriage which has been far too long delayed. It is high time his only son took a wife and got progeny upon her. Yet it would seem the wife his father has chosen is not to his taste.'

'Perhaps the woman who would be to his taste does not exist,' another quipped.

'Indeed,' said a third. 'He arrived from Birjand two days ago with a bosom companion, a man five or six years his senior, and ordered a feast to be prepared in his private residence.'

'There were to be garlands of flowers, a carpet of ostrich feathers and ornate pastries of honey and almonds, exactly the presents with which a rich man of this city welcomes his wife into his house,' resumed the first. 'Ka ought to have called upon his father before removing his riding cloak and washing the filth of travel from his body . . .'

'. . . Before even crossing his own threshold . . .' put in his neighbour.

'. . . Whereas all he did was send the Caliph a terse message. His father's summons was ignored, such was the hubbub of preparation for the party . . .'

'. . . And within the hour a company of guards arrived to haul the wayward boy into our Caliph's presence.'

'What happened to his companion?' put in Dashkur.

'He was thrown into a dungeon,' said the first man, 'and he languishes there still.'

He gave this piece of information with an air of deep satisfaction, implying that no more appropriate course of action could have been taken where Leflef was concerned. He underlined this impression with a puff at the long tube of his hookah pipe, so energetic it set the water in the shared vessel the tube fed into bubbling, as furiously as if it had been boiling.

'Who is the bride?' asked Shiram. He was listening intently, missing not a single word that was exchanged.

'Shian-Tal,' came the reply, 'daughter of the Great Khan of the nomad tribes in the desert to the north.'

'And was she in such a hurry to be married that she arrived the moment the contract was drawn up, without even waiting to find out whether her bridegroom had returned to Tabriz?'

'Ah,' said the fourth man in the group, who had not spoken up to this point. His voice was deeper and richer than that of his companions. 'I see you know little about the ways of the horse people. Their movements are as unpredictable as the storm winds which unceasingly mould and remould the dunes, and their disposition changes as rapidly as the outline of the vast wastes they inhabit.'

'They have never yet attempted to plunder Tabriz,' said another. 'The walls of the city are too thick, and their circuit too immense, for the horse people to mount a siege. In any case, they lack the patience and application for such tactics. But none of the towns within a day's ride of the desert's edge can count itself safe without paying a yearly tribute to the Great Khan. How long have you been travelling?'

'Four days.'

'Were you to travel for twenty times as much, you would not reach the limit of the territories he reigns over. They say he dictates law in distant Mongolia.'

'And he is fabulously rich,' broke in another of the group. 'I have it on reliable evidence that his treasure hoard is concealed in a subterranean palace below the dunes . . .'

'. . . Impossible for human skill to trace . . .' burst in another.

'. . . And so the Great Khan keeps a genie by him, imprisoned in a magical mirror. The only place the genie can get food or drink is in the underground retreat . . .'

'. . . For it lives on diamonds, and on pearls dissolved in vinegar. That is why, time and again, it guides the Great Khan to the hidden chambers.'

'I have heard genies will feed on human blood, provided it be fresh and uncongealed,' put in one of the company.

250

'Rubbish! No divine creature, however low the order it belonged to, would take nourishment so base!'

'Your Caliph has found an unusual bride for Ka,' observed Dashkur.

'Thanks to the wedding contract, the tradesmen of Tabriz are assured free passage through the desert in all directions, with the guidance of no fewer than two tribesmen, for as long as Ka and the children of his marriage bed live,' the first man announced triumphantly. 'If our city were not already the richest from the Caspian to the borders of China, this contract would make it so.'

'I have heard,' said the man who had furnished the disputed detail about the diet of genies, 'that the women of the nomad tribes refuse to accept their husbands' authority, that they are excellent archers, and that for this purpose it is their custom to cut off the left breast . . .'

'Al-Hujan would never accept a mutilated bride for his son!' the first man said indignantly.

'Nevertheless, there can be no doubt that the woman has a mind of her own,' said the man with the rich voice. 'Along with her dowry, she brought to Tabriz a casket filled with gold and silver. It is to be offered as a prize to the finest musician to perform at their wedding feast.'

'Her father-in-law to be,' said the first man, 'explained to her that this was not a custom in Tabriz.'

'She flew into a rage, and told him,' another of the group went on, 'through her interpreter, that she had not come to our city to offer obedience to any man, not even to its Caliph.'

'Apparently she said even more shocking things,' said another, 'such as, that marriage must not be a form of slavery, that she had not sold her body to her husband, that she herself had drawn up the terms of her marriage contract, and that she intended to follow the ways and customs of her people till her death.'

'A prize for the finest musician,' murmured Dashkur, who had practically ceased to pay attention once these words were pronounced.

'You know why our Caliph hates the idea of a musical contest,' said the first man who had spoken to them, casting a knowing grin around the table. Everyone except the two travellers nodded gleefully, as if savouring in anticipation the inevitable discomfiture of the man whose rule they lived under.

'Why?' Dashkur asked.

'For many moons now, Al-Hujan has been locked in conflict with the Chief Assessor.'

'And can he not throw him into a dungeon, as he did with Ka's companion?' Dashkur asked, careful not to mention Leflef by name, in case that should reveal how closely the prisoner's fate concerned him.

'There are limits to our Caliph's power. The Chief Assessor is rich, intelligent and without scruple. He controls the complex mechanism by which taxes are assigned and collected in Tabriz and all its subject territories. He has allies, hidden and declared, in every guild and corporation in the city.'

'Were the Caliph to make an attempt on his life or his liberty, a hundred voices would be raised in protest,' said the man with the rich voice.

'His library is rivalled only by that of the Caliph himself...' another of the group burst in.

'... At this very moment, twenty copyists are busy adding to its wealth by the light of candles of purest beeswax. I have been told that last week a further convoy of manuscripts arrived on loan...'

'... Sent by the learned men of Afram-Dai. The Chief Assessor is their most generous patron.'

'Soon,' the man with the rich voice predicted, 'his collection will outstrip Al-Hujan's. And it is an acknowledged fact in Tabriz that his private chapel of musicians is superior to the Caliph's own.'

'A band of shawms and rebecks goes before him through the streets,' said the man next to him, 'each time he proceeds from his residence to the Caliph's.'

'And trumpets and kettledrums bring up the rear, along with tinkling triangles.'

'That is why,' the first man to have spoken concluded, 'Al-Hujan took the announcement of a competition as a personal insult.'

'In the course of the last two days, the Lord of Masques has scoured each school of music in the city, co-opting its most gifted pupils to perform at the Caliph's behest.'

'None of them will play better than Vendlin.'

All four men shook their heads sagely from side to side. Silence fell.

'And who is Vendlin?'

'The leader of the Chief Assessor's private chapel, of course.'

'What is his favourite instrument?' hazarded Dashkur.

'Which do you think? The rebeck, naturally.'

'And what does he play on it?'

'Chaconnes. No one can construct variations of infinite complexity and charm on a ground bass better than he.'

'And where can I find a rebeck?'

'You intend to enter the competition?'

Dashkur had already risen to his feet.

'Take me to an instrument maker. Quickly.'

'Do you have gold?'

'I have a horse.'

'You seem little more than a stripling, though you have the beginnings of a beard. How could you possibly defeat the greatest virtuoso in Tabriz?'

'If he were to win the competition, and humiliate the Chief Assessor, there is no gift our Caliph would think too generous for him,' one of the men said to the other three.

'Wait,' said the man with the rich voice. 'I have a rebeck in my house no hand has touched since my wife died. Her favourite pastime was to listen to ballads of happy and unhappy lovers sung to its accompaniment. When I lost her, I thought it fitting that it should fall silent. If you wish, strange youth, your skill may waken it again.'

Dashkur said nothing, only bowed, slowly and deeply, in the sign of acknowledgement that honours the receiver as much as it does the giver. He completed the movement with such consummate elegance that the onlookers gasped.

'Are you a king?' asked one. 'A prince travelling in disguise? Where did you learn such courtly ways?'

'I am a lover who has been bereft of that which he most treasures,' Dashkur answered gravely. 'Sorrow brings suppleness to my body, for only those who bend and yield as reeds do can withstand the onset of a grief like mine. That grief, if it is the will of the goddess who protects me, will spur me to such eloquence tomorrow, that even the head of your Assessor's chapel will fall silent upon hearing me.'

'Come to my house in the hour after dawn,' said the man with the rich voice. 'That will give you time to restring the instrument and to learn its ways before going to the palace.'

'How shall I know the place?'

'Ask to be directed to the House of Butterflies. A compendium of every kind of butterfly human eye has seen in Tabriz is painted on the tiles of its inner patio. The Caliph's gardener brings his pupils there, when they are learning to identify the different species.'

'Would you have allowed me to sell your horse in order to buy a rebeck?' Dashkur asked Shiram, once they were outside the tavern.

'I would,' said Shiram. 'Where do we go now?'

'To the temple. No matter how crammed the city is with guests, there we shall find peace and quiet. We can wash the dirt of travel from our bodies. They will let us bed down in the shadow of the trees on its perimeter. And even if the night is cold, we can wrap our bodies in one single mantle to keep warm.'

The two did as Dashkur said. They were given food for nothing, and he used the coins he carried to pay for ten white pigeons to be freed in the name of Wu. The grass they lay upon was dry and fragrant. In the branches over their heads, the sacred goldfinches chirruped contentedly, now and again dislodging a leaf with their flutterings.

Shiram was close to tears. He placed unquestioning faith in Dashkur's skill. Not for a moment did he doubt that the youth he loved would win the competition, using the victory to gain freedom for Leflef. This was the last night they would spend in each other's company. He found it too painful to bear that the first time he held Dashkur in his arms must also be the last.

He noted with embarrassment, as they drew the mantle around them to shut out the evening chill, that his sex was rigid with excitement. Dashkur did not pull away. Instead he began to sniff at Shiram like a puppy, examining the different odours of his neck, his armpits and his chest. Suddenly Shiram realized that there was not one, but two hot rods inside their bundle. With a confidence whose source he could not have accounted for, he eased Dashkur's garments from his limbs, shaking them out onto the grass, and then removed his own. The youth did not resist when he climbed on top of him. He appeared to welcome it.

Until the stars faded into dawn, Shiram took all the pleasure he desired with Dashkur's body. And the pleasure he took was no more intense than the pleasure he gave.

'Walk behind me like a servant,' Dashkur told him, when they had washed at the fountain and adjusted their clothes. 'We shall go, first to the House of Butterflies, then to the palace of Al-Hujan. Remember that you are to do my bidding.'

'What we did this night was not of your bidding.'

'No,' said Dashkur, 'it was not of my bidding.'

23

Brian was aware of a figure standing right in front of him. He lifted his eyes from the page. It was Kieran. In one hand he held two glasses, in the other the last of the bottles of red wine Nicol had brought, still almost full.

He had found the study door ajar. Brian had unfolded the double wooden panels from the cavities on either side of the long, high window they fitted into so precisely, and they formed a partition against the glass, shutting out the ephemeral summer night. From the top of its slender, delicately fluted brass column, a standard lamp shed a pool of warm gold onto his lap, flooding the pages of the book that lay open on it.

'I thought you might like a drink,' said Kieran. 'We've been having a toast. You can join in.'

'What sort of toast?'

'We couldn't decide what to drink to. So each of us mentioned something or someone, then we all raised our glasses.'

'How original. Who was your toast to?'

He is being deliberately difficult, thought Kieran, yet I like him. He is even more handsome than Gordon. I would not have believed that possible.

'My mother.'

Brian laughed. More than a laugh, it was a splutter. Kieran filled two glasses.

'Come on,' he said. 'Let's drink to something together.'

'I want my twin to wake up soon.'

They drank.

'What's the news? When did you fly in from London?'

'Gavin picked me up at the airport on the way here. That's why I was so keen to get back home tonight. I haven't slept in my own bed since the start of the week. I was actually booked on a Glasgow flight this morning. I had half a mind to go to the rehearsal after lunch. I thought it might take my mind off things. But I couldn't face it. Everybody will know what has been going on. You have no idea what a gossip shop the orchestra is. They might not ask me but they'd be scrutinizing my face to find out what the latest news was.'

'Have they given you time off?'

'Until the middle of next week. I had leave owing in any case.'

'And what's the prognosis?'

'He'll come through all right. His loving parents and his estranged, but still loyal spouse are at the bedside, along with one of my sisters.'

Kieran noted the heavy irony, presumably a provocation he was expected to respond to. He chose to ignore it. He had other business on his mind. He coughed nervously.

'I made love with your twin.'

There was a silence.

'So did I,' said Brian.

It could have been the most normal conversation in the world.

'Why don't I shut the door properly,' Kieran said.

He did so and returned to his place opposite Brian.

'I didn't think you could be better-looking than he was. I didn't believe it was possible. But you are.'

'It's not something I give much thought to. Don't we look exactly the same?'

'Not exactly.'

'You know about the birthmark?'

'A dark smudge like a tear, underneath the right armpit.'

Brian nodded. Kieran noticed he had started trembling, ever so slightly.

'Shall I go first then?' he asked.

'Yes, you go first,' said Brian.

'It was in London. I hated London. I'd been working in the Civil Service for nearly four years. They offered me a further change of grade if I would agree to move down south. I thought it was Scotland I wanted away from when in fact it was the job itself. It struck me as a good idea at the time. You know, the lure of the big city and so on. I had sort of come out, but not to anyone at work, and not to my mother or other people in the family.

'London offered better chances to explore things. That's the funny thing about being gay. You sense that there is something but you don't know what it is. Like a language only you can speak, but language is a social thing, and you are aching to get to the place where everybody speaks that way. For many years I believed it was something that already existed and all I had to do was to discover it. You know, I thought I would come upon a man or men who would demonstrate how I had to be, who would have got there before me and could light the way. In fact, it's not about discovering at all. You have to invent. To choose and to invent.'

'And it means Dougal to you now?'

Kieran paused. He had not thought about it in those terms.

'Yes, for me it means Dougal. That was a choice. Does it mean Gavin for you?'

Brian nodded and smiled.

'I don't know how he manages to put up with me.'

'Look at yourself in the mirror.'

'You're being superficial. And I don't believe he finds me that stunning anyway. Looks have never been important to him. You should see the photographs he has of Colin. Hardly Richard Gere. But we're getting away from the point. You were telling me about London.'

'They hadn't quite made us legal in Scotland at that time, whereas down south the law had been changed for over a decade. There weren't more than three pubs in Glasgow you could go to, plus a disco, and that got depressing within a month, because you inevitably encountered the same familiar faces. Drinking heavily didn't make them look any more attractive.'

'How long did you stay in England?'

'Not quite a year. The first four months were the most difficult bit, till I got home at Christmas. It was while I was back visiting my mother that I decided to do further Highers, even if it meant studying on my own and at a distance, and to apply for university. So I suppose London sorted my ideas out for me. She was appalled.'

'Was that because you were supporting her?'

'I've never supported my mother,' Kieran said quickly, as if Brian had insulted her. 'Most of the money I sent went straight into her savings account. I imagine that's where it still is. No, it was just unknown territory. I was giving up the safest career I could have had. And she thought studying would cut me off from her. She reads scandal magazines. I don't think she has ever got to the end of a book in her life.'

'What did you find so hard about London?'

'The loneliness. I had a bedsit, a nice enough place in Notting Hill. It was the realization, when I travelled home on Friday evening, that unless I went round the gay pubs, I might not speak to another living soul till I went back to work on Monday. That's partly what sent me out. The problem is that sex is sex and intimacy is intimacy. And having sex with someone because you're lonely can simply make you feel that much more isolated. Once it was over it was as if they were waiting for you to go. Sometimes I stayed for coffee and cornflakes the next morning. Mostly I beetled off halfway through the night and spent far more than I could afford on a taxi to get home.'

'How many people did you go with?'

'Not that many. Don't get me wrong. Have you never been . . . promiscuous?'

Brian looked perplexed and they both started to laugh. He took the bottle and filled their glasses once more.

'It's not the right word, is it? Did you try the leather bars?'

'I think I tried everywhere. What I liked most was a pub in the East End where they had a drag show on Thursday evenings. It lessened the tension. People stopped worrying so much about who they were going to go home with and started enjoying themselves. Do you know, I actually had difficulty in understanding what those guys were saying?'

'I'm sure they found your accent problematic, too.'

Kieran shrugged his shoulders.

'The conversation wasn't an important part of it. The one leather place I went to scared me stiff. It was festooned with chains and handcuffs and they served your drinks through metal bars, as if it were a prison. Not a lock of hair in sight, excepting forelocks. They all had shaven heads. I'd never have dared to spend the night with one of them.'

'You'd probably have been asked to take your shoes off the moment you got in the door, so as not to spoil the exquisite Afghan rugs. And you'd have had your nipples pierced behind a priceless Chinese silk screen.'

'I didn't have the nerve to find out. And in any case, I think my ideal is having a friend, rather than a master.'

'So you didn't see Gordon there.'

'No, he trawled me at the London Coliseum. I remember the night well. They were doing *Madame Butterfly*.'

'In English!'

'Don't be such a snob! How good is your Italian?'

'I hardly understand a word. It's just that English sounds so stupid when they sing it. And I detest Puccini.'

'I can't say I much care for him either.'

'Did you meet him in the bar? Wasn't he with his wife?'

'No, I didn't know about any of that then.'

Brian was struck by the force of the word 'then'. It made him wonder how Kieran had found out about 'that' and what 'that' meant for him. Were people in the habit of gossiping about Gordon here in Scotland? Had they been sneering at his twin behind his back? Once more he turned his attention to Kieran, who had carried on without a break.

'That night was a sell-out. I had come on the off chance of getting a return. I was standing in the street outside and suddenly your twin was right there in front of me, offering me a ticket. He wouldn't let me pay and I nearly said no. Then the expression in his eyes told me it wasn't just the seat that he was offering. I got that sick feeling in my stomach that meant I wanted to sleep with him. I hadn't experienced that since coming down to London or for many months before. That's what I'd been doing wrong, you see, more or less forcing myself to go with people because it would be educational, not because I really wanted to. I understood you were supposed to behave that way.'

'But you didn't have to force yourself to go with Gordon.'

'No, though it was a far from successful night. And then there was his Glasgow accent. It was unmistakable and made me feel so homesick. The funny thing was, we could have been talking about different cities. Me in Drumchapel at St Ninian's High and him going to Hutchie Grammar on the south side of the river and living in a big detached house with a garden.'

'You're not a social climber, then.'

'Why are you being sardonic? I'm trying to tell you something really important and you keep making sarcastic comments!'

'I'm sorry. It's a way of defending myself. It's because you mention the house.'

'Why is the house so significant?'

'It's like a theatre. I can't stand going back there. When I do, I have to pretend that everything is normal, and nothing is. It reminds me of a theatre because it was a stage things happened on. Everything meant more than itself. Even the most humdrum gestures had a kind of horror about them. And' – Brian was feeling his way towards something he had never before articulated – 'the terrible thing about a theatre is that the performances never stop. You can have the same play on night after night and year after year and it is different but identical. A ritual. As long as the house is standing, it will be as if the show was still going on. The only way to put an end to it would be to burn the theatre down.'

Kieran shivered. He got up and opened the inner wings of the shutters, so that the light of the standard lamp found an echo in the glass. There were two lamps now.

'Why did you say the night was unsuccessful?'

'He didn't want to be touched. He undressed and got on to the bed and wanted me to look at him. That was all. I had to watch him wanking off.'

'And you found him beautiful.'

'Not then. He scared me at that point. Not because of what he might do to me but because of what he was doing to himself. When he came up to me outside the theatre, I suppose it was like every homophobe's dream.'

'I don't get you.'

'You know, gay men who aren't happy with themselves often fantasize about getting off with someone who isn't really gay. Or doesn't look it, at any rate. And Gordon didn't. He looked like an ordinary married man.'

'That's what he was. Or what he claimed to be.'

'I guessed that, from the way he slept. It never occurred to him not to stay the night. I could sense he was used to sharing a bed. He went out like a light. I didn't close my eyes until it was nearly dawn. When I opened them again he wasn't there any more.'

'So how did you find out about Melanie and the children?'

'He rang the doorbell one evening early the next week. Repeatedly. He had been drinking. I could smell it off his breath. There were bedsits on three floors, all the way up to the attic, and people were putting heads round doors to see what was happening. The easiest thing was to invite him up. And, to be honest, I was lonely myself. I hoped things might work out better than they did the time before. During all those months in London, your brother was the only man I slept with more than once.'

'Did he want to penetrate you?'

Kieran was perfectly aware of the intensity of Brian's listening. He knew that, after its fashion, each of Brian's questions was a statement, an indication of another story, neither parallel to his, nor necessarily similar, but sharing a protagonist. It would be a shock were they to discover they were actually talking about different people. But the physical identity made that impossible.

'No, he wanted me to penetrate him.'

'So he'd got over the thing about touching. And you refused?'

'I wasn't into that. It was something I excluded at that time, either way.'

'How did he take it?'

'He got violent. He called me a poof and raised his hand to hit me. I reached for the only weapon of defence in sight. It was an umbrella. When I grabbed it I inadvertently pressed the button on the handle and it opened out just like a parachute. The whole situation became comic and he calmed down.'

'Why didn't you throw him out?'

'I felt sorry for him. I could tell something had happened and I was curious to know what it was.'

Kieran paused, for he wanted Brian to prompt him. The blood was thundering at his temples. He had given up trying to work out what his own emotions were. He had not seen the man in front of him before this evening. His twin, much older now, and who could tell how ravaged by unhappiness and drink, lay motionless in bed in a London hospital. Telling Brian was like telling Gordon, almost like being able to punish him, to have revenge. No, that was not it. Kieran corrected himself. Brian might not have been there in the Notting Hill bedsit. But he was implicated in what went on. And the way he listened now was an acknowledgement of Kieran's part in things, in his family and in the connection to his twin. It was odd, he reflected. I have a relationship with a man I had never seen, because he is identical to another man I once made love with. Does that mean I come between them?

'Why have you stopped?'

'I don't want to hurt you.'

'You aren't hurting me. Nothing you tell me can be more terrible than what I already know. All I ask is that you should hear me out when my turn comes.'

Kieran did not understand. It was too late to turn back.

'They had had a threesome that weekend. I don't want to be crude but I don't exactly think his wife found their marital relations satisfying. They had agreed in theory that, if she wanted to have other men, it was allowed. Gordon, however, had to meet them, to give them the once over, as it were. Make sure they were OK. That was the first time and they ended up all getting into bed together, without more ado.'

'Where were the children?'

'God knows. He didn't tell me.'

'Maybe at their grandparents' house. Go on.'

'It was fascinating listening to him. He was finding out about it all as he went on. I was hearing something no one else had ever heard. This man had nobody to talk to, had had nobody to talk to for years. Maybe we were equally lonely, but in very different ways. I couldn't stop watching his hands. Later that week I saw his picture in the newspaper and read that he was big in autopsies. Cutting up dead people. His hands had the grace of a flower arranger's or a pianist's.

'Anyway, his front had collapsed. No sooner had they got into bed than the guy made it clear it was Gordon who interested him, not Melanie. You don't seem to realize what beauty such as you possess does, Brian. I noticed it that first night at *Madame Butterfly*, the way people looked at Gordon during the interval. The way they looked at *us*. He wasn't just a beautiful man, he was a living statement. As if he were carrying a torch for all of humanity. Beauty of that sort is like courage. People can't remain indifferent to it. What's more, it creates a space around itself, transforming everyone nearby into an audience. They are afraid to come close, so they spectate. I don't know what makes me say all this. I never spent more than ten hours at a time with your brother.'

'The time doesn't matter,' said Brian. 'It's the intensity.'

'He wore his beauty like a suit of clothes he couldn't get comfortable in. Or a burden he only just managed to carry but longed to put down, to get relief from. Has it never been that way for you?'

'I always felt I was my brother's shadow. A reflection of him. That everything I was really belonged to him.'

'He never played the cello!'

'That's what saved me. He was in the light. I was in the darkness. The cello was my other body. The body he could not have.'

Once more Kieran felt out of his depth. He was unwilling to demand an explanation from Brian at this stage. Let him tell whatever he wanted to, in the order and at the time he chose. Yet Kieran had an urge to help.

'He's in the darkness now.'

'He's going to emerge from it!'

'Will things be different?'

'Oh yes,' Brian insisted. The certainty in his voice was veined with anger. 'People who come back from the dead don't stay the same.'

'How can you be so sure?'

'From the expression on his face. Even when somebody's unconscious, they have emotions, things are happening inside them. His face is quite changed now. No one can gauge that more accurately than me. When he awakens, something will come awake in me, and I will be different too.'

There was another silence.

'What is the house like? Gordon mentioned the area and named the street, without going any further. I tried to imagine the place in a general sort of way.'

'I suppose it's the kind of home many families would long to

264

have. For me it was a chamber of horrors. And the worst horror was the absolute conventionality of it all. Our father' – (the adjective brought Kieran up short, as if Brian had never felt able to say simply 'my father') – 'owns a building firm. He inherited it from his father, who was also the eldest son, and inherited it in his turn from our great-grandfather. He was the one who started the business and put together enough money to have the place built.

'It's not that striking from outside. There are streets of mansions of similar design in Glasgow's leafier Victorian suburbs. It's quite special once you get in, though. The hall takes up the space of the first two floors. A stained glass window is let into the back wall, with two long, thin panels, curving at the top. The sort of thing you'd expect to find in a church, rather than in a private house. Upstairs there are five bedrooms and two bathrooms. The ground floor has a sitting-room, a dining-room and a study, a kitchen and a toilet, plus the servants' quarters.'

'Your family had servants?'

'Of course we didn't! My mother had a woman come to clean for four hours every day. She was a primary school headmistress. Her hands were full with that, so she got the woman to do most of the cooking as well.'

'Was it good?' Kieran put in.

Food always appeared to him a crucial element in any situation.

'I don't remember. There were six of us at meals. The older sister and the younger sister and me and my twin. Plus our parents. We mostly sat in silence. On Sunday we all went to church together. Then my father read the newspapers. My mother worked in the garden, or did embroidery. She said it helped her forget the strains of running a school during the week. The two girls went out cycling or called on friends.'

'And you and Gordon?'

'We had sex.'

'Right from the start?'

'From when we entered secondary school. It's hard to talk about it even now. Shame is a funny thing. They say it starts outside you, then it becomes part of you. The way to overcome shame should be to talk. But the shame stops you from talking.'

'I'm going to light a candle,' Kieran said.

Two green candlesticks stood ready on the mantelpiece, containing carefully chosen candles of an identical shade, their wicks as yet a virgin white. Ignoring them, he extracted a half-consumed, stocky and slightly misshapen candle from the corner of a bookshelf where he had hidden it. Unsightly and therefore somehow trustworthy, it had escaped the tidying attentions of both Dougal and the cleaner. A match scraped briefly and the wick leapt into flame.

'What makes you want to do that?'

'It'll help shed light on things.'

Brian grunted and went on.

'He kept saying it was me that wanted it. I was the abnormal one, the pervert, according to him. Gordon was born first of the two of us. He and my father made sure I never forgot that. My father used to joke I was a poor quality carbon copy, a replica he neither wanted nor needed. Gordon claimed he had sex with me to keep me happy, otherwise I would have started pestering the other boys. It was a charitable activity he engaged in for the general good.

'Even though I knew it wasn't true, I pretended to believe him. It was easier than contradicting him. And I enjoyed it. Can you imagine what it was like? All the curiosity you have, all the experimenting gay teenagers long to do – not just gay teenagers, I suppose, but then the straight ones have more opportunities – and there he was, as close to me as anybody could be, almost myself over again, ready and waiting.'

'Was his dick just like yours?' asked Kieran.

The question led to laughter, though it had not been intended to, and the atmosphere lightened.

'No. Mine's slightly bigger, actually. And they point in different directions. Both to the left side, but mine is angled higher. At least, that's how it was the last time I saw them both together.'

'So what was bad about it all?'

'There was a kind of humiliation at the core. And now I finally know what really happened.'

The candle flame was burning steadily. Kieran had started to feel scared again. It soothed him to watch the wax soften, then liquefy, gathering in a pool whose shores drooped inwardly, like the well-thumbed pages of a book. Now and again the liquid made a breach for itself, overflowing like lava from a volcano.

Candles were hard and solid. Yet they transformed themselves into light the moment you gave them the chance. You would think they had been waiting, and leapt at the opportunity. There was no rigid boundary, then, between liquid and light. Did pain turn just as easily to tears? Could it find definitive release? Or was the movement reversible? There was no way you could gather light and turn it back into a candle, imprisoning it in that rigid shape again. Perhaps that meant the movement was indeed in one direction only – that shed tears would not return to trouble those who shed them.

As if from an alien planet, a murmur of raised voices drifted from the dinner table at the other end of the corridor, through two doors. The laughter of ghosts. Brian took a deep breath.

'That house, and everything that happened in it, all that normality, served to mask a crime. I have felt that for as long as I am able to remember. Gordon convinced me I was the one responsible. I took the burden upon myself in order to absolve them of blame. If I were guilty, they could remain innocent. It was like sucking the poison out of a wound.'

'But then the poison risks killing you.'

'I know. The unreality is what makes it so awful. From the outside, everything looked perfect. The minister and his wife came for dinner three or four times each month. They all sat round the table, discussing the outlandish nature of Catholic doctrine and their concern for the moral welfare of the community. You know how it is in Glasgow. The barriers between different social classes are more fragile there than elsewhere. Our home was barely a street or two away from a council estate. The minister was forced to deal with people from a different income bracket and with a very different attitude to religion. So was my mother, being headmistress of a school. The conversation would range from the horrors of alcoholism to the dangers of single-parent families. My father insisted that, if young girls got pregnant, it was their parents' fault, for not keeping them on a tight enough rein. Time and again I heard him speak of us as a model for the way children should be brought up.'

'Didn't you want to cry out? Say it was a lie?'

'Quite the contrary. I was terrified we would be caught. I did everything I could to protect us. Not just me and Gordon though, the whole family. I was the canker at the core and we were all corrupted. If they decided to root it out, they would either start with me or reach me in the end.'

'There's something I have to tell you, Brian . . .'

'Wait. Give me time. I'll hear it later. You see, my mother knew.'

Kieran restrained himself with difficulty.

'How can you be sure?'

'She opened the door once. Gordon was on top of me, on the bed. He neither heard nor saw her. We were still wearing our shirts and jumpers but we had our trousers down about our knees. I caught the merest glimpse of her face, then it disappeared. I tried to persuade myself it never happened. Or else that she didn't realize what we'd been doing.'

'Did you tell Gordon?'

'Of course not.'

'Why not?

'We never talked about it.'

'But you said he blamed you.'

'That was before we did it. Each time. It wasn't really talking, it was a sort of routine. A little number we ran through together. He would say "Oh, I can see you're needing it again," or other words to that effect. I used to pretend to resist, then he would say things like "Don't try to deceive me, you little pervert" or "I know what you're really after" or "Think you can kid your brother Gordon?" or "We've got to make society safe from people like you!" The way he uttered them they sounded almost tender, as if he was complimenting me. Like a ritual of seduction that had to be observed. They do that in some porno magazines, you know. I mean, insult each other while they're having sex. I couldn't think of anything to say that would break the pattern rather than fall into it. It felt like protesting would only encourage him even more.'

Kieran nodded.

'Do you understand?'

'It's not something I've experienced, not in that form. But I understand.'

Kieran gulped and took a quick look at the candle.

'It was your father, Brian. He started it. I have to tell you.'

'I know. That's what you came through here for, isn't it?'

Kieran nodded glumly.

'Did Gordon tell you?'

'Yes.'

'Did he mention me?'

'Not once. He gave me no reason to think he might have a twin.'

'Any idea why?'

'He wanted to present himself as the prime victim. To do that he had to exclude you.'

'So when did you discover I existed?'

'Several years later, I caught sight of him in a pub in Edinburgh. Not a gay pub, the one on Rose Street with the lovely woodwork . . .'

'The Abbotsford . . .'

'Yes, the Abbotsford. The next day I read in the paper that there was a big medical conference on. He was sitting with a crowd of men in suits and ties, winding down at the end of the day's session.'

'You didn't say hello?'

'No. I noticed and said nothing. But the person I was with that night knows you and knew you had a twin. We got into this long, involved discussion. Eventually I worked it all out.'

'How much of what you knew did you pass on?'

'Not a word, Brian. What do you take me for? It's not the kind of stuff you spill out over a pint. I'm really sorry I didn't find a way of telling you earlier.'

'Don't apologize. It's not your fault. And it wouldn't have been enough. I needed evidence. I've got it now.'

'What do you mean?'

'It's in the letter. The one he wrote before trying to kill himself. He left three: one to me, one to my parents and one to Melanie. At some level, I knew about him and Dad, without being able to formulate it clearly. I could never have asked Gordon. After he left home, there was a complete taboo on talking about sex of any kind, especially once he was married. Rather than admitting he had screwed our father, he'd probably have denied everything the two of us did. That would have been more than I could handle. I had enough trouble holding myself together without taking on his denial, too.'

'And your mother? Did she do anything to make you stop?'

'Far from it. She was desperate not to rock the boat. Her attitude changed after that day. I had a vague hope she would intervene or, at the very least, say something. What she did was show me a kindness I had never experienced in the past. Soon I realized she was afraid of me. Afraid I might crack up.

'I didn't realize at the time, you see, but I had a huge amount of power inside that family. I was the only one who never lied about what was really going on. My mother had always known. The only consequence of her opening the door that time was to show me she knew. She was perfectly aware of what my father was doing with Gordon, though I didn't begin to suspect that till a long time afterwards.'

'Gordon couldn't remember when it started. There wasn't a time when it hadn't been like that for him.'

'I always knew he was my father's favourite . . .' said Brian.

The smile on his face made Kieran feel sick.

'. . . Just didn't guess what form it took.'

'How did your mother show her kindness?'

'She insisted they had to buy me a cello. One of the teachers at the Academy was my salvation. He was married, but I'm sure that he was gay. I got invited to his home in Helensburgh for afternoon tea, the summer of my Highers. It wasn't a big place, one of the top flats in a converted seaside villa. His wife could not have been more boyish. She wore no make up. She had a sharp chin like a bird's beak and she kept her hair drawn tight in a bun at the back of her head. Come to think of it, she hardly had a body. Maybe he was more comfortable with that.

'She was very active in the anti-abortion movement and talked about it endlessly over tea. He kept his distance. I had the distinct impression she embarrassed him. Afterwards we went for a walk along the sand, just the two of us. He spoke about E.M. Forster, how he hated school and how much happier he was once he had left home. He lent me a book by Gide. I think it was a kind of code.'

'Which one?'

'The Counterfeiters.'

'That's a marvellous book. Remember Olivier's suicide?'

'I could never understand that. Trying to kill yourself because you are so happy. Thank God Édouard found him in time.

'Anyway, this guy was our music master and he ran the school orchestra. It was thanks to him I started on the cello. He had been on at my parents to buy me a proper instrument and pay for lessons outside school hours. They wouldn't hear of it. And then my mother changed her tune. You know,' (the bitter laugh rang out again) 'I still wonder how she put it to my father. If they actually acknowledged what was going on. I was keeping Gordon stable. Gordon helped the dynamic of their marriage, though I cannot fathom how. I know he was important. He was sacrificed as well. That's what has made me able to forgive him. It was a turning point for me, Kieran – the day I realized that, deep inside, I consider my parents' relationship to be a crime. Not to have *been* a crime. To *be* one, still. In a sane society, they would be taken to court and made to stop. Even now I cannot put into words what it is they ought to stop doing. All I know is, someone should put an end to it.'

'And nobody has done.'

'Nobody! It's still going on. Right up until today. They haven't been exposed.'

'We could put an advertisement in the paper.'

The joke was well intended and well taken. Brian grinned.

'Society doesn't prevent that kind of thing. It protects and encourages it. Do you think the other letters will bring it all out? Do you think he wrote it down there as well?'

'How could he not have done? What more had he to lose?'

The candle had almost gone out. It risked drowning in the pool of its own tears. Kieran took a match from the box to open a rift in the barrier of still undissolved wax. The contents of the pool rushed out, down the side of the candle and into the dish that held it, chilling and hardening as they went. Not all the column would be turned to light.

'Does Gavin know anything of this?'

'Practically nothing.'

'I find that strange.'

'What?'

'That you should be telling me all of this and have said nothing to him.'

'He guesses. He picks it up in other ways. To begin with, he cannot bear having Gordon around. The few family occasions when we were all together have been horribly difficult.'

'So your parents know? They have met Gavin?'

Kieran nearly got up he was so surprised.

'But of course. They are so enlightened. People keep telling me how lucky I am. Don't you see that it plays into their hands? Being gay accounts for me being so difficult, so hostile to them, so resentful, failing to fit in. And by having me and my partner round they can demonstrate their truly Christian spirit. Pretend they rise above it all.'

'And you haven't talked about any of this with Gavin?'

'After the first visit to the in-laws we had the most tremendous fight. I accused him of fancying Gordon. For an instant I thought he was going to hit me. I could see it flash across his face. Then he calmed down and moved away.'

'Did you apologize?'

'Yes, later on. He said he hated the family and especially my twin. That he would only go back under extreme duress and that the less I saw of them the better it would be for me. Then he went out and slammed the door. Do you know what I say to him, Kieran? On the days when it is difficult to let him near? I tell him I feel like a heap of broken glass. Sharp, wounding, jewel-like shards. If he touches me he will get cut. There's no way he can hold me and be safe.'

Kieran was following his own train of thought.

'It makes me furious, Gordon never mentioning you. All he wanted to talk about was your father and Melanie. She disgusted him. He spoke so much about her he began to disgust me in turn. He dreamt again and again that he'd been sleeping with a monstrous creature who had hair in all the wrong places, the body of a man and the sex of a woman. He told me screwing her made him hate his body. He had been corrupted, that is how he put it. He hoped that marrying her would sort him out. Instead it made things worse.'

'Of course.'

Another pause.

272

'What did they do?'

'What do you think? The usual things, I presume.'

'No,' said Brian, on a different tack now, 'not Melanie and my brother. My father and Gordon. What happened between them?'

'It's funny,' said Kieran.

He twisted his face, as if he were about to spit out a particularly repulsive morsel.

'I fell asleep at that point. Not that I didn't care or wasn't interested. It was a way of protecting myself – hearing no more than I could cope with. All I remember is that your father used to put his finger up Gordon's backside. Finger or fingers, I can't be sure now. I'll never forget how he described it to me. The family round the dinner table on Sunday evenings and your father reaching out, with that hand, for the cold roast joint. Or asking for the gravy boat to be passed and hooking his index finger into the curved pottery handle. And Gordon remembering where the finger had been.'

Behind Brian's shoulder, the door had opened ever so gently. Now Dougal's features were peeping through. Kieran froze. He did not know what to hope for. Part of him wanted to flee, wanted Dougal to break in and put an end to the discussion. Another part feared that if he destroyed the spell, what needed to be said would never emerge. It would stay walled up inside Brian, rotting, turning him rotten.

The door closed again, without a sound. Kieran knew exactly how to do that, how you had to press the handle inwards before turning it, so that it would not even squeak. He had done it innumerable times, when Dougal fell asleep there on weekday evenings, and he came looking for him. Blessing his partner silently, he said aloud:

'I find this hard.'

'*You* find it hard!'

He refused to be antagonized.

'Tell me how it ended. How did you survive?'

'Music helped a lot. My father objected to the racket I made practising. For a while I was afraid they would take the instrument away and force me to give up. Then they decided I could use the attic. It was insulated and that stopped the noise getting through. It was pretty cold, mind. But at least I had a place where nobody disturbed me.'

'Not even Gordon?'

'He tried to come up once, not long after I had settled in. We had a hand to hand at the trapdoor. It was peculiar. Deep inside I realized how crucial that fight was. Yet we kept bursting into uncontrollable fits of laughter. I shouted I was a captain defending my ship from attack by pirates. He didn't stop until I actually stood on his fingers. We heard a crack and he let out a genuine yell. Luckily no bones were broken. I'm amazed he didn't fall down.'

'So you had your own territory.'

'Physically and in my head as well. My father bought a new stereo system. He liked listening to opera. One of his jokes was, that he used to enjoy listening to stringed instruments, to violin and cello concertos and quartets but, when I took to practising at home, he couldn't bear the sound of them any longer. I was allowed to take the old record player up the ladder into the loft.'

'What did you do for records?'

'I rifled them from downstairs. My father got furious when there was one he wanted to put on and he couldn't find it. My mother would take my side and then they'd send me off to bring it down. I try not to listen to music so much these days. Partly because it is too like work, partly because it gets me right into my head. As if, when I listen to music, I can stop being in the world.'

'I understand that.'

'Kieran,' Brian said suddenly, and Kieran understood from the tone of his voice, with a rush of pleasure, how close they had become, 'do you think I should have stopped them?'

'Could you have?'

'But wasn't it up to me to do something?'

'You might only have made things worse. You had nobody there to defend you. What if you had gone under completely? They could have had you sectioned. You held out for as long as you needed to. Then you escaped.'

'I feel that. I feel I did the right thing.'

'What matters is . . . What matters is . . .'

'Tell me.'

Kieran knew what he wanted to say. It surprised him so much that he hesitated.

'Never stop hating them. Hold on to your hatred. That's what makes you safe. It makes you safe for Gavin too. Remember that.'

He paused, before asking:

'How *did* you escape?'

'It petered out. Not with a bang but a whimper. I left school a year before Gordon and started at the Academy of Music. By the time he finished sixth year I had already moved into a flat in Ruskin Terrace, just off Great Western Road.'

He smiled.

'I shared it with three women. All my friends were women at that time. That was another thing. At school I was afraid to have a friend because of what Gordon kept telling me. I thought I might get out of control, you know, and end up raping him or something else along those lines.'

'So when did you meet Gavin?'

'Not for a long time. For many years I had no sex at all. A long and sleepy convalescence.'

'And nobody suspected you were gay?'

'Oh, everybody I was studying with knew. I saw no point in making a secret of it. They called me "the untouchable". It wasn't meant unkindly. The thing was nobody got to lay a finger on me, either boy or girl. And that was quite unusual. It wasn't the fact I was gay that bothered them. They found it frustrating that I never pitched into the sexual free-for-all.'

'You make it sound exciting.'

'Maybe it just looked that way because I wasn't involved.'

'Gordon screwed around a lot.'

'Did he?'

'Mostly girls until he got married. More men afterwards.'

'So it was him society needed protection from, not me.'

All of a sudden Dougal threw the door open with a theatrical gesture and entered brandishing a bottle of sweet champagne. His joviality was forced. Kieran worried whether Brian might guess this was not his first visit.

'Is this an alternative dinner party?' he asked.

Kieran could tell, from the tone of his voice and the look in his eyes, that he was not seriously annoyed. It might even be an offer to rescue him. Dougal filled their glasses and put the bottle down next to the empty one on the table.

'So are you going to stay the night after all?'

'Looks like it,' Brian answered, in his habitual, vaguely arrogant way. 'I'm drinking, amn't I?'

'The spare bedroom is made up, with towels and everything. I'm sorry it doesn't have an *en suite*. The bathroom's just across the corridor. You and Gavin can turn in whenever you feel like it. God knows when breakfast will be. I don't know about Kieran, but I'm going to have the most appalling hangover tomorrow. Don't feel you have to wait up for the other guests. We all know what Rory's like. He may never go unless his Catalan man drags him off.'

Dougal was blustering in a way that showed how insecure Brian made him feel. There was a moment's silence. He headed for the door.

'Come and join us when you're ready.'

'Oh, I think we're ready now,' said Kieran.

'If you don't mind,' said Brian, 'I'll stay on for a bit and finish the story I was reading.'

24

Dashkur and Shiram had no difficulty in finding the House of Butterflies, whose owner's name was Hyundar. When he learnt that they had spent the night in the open, on the temple perimeter, his face flushed with shame.

'Why did you not tell me you had nowhere to go? You could have had a chamber to yourselves beneath this roof.'

Shiram noted how Dashkur grew silent and absorbed when the rebeck was placed in his hands. He turned it slowly round, so that the light, penetrating from the courtyard into the shadowy room where they stood, ran caressingly, like ripples of water, across the wood.

'Cherry,' was all he said.

Only one string was unbroken. He patiently disentangled the remnants of the others, then asked for seed oil to lubricate the tuning pegs. Hyundar had strings of finest gut laid ready by. When they were in place and taut, Dashkur reached out, without a word, for the bow that Hyundar held. He surveyed it carefully, rather as Shiram might have observed a horse.

'Resin?' he enquired.

That took a little longer to find. A servant was despatched and eventually brought a small block from the kitchen, where it had been destined to a different use. Shiram wondered if Dashkur would immediately break into melody, but no, he drew the bow across each string in turn, then plucked it with his finger, until he was satisfied with the tuning.

'It will have to be done again before I play,' he said. Then, looking at Shiram: 'I had sworn not to use a bow again until . . . But my redress is close at hand, I do not doubt it. This bow will help me right the wrong. I cannot believe the gods will punish me for breaking my oath.'

Hyundar had understood not a word of this, and did not seek enlightenment. He found the intimacy between Dashkur and his servant rather odd.

'Do you like the instrument?' he asked.

Dashkur nodded, and Hyundar placed one hand gently upon his shoulder before saying: 'It is yours for today. But if you choose to share my bed tonight, it can be yours for ever.'

A smile flitted over Dashkur's features.

'I have plenty of gold and silver, and lands between here and the mountains,' the older man insisted. 'My humour is not changeable. You will find me a faithful lover.'

'Wait until the result of the competition is known,' said Dashkur.

They placed the rebeck in a case of supple calf's leather, knotted the thongs on it, then set off for the Palace, two of Hyundar's household following on their heels.

A crowd had gathered around the gateway. When, however, the guards saw Hyundar, they formed a passage for him and his companions. They proceeded past the fountains of the outer courtyard and the gardens of the inner to a vaulted chamber, whose walls were of brilliant white, lit with windows of alabaster. The Caliph's throne stood vacant and, next to it and only a little smaller, that of the Chief Assessor. Guests clustered round a rectangular cleared space in the centre of the room, marked out in the geometrical patterns of the tiled floor. Hyundar was accommodated in a carved, high-backed wooden chair, inlaid with mother of pearl and decked with brightly coloured cushions. Dashkur sat on a low stool in front of him, while Shiram and the other two servants tucked themselves into the standing crowd behind.

There was a flourish of trumpets from the musicians' gallery. All those who were sitting, or lounging on cushions, rose as the Chief Assessor entered from one door. Another flourish, and Al-Hujan appeared in solemn procession from the opposite side, wearing a particularly magnificent turban of interwoven cloths, topped with a diamond, which it must have taken a good part of the morning to assemble. Behind him, dressed with simple dignity, strode a youth Dashkur realized must be Ka. The beauty of his rival took his breath away, enhanced as it was by the

278

unequivocal melancholy of his expression. His looks were of a kind rarely seen in Birjand: hair as black as a crow's wing, with here and there the glint of a premature white strand emphasizing the liquid sheen of all the rest, long, dark eyelashes and piercing blue eyes. He was cleanshaven. Dashkur thought everyone was going to sit down when there was a further, unexpected blast of trumpets.

As it died away, another music was heard, from fifes, Jews' harps and plucked strings. A chapel of small children danced barefoot into the centre of the room, wearing baggy trousers of pink silk and pale blue singlets. Dashkur recognized the first two instruments. He had never seen the third, two cords strung across a tortoise shell to act as sounding-board. He was struggling to identify the modes of their strange music when the chapel fell silent, the children stood stock still and a chiming of tiny bells filled the air. Shian-Tal had arrived.

She, too, might have been dancing. In fact, she was moving with the steps obligatory for a prince or princess of the horse people on ceremonial occasions, sliding the sole of each foot forward along the floor while maintaining her torso and her shoulders in perfect equilibrium, and moving her head slowly from side to side to scrutinize the assembled company. Her sandals had long, curving tips, like the tendrils of a climbing plant seeking support. She was clothed in a single garment of blue, but such a blue as had never been seen in Tabriz till that day. Perhaps the divers who hunt for corals, in the ocean far to the south, might have recognized it, although even when the sun's rays at midday strike the surface of the waves directly, and the movement of the currents refracts its light below into a hundred different shades, it is hard to believe their magnificence could rival Shian-Tal's mantle. Had she stood in the middle of the desert in the hour before sunset, when the descending planet sets fires burning all along the horizon, and on every side the tent of the sky turns to an incandescent, throbbing blue, stealing that great arc to make her fabric, she could not have obtained a more splendid robe.

On her head she bore a tapering structure of whalebone, just like a tree whose branches are long at the base, then grow shorter towards the summit. To each extremity a bell was attached,

279

giving out a clear note when it chimed. So perfect was her deportment that the bells made no sound as long as she sat still. But when she walked, or danced, or laughed and threw her head back, their music cast an enchantment on the company more powerful than that of the trumpets, or even of the chapel of nomad children.

An odd, ungainly figure waddled along behind her, a dwarf not more than half her height, tonsured, with a beard and rigid, twirled moustachios that made Dashkur think of a cat's whiskers. His tunic was of pale grey with golden braiding, his arms concealed by its long, floppy sleeves. He was the princess's interpreter. When she sat down, his mouth, as he stood next to her on tiptoe, was at the level of her ear. Throughout all that followed, he muttered to her ceaselessly, until the music began. From the expression on her face there could be no doubt she was listening to every word. From time to time she would laugh, or nod her head, and on each occasion the bells chimed out a different symphony.

The formal speeches were got through at record speed. Everybody present was in a hurry for the musical competition to start. Dashkur noted that the Caliph and the Chief Assessor did not look at one another so much as once. Each appeared to be totally oblivious to the other's presence. The casket filled with gold and silver she had brought with her as a prize was set at Shian-Tal's feet. The three chosen judges were led in, blindfolded, and given cushions to sit cross-legged on. In front of each an abacus was placed, so that they could register their verdict on the various contestants.

The tune that had been fixed upon as a basis for the variations was familiar to Dashkur in a slightly altered form. One by one, the six competitors the Lord of Masques had selected performed their chaconnes. When each had finished, deft hands set the wooden beads on the abacuses rattling back and forth. A scribe recorded the verdict with a goose quill on a roll of parchment. Dashkur found them gifted. They managed the ornaments of the third, fifth and seventh series excellently. However, when they reached the twelfth, and double ornamentation was demanded, the limits of their skill became apparent. It was as much as they could do to meet the requirements of the form, and they were so exhausted that the closing restatement of the theme in double measure came as an anti-climax.

At the end of each chaconne, Shian-Tal and her interpreter patted the palm of one hand with the second and third fingers of the other. This was their equivalent of clapping. The Chief Assessor sat impassively through all of it, giving no sign of impatience, while Al-Hujan listened with growing concern. At last Vendlin was led on.

'You did not tell me he was blind,' Dashkur murmured to Hyundar.

The leader of the Chief Assessor's private chapel was a man aged fifty or over. The lids flickered ceaselessly over his sightless eyes and a continuous tremor shook his hands, until they grasped his instrument. Then he was like a fish which has panted on the beach and is restored to water, or a bird released from its cage into its native element. From the very first stroke of his bow, even the most uneducated listener could detect a master's touch. The Chief Assessor followed his every movement with lively interest, almost as if he himself had been generating the variations from his own head, while Al-Hujan wrung his hands nervously.

When Vendlin had concluded, thunderous applause drowned out the rattling of the abacuses. The points awarded by the judges were nearly double those of the previous contestant. Shian-Tal and her interpreter engaged in a heated exchange. The princess did not appear content with the outcome of her competition. Al-Hujan hid his face in his palms. The Lord of Masques, whose thankless task it was to preside over his employer's discomfiture, had risen to his feet to proclaim Vendlin the winner, when Hyundar interrupted:

'One player remains to be heard.'

'And who may that be?' asked the Chief Assessor.

Without saying anything, Hyundar gestured towards Dashkur, who had stepped into the cleared space.

'Impossible. The list of contestants was drawn up three days ago. Additions are excluded.'

'Who is the player?' Vendlin, the blind virtuoso had spoken, inclining his head strangely to one side, like a bird contemplating a seed before picking it up to swallow it.

'Dashkur, son of Sherepnan.'

Ka started, and his mouth fell open in astonishment and alarm. Only Dashkur noticed his reaction. All other eyes were turned to the main actors in the scene.

'And who may he be?' asked the Chief Assessor, his voice full of contempt.

Al-Hujan was looking up, hope of victory rekindled.

'My father is Lord Advocate of Birjand.'

'The school of rebeck players in Birjand,' Vendlin said, 'was once renowned in all of Persia. I myself studied there in my youth.'

'And it shall be again,' said Dashkur stoutly.

'But whose instrument will you play upon?'

Shiram removed the rebeck from its case. Dashkur held it high so that all present could see it.

'His instrument,' said Hyundar, 'is the twin of your own, Vendlin. Like babes from the one womb, they sprang from the same tree, and the hands that made yours, like a just parent, did not stint one in order to favour the other.'

'I had believed that rebeck lost,' said Vendlin. 'Then the man must play, for nothing could be more welcome to my ears than to hear the tones of an instrument whose harmonies must rival mine.'

'How can this be?' the Chief Assessor roared. 'All Tabriz knows that my minions sought that rebeck high and low throughout one spring and summer. Why did you not produce it then, Hyundar? How dare you keep it hidden from me?'

'To honour my wife's memory, I had sworn it should be silent. Not until my eyes fell on this youth did I alter my resolve.'

'Useless,' said the Chief Assessor, turning to Al-Hujan with a menacing air. 'The rules of the competition have been set and cannot be altered.'

'I think,' said the Caliph quietly, 'the princess must judge whether this youth should play or not.'

The message took a moment or two to be conveyed to Shian-Tal. Her reply made the interpreter beam.

'Let him play,' he pronounced in his peculiar, sing-song accent. 'He is to play three times. After each piece the blind man may perform again if he wishes, to see if he can match the young man's skill.'

282

Dashkur turned towards Al-Hujan.

'What,' he asked, his voice trembling at first, then steadier, 'will you give me, my lord, if I should win the competition?'

'Both your fists full of gold and diamonds,' the Caliph replied, without hesitation.

'I wish for neither gold nor diamonds,' said Dashkur.

'What do you want, then?'

'For each piece that I play, I shall formulate a request. And if I am judged the winner, you shall meet them.'

'You are bold, young man. What might these requests be?'

Ka leapt to his feet.

'Stop him, father. Stop him. Don't let him play!'

The Caliph's cheeks flushed with anger.

'What is your part in this? Am I to follow your commands? What son dictates his father's actions?'

The cunning man put two and two together.

'Is this youth known to you? Has he followed you from Birjand?'

Ka was afraid to speak out. As he hesitated, there was a massive tinkling and jangling of bells, and Shian-Tal rose from her chair. What emerged from her lips was a not unpleasant croaking, like the dialogue of frogs in a mud pond at twilight, or like the cries of storks as they lift themselves into the evening sky for one final circuit, before settling on their chimney top nests to sleep.

The interpreter looked anxious.

'What is the princess's will?' put in the Lord of Masques.

'She says, what great lord pauses to find out the nature of a request before he grants it? Is the lord of Tabriz so poor, or so craven, that he thinks a youth may harbour wants he cannot satisfy? An end to this bickering. On with it. Let him begin.'

In the silence that preceded Dashkur's playing, the falling of the water in the fountains two courtyards away could be heard distinctly. A sensitive ear could even have detected how the wind frayed the descending jet, scattering it in a rain of drops that tore the surface of the water as rough sand can graze the skin. Shiram had been feeling acutely nervous. Once Dashkur began, all apprehension vanished. With the earlier competitors, he had been in constant tension as to whether they would bring their chaconne off or not. Even when Vendlin was performing, his attention was taken up with admiring the blind man's virtuosity and the deft movements of his fingers as they stopped the strings in different places.

When Dashkur made music, Shiram forgot everything but the tones themselves. It was a component of Dashkur's gift that he should totally eclipse himself in this way, pointing, as it were, beyond himself and his ability to the sounds that he produced. Never had complexity been made to sound so simple. The double ornamentation of the twelfth series rang limpid, crystalline, so that Shiram had the illusion he, too, could have managed it after barely a month of lessons. Restated in double measure, the theme made a new impression, as if the experience of the variations it had undergone had altered it irrevocably.

Utter silence greeted the ending. All eyes turned to Vendlin.

'Let him play on. I cannot rival that.'

Dashkur sang next. He chose a ballad that is particularly beloved of the washerwomen of Birjand. It speaks of the sitar, a race of spirits who dwell in knolls and hollows at the edge of the steppe and often assume human form to meddle in the dealings of men and women. A man of the sitar sings the song. He has got a human girl with child and she, to conceal her dishonour from her family, brings it from the city to the knoll where they made love and leaves it there for him to find. As the spirit strives to quieten his son, he recounts the story of their courtship and its birth.

Vendlin had difficulty in speaking this time. His mouth and lips were dry and he struggled to bring forth words he could not form. The Chief Assessor could control himself no longer.

'Play, you vile knave!' he shouted. 'Do you intend to shame me in front of this whole assembly? What do you think I pay and house you for? Are you to thwart me so late on in life?'

'It is not I that thwart you,' Vendlin said, 'but this youth's skill that binds me to silence.' And then, to Dashkur, in tones of infinite gentleness: 'Play once more, man of Birjand.'

The last piece Dashkur played was in binary form, its two contrasting, yet complementary halves like husband and wife, or dear friends whose affection never wavers. He moved repeatedly from one to the other, discovering resemblances his listeners had never suspected, so that there were moments when it seemed he played one theme, not two. In the final variation it was as if one waited for the other after death and, in the end, they were reunited at a level where further separation was not possible.

Silence again. Everyone waited to see what Vendlin would do. There were tears on the old man's cheeks.

'Bring him close to me,' he ordered and, when Dashkur stood in front of him, leant forward, grasped his ankle, and bathed his feet with kisses and with tears. The triumphant outburst of the onlookers set the vaults ringing in response.

'What, then, are your requests?' asked the Caliph sharply.

'First,' said Dashkur, 'there languishes, in a dungeon beneath your palace, a man who arrived from Birjand three days ago. Let him be freed and brought before us.'

Leflef was unwashed and unshaven, with a two days' stubble on his chin. His every feature evinced terror and despair. When the guards brought him in, he fell to his knees before the Caliph and then, raising his head, caught sight of Dashkur.

'Your second request?'

'That he should be allowed to remain here, as your son's faithful companion, for as long as both of them desire it.'

'This cannot be!' cried Al-Hujan.

'My lord,' the Lord of Masques said gravely, 'you are bound by your promise, given in the hearing of all present in this place.'

'What does the princess say to this?'

Shian-Tal rose to speak. The dwarf interpreted her words.

'It is not my mistress's intention to dwell here in Tabriz. By the terms of her marriage contract she will visit her husband's bed no fewer than four times each year, for as long as it may take to bear three children. Her home is in the vastness of the deserts and her natural place is on a horse's back. What her husband may do in her absence and who shares his bed is no concern of hers. Nor should he inquire into her doings when she is far from this city.'

He sat down again. Al-Hujan tried to think of a rejoinder to make to this speech but none came to mind. The treaty with the Great Khan was too precious for him to baulk at any subsidiary conditions, no matter how oddly they might strike himself or his subjects.

'And your third request?' he asked, a little lamely.

285

'A horse,' Dashkur said simply, and pointed to Shiram. 'The man who acts as my servant is not my servant, but a son of Wek the carpet-seller. We rode here on a single horse but we shall ride away on two. This night I was united with him as I have been with no other man. From henceforth we shall walk through life on neighbouring paths, until death takes the luckier of us first.'

'And Shian-Tal's treasure chest?' asked the Lord of Masques.

'Perhaps the Caliph will be good enough to have it conveyed to Birjand under armed guard. I have not forgotten the daughters of Shisnal, languishing in their garden. Thanks to Shian-Tal's munificence, each of them can buy the bridegroom of her choice.'

25

When Kieran and Dougal got back to the dining-room, an important connection had been established.

'We've discovered we're related,' cried Ramon.

'What do you mean?' asked Nicol.

'One of Rory's lovers has been living with my uncle Josep for the last fourteen years. What does that make us?' said Ramon, laughing and looking at Rory. 'Am I your cousin? Your nephew?'

'They met in the Palau,' said Rory, embarrassed by Ramon's enthusiasm and wanting to divert attention from himself.

'That's not quite accurate!' Ramon protested.

'What's the Palau?' asked Gavin.

'It's a concert hall,' Rory answered, 'the most beautiful concert hall in Europe. Concert halls are usually designed to put you into subjection, so that you listen to the music with the right sort of cowed seriousness. As if you weren't entitled to be there and certainly were never intended to enjoy yourself. Instead this one looks like an ice-cream parlour designed by a Mediterranean Charles Rennie Mackintosh. It has a ceiling of garish ceramic tiles. All the pillars are clothed in glittering mosaics. It's like the Arabian Nights conjured up in a Catalan farmhouse.'

'Is he right?' asked Gavin. 'Is the building really in such bad taste?'

'No,' said Ramon, not a bit offended. 'It was designed for a patriotic choral society. Not long after they put it up, the style went out of fashion. A strong current of opinion in Barcelona was in favour of pulling it down again. Josep Pla despaired of the place because it was so poorly soundproofed. All it needed was for a horse and cart to drive past and you could no longer hear the music properly. Luckily it survived. Nobody would think of altering it now. It's even been extensively renovated.'

'The walls on either side are of coloured glass,' said Rory. 'It's in a very awkward site, squeezed into the corner of two narrow streets. The architect wanted to make as much use of the daylight as possible. You can't get a proper view of the facade because of the position of the building. All you can do is crane your neck and imagine how it would look if there was a cleared space in front of it. The best time to go is on a Sunday morning. In spring and summer they have no need of artificial lighting. The architect put the auditorium above street level, on the first floor, so that you have to climb stairs to reach it whatever part you're sitting in. Entering is always a surprise. There is a glorious central glass lantern, a constellation of female choristers, ranged in a circle like the petals of a flower. The middle part projects downwards. It is shaped like a huge drop of liquid, gathering and about to fall. It makes me think of Klimt, or the different orders of angels in a frescoed dome in Italy.'

'High up to one side of the stage four Valkyries charge out from the wall, complete with horses, leather bridles and spears,' Ramon put in, 'just in case anyone in the audience might be tempted to fall asleep. There are two other horses above the raised seats at the back. When I was a child I used to want to jump up and swing on an outstretched hoof.'

'You'd probably have broken it!' said Rory.

Ramon shook his head.

'No, no. I wasn't heavy enough. The seats at the back are the cheapest seats but you hear best from them. The tiles on the wall are dark crimson and have an odd visual effect. There are big squares with smaller squares stuck on at each of the four corners. If you see them from a distance, although all the lines are straight and there are only right angles, it looks as if they are spinning round, like Catherine wheels, or like windmills, with the smaller squares threatening to fly off at any moment.'

'Behind the stage,' continued Rory, 'the wall curves in a semi-circle. It has pottery busts set into it, nine on either side, of women playing traditional Catalan instruments. From the waist downwards they are flat mosaic, with feet peeping out underneath their dresses. One of them is dancing, and the fabric swirls so convincingly you could almost believe she was actually moving. The wall behind is deep ochre, with glistening fragments of tiles pasted in at different angles . . .'

'*Trencadís* is the Catalan word,' Ramon interrupted. 'Smashed-up pots. It's what Gaudí used for the chimneys on the Güell Palace.'

'It could be sunlight on the roofs of houses,' Rory went on, 'if roofs were able to shift and shimmer like the surface of the sea.'

'The stairs are a marvellous place for cruising,' said Ramon.

'I never noticed that! What do you mean?'

'There are twin flights opposite each other. At each landing you have to decide which direction to go in, because they move out from the centre and join up again on the next floor. It's a vertical zigzag. The notices telling you which floor you are heading for reflect everything just like mirrors. Thanks to them, as well as sizing up whoever's on the other side, you can make eye contact with people in the crowd immediately behind you. It's the perfect way to decide if someone's really interested or not. That's where Toni first *saw* my Uncle Josep. They met somewhere quite different, however.'

Cruising was the last thing on Toni's mind when he attended the Sunday morning concerts. Once or twice he managed to persuade Rory to accompany him but, while he loved the building, and was passionate about opera, the Scotsman had little patience with orchestral music. His barely disguised lack of interest troubled Toni, interfering with his enjoyment of the occasion.

The autumn after his breakdown his mother bought him a season ticket for the whole year, in the hope that it would help him regain a measure of inner peace. The concerts punctuated the gradual but inexorable changes which took place in Toni's life and laid the basis for what came afterwards. Like all repeated actions, they belonged to a time scale of their own, and could make moments that were really very far apart seem juxtaposed. Toni kept the programme of that year's season. Merely by glancing over it and remembering the pieces he had heard, he could evoke those months with absolute clarity. A benevolent god watched over the place, he sometimes thought, allowing concert after concert to unfold as if turning the pages of a book already written, whose contents Toni could only discover at the appropriate time, according to a predetermined rhythm he was powerless to alter.

The concerts are a core ceremony of bourgeois life in Barcelona. Perhaps that is why Toni's mother assumed that they would steady him. While all three sons had been baptized, the family never attended mass on Sunday. Toni's father was a lapsed Catholic of the secretly nostalgic kind, a man who gave up going to church because others would have considered it unenlightened in one with his social and political convictions. At most, he could have become a Catholic militant and made a great song and dance about it. But he was not a man for outward show, and desired nothing more than peace and tranquillity in his family, however high the price he had to pay.

He died, mercifully quickly, of a cancer of the throat, when Toni was twenty-three. His wife nursed him at home throughout the final weeks. More than once his lips quivered, as he rehearsed the phrases he would use to ask her to summon a priest. It would have soothed him to receive the last rites before embarking on that final journey. But he could predict the expression her face would assume on hearing them. It was enough to stop him.

Toni's mother was a convinced atheist who subjected the church, and all its practices, to open scorn, both within the family and further afield. Her parents were agricultural labourers and had experienced extreme poverty in the years during and after the war in Spain. While she appreciated to the full the comforts and privileges of the middle-class life style she had achieved, the move to Barcelona had never quite extinguished the egalitarian notions she absorbed in her early years. They continued to haunt her just as religious nostalgia haunted her husband. As she had a very different character, she insisted that those close to her should assume, or at least mimic, her own attitudes.

Her two elder sons were married and settled by the time her husband died. For reasons he did not discuss, Toni went to university in Madrid. When his mother became a widow, he got a transfer back, taking his final exams in his home city. As the youngest son, he had always been her favourite. She, in her turn, was aware of a different quality in him, one she liked, even admired, yet at the same time feared. Not until he first left home did she dare give it a name. She kept the label to herself, never mentioning it to her husband. A woman of endless intellectual curiosity, she had read and admired both Wilde and Gide, and knew from newspapers and magazines about the mushrooming of gay organizations in the States and in Catalonia itself. So when she and Toni found themselves sharing the family flat, it proved a relatively simple matter to talk things through and place everything in the clear light of day.

As well as rooted political radicalism and a deep respect for culture and education, she imbibed from her father a sense of the right of each individual to be different, to command his or her own chosen space. So she rarely questioned Toni about his comings and goings. When the relationship with Rory was at its most intense, he might only call in at the flat once or twice each week, to collect some papers or track down a shirt, or a pair of trousers he particularly wanted to wear. He never brought home dirty washing or expected her to prepare a meal for him. Nevertheless he phoned her unfailingly each day, not long after the late lunch which is customary in Barcelona, to hear how her morning at the office had been, the details of a card party with friends the previous night, or the latest vicissitudes in the life of an alcoholic cousin, whose family was inexorably falling apart.

Toni was convinced you heard music better in the mornings. The ears were more alert, more finely tuned in the hours immediately after wakening. It might have been an effect of the medication he was taking, or because his dose was rapidly decreasing, restoring to him the full gamut of emotions and sensations, that throughout that spring he greeted each day, not with dread, but with excitement. There were moments when he conceived of himself as poised on a hill of happiness, ready to take flight. It was not a happiness he could account for easily. Rory's relentless infidelities, and the sheer nastiness of the man he tried to replace him with, had so weakened his defences that in the end the only thing he could do was let them be washed away completely.

He expected that would cause a kind of madness, and indeed, for several weeks he was unable to carry out the simplest of everyday tasks, to bring himself to wash or shave, to find clean clothes, or even rise from his bed. That was gone now. When he awoke, his hearing was like a virgin page, a luxurious sheet of textured paper that would ruffle at the slightest noise, the way static electricity raises the hairs on a woollen blanket, if you pass your hand across it. He awaited the first sounds of the day as, in a Chinese calligrapher's workshop, a page might anticipate its first contact with the brush, watching the black ink glisten on the hairs with a mixture of voluptuousness and terror.

His bedroom looked on to an inner courtyard not far from Passeig de Gràcia in the Eixample, one of those courtyards that are inexplicably silent, despite the relentless flow of traffic in the geometrically patterned streets they offer refuge from. The first noise of the day might be the barking of the downstairs neighbour's poodle, rejoicing at being released into the sunlight, or birdsong from the caged thrushes two balconies away to the left. Yet Toni imagined that the light itself had a vibration, that its throbbing could translate itself into sound, that the silence was not uniform but differentiated, endowed with a texture of its own so that, if he paid close attention, he could guess the aspect of the skies, and even the temperature he would encounter when he opened the window and stepped out onto the balcony.

He was convalescing and he knew it. That awareness helped him to let go of time. There was no way he could dictate the pace of healing or take responsibility for it. He watched the process with a detachment he maintained, even on days when he plunged back into the cruellest stretches of his breakdown, as if nothing had changed at all. He did his best to reassure himself that, if he could only endure it, the nightmare would vanish definitively, like an island in the middle of the ocean an aeroplane circles repeatedly over, spiralling up into the sky till it has reached a sufficient altitude to depart for good.

For several months he felt too vulnerable to have sex. He was unwilling to go back to the bar where he had picked Rory up because, though he was preparing to leave Barcelona and return home, the Scotsman would almost certainly be cruising in a corner, neither glamorous nor even carefully dressed, but with a characteristic intensity and skill that meant he rarely failed to score the nights he wanted to. There were other bars Toni could have gone to. The problem was, the man who had abused him was a regular customer at several of them. Toni knew that, if they bumped into each other, the man would try to start things up again, as part of what had been a regular pattern. He lacked confidence in his own ability to resist. That would have begun a downward spiral. Now he understood only too well where it would lead.

In the end he decided on the sauna. It was a place where he could spectate harmlessly until he felt strong enough to get involved. And he enjoyed the physical comfort of it, the warmth, the repeated showering and the stifling intensity of the closed room with its electric brazier, which always made him feel as if his nostrils were being pinched.

He used to argue about it with his friend Oriol.

'You have to grasp the fact that gay men fall into two classes,' Oriol would explain. 'There are the ones who make commitments and try to build relationships. The other ones go to saunas and parks and station toilets. They hate themselves and are promiscuous and never make anything of their lives. My fear is that you're moving from one category into the other. The very idea of a sauna disgusts me. How could you possibly meet anyone there you would want to get to know better? Most of the regulars only use the place because they are too ugly to show themselves in the light of day.'

'You can't be certain if you've never been,' Toni replied. 'I go, don't I? I may be nothing great, but I'm certainly not so ugly I'm afraid to walk down the street and eye up a man or two.'

'But it's anonymous and indiscriminate. That's not what sex is for.'

Toni was extremely fond of Oriol, who had spent his adolescent years in a seminary in Girona, never quite managing to shake off its influence. Patiently he tried to make him see reason.

'I consider it to be a kind of sex temple.'

Oriol spluttered with disbelief.

'No, seriously, in a society that had a proper culture of sex it would be available to everybody on demand, like food or medicine. People in general would be much happier if they could have easy access to touching and closeness whenever they felt the need of it. It's been proved that orgasms are good for you. And that's what a sauna provides.'

'First of all, it's not for everyone. Secondly, it leads to a distortion in people's sexuality. Who ever goes there just to have one contact? From what I hear, nobody knows when to stop. It's Sodom and Gomorrah all over again.'

Toni would lose his temper.

'What makes you so sure you know what sex is for? You can't transfer your Catholic dogma lock, stock and barrel to gay men, as if we were no different from heterosexuals!'

He met Jaume in that sauna. It lies in the oldest part of Barcelona, on the same side of the Ramblas as the Cathedral, down an innocent-looking lane which turns into a dead end when the iron gate at the bottom of it is locked. Each time Toni turned the corner, he found the surroundings so silent it made him wonder if the sauna had closed down, or if he was going to find it deserted that particular afternoon. It gave him a strange feeling, when he passed the end of the lane last thing at night, having bid farewell to a group of friends, or on his way back to work after lunch, to see the lamp above the door still burning, a sign that that world persisted, with its own rules of behaviour, parallel to the world outside, but so distinct from it. The continuity was reassuring. Like international trains, the sauna was indifferent to the calendar, to night and day. Its uninterrupted service showed no respect for holidays or feastdays. A friend had told him the place closed for a few hours on Christmas Eve, then stayed open without a break until the day after Boxing Day.

Once he was inside, he might have been on the platform of a major railway station. Longing for sex, and the likelihood of getting it, produced an anxiety that kept everyone in ceaseless motion. The clients could have been zealous young policemen on the beat, aching for promotion, or frenzied postmen combing the streets, in search of an address where they can finally deliver a letter they have long been desperate to get rid of.

Oriol could not have been more wrong about the quality of the men. Wearing nothing but a towel about their loins, many of the clients revealed a beauty which made Toni gasp. It was comforting to reflect that this source of joy, at least, would not dry up. Each generation of school leavers, each military levy paid its tribute to the sauna. And if a small proportion of the users were beyond retirement age, surely they had not lost the right to enjoy themselves all the same.

The corridors were labyrinthine. The facilities took up two floors, with stairs at either end. If Toni concentrated, he could always find his way to the showers or the bar, the Turkish baths or the darkroom, which was never more than semi-dark. But he never quite managed to get the hang of the sauna's geography. Once inside, he lost all sense of time. Sunday was a timeless day anyway, without the structuring of office hours, or shops opening and closing. More than once he shut himself carefully in a cubicle, rolled one of his towels up for a pillow and slept, with the endless rhythm of that pacing, just beyond the partition, as a background to his dreams.

That was the pattern of his Sundays: first the concert, then lunch with his mother, then the sauna. It was a day he especially relished. He soon became acquainted with the faces of the other season ticket holders at the Palau. By the time the spring days lengthened and Easter arrived, he had pieced together the stories of the groups he saw around him. There were couples, extended families, individuals of all ages and sodalities of older women, who resolutely donned their furs until the temperature outside rendered such precautions preposterous, even for them. If they slumbered during the pauses between movements, the resumption of the music stirred them to furious activity. They rummaged in a pocket or a handbag for a handkerchief or a bag of sweets, unwrapping the cellophane with painstaking slowness, ostensibly to reduce the disturbance but, in Toni's opinion, because this protracted the crackling for the longest possible time.

Amongst the regulars was a man who never brought his wife. He came accompanied by two boys on the verge of puberty, presumably his sons. Their father was affectionate towards them, placing a hand on the shoulder of one when he showed impatience or gently ruffling the other's hair, to alert him to an important section of the piece that they were hearing. More than once the older boy arrived with a pocket score under his arm, turning the pages with excitement and circumspection, as he traced the link between what was written there and what his ears perceived. The father took notes in a small notebook with a spiral binding. Toni was immensely curious about the content of the notes. Was he a writer? A poet?

During the interval Toni would make his way down the stairs

which filled Ramon with such enthusiasm to buy himself a glass of champagne at the bar. Leaning against the wall, he could observe the father and his sons as they pored over the programme, discussing with considerable animation the standard of the performance and the music that was still to come. As far as Toni could make out, the older boy was more than willing to argue with his father. The younger one was dreamy and withdrawn, perhaps jealous of his brother, although his features resembled the father's more closely. If he added the boys' faces together, then subtracted the father's, what was left must represent the mother. Time and again he hoped to see her so as to check the accuracy of his deductions. She never appeared.

'It sounds like you're falling in love with him, the way you talk,' Oriol observed wrily.

'Who do you mean?'

'Don't be disingenuous. You know perfectly well I mean the father.'

'If I am, then it's Platonic. He's as straight as a die. What more proof could you ask for than two sons? Let me daydream about him, seeing there's no possibility of anything happening. It isn't going to do me any harm.'

Even in his worst moments, Toni's ability to draw did not desert him. There were sketches from the bleakest part of his breakdown he could only look at on good days, because they brought back the horrors that had possessed him with exceptional vividness.

The restraint normally prevailing in his relations with his mother had slackened when he came out of hospital, not least because Rory became a regular visitor to the flat during the next few months. One barrier between the different parts of Toni's life collapsed. Initially suspicious, she came to treat the Scotsman with respect and even a kind of formalized affection.

She admired the drawings no less than Rory. Toni knew they were of exceptional quality and heralded a new phase in his work. He and his mother discussed his employment situation at length. He was eager for a change. To his surprise, he had been taken back into the same office without demur after his breakdown. They even gave him half pay for the weeks he had been absent.

'That's because you're so talented. Don't you realize?' Rory pointed out.

Now that things were in full swing again, he experienced fewer twinges of embarrassment at the thought that the people he rubbed shoulders with each day knew what he had been through, knew about the hospital and the medication and his sexuality. The job frustrated him. All he got to do was develop other people's ideas or put the finishing touches to material he considered clumsy and outdated.

With his mother's full approval, he took a daring step. He assembled a portfolio, included the darkest of his drawings, and sent it to a successful graphic designer he particularly admired. That was late in February. A month, a month and a half passed, then one day a phone call came. His mother took it. Toni was summoned to the designer's studio for an interview the following Monday afternoon.

Maybe it was nervousness and excitement that made him lose one of his contact lenses the preceding Saturday. The goggles he used to protect his eyes when swimming had sprung a leak. He took the lenses out before going for his shower and, when he opened the case on returning to his cubicle, found only one inside. No amount of hunting could unearth the lost one. Toni left his home number with the janitor at the swimming baths, who promised he would phone immediately if it came to light.

He turned up at the concert the following morning with a pair of glasses he had not used for years. His mother did not tell him how attractive he looked in them and there was nobody else to enlighten him. He still wore a black jacket, though not the one Rory had first seen him in. His cotton shirt with its thin, vertical blue lines was unbuttoned at the neck. It was enough to have to wear a tie during the week. Anyone who wished to could observe how sturdily his neck rose from his shoulders. Perched on the sharp nose, the old-fashioned glasses gave an academic look to his heart-shaped, Italianate face, the dark curls framing it as plentiful as ever, accentuating the mixture of fragility and strength which was the secret of his charm. He would have distracted the music critic, sitting only a few rows away between his sons, even more than usual that day, oblivious as on other Sundays to the effect he was producing. Inexplicably, the man was absent. It made the concert somehow incomplete.

Toni left his glasses in his inside pocket, settled the jacket on a hanger, slipped the hanger into the locker next to his remaining clothes and his shoes, which had his socks tucked carefully inside, then turned the key in the lock. He had decided that there was no point in wearing glasses in the sauna. They would steam up for the first quarter of an hour and he had nowhere safe to leave them if he should wish to take them off. He fitted the elastic band carefully around his wrist. He was accident prone these days and it would really be a nuisance for him to lose his locker key.

He had to admit he could not see a great deal. To be honest, that added excitement to the experience. He was not quite short-sighted enough to run the risk of knocking into people as he sauntered down the corridors. He could make out the shape of each body – amused, as always, at the way so many men lose control of their bellies the minute they bid farewell to adolescence, while others, by natural advantage or thanks to self-discipline, keep that expansion within reasonable limits. He felt confident he could tell which faces pleased him, by the regularity of their features, the set of a head, or the particular quality of a smile.

Returning interrogative glances was impossible, however. He was uncertain which were aimed at him, blind to whether the eyes betrayed interest, arousal or disdain. He started counting the months that had passed since he last had sex. For a considerable period he had been too depressed even to masturbate. It brought back Rory's image, memories of the Scotsman's body and of how they had fucked together. The pain had sometimes been nearly unbearable. Today the thought of it left him curiously indifferent. That disturbed him, made him feel disorientated.

He broke his fast in the most banal way imaginable. He was standing in the darkroom, curious but uninvolved, careful not to go too close to the knot of bodies in the far corner, wondering at the confident indiscriminacy of it all. He had grown tired of the corridors. There was little point in peering into open cubicles today because he could see so little. In any case, the scenarios would be the same. Here two men chatted over a friendly ciga-

298

rette, there another smoked on his own. A third played with himself, though without glasses Toni could not make out how much he had to play with, while a fourth lay stomach down, buttocks exposed. The request was so explicit it made Toni's head reel. It would have been rude to stop for too long at the door of a cubicle and the person inside could easily get the wrong idea. That might provoke either a rejection or an invitation, neither of which Toni felt ready to deal with. Here in the darkroom you could stand still and get lost in your own thoughts, without feeling lonely or conspicuous.

He was enjoying the relative peace when he nearly jumped out of his skin. A man sitting behind him, to his right, had run the back of his hand down the hairs on Toni's thigh, with infinite gentleness. He heard suppressed laughter.

'Don't be scared,' the man murmured. 'I won't eat you.'

The hand moved down his thigh again. The pressure was deliberate now. Toni stood stock still. Reaching over to grasp his wrist, the man pulled Toni down to sit beside him. He offered no resistance. The man nuzzled into his shoulder then kissed him slowly on the neck. His hand was in Toni's crotch, investigating the response, taking the measure of his success.

'That's some dick you've got,' he whispered. 'I'm a bit pushed for time. My last train goes at half past eight.'

Toni had lost any sensation of clock time a while ago.

'Why don't we look for a cubicle?'

Not long before there had been plenty of empty cubicles. Now they were all occupied. Had everyone scored simultaneously? Toni felt an urge to giggle as he obediently followed a man whose face he could not see precisely. He walked awkwardly because of his erection. The consummation was comforting, if perfunctory. They even had leisure for a brief chat afterwards. It turned out the man ran a chemist's shop in a provincial town. Although he was in his late forties, he lived with his mother and travelled into Barcelona once a week to visit the sauna.

'Why don't you bring your car? That way you wouldn't be tied down by the trains.'

'Too much trouble. Parking in the centre of Barcelona is a hassle, even on a Sunday,' answered the man.

What about the underground car parks, Toni thought. You can

always get into one of those, especially at weekends. But perhaps everything the man was saying was invented.

'I've seen you here before,' the other said.

'Does your mother know?' asked Toni, cutting him short. He did not want the encounter to mean more to the man than it had to him.

'No. She has problems enough with my brother and his family without having to cope with me as well. She thinks I'm playing five-a-side football. My strip is in a bag down in the locker room.'

Toni smiled, a little bit incredulous.

'Doesn't it make her suspicious? I mean, that everything stays clean?'

'Oh, I stop off on the way home and rub a bit of dirt into my outfit. She hasn't noticed anything so far.'

The man had a nice body smell. The hairs on his chest were springy, just like the curls on Toni's head, if less profuse. A moment later he was gone. Toni stretched out on the couch and lingered for a further quarter of an hour, savouring what had happened, before making his way straight to the showers. He was beginning to get nervous about the meeting the following afternoon. What had the designer made of his work? Maccarese was his name. He was of Italian origin.

Was it too much to hope that there might be an opening? Toni felt ready for a change. He pressed the jet repeatedly, letting the water splash onto his head, cascade over his shoulders, then flow down his arms and sides, moulding his body. He adored standing there, dripping from head to foot. The pleasure made him want to laugh out loud. The man next to him appeared to be enjoying himself too. Toni could have sworn he was smiling in his direction. But he couldn't rely on his sight, and in any case water kept getting into his eyes. When he moved off to dry himself, the man was waiting, completely naked, a towel around his neck. Toni took his body in at a glance. He was slightly taller. Something about his body, the tightness of his hips, set Toni's heart thumping. He realized he could not speak. Was he in the running for another encounter? What would Oriol have said? This might never stop. His dear friend's direst prophecies were being fulfilled. He was addicted.

'My name's Josep,' the man said.

300

Toni said nothing. His mouth was dry.

'Shall we find a cubicle?'

Toni asked himself why it should feel so different this time. The man hardly had leisure to spread their towels on the pallet with its red plastic covering, before Toni was upon him, pushing his knee between his thighs, hugging him tightly, as if what he wanted was to blend with him, to get inside him. Why do I feel I know you, he wondered, when we have never met before?

'Hold on,' the man said, delight in his voice. 'Just take it gently.'

He lifted Toni's face in his hands and touched the lips with his, not opening them, probing, questioning, like the first words in a conversation. Toni relaxed. Words formed in his head. He was afraid the man might slip away, might disappear. He did not tell him so. It would have been too dangerous to expose himself so much this soon. There was an urgency within him he had not known for months. He lay still and the man's lips moved across his cheek, along his chin and down onto his neck, testing the closeness with which he had shaved that morning, learning the contours of his dimpled chin. Toni concentrated on the stranger's smell, as if it told him all he needed to know. As if he could have used it to identify this man for ever after.

'I was sorry to miss the concert this morning,' the man said. 'I'd been looking forward to seeing you.'

26

Toni sat bolt upright. This wasn't possible.

'But you're married,' he almost shouted.

'Easy now, easy now,' Josep murmured, holding him.

Toni broke free and made for the door. He did not know what made him pause. Josep caught his arm.

'I won't let you disappear now I have found you at last,' he said.

'What are you trying to get me involved in?' Toni nearly shouted.

There were concerned voices in the corridor. Someone rattled at the door.

'Nothing. I'm gay, I tell you. I live with my two sons. Where do you expect them to live?'

'What about the mother?'

'She's with someone else. She left them with me. They're my responsibility.'

Toni's hand was still on the doorknob. Uncertain whether to stay or flee, he had one heel on the ground, the other poised for movement. Josep gave his hand a light tug.

'Come back and tell me about the concert. It was Prokofiev, wasn't it?'

Toni's head was in a whirl. He knew he wanted to stay. So why was he resisting? Hadn't he given himself away already by the strength of his reaction? If a married man had come to the sauna for a casual shag, what was there to be so shocked about? He had never thought of himself as a Puritan before. Why not just enjoy it, taking the experience for what it was worth? But he kept seeing Josep, fully dressed, sitting in the Palau with an intent expression on his face, his sons on either side of him.

The next thing he knew he was squatting on the couch again,

in almost exactly the position he had assumed in Rory's bedroom many months before. Putting one arm round his shoulder, Josep laid his other hand on Toni's thigh. He gave his voice a security that did not correspond to what was going on inside him.

'So tell me,' he said. 'Was it good?'

Toni said nothing. Suddenly Josep spoke with a quite different tone.

'I hadn't heard your voice until today,' he said. 'I thought I might never hear it.'

There was a silence and, in the silence, unmistakable, the sound of tears. Unable to believe it, Toni raised his hand and touched Josep's left cheek. He was indeed crying. All at once, like a warm flush rising from the soles of his feet, he was invaded by a glorious sense of power, of a kind he had never experienced in his life before.

'What's the matter?' he asked, incredulous. 'What's coming over you?'

At the back of his mind a voice, bemused, commented that, whatever he might have been expecting, he was no longer in line for sex. Things had taken a very different turn. They had slumped down on the couch now and were lying stretched out next to each other. He held Josep gently, letting him cry till he had had his fill. The tears took a long time to stop. When Josep was perfectly calm, Toni picked up one of the towels, which had fallen to the floor – he could not be sure if it was his or the other man's – and wiped his cheeks then his eyes, as he would have done with a child. Deep inside he was smiling broadly, happy and confident. He squeezed Josep's nose in a fold of the towel, as if he were needing to have it blown.

Josep shook his face free and laughed.

'My God,' he said, 'I wasn't expecting that.'

'Sounded like you needed it. Of course I don't believe a word you say.'

Toni was adopting a cynicism alien to his character. Luckily, even at this early stage, Josep had a clear enough perception of him, and sufficient sensitivity to his tone of voice, to know that he was bluffing.

'What do you mean?'

'Have you any idea how many happily married men come to

303

the sauna on a Sunday afternoon, or any other afternoon in the week, invite someone into a cubicle, talk a load of bullshit to them, and disappear for ever?'

'And that's what you think I'm doing?'

'It doesn't look good.'

'Come home with me, then.'

Toni was startled. He had not expected to be taken seriously.

'Come home and I will show you the evidence. My room, the boys' room. I can even let you see a photograph of my wife.'

'So where are the boys?' asked Toni. 'Why weren't you at the concert today?'

He did not want to move. Josep lay flat on his back now, his right arm supporting Toni's head. Turned on his left side, Toni had his dick cradled comfortably between his crotch and Josep's thigh. As they talked, he moved his right hand gently, unobtrusively over Josep's body, investigating a new geographical territory that had unexpectedly opened up for him, checking out its exposed and its secret places, making a map of touch he could coordinate with the visual memory he had of this man, sitting in the Palau de la Musica between his two sons, and with the smell he was still breathing into his nostrils.

'They're with my brother, my eldest brother Ricard. I'm the youngest of four boys and he's the only one who knows.'

'Knows what?' Toni put in, wanting precision.

'Knows about this. About wanting men and coming to the sauna. He's got three kids of his own. He and his wife have a place in the country, in the Priorat south of Montblanc, and when they go there they often take my two with them.'

'So why did you miss the concert?' asked Toni, struck and a little startled by the man's openness, his absolute willingness to deal with questions. I could ask him almost anything and he would tell me, he reflected.

'We can't all fit into the one car. I ran them down on Saturday and stayed the night. I have never been to the sauna on a Sunday before. It wouldn't cross my mind. And anyway, it's not a time I'm free. Usually I come on a Thursday evening. Pere has football and Maurici goes to music theory classes. That gives me a couple of hours between dropping them off and picking them up again. But the house felt so empty today when I got back I couldn't settle to anything. I'm missing them already, you see. They take up all my time and then, when they're away, I just can't cope.'

Josep moved on to his side and took Toni's face between his hands.

'Look me in the eyes,' he said.

'I can't,' answered Toni, close to laughter. 'I've lost one of my contact lenses and I left my glasses in the locker room.'

Josep went on, as solemn as before.

'I didn't want to meet you here. Not in this place.'

'Is it such a terrible place?'

'It's a place you come to do a piece of business and then go. I'd built up hopes around you.'

'What kind of hopes?'

'Hadn't you noticed me watching you at the Palau?'

Toni shook his head. He still found it hard to believe what he was hearing. Or rather, disbelief was the only reaction he would permit himself at present.

'Hopes that something more was possible. That I could have something more than what I've got. With you. Or with somebody like you. I fantasized about the places we would meet. There's a bookshop I particularly like, when you walk up from the Ramblas, just opposite the Liceu, curving round to San Josep Oriol where the buskers often play. You know the one? I used to think I'd be browsing in there, and I'd lift my face from the book and you'd be next to me, and we'd nod and say hello, and that would be it. I noticed you watching me,' he went on.

'When?'

Toni was defensive now.

'During the intervals at the concert. You invariably placed yourself at an angle where you could see me and Pere and Maurici and observe everything we were doing. I wondered if you were planning to write a book about us. I even thought you could be a private detective.'

'That's crazy!'

'Call it paranoia.'

'What do you have to be paranoid about?' asked Toni, and suddenly a thought occurred to him. 'Your wife?'

'No danger there. If there were to be any chasing, I'd be doing it, not the other way round. No, I sometimes lie awake at night and imagine that my visits to the sauna will be exposed, that people will say two boys just entering puberty are not safe with a father who's queer, that they'll be taken away and put in a home or something. The next morning I can see it's crazy but at the time it's frighteningly real.'

'And are they safe with you?'

'As safe as teenage girls are with straight fathers. Yes, they're safe.'

Toni was calmer, now that the conversation had moved away from what he might, or might not, have felt for Josep before that day.

'So where is your wife?'

'New York.'

Toni burst out laughing.

'Why do you laugh?'

Toni shrugged his shoulders, filled with delight yet again. He kissed Josep on the lips and Josep's rose to meet his, anxiously responsive.

'Because it's so classic. You say exactly the things a married guy would say if he were trying to pull the wool over the eyes of a gay guy he'd got off with. What could be more convenient than a wife in New York?'

'You mean you don't believe me?'

'You said you were going to take me home and give me proof.'

Toni expected Josep to balk at what was more or less a demand. And instead, with a naivety that surfaced time and again, so automatic it almost wounded Toni to behold, Josep sat up on the edge of the couch and started looking for his plastic sandals.

'No, let's wait a bit longer. Lie down again. Tell me what happened. Finish the story.'

'Have you ever been with a woman?'

'Not since I was fifteen.'

'You began that early?'

'Does it seem early to you?'

'My wife and I starting going out together when I was sixteen and she was seventeen. When I married her she was still a virgin and so was I.'

'Is your family very Catholic?'

'No, it was just that neither of us was interested in anyone else. Now, when I look back, I think I put if off because I knew.'

'And didn't she suspect?'

'No, not at all. She has assured me of that.'

'So how did you find out?'

'It was when Maurici was aged two and a half. Carme – that's my wife's name – my ex-wife's name, I mean – was acting with a fringe theatre group.'

'So who looked after the child?'

'We both did. I've never had any problems about that. I was rather better at it than her, as it turned out.'

'And you lived off the money she earned by acting?'

Josep laughed.

'No way. I had a part time job in a government office. And I was already writing about music at that point. That's what I do now, I teach music and write about it.'

At last Toni understood the notebook and the scribbling during the concerts. A suspicion crossed his mind.

'Which paper do you write for?'

Josep named a prestigious Spanish-language daily, edited and printed in Barcelona.

'So why don't you sit up nearer the front, in an expensive seat? That's where they normally put the critics.'

Josep was unperturbed and explained patiently.

'It's because of the boys. I feel awkward about putting them in the limelight. And when they were younger they used to mess around a lot. I remember sitting through one concert when Pere – he's the little one – wriggled like a worm. I could have been holding Proteus, or a cat that is desperate to get down from your lap and go exploring.'

'Didn't you lose patience?'

'No. I just kept kissing him to let him know it was OK. He likes having his head stroked. That calmed him down a bit.'

Josep paused, trying to find the thread of his interrupted tale.

'Anyway, I used to take Maurici to rehearsals. And I fell in love with one of the actors. His name was Anselm. He had fair hair. He could have been a German.'

'Was he gay?'

'Oh, yes. Carme accused him of seducing me. But he didn't. It was like seeing your first film in colour, when all you have been accustomed to is black and white. I fell in love as I had never done before and haven't done since. I fell in love with a person,' he said with special emphasis. 'It didn't strike me as an issue at the time that he was a man and not a woman. I thought about him every minute of the day. If two hours went past and I didn't see him, or at least speak to him on the phone, I felt ill. Sometimes I would just sit in the kitchen and cry. As if I had been thawing out. As if something in me that had always been solid and congealed was loosening up at last.'

'How did Carme find out?'

'She didn't need to. We made no attempt to hide anything. The whole thing happened under her eyes. When you fall in love like that it never crosses your mind to hide it. I wanted the whole world to know how much I cared about Anselm. I used to fantasize about putting banners all the way down the Ramblas, so that every single person in Barcelona could be informed. They were going to alternate: "Josep loves Anselm", then "Anselm loves Josep". From Plaça de Catalunya right down as far as the Drassanes. Sometimes they said "Anselm phoned Josep six times today", or "Ours is a love that will last for ever".'

Josep paused to think and Toni, as he waited, realized that he was jealous. The jealousy failed to make sense for at least two reasons. It was about a man from the past and that man's relationship to someone who might, or might not be part of Toni's future. The latter still hung in the balance. Yet the jealousy was strong.

Talking about Anselm had brought Josep to a plateau of remembered happiness he was not in a hurry to leave.

'Let's go,' he said to Toni. 'I could do with a bite to eat. Then I'll take you back.'

Beyond the door of their cubicle, the timeless, otherworldly bustle of the sauna had lessened only slightly. Yet the place struck Toni as radically different. What had happened since they locked themselves in had changed his relation to it. It somehow did not surprise him that, as soon as they were in the corridor, Josep took his hand and led him happily away. They trooped downstairs together. Heads turned to watch them.

The locker room was colder, an antechamber to the outside world. Toni did not turn to look at his companion till they were both fully clothed. He reached into his inside pocket for his glasses.

'This feels so momentous,' he said.

'Why?' chuckled Josep.

'I'm afraid it's not really going to be you. Or that you will dissolve before my eyes.'

He put them on. Josep did not flinch.

'Reassured? Is it me you can see?'

'Oh, yes,' said Toni, drawing in a deep, deep breath. 'I see you properly now. You're real.'

'*Soy realidad,*' said Josep.

They had been speaking Catalan but he said it in Spanish, because the words were from a song that had reached the hit parade during the last few weeks and could be heard in bars and workplaces all over the country.

They kissed.

'You look different from the way you do in the Palau.'

'That's because I'm with you now,' Josep answered, quick as a flash.

He's falling in love, thought Toni, with a mixture of resentment, trepidation and envy. He's falling in love with me. Look how easily he lets himself do it. Without considering the consequences, the terrors or the disappointments that may lie ahead. He's crazy. Or maybe he's just confident. He trusts me. And with the last thought, again the sensation of tremendous power, flowing up in waves from the soles of his feet, filling him and warming him.

They stopped in a restaurant on the other side of Portal de l'Àngel. From the way the waiters welcomed them it was clear Josep was a regular customer.

'Do you often come here?'

'I call in most Thursdays. Before or, more usually, after. I feed the boys at home but that's too early for me to eat. So I'm ready for something when I leave the sauna.'

Again Toni felt a pang of jealousy. I have to stop this, he told himself. It is ridiculous to carry on this way. I cannot cope with worrying about all the men he may have had on his Thursday evening visits. And the ones he may be going to have?

'So what happened with Anselm?'

'Carme persuaded me to break it off. We had one kid already

and we agreed to have another immediately. We had the best intentions. Both of us saw it as a way of strengthening the relationship. She pleaded with me because of the family and our commitment. And anyway, she couldn't have gone on acting without my help. I was supporting both of us, though we lived meagrely enough.'

Toni thought about the younger of the boys and how marginal and excluded he had looked in the company of his father and brother. That is the problem, he observed to the child in his head. You came here not for yourself, but in order to cement the bond between your parents. You were a pretext. About something else.

'And Anselm?'

Josep put his fork down. He had been tucking into a plate of spinach fried with garlic, pine nuts and raisins, a steaming knot of tangled green, veined with gold and black.

'He left for Madrid later that year. I heard he found someone there. He's back in Barcelona now. I saw him in the sauna once.'

'How was that?'

'Horrible. I've seen him other places, too. A couple of times in bars – straight ones – and once at the theatre. He pointedly ignores me. I take it he has not forgiven me and I can understand.'

Toni continued to find elements of the story hard to believe.

'But didn't you realize you were gay? That there was no point trying to continue with a woman once you had found out?'

'None of the three of us looked at it like that. I had been in love with a woman and now I was in love with a man. That didn't prejudice the future in any way. Or so it seemed at the time. It was the people that mattered, not what sex they were. The months when Carme was pregnant with Pere were very difficult.'

'She had to leave the play, of course.'

'Oh, the company fell apart long before the date for the performance. Too many internal feuds. And when Carme refused to speak to Anselm offstage, it became very hard for them to talk to each other using someone else's words, when they were on. She attacked him physically in the midst of one rehearsal. It was awful.'

'Don't you regret it? Agreeing to stay? Agreeing to have another child?'

Josep enunciated the next words carefully, like a politician fielding a difficult question he has been waiting for, one he has had plenty of time to find an answer to.

'I can't do that, Toni. I can't regret the marriage or anything. That would mean wishing my boys had not been born. There's no way I can let myself do that.'

They munched morosely for a while. Toni continued to envy the other man's ease of self-disclosure. When will he ask about me, he thought. Does he think I have nothing to tell? Does he see me as just another *maricón*, with the trail of broken romances so many of us have?

'What's the matter?' Josep asked.

'Nothing.'

'Something is. I can see,' said Josep.

He flipped his tie, which had been getting in the way of his food, over his shoulder. The problem was, the man's inane confidence made Toni want to protect him: to make sure he did not discover how misplaced it might easily have been, make sure that he would stay that way. For other men? Or just for Toni?

'I have a job interview tomorrow afternoon. I've just remembered,' he said, lying.

He still preferred to use masks, to keep to himself the things he was experiencing.

'Do you want to go home to your own place?'

'No,' said Toni slowly. Then, more definitely: 'No. But I'll have to phone my mother.'

'And I think I've got problems!'

'Point taken.'

Josep's flat was in the lower part of the Eixample, not far from the university. They walked back in silence. If Josep displayed more and more energy the closer they got to the door, quickening his pace, Toni had the sensation of wading through matter that grew increasingly resistant. The urge to run for it was so strong he had to stop worrying about whether he really wanted to be with this man or not, and concentrate on placing one foot after another on the pavement. Josep's undisguised elation made his turmoil all the harder to bear.

It got more difficult still once they were in the flat. Toni told himself that he was crazy to prejudice his chances at tomorrow's meeting by letting himself in for an overnight adventure of this kind. He had not gone back with anybody for more than two years, since the night he picked up Rory. Experience told him he would get practically no sleep. More overwhelming was the sense he should not be there, that he had no business invading this man's life and his intimacy, letting Josep fall in love with him, when it was clear there was no serious prospect of continuing. The boys were coming back the following Sunday. The most they could hope for was a week's headlong romance, exploiting whatever energy and time they had left over from work.

That was another thing. He had to be in the office for nine the next day. Normally he went back in the afternoons, after a long lunch hour. He would be unable to do so tomorrow. It would not be fair for him to neglect the project he was engaged on, because of a secret meeting with a prospective new employer. So he was determined to report for work first thing the following morning.

Josep got a couple of beers from the fridge. Toni was silent.

'Tired?' Josep asked.

Toni nodded.

'Then let's go to bed.'

Josep cast his clothes on a chair next to the fitted cupboard. Toni undressed with his characteristic, meticulous slowness, folding his shirt and trousers neatly and rolling the socks into a single bundle. When he turned round, Josep was standing at the other side of the bed, that beauty unveiled again as in the sauna. Toni had his glasses on. Not a trace of sexual excitement. There was a moment of embarrassment for both of them, then Josep lifted the sheet and leapt in. Toni put his glasses on the bedside cabinet and lay down near the edge of the bed. To his surprise, Josep moved close, turned him round so as to hold him from behind, reached over to put out the lamp, and gave him the chastest of kisses on the nape of the neck. Even more to his surprise, they both slept.

Toni had not bothered to work out where the window was when he entered the room that evening. When he awoke, morning sunlight was already piercing the slats in the shutters, casting a regular pattern of blobs on the opposite wall, with the indistinctness of an image seen through water. As if shuffling through a pack of cards, his consciousness, alarmed, reviewed a range of rooms he might have been in. None of them corresponded to what he saw. Then the events of the previous day came back to him. He was in Josep's bed, in a flat in the Eixample. His eyes went to the radio alarm. Half past five. Josep was still holding him from behind, one leg between Toni's, straddling him. He could feel a distinct pressure.

'Awake?' murmured Josep.

'You've got a hard-on,' said Toni.

'Mmh. The mornings are the best time for me,' said Josep, and thrust a little.

'That's nice,' said Toni, not moving.

He let Josep draw him in closer. One hand played with his belly button, then moved down to the tangle of hair above his sex. Toni swung round and plucked a kiss from his mouth, like picking a flower from a trellis of roses, with just that definiteness and certainty. Rory smoked, and his mouth had tasted horrible after he slept. Josep's breath was so fresh he would have liked to draw it directly into his lungs, to get his oxygen from that source.

Josep was investigating Toni's backside with the middle finger of his other hand, pressing, looking for the right place, preparing it.

'I haven't done this with a man before,' he said.

'But you've done it with a woman?'

'Oh, yes. It was something Carme liked.'

'Not Anselm?'

'No, I never did it with Anselm.'

'Not in the sauna?'

'No, not in the sauna.'

Toni's reserves of cynicism were almost, but not quite exhausted. Josep found the right place and, as he pushed, Toni first winced, and then relaxed.

'Now you are inside of me, just pause,' he said. 'Stay there peacefully. It's what I like best.'

'Just whatever you want,' Josep said, in a tone of voice that was different now, but that sounded as if he meant it. Then, almost without meaning to, he came.

313

27

They showered afterwards. It was not quite seven o'clock. Josep pulled on a frayed blue T-shirt and a pair of shorts. The flat was overlooked, and they could not wander around naked if they wanted to open the shutters and let the morning light in. After a bit of searching, they found a smarter shirt and another pair of shorts that fitted Toni and looked good on him.

'Now I can show you around,' said Josep.

'He supports Barça!' Toni cried out in pleasure when they entered the boys' room.

The space above Pere's bed was a collage in homage to the city's team, with festoons of photographs, banners and posters.

'I find football so boring,' said Josep.

'I don't understand how you can live in the city and not support its team,' said Toni. 'Don't you care what happens when they play Real Madrid?'

'Not in the slightest,' said Josep, quite calm.

It was on the tip of his tongue to say, you can take him to a football match if you want to. He stopped himself. That felt too dangerous. It meant venturing into unknown territory. Maurici's side of the room was more sombre. There was a framed picture of Beethoven, irate and with a shock of unkempt hair, upon the bookshelf.

'He's the musician,' said Josep. 'He plays the piano and the fiddle.'

A music stand had been pushed up against the wall at the end of the bed. A baby grand piano took up nearly a third of the small sitting-room. Josep was making coffee.

'Do you play that?'

'Yes. I teach piano repertoire. That means, I don't teach students how to play, but talk to them about the available literature.'

Toni was feeling out of his depth. Despite his love of music, he had never played an instrument in his life. He picked a photograph from the piano top. Now at last he had the answer to his question. Maurici was like Carme, Pere much more like his father. He squinted at the woman with a sense of dislike that struck him as entirely natural.

'So this is your wife,' he said.

'My ex-wife,' put in Josep.

He took the photograph from Toni and looked at it as if he found it altered.

'Why don't you finish the story?'

Coffee was bubbling up in the espresso machine in the kitchen. They sat at opposite sides of the table, cradling the cups in their hands as they drank. Toni had to keep recalling his attention to what Josep was telling him. The daylight had a special quality to it that morning. Josep had his back to the window, with the sun behind him, so that its rays picked out each detail of the hair framing his face. Toni was mesmerized by the movement of the lips as much as by what they said. He rejoiced in Josep's solidity, the symmetry of the triangle formed by his collar bone and the shoulders gently ascending towards the neck. He knew what it was like to have that body close. His backside was sore. If he closed his eyes for a moment, he could imagine he still had Josep inside him.

'Pere had a difficult birth. Carme had to have a Caesarean section and she bitterly resented it. She told me the child had not been meant to be. That was why they had to cut him out of her. Breastfeeding was painful. Then the milk dried up. When I look back now I realize she must have been seriously depressed. At the time it was as much as we could do to get through the day, looking after Pere, trying to make sure Maurici didn't feel too neglected, and keeping a very shaky relationship on its legs. We struggled on until the summer. That was when it all fell apart.'

Josep sighed deeply. He was playing with the spoon in the sugar bowl, digging down then turning it over, digging and turning it over, emptying small shovelfuls of the white powder towards the side of the bowl. Digging for something he had never been able to find and would not find today.

'Her parents have a holiday apartment on the outskirts of Sitges. Nothing grand. It's tall and narrow, on three floors, and has a garden at the back. The apartment next door had been rented out to Americans from New York. A married couple and a lawyer, recently divorced. All middle-aged. They didn't have a pool and we did. So one day, in the course of a conversation over the fence, Carme invited them to have a dip in ours.'

'Do you speak English that well?'

'I don't,' Josep answered, with a shrug of the shoulders. 'Carme does. I got a bit suspicious at the beginning, but she said she wanted to practise the language. It would help her get a job later on, when Pere was a bit older. You see, the depression made her very negative about acting. She swore she would never set foot on a stage again. And she didn't want to be stuck at home with the boys. I was unwilling to contradict her. I had invested a lot, maybe even more than she, in making the marriage work. After all, I had sacrificed Anselm to it. She was holding on to the only thing she had. I gave up something else I already had. So, in the last analysis, whatever she said, went. I was more afraid of things not working by that stage.'

'And then?'

Toni could tell that it was painful for Josep. But he needed to know. He had an image of Carme clear in his mind. He was setting the scene in an apartment belonging to friends of his, very similar to the one Josep described, though not in Sitges.

'One morning I took the boys down to the beach. Carme was supposed to catch up with us later on. The Americans were to leave that day and we had dined together in style the evening before.'

'What about the children?' Toni asked.

'Maurici has always been a good sleeper. We dined in the back garden, on the Americans' side. From time to time I got up to check he was OK. Pere was in a wicker basket next to us, lifted from the ground on a couple of chairs. I had bottles prepared. It was no problem getting him back to sleep when he woke up. Anyway, I waited and waited on the beach. The funny thing is, it didn't cross my mind to worry. I presumed Carme had gone back to bed or was just taking some time to herself.'

He stopped.

'She left with them,' said Toni.

Josep nodded.

'So what did you do?'

'I dropped the boys off at my parents' house in Barcelona and got a plane to New York the following day. All I knew was the lawyer's name, his surname and his job. The people who owned the apartment next door refused to supply me with the address of his friends, the people they had rented the apartment to.'

'How did you know Carme had gone off with him? Did she leave a note?'

Josep nodded again. Toni did not press him to repeat the contents.

'I got through to his office on the afternoon of the second day.'

'I thought you didn't speak English!'

'I don't, not really. But it's amazing what despair can drive you to. If you have something important to say, you'll get it over whatever the language barrier. His secretary told me he was at a meeting. Maybe it was true. I left my name and number and he rang back within the hour. "Yes, Mr Roig," he told me in that measured, Anglo-Saxon way. "Your wife is living with me now. She is not coming back to Spain. And I must ask you to return home as soon as possible and never bother us again." I was going off my head, Toni. I had that frenzied energy people get when everything is collapsing around them. I waited outside his office and managed to follow him to his apartment block in a taxi. I stood outside the main entrance until they both emerged. A hooker went by and started baiting me. I nearly went for her with my fists.'

'But you got to speak to Carme?'

'No. She turned and ran the moment she saw me. And I tore after her, with the lawyer on my heels. He wasn't quick enough to keep up with us. I lost her in the end. The next morning the police came to my hotel and cautioned me for molesting her. They told me I had to leave the country within twenty-four hours. The lawyer told them I was homosexual and that seemed to make me an undesirable alien.'

'So you left?'

'First,' said Josep, shaking his head with a wry smile, 'I bought a tube of sleeping pills and a bottle of Bourbon. I sat in the hotel room until well after lunchtime, looking at them. You know, I kid myself I can still feel what it was like to hold that bottle in my hand. I poured the pills into a pile on the table and played with them, the way I am playing with the sugar now.'

He stopped and gazed at Toni. Toni could see no desperation in his eyes, only incredulity and a kind of amusement, as well as a touch of provocation.

'So what stopped you?'

'What do you think? I have two sons. I had spoken to Maurici on the phone after arriving in New York. He was distraught. You can't kill yourself if you have children.'

'It doesn't stop some people.'

'Well, it stopped me. What's more,' and he gestured towards his crotch, his features broadening into a smile, 'I like all that far too much. I'm in love with life. I'm not the kind of man who lets it go.'

The kitchen clock was ticking in the background. In the bedroom the radio alarm had switched itself on. An agitated voice in Catalan discussed traffic problems on the access routes into the city centre. Toni realized Josep would say no more. The openness had vanished. He had reached a place that was not permeable to him. Josep pushed his chair back and, almost instinctively, Toni rose at the same time. He leant against the sink and Josep put his arms around him. They were both aroused again.

'I have to go,' said Toni.

'I know.'

Josep reached for the pad by the phone.

'This is my number,' he said, writing. 'You know where the house is.'

Toni took the slip of paper.

'And yours?'

It was more of a demand than a request. Toni wrote the digits down, overcoming a reluctance whose cause he could not define. The thought of changing one of the digits crossed his mind. Such dishonesty would have been out of character. Josep blew him a kiss as he clattered down the stairs.

He called in at home to get fresh clothes for work. His mother was not angry. She had only too shrewd an idea as to why he

318

had failed to come back that night, and was still enough his mother to note that the clothes he was wearing were not the ones he had left with on Sunday afternoon. While not exactly embarrassed, it terrified her that her son might refer to the business directly, or even wish to discuss it with her. So she bustled around him without interruption, careful to avoid sitting down with him to breakfast. Their conversation had a stiltedness alien to it since before Toni's breakdown.

Toni loved his city with a fierce pride, and his affection for it grew even stronger that morning. He could not have guessed how many people he would normally set eyes on during his journey to work. A hundred maybe, even two. It seemed to him each of them was living with the same intensity as himself, their stories parallel and interweaving, and he experienced an urge to turn to an utter stranger and give an account of the previous night's events. Can't they tell I am a man who has just fallen in love, he thought, then chided himself for using such words. He had been hurt too often. It would be stupid to risk all that pain again.

The need to unburden himself was so powerful that he did not go home directly at lunchtime, calling in instead to see his friend Beatriz at her workshop in Gràcia. As usual, she did not even turn to greet him, but continued painting the piece she had in front of her, an enormous pitcher she was decorating with flowers in a vaguely Latin American style. They sold the pottery at the front of the shop. Alicia, who handled customers, let Toni in just as she was about to close for lunch, a cursory smile on her thin lips. Alicia was invariably there at half past nine to open the place. Beatriz came in late but, on the other hand, frequently worked right through her lunch hour, and far into the night.

She was a big woman who towered over Toni when she stood upright. She kept her mass of knotted, corvine hair on the top of her head, bound with a brilliant scarf. It poised there as if contained in a basket. One of her more lovable eccentricities was to stick brushes in it for sheer devilment. They would poke out, like flowers hastily arranged in a vase, blue, orange or vermilion at the tip. Beatriz washed her hair most days, so it was scrupulously clean. But she found it hard to get the paint off, and blotches of incongruous colour punctuated the metallic black sheen. In her late thirties, and classified an irredeemable fag-hag by her circle of friends, she had recently taken up with a divorced businessman named Vicenç, barely half her size. Somebody pointed out that there was enough of Beatriz to make at least two of Vicenç. The jokes about how they got on in bed are better not repeated.

'That's not all,' Beatriz said, when Toni had finished telling her about his interview that afternoon and the portfolio of work he had sent.

'What do you mean?'

'There's something else. You've been making love.'

'How can you tell? You haven't even looked me in the face.'

A car went past in the street outside, tooting its horn. Gràcia is an old working-class quarter in the throes of gentrification, and the streets are so narrow that every noise in them is magnified. Beatriz waited.

'I don't need to look at you. It's enough to hear your tone of voice.'

'He's a married man.'

'So what else is new? You met him in the sauna?'

'Mmh.'

'I thought you only went as a spectator?'

'That was till yesterday.'

'I knew it couldn't last. Big dick?'

'Beatriz! He has two boys.'

'And where was the missus?'

'She's supposed to be in New York.'

'You don't believe him?'

'I don't think I can afford to.'

'Funny basis for a relationship.'

Maccarese did not offer him a job that afternoon. Only once he had been disappointed did Toni admit to himself what he had been hoping for. Taking barely five minutes from his work, the designer presented him with a portfolio.

'This has been botched,' he said. 'See what you can do. Ring me when you are ready.'

The pipe went back into his mouth. Evidently the interview was finished.

Toni felt horribly depressed. He had been riding on the crest of a wave since speaking to Josep in the sauna. Now he hit rock bottom with a vengeance. He could not face going home to tell his mother that, in effect, he had nothing to tell her. So he went and sat in his favourite *granja*, a cakeshop just off the Ramblas, close to the art dealers in Carrer Petritxol. Gradually the intense coming and going of other customers revived him. Adolescents dipped sausage-like confections in cups of hot chocolate, while single businessmen consumed plates of whipped cream they first had scattered generously with sugar.

When he opened the portfolio he had been given, he was so astonished he nearly let it fall from his hands. It was a commission from a major chain of clothing stores, with branches all over Spain. Leafing through the sheets, he thought he could see what was wrong and how it could be improved. Ideas started crowding in on him there and then. He took a pencil from his jacket pocket, ground it in the sharpener he always carried with him, and made a sketch or two in the margins of a newspaper somebody had left on a nearby table.

'A man called Josep has been trying to find you,' his mother said when he got in. 'He'll ring back later.'

Josep phoned every night that week, around bedtime. Toni found the days that followed a battle. His present bosses loaded him with work, as if they sensed he was thinking of abandoning them. He was rarely able to get home before the middle of the evening, which in Barcelona meant not earlier than ten o'clock. After grabbing some food, he would sit at his drawing table until two or three in the morning, working without respite on the revised project. What he produced gave him a joy that would have been its own reward, if it had led no further. Josep did not protest when Toni explained they could not see one another before the weekend. He chatted about the minutiae of his day, wished Toni well and then rang off. On Friday night, he stood waiting at the door of the restaurant where they had booked a table, his arms full of flowers.

'We can't go in with these!' said Toni.

'Why not?'

'But what will people say?'

'The waiters can look after them.'

And so they did, without the slightest sign of surprise, producing them along with the coats at the end of the meal. By then the atmosphere was more serious, perhaps more sour.

'I can't come back with you tonight,' Toni said.

'Why not?'

'My mother's not well. Something in her chest. And I have to work tomorrow. What about Saturday night?'

A look of desperation settled on Josep's face.

'The boys are coming home tomorrow afternoon. It's impossible.'

'That's that, then, isn't it?' said Toni, getting up.

'Give me time,' said Josep. 'I need you to give me time.'

'Time for what? I live with my mother. She knows all about me but I'm not going to start bringing people home.' (That 'people' really hurt.) 'You live with two sons who don't know you're gay and you have no intention of telling them. There isn't a way forward.'

Josep clasped his courage in both hands and explained, in a shaky voice, the idea he had had. Toni never told Oriol. When Beatriz got to hear about it, she was enormously amused.

'So you're going to meet each other in the sauna on Thursday nights? And have polite conversation with his sons over a glass of champagne at the Sunday morning concert? You agreed to that?'

She hooted with laughter, swung round from the wide, shallow dish that she was painting, and lit a cigarette to celebrate.

'Do you think it's wrong?'

'I think it's absolutely priceless! Don't you realize? You're going to the sauna once a week to have a monogamous relationship!'

When she put it like that Toni saw the funny side. The reality was harsher. He hated the arrangement and hated himself for accepting it. Dissatisfaction gave an aggressive edge to his treatment of Josep that expressed itself, at the Palau, in a football supporters' alliance with Pere, formed so as to bait the intellectuals, Maurici and his father. When they made love, in a locked cubicle in the sauna, quieter and alien on a weekday night, the situation was more complicated. On each of the four occasions that they met there, Josep had to ease his anger from him, loosening it and lifting it away as if it had been a suit of clothes Toni himself was incapable of removing. Then they made love, in a manner that had him aching for the next Thursday to arrive.

They were weaving a fabric that united them and bound them. Each time, as they were about to start, Toni would refuse, and Josep had to take time patiently to persuade him, to disarm him of his fear and mistrust, even though he himself was no clearer as to what the finished cloth would look like, the sort of garment their lovemaking would in the course of time become.

Toni told him it was over on the doorstep of the sauna, as they were leaving, on the fourth Thursday. He had started work for Maccarese the previous Monday, at nearly double his former salary, but the pressure was enormous. Getting rid of Josep was part of his new life. Josep said nothing, only hung his head. Toni waited for a moment, then realized he was waiting, decided it was inconsistent on his part, and walked away.

'There was no future in it,' he told Beatriz.

'But you love him.'

'He was tormenting me.'

'But you love him.'

'I deserve something more.'

'So does he. And you love him.'

Ricard phoned within a fortnight, at the office. It transpired he had done business with Maccarese, who used the bank where Ricard was employed. He had an impeccable telephone style. Toni was desperate and would have clutched at any approach. It hurt him more than he could believe that Josep should make no attempt to fight back. They met in a trendy cocktail bar. There was a play of lights in the gents' toilet so that when you peed, the liquid flowed down like a mixture of differently coloured paints. Toni was already feeling slightly sick and the sophistication of their surroundings made it worse. Ricard was taller than Josep. Everything about him seemed out of proportion. Toni would have liked to take him in his hands, like a piece of plasticine, and remodel him into the other brother, the one he loved.

'Josep's back on medication,' said Ricard.

Toni was chastened. It didn't make sense. He shouldn't feel

responsible and yet he did. It came again, the warm flush rising up through the soles of his feet, just like that first night in the sauna. I am the remedy, he thought. I can do that.

'I didn't know he was on pills.'

'He hasn't been. Not for years. I think he's on the point of cracking up.'

'What can I do?' asked Toni. What he intended to put across was the conviction he could do nothing. The way the words came out, it sounded like he was ready to do anything.

'Give him time, that's all he needs.'

'Do you know what we were doing? Do you know where we met?'

Ricard's face broke into a smile.

'You think that's funny?'

'No, it isn't funny. It's unusual. It shows you really love each other.'

'Where do you think this will lead? I can hardly move in with him and the boys.'

'Why not? It would be an intelligent solution.'

'What kind of a family would that be?'

'It could be a very happy one.'

'I don't believe in you,' Toni said. 'I've never heard a straight man talk that way.'

'I don't believe your prejudices,' said Ricard.

'You mean you want your nephews to have two fathers?'

'What I want is for my brother to be happy. Look, why don't you come to lunch on Sunday?'

Toni had pushed his chair back. Ricard stretched out a hand and grasped Toni's across the table. Toni tried to pull his smaller hand away, but Ricard had quickly slipped his fingers between Toni's and was gripping tighter. Toni's other hand went to his face, to cover his eyes. He did not want Josep's brother to see him crying.

'The problem is, he loves his children too much,' Toni said at last.

'Lying about yourself is a funny way to love your children,' said Ricard.

When Toni emerged from the lift on the third floor of the apartment block where Ricard lived, the following Sunday, Pere and Maurici were waiting for him on the landing. A shamefaced Josep was just inside, whiter than Toni had ever seen him, so white Toni was afraid. He counted the guests. All four brothers were there with their families. Their mother was busy in the kitchen and Toni did not meet her until she took her place at table after the first course. There were twenty-two people sitting down to eat. His tension, and Josep's, dissolved in the general uproar.

'You'll come back with us,' said Josep, when the time came to get their coats.

The boys forgot about them once they were inside the door. Pere had videoed that day's football match and settled to watch it in the bedroom. Maurici sat down to practise the piano, beginning with his scales. Toni and Josep retreated to the kitchen. Josep started making some coffee but Toni had been panicking since they arrived. Being there evoked their first night together only too clearly. Things were so different now.

'I'm going to go,' he announced. 'This is hurting more than I can bear.'

Josep stood with his back to the door, slammed it shut with his backside and stretched his arms on either side of him, as if he were taking the weight of a collapsing mountain on his shoulders. Maurici had got on to his arpeggios now. His hands stalked up and down the keyboard, like spiders which only occasionally put a foot in the wrong place. Toni approached, half intending to fight. The electric light·caught Josep's trousers at an angle. He put his hand to the crotch. Josep's taut sex was tantamount to a declaration of love. Fireworks were going off inside Toni's head. He paid no attention to them, squatted down, unzipped Josep's flies, and took it in his mouth. Josep's hands were caressing his head, stroking the nape of his neck, cradling him as his lips cradled his sex. Incongruously, he remembered what Josep had said to him about Pere wriggling all the way through a concert, and how he loved having his head stroked.

'Was that crazy?' he asked Beatriz afterwards.

'Why?'

'With the boys just the other side of the door. What if they had tried to come in?'

'Did they?'

'Thank God, no. And we were in there for three quarters of an hour. We jammed the table up against the door.'

'They probably had a very shrewd idea of what was going on. Married couples do that all the time. They must do, don't you think?'

'But we're two men.'

'I don't see that makes much difference.'

'I've never had sex in a kitchen before.'

'Toni, sometimes you worry me. What will you get up to next?'

'It was incredibly exciting. I've never made love with such . . . love.'

'Darling, you've done nothing until you've had sex leaning against a washing machine which is going through the spin dry part of its cycle.'

'You've done that?'

'Mmh-mmh. With Vicenç's daughter copying out her English homework on the dining-room table through the wall. We were waiting to unload the machine and hang the washing up. Vicenç came on all strong.'

All of a sudden Toni saw Vicenç in a new light.

Once they were finished, Josep had looked at him quizzically, wondering what they could use to wipe themselves dry. Toni picked a dishcloth from the edge of the sink. His lips were so sore from kissing and sucking he was convinced they must look different, that the boys would notice something. Engrossed in the last movement of a Beethoven sonata, Maurici nevertheless broke off to say goodbye, ever the soul of politeness. Pere did not even look round from the television screen. It was all he could do to mutter a greeting over his shoulder.

Josep had won a stay of execution. Time was running out for him and he knew it. He discussed the weeks ahead with Ricard. Together, they concocted something very much resembling a plan of campaign. As it was, events themselves took over. School finished the following week. Ricard and his wife were to take the boys to Siurana, in the Priorat, for a fortnight. Josep tripped over a piece of luggage just outside the main door as the convoy was getting ready to depart, fell and sprained his right ankle. It was a spiral fracture and would be slow to heal. Toni came immediately, and took affairs in hand. What he would never have dared propose became sheer common sense. He moved in for two weeks.

He even agreed to drive Josep out to Siurana, when the time came for the boys to return. It was a Saturday morning. Neither of them had slept. Toni had a heavy heart. Back to square one, he was thinking. How long can we keep this up? He had to call in at the office. He had packed his bags the previous night and he took them down with him and stored them in the boot. It was illogical, but he couldn't bear to drop them off at his mother's there and then. That would have been an acknowledgement that the separation was inevitable. Although it meant there would be less room for the boys' things, he decided his bags could stay in the boot till they all returned to Barcelona that evening. He took the underground to work to save on time. It was a nightmare trying to park outside the office, even at weekends.

When they drove off just before noon, Josep's face wore an oddly lighthearted expression which irritated Toni. The day, however, was splendid. In spite of its being July, the weather was neither as muggy, nor as burdensomely hot, as it ought to have been. They had had a thunderstorm the previous night. The air was clear, the sky a pristine blue. The usual roadworks created lengthy queues on the motorway leaving the city. Once out of sight of the sea, they were able to speed up. Toni loved driving. It was a powerful car and his mood lightened. They hardly spoke to each other. In his head Toni was preparing a speech, without being sure whether or not he had the courage to use it. About how it was better if they became good friends rather than lovers. About how he had never loved anybody yet as much as he loved Josep but, given the way things were, it was a love that couldn't find proper expression. He couldn't face waiting years and years, he would argue, until the boys had both left home. He managed to put it all with a clarity that impressed even himself. Next to him, Josep had dozed off. Again, Toni found his complacency slightly insulting.

'Let's call at Poblet,' Josep said, waking up.

Toni was ashamed to confess he had never visited the monastery, a shrine of Catalan nationalists since late in the last century, its royal tombs reconstructed with mathematical precision from drawings and written accounts. They went on a conducted tour, Toni growing more and more impatient, partly because he was hungry, partly because he saw no point in prolonging the agony. All he wanted was to keep his promise, to be polite and even affectionate with Ricard and his wife, gather the boys and their belongings, and see Josep settled back in the only style of life that was feasible for him, one which excluded Toni.

Josep suggested they stop at a bar in Prades in the hills above Poblet. It was under the arcades on the central square, opposite the church. There was an expensive restaurant a little further down but they both preferred the homely feeling of the bar. They were the only people lunching. A woman in her fifties brought them freshly made *tortilla* with roasted peppers and a salad of furry green leaves Toni could not identify. When he asked what they were, she told him she had gathered them outside the walls that morning. He did not recognize the name she used. Like the walls, the rest of the town was built of uniform red sandstone, friable and glowing. It enchanted Toni. The coast of Catalonia, he reflected, could not compare with this rugged landscape of gullies and thorn bushes, the hillsides clothed in a rich green even summertime was powerless to bleach. The delight he took in the architecture gave him courage. He put his fork down and looked hard at Josep.

'We have to talk,' he said.

'I know we do.'

'I'm going back home tonight and . . .' Toni's voice cracked. He could not say it. He did not even know what he wanted to say.

'You're not going back. I don't want you to go back.'

'What's the alternative?'

'We'll pick the boys up and go home. Go to our home. Just like an ordinary family.'

'But we're not an ordinary family!'

'Does that matter?'

All Toni had left to resist with was his pride, the pride that stopped him admitting this was what he had always wanted, even though he had not thought it possible.

'You've planned it all out, haven't you?'

It was supposed to be a challenge. Josep seemed not to notice.

'Yes, I have.'

'Then why are my bags in the boot of the car?'

'They're not. I got the concierge to take them upstairs while you were out.'

'Oh.'

Toni felt he ought to say something momentous, a yea or nay. He could not think of anything.

'You've told the boys?'

'Ricard told them.'

'The Roig family has thought of everything.'

'But you're part of the Roig family,' Josep added, as if the doubt had entered his mind for the first time. 'Isn't that what you want?'

'Are you doing this for the boys, or for me? Who comes first?'

'I don't know. Does there have to be a first and a second? It's for the four of us.' And he added, as if he had pulled an object out of his pocket which was extremely precious, but which he never knew he carried with him: 'I can have all of you.'

'And we'll sleep in the same bed?'

Toni felt like a child being promised an eternal summer holiday, the details of which he cannot quite believe.

'Where the Hell do you imagine we're going to sleep? I want to wake beside you. Can you hear the swallows?'

The teenage son of the family from Córdoba who ran the bar arrived with two cups of coffee. Josep drank his in one gulp.

'We'd better get moving,' he said. 'They'll be wondering what has become of us. I'm glad we got that sorted out.'

They could see Siurana long before they reached the ridge it sits at the end of. It dominates the countryside around, one of the last strongholds the Moors were able to defend when the tide turned, and the Christians began to drive them back towards the south of Spain. Josep started talking about Roland and Roncesvalles and Wagner's *Parsifal*, how this was the kind of landscape he always imagined for the knights of the Grail, with Klingsor's enchanted garden on the slopes of the mountain across the reservoir, on the far side of the valley to the east.

No longer in a hurry to reach their destination, Toni parked the car outside the entrance to the village. It was a marvellous viewpoint, a kind of cockpit commanding the countryside for miles around. Anyone within twenty kilometres of Siurana would be able to see them where they stood. Josep commented that there were three distinct kinds of swallow in Siurana. One of them did not migrate, but spent both winter and summer on these mountains.

Toni put his hands on Josep's hips and drew him close, slipping his fingers into the belt loops on his trousers, kissing him on the lips and in the mouth, silencing him so that all they could hear now were the swallows, there where nothing was hidden any longer, where all the world could see what they were doing.

28

People had started getting up from the dinner table. With Nicol's help, Dougal pushed back the folding doors which connected the dining-room and the lounge. They moved the chairs up against the wall so as to make space for dancing. A man Ramon did not recognize, whose arrival he had failed to notice, squatted down to examine the collection of CDs.

'Who is that?' Ramon asked Alan.

'It's Andrew, Nicol's boyfriend. He's famous for being the hairiest man in Edinburgh.'

'And what is Nicol famous for?'

Alan stopped to think.

'For only ever having slept with Andrew in all his life. That's unique.'

Ramon had a further question, which he preferred to put to Rory.

'Barry,' he said, 'why was he so silent when you were all talking about Robert?'

'Barry looked after Robert in the weeks before he died. It was something none of us could have predicted. Robert refused to talk about AIDS or anything connected with it. The one time Kieran mentioned HIV, he tried to punch him, but he was too weak by then to do him any harm. We were supposed to keep up a ridiculous pretence with his family, and because he insisted so much about it, we did. Even at the funeral, nobody mentioned AIDS. It was a travesty. We organized a pretty effective rota, so that he was never alone in the house. And then, one weekend, Barry simply moved in, and nursed him till he died.'

'What about his job?'

'He must have used up all his annual leave. It was his decision. He never consulted anyone else about it. Kieran and I even got quite jealous. It felt like Barry was hogging Robert, keeping him to himself, whereas we had all known each other long before Barry appeared on the scene. Andrew went to pieces around that time and went to have the test. I got very impatient with him. All we needed was somebody else falling apart in the midst of it all. One more drama queen! As if Robert, in his sardonic way, was not enough.'

'Was Andrew OK?'

'Of course he was. It was years since he'd slept with Robert.'

'And Barry?'

'What did he have to worry about? Robert would never have looked twice at him. He was very choosy about his lovers. Barry was way below his standards. He could be very cruel. Very cruel and very funny. For a while he referred to us all as members of the Royal Family. Robert was Her Majesty in person, naturally. Going down to the pub to trawl was called "reviewing the troops". Kieran was Princess Margaret, Dougal was Princess Anne, I was the Duchess of Kent and Nicol was the Duchess of Gloucester. Andrew, for some reason I never understood, got to be Prince Philip. And Barry was the Queen Mother. Robert kept trying to persuade him to pose for a photograph holding a hand-bag, wearing a white hat with a fascinator veil and pink butter-flies stitched across it. He managed to get Barry to put the hat on, but the photograph was too much for him. It never got taken.'

Kieran had been busy in the kitchen, scraping leftovers from plates into the pedal-bin and carefully covering with clingfilm the food which had not been eaten. It would save him cooking so much over the weekend. On his way back to the dining-room, he was stopped in the doorway by Mark, thoroughly the worse for drink now, determined to make one last attempt.

'I just don't understand what it is you see in him.'

'In who?'

'The lawyer.'

'You wouldn't,' Kieran observed drily.

'This isn't the right setting for you. Look at the flat! God knows how much he spent on those curtains, or on the precious knick-knacks littering the antique tables. Not to mention the oil paint-ings by Scottish artists. He's such a materialist. And you know what? You're another piece in his collection, nothing more than that. He thinks you fit the bill.'

Kieran wondered what he could do to stop the flow. From where he was standing, leaning against the door frame, he could see Alan, pretending to talk to Barry, but actually observing Mark's agitation with the greatest interest. It was inappropriate for Mark to be raking over all this on such an occasion, and perhaps wrong of him to be listening. But he sensed that, if he let the argument develop, it would give him the chance to tell Mark several things he had been wanting to get off his chest for quite a while.

'But he's wrong. And when he realizes, though it'll be a shock for him, it'll be a worse shock for you.'

Mark took a hurried slug of his wine, so hurried that it dribbled down his chin and he had to wipe it off with the back of his hand. He thinks I believe him, Kieran reflected. He thinks he's winning me over.

'Just now everything's hunky-dory. You preside at the dinner parties, do the cooking, provide intelligent conversation and generally look decorative. But how many of Dougal's friends are here? Do the people at the law firm know about you? Just how carefully does he hide you away? His friends can't stand you, Kieran, let me tell you. I've heard the kind of things they say about you. You haven't got the right background or the right accent or the right size of pay packet. And have you asked yourself what will happen when he comes to and you get the boot?'

'Mark,' Kieran said, 'I'm not coming back. Not with you. Never again.'

Mark pretended not to have heard.

'His eyes will fall on someone younger and more suitable. And then you'll be out. Do you have a share in the flat? Do you know how much he's worth? Would you even dare to ask him?'

Kieran was ready to butt in, but they were rhetorical questions that did not expect an answer.

'Use and abuse, that's the rule in these kind of circles. Kieran, you aren't tough enough to make the running. Take my word for it. The risk is too great. Get out while you can.'

Alan had moved away from Barry. Kieran prayed that he would not join them and, providentially, Nicol intervened, drawing him to one side. They disappeared into the lounge to join the dancers.

'Mark,' he said, 'you do not deserve an answer. And, in spite of that, I'll give you not one, but two.'

Kieran himself was less drunk than he thought and, as he spoke, he wondered at his own articulacy. He did not merely wonder, his eyes filled with tears, but he was determined not to cry. What he had to say was too important, almost more so for him to hear than Mark.

'It's about love,' he said. 'Have you ever come across the word? Four letters, but it's not a swear word. L-o-v-e. I don't care about his mortgage or his background or his paintings. It's the privilege of waking up next to him in the mornings that matters to me. There he is when I come round, week in, week out, come winter, come summer. Even five years on I still can't quite get over my surprise. He doesn't find it a bit surprising. Sometimes he pretends to carry on sleeping, just for fun, and then he jumps on me. He puts his head on my chest before getting up, looking for comfort, or maybe it's because he wants to hear my heart. And my heart is beating, Mark, oh yes, it beats for him. So the first answer is, I stay with him because feeling that love gives me such joy. Not for anything I get from him. Because of the way being with him makes me feel.'

Alan sauntered past them on his way to the bathroom, nodded, but did not stop. Maybe he felt calmer because Kieran and not Mark was speaking. Mark's head was bent but Kieran was not deceived. He knew his former partner was listening intently.

'I know so much about him now,' he went on. 'I know what he's like at the wheel of the car, the way he tenses his body when he's about to overtake, as if he were riding a horse rather than steering a machine. When we're out in the pub for a night, I can judge how far he's gone in drink by the degree of bleariness in his blue eyes. Between leaving the pub and reaching our front door, I know there's going to be a declaration of love, unfailingly, each time, though I cannot tell when exactly it will come, or which words he will choose. The predictability makes it not a bit less precious. When we're going home along Heriot Row, I try to make sure I walk on the inside of the pavement, because I'm afraid he'll trip and tumble down a flight of steps into a basement. And next morning, even if he has the most God awful hangover, he still wants to make love to me.'

Mark had lifted his eyes.

'But I love you, Kieran. I made a mistake and I know it now. I've learnt my lesson.'

The strains of Wet Wet Wet rang out from the sitting-room. All the guests except Gavin and Barry were dancing.

'The other answer is the love he gives me,' Kieran went on, refusing to be deflected. 'Do you know that everything I do is of interest to him? What the secretary says to me at work, the bumph I get through the post in the morning, the girl student who walks in to talk about her essay and I can tell she's about to burst into tears because I know the signs, and I curse myself for forgetting yet again to lay on paper hankies? He even remembers their names, God love him!'

Kieran had raised his voice. Rory, on his way to the bathroom, caught sight of them, raised his eyebrows and smiled. He was not averse to a bit of drama. He had seen Mark making up to Kieran once too often. It was about time they got things sorted out.

'He's like . . . he's like the soil I sink my roots into,' said Kieran, relieved he had found the image that he needed. 'I get nourishment from him and a place that I belong.

'There are people who cope fine on their own. But I'm not one of them, Mark, I've come to realize that. Did you guess how wretched I was when you went off? Have you any idea what you put me through? I was wandering around as if I only had one leg. But no, that's not the point, it doesn't matter any more. I've found what I spent so long looking for. It may not be exciting, it may not be glamorous, you may not understand it, but what does that matter to me? It's where I am and where I want to be.'

'You should have been a dancer,' muttered Mark. 'A painter or a writer, not a bloody teacher laying dinners on for queens!'

Just then Dougal's face appeared over Mark's shoulder.

'Fancy a dance, darling?' he said.

Brian passed Kieran and Mark, framed by the kitchen doorway, as he went down the corridor towards the dining-room. He had replaced the volume of tales carefully on the shelf and switched the standard lamp off, but preferred to leave the candle burning at the centre of the dark study.

Gavin was still seated at the table, tired and a little dazed, staring into space, occasionally squinting at the dancers through the door into the lounge. When Brian arrived, he paused behind him, placing a hand on each shoulder. As he bent down to speak into his lover's ear, he rubbed the outer side of the joint of his right thumb up and down the nape of his lover's neck, between the hairline and the collar of the white work shirt he had not had time to change.

'Don't worry,' he said. 'We're staying.'

'That's good news,' Gavin murmured.

Brian moved on to join the dancers.

Nicol disengaged himself from Andrew and took a seat next to Ramon, who had been watching.

'What was that you said when we had the toast? About the Night of San Antoni?'

'Not Ántoni, Antóni,' Ramon corrected him. 'That's how we say it in Catalan. It's a Mallorcan feast, actually, rather than a mainland one. They celebrate it at the end of January. It's supposed to be the coldest night of the year.'

'And do you come from Mallorca?'

'No, from Barcelona. But there are plenty of Mallorcans in the neighbourhood I live in, Gràcia. They cordon off the streets, then make small bonfires at the crossroads and a big one in front of the church, in Plaça de la Virreina. A band plays in the square on Saturday night and the singing and dancing goes on into the early hours of Sunday morning.'

'So why did you want to toast that particular night?'

'Because of what happened on that night when I was 15. A whole crowd of us went from my secondary school, boys and girls together. I sort of realized I was gay already but had only told one friend, Lluc. It was like a fish or a seal, gradually making its way to the surface of the sea without popping its head out of the water yet. It needed to emerge but I didn't know how it would.

'They were having a folk concert in the square and the dancing wasn't going to start for another hour or so. Lluc and I went for a wander round the streets nearby. It was as cold as you could hope for on Sant Joan. People huddled at the corners to warm themselves at the fires. The big one in front of the church gave out so much heat no one could bear to stand close to it. They had had *gegants* out earlier that evening. That means giant puppets, two or three times life size. Although they are so big they are made of very light material so that one single man can carry each along, hiding beneath the folds of the costume. They are paraded through the streets with a band marching in front. The *gegants* had disappeared but there were still figures here and there dressed up as dragons or demons, mingling with the crowd, letting off firecrackers and generally creating mischief. Right next to where we were standing one of the demons removed his headpiece. It must have been stiflingly hot for him with it on. The head was painted black and red. It had an outsize nose and horns and pointed ears. There was a diabolical grimace on the lips. He carried a pitchfork too. Anyway, the head came off and the most beautiful youth I had ever set eyes on was revealed. It took my breath away.

' "What's up with you?" Lluc asked.

' "Didn't you see? That demon. He's so beautiful!"

' "It's Àngel. He's a friend of mine. Shall I call him over?"

'And before I could say no, Lluc did. He was in the same year as we were but went to a different secondary school, because of the street he lived in. Otherwise he and I might have been sitting next to each other in class!'

'What happened next?' asked Nicol.

'Lluc did it all. Maybe he knew about Àngel, or suspected. I never wormed that out of him. Later in the week we met up at the swimming pool. That was Lluc's idea. He said I had to see a bit more of Àngel's body, to make sure I really liked him. I was head over heels in love already. When we were in the pool he insisted on playing games, swimming between my legs under the water and getting me to sit on his shoulders. The following Saturday we went to the cinema in a group of ten. Àngel sat next to me. During the second half of the film he put his arm across the back of my seat, then on my shoulder, then he cupped my cheek and turned my head round so we could kiss. And that was it. We were boyfriends for the next three years.'

'What did the others say about it?'

'One girl, who had been making up to Àngel, kicked up a bit of a fuss. The others just accepted it. What else should they have done? The problem was finding somewhere to go. Neither of us was out to our families yet. And even if we had been, it would have been hard to feel comfortable having sex together with our parents on the other side of the wall. That's where Uncle Toni came in.'

'Wait a minute. I thought Toni's partner was your uncle.'

'That's right. But we call both of them uncle just the same. Josep is my father's youngest brother and has always been his favourite. So from the time when I was very small we were used to the two of them coming to the house, mostly with Pere and Maurici, but sometimes on their own, without the boys. My father – that's Ricard – took me aside once and explained very gravely that Josep loved Toni the way he loved my mother. Although the sexes were different, the love was the same and that was all that mattered. I found it hard to take him seriously. It was so much a part of things it hardly seemed to need an explanation. I'd always known the way they felt about each other, since I was a toddler.

'Not long after Àngel and I got together, Toni noticed there was something wrong. We had a family do at their house and I was helping him wash up in the kitchen. Everything came tumbling out, about how we really loved each other and had nowhere to go and all of that. As far as I could tell, he wasn't a bit surprised. When we were leaving, he asked me if I wanted to pop over for lunch the following Saturday.

'"Bring your friend Àngel along," he added. "We'd like to meet him."

'Àngel played the flute and was really into classical music. So he and Josep had plenty to talk about. Pere and Maurici were away for the day. I can't remember what they were doing. When lunch was over, Toni said:

'"Josep and I are going up to Tibidabo for a stroll. Then we have to collect the boys. We won't be back before six or seven. I'm sure you two are needing a rest. You can use our room. Just let yourselves out when you are ready to go."

'It was as simple as that. I couldn't believe it. Àngel was as cool as a cucumber.

338

' "This is what we've been waiting for!" he said. And we made good use of the opportunity. Then later on I told my parents and things became easier.'

'And where is Àngel now?' Nicol asked.

'Married. With two children.'

'What?'

'He'd carry on with it still, if I agreed. But it wouldn't feel right. He was my first great love and you always have a special feeling for someone like that. I couldn't have a surreptitious thing with him, on the side.'

'But is he gay or straight?'

'If you ask me, he's basically gay. He might not agree, though. He's not here to be asked.'

Gavin was electrified by Brian's touch. Conscious or unconscious, it was a signal that they would make love that night, under Kieran and Dougal's roof. It had been the gentlest of frictions, hidden from anyone but themselves. Yet it was sufficient to fill Gavin with a sexual excitement so intense he felt in danger of exploding. That was one reason he stayed sitting in his chair, waiting for it to subside a little.

He had had a difficult week. Two separate cases at the hospital were causing him concern. What was more, on top of the worry about Brian's twin and what would happen to him, Gavin had difficulty in sleeping when he was on his own. It did not stand to reason. Brian had been away for three nights and, instead of enjoying having the bed to himself, Gavin had struggled to get even as little as four hours' sleep on each occasion. When Brian was there he would fall asleep in a matter of minutes, and if he awoke during the night, it was only for long enough to hear the chiming of the grandfather clock in a neighbour's flat through the wall, or to slip out for a pee then snuggle in again.

On top of that, instead of flopping on Friday as he was used to doing, he had had to drive through to Edinburgh, in rush hour traffic, to meet his lover at the airport. He had not expected it to be easy. Brian's mood proved even grimmer than he anticipated. Their near-quarrel in the car, and the prospect of being driven back home long after midnight, meant Gavin started the dinner party in a very gloomy frame of mind indeed.

Now, without him doing anything but eat, drink, and listen to the talk, it had all sorted itself out. The tone of Brian's voice, in the few words he had spoken, and the quality of his touch, told him all he needed to know. The bed where they would sleep could only be a door or two away. But right now setting out from his chair to reach that pillow was a hardly less daunting prospect to him than setting sail for Ithaca was to Odysseus. He filled his wineglass again, shut his eyes, and spoke to Brian in his head, in a fashion he often did, telling him things he could never have said out loud.

I am as excited as the first time (he thought), four years ago. And that's saying something. You were such a mystery to me then. You almost scared me. I had no idea what you might be like, what it might be like between us. And I wanted it so much.

You haven't really changed. If anything, you're better-looking now than when we first met. You've lost weight and you take more care of yourself. No more dark rings under the eyes, or at least not so often. And I've got you to floss your teeth so your mouth tastes fresher. Now that I know every bit of your body, that there's not an inch of you I haven't smelt or licked or kissed or sucked, I feel I want it even more. Because you're always different. I hate it when you demand that I declare how much I love you. And it's worse still when you ask me to say why. I can't put things into words to order like that. It feels insincere and sounds it, too. Nothing I could come up with would satisfy your longing to be loved, to have me spell it out to you. That's how it feels when you are pushing me, at any rate.

And yet I do love you, more than you have any concept of. More than you are capable of taking in. In spite of your being difficult, sulking, resenting and complaining. I don't know what the darkness in your family is and I don't think you'll ever tell me. I sense it in you, like a core of blackness, or a cloud suspended above your head. Not all the time, thank God. But when it's there I can tell. The things it makes you say! Do you remember when you told me you were like a heap of broken glass, and if I lifted you up or even tried to touch you, I'd get cut and bleed? And I wanted to say, and didn't say it (even tonight I couldn't say it to your face, I'm not a poet and it would sound stupid, but I can think it): You may be broken glass. But the fire of my love is so

340

strong, its heat is so intense, that no matter how many fragments they shattered you into, I can melt them down and forge them all anew. You'll be whole and glowing and transparent, standing there for everyone to see, the light shining through you, not a patch or a speck of dust or shadow! That's what it feels like when we fuck, at any rate the best times. And the more it happens, the more I want it to happen.

You see, I can't tell you I love you for specific things. Because you could lose any one of them. You're handsome, of course, everyone comments on that. I can see people looking at you then looking at me and thinking, what does he do to get a guy like Brian? And yet the handsomeness wasn't the thing I noticed about you. It almost gets in the road at times. Even your looks will fade with the years. I could say I love you because you're a musician, or because you cook well and feed me, or because you get a hard on when I touch you and enjoy the things I do to you.

You make me feel so capable, so skilful. But what I love you for is different from all of that. If you change every day, then it changes every day too. That is the thing I love. You cannot control it or alter it or shape it. It is you but you do not make it. It flows right through you, like water in the bed of a stream. Each time I look there I see the same reflection, but the water is not the same. I see your face, but the you that is there is different. That is why I am able to continue loving you.

It was so achingly difficult, the first time. I had got to thinking it would never happen. We met at a party and although you hung on talking in your rather unnerving, ironic way, I had no clue whether you were interested in me or not. They told me your nickname, the one that stuck until we got together – "the untouchable" – and I practically gave up hope. Then we met in Safeways at the top of Byres Road, pushing our trolleys down the aisle one evening in the middle of the week, surrounded by university students stocking up on sausages, pizza and beer. Not quite knowing what to say, I commented on the stuff that you had bought. As if taking offence, you said: 'I'm quite a good cook actually. You must come for a meal sometime.' For the rest of the week, each time the phone rang, I was sure it must be you, calling to invite me. It never was.

A three weeks' silence followed. You were away on tour, in

Italy. I didn't know. Only a couple of days after you returned, I saw you in the pub after a performance, still wearing formal dress. You hadn't changed after the concert. You came over for a chat and once again I couldn't stop thinking about you. So I gathered all my courage, got your phone number and asked you round for a meal the next weekend. You couldn't manage Friday or Saturday because of concerts so it had to be Sunday. Not the most auspicious night for starting a love affair.

When you arrived, you were carrying your cello. An extra rehearsal, you said, and if you had gone home, it would have made you late. I sensed something was troubling you but you never mentioned what. The meal was awkward. I was nervous about the food and we kept starting up a conversation, then breaking off after a few sentences. All I did was look at the light catching your cheek and long to touch it. I was at my wits' end. Then I had a bright idea. Would you play something for me on the cello?

You sat in the bay window, the place that has been your favourite since, and played a Bach suite. Or rather, the first two movements of one. You didn't get any further. Later you told me it was just as well. Those were the only two you had mastered at that stage. You could play them both from memory. It was the last suite of the six, the one in D written for a five-stringed instrument, so that it sounds shrill, almost frantic on the four strings of a cello. The prelude ends in a torrent of notes. Then comes a dance movement, slow enough to be a sarabande, though it is not. I was listening with such concentration I lost track of the repetitions. A longer silence came and I could not tell if you had finished or if you still had to repeat the second half. Then in a flash I understood what needed to be done. I got up, took the cello from you, and put my body where it had been.

'Are they ever going to go?' Dougal asked Kieran, in the kitchen. 'I'm knackered. When are we going to get to bed?'

'Don't worry. Some of them want to go up onto the roof.'

'But that'll take ages!'

'No, it won't. I'll give them the key and they can put it back through the letterbox. The stepladder can stay out on the landing till tomorrow morning.'

'Who wants to go up?'

'Mark's not here. He must have slipped away without telling anyone. He's done that before, it's not the first time. Rory and his Catalan, Nicol, Andrew and Barry.'

'Barry doesn't usually stay out so late. What about Gavin?'

'He looks so tired Brian may have to carry him to bed.'

'And Alan?'

'Now Mark has gone, he won't be staying very long either. When Mark goes off like that it means he's feeling bad. Alan is as sensitive to that as I am.'

Dougal and Kieran's flat was the only one on the top landing. You gained access to the roof through a padlocked trapdoor to one side. They leant a stepladder up against it and Andrew went first with the key. Once the trapdoor was lifted, he hauled himself through, then turned to help the following person up. The ladder was relatively steady. Nevertheless, if you had fallen from it at the wrong angle you might just have missed the banisters and tumbled into the stairwell, hitting the stone pavement three flights below with regrettable consequences. Nicol held the ladder while the others climbed, then shrugged his shoulders and went up on his own.

Behind them the slate roofs of the New Town rose towards George Street, punctuated with spaces for the Queen Street gardens and the circuses at Moray Place and Ainslie Place. The sky to the south was a sluggish grey colour, like a liquid that requires vigorous stirring to clear it. They did not look in that direction. Northwards, in contrast, above the low line of the Fife hills, the sky was an incandescent yellow, as if a huge conflagration were taking place somewhere over the Shetlands and all they could see of it at this distance was the light it produced, distilled and purified so that no trace of burning or of flames remained. The hills were in shadow, from Craigluscar and the Cleish Hills on the left to Largo Law on their far right, where the peninsula pans out, subsiding into the East Neuk with nothing but the chill North Sea beyond it. Thanks to a trick of the dawn, the waters of the Firth had caught the light. They could have been a sea of quicksilver beneath a curtain of grim stone, the island of Inchkeith an eerie blob of darkness to the east.

Within an hour, the land would turn from black to green. At their backs, the morning light would soften the contours of the castle and the volcanic ridge the Old Town struggles up to reach it. Early walkers and insomniacs hiking to the top of Arthur's Seat would be rewarded with glimpses of the hills north west of Stirling, for centuries the gateway into Gaelic Scotland, of the outcrops of the Grampians that frame the Angus glens, perhaps even of Schiehallion, the mountain at the centre of the country.

The five men stood in silence, awed to be reminded that the evening they spent together had as its corollary this miracle, perceptible so far south – the light that never fades from the June sky.

'Do you think,' Ramon murmured, 'they realize?'

'Realize what?' asked Rory.

'That we are here.'

'Who?'

'Them. The others. The normal ones.'

'You mean,' said Andrew, 'has anyone noticed that an alarmingly high proportion of the individuals in Edinburgh who are awake at this precise moment are homosexual?'

'Exactly,' said Ramón.

'I don't think they ever notice us,' said Barry, his mind preoccupied with the image of Robert and the decision it demanded from him. 'They go about their lives as if we didn't exist.'

'That's what they like to pretend,' said Rory. 'You know, I was listening to a programme on the radio this morning – yesterday morning, I mean – about gay adoption, and a woman actually used the phrase "host community".'

'As if we were immigrants, and could be deported,' said Andrew.

'Where do they think we arrived from?' Nicol said.

'That's the dream, isn't it?' said Ramon. 'A world without homosexuals.'

'A country without jessies,' said Andrew. 'A denellified Scotland.'

'It's so ridiculous,' said Nicol. 'If only they had eyes to see. Who do they think sold them the newspaper they are reading? Did they look at the man who punched their ticket on the train?'

'Who comes to read the meter?' Andrew said. 'Have they ever

344

wondered why the dentist they use is so particularly gentle? When are they going to acknowledge the extent to which they depend on us to get through an ordinary day?'

'We are their sons and brothers,' said Ramon, 'their uncles and their cousins.'

'Fathers and husbands and lovers too,' said Rory.

'What worries me,' said Barry, who had almost understood, almost glimpsed the answer, 'is that all of this may be an inter-mission, just a bleep. You know, like Germany before Hitler. That there will be a catastrophe and we will disappear from view once more.'

'Even so, there would be that unmistakable limp wrist in the cradle,' Andrew said. 'A suspiciously camp glint in baby's eye.'

'It's gone too far,' said Nicol. 'We'll never go underground again. We're here to stay.'

Barry would take the test. He knew that now. He could ask Andrew. Someone had said you could get the results back within twenty-four hours. That would cut down on the torment of wait-ing. He had been too long a eunuch. All through the evening, he admitted to himself, he had been struggling to take his eyes off Ramon, riveted by that Mediterranean charm, beauty on a miniature scale, manly and yet boyish too. Whatever the result, things were going to change. The time had come to inhabit his body at last, and learn its ways.

'Looks like today will be a splendid day,' he said.

'We'd better get some sleep then,' said Rory. 'Otherwise we won't see much of it.'

Kieran glanced at the red digits on the radio alarm as he pulled back the downie and slid, exhausted, into bed. It was quarter to three. Dougal was brushing his teeth in the *en suite* bathroom. He put the bedside lamp out and followed the familiar sounds, through a distinctly tipsy haze, as the toilet flushed, Dougal washed and dried his hands, then turned the other lamp off too and leapt into bed.

'I think it went OK.'

'Oh, yes, it did,' said Kieran, moving closer.

He was thinking how nice it was to have a hard-on and be too tired to do anything about it. He could not be sure exactly what

345

it was that enveloped him. The warmth of the downie? The warmth of his lover's body close to his own? Or the unmistakable, familiar smell of Dougal's skin, the fragrance of his breath? Drifting off into sleep, he thought: you carry that fragrance around you like a cloud, like love emanating from you. I can warm myself at you, as if you were the sun, a gentle sun that cherishes and nurtures without scorching. You are my port, he thought, as Dougal burrowed into the mattress, closer to him, putting an arm around him that settled like a latch on the inside of a door at nightfall. When the day is over, thought Kieran, I can guide my ship inside these safe, protecting walls and rest it there.

Port, Dougal was thinking, nearly asleep himself. I'm sure it was port they spilt on the rug in the sitting-room. He awakened with a start. That wasn't tonight. It had been at another party, in a different flat, the one with two advocates and their wives and his schoolfriend Beryl in Darnaway Street, that got out of hand and rather ribald. The two couples started touching each other up and he had no idea what to do. Maybe an orgy was on the cards and Beryl had been hoping he would follow suit. He never got the stain out of that rug and hadn't brought it with him to his new home.

Nobody had spilt anything tonight. They had run out of port, that was it. The bottles they put it in nowadays, he thought, are so dark you can hardly tell if there is any left or not. And I felt such shame when Rory asked for more and there was none to give him. When guests come to our house, he thought, I want there to be an abundance of everything they ask for. I want to be able to share my happiness with them.

Kieran was asleep in his arms. Not long afterwards, Dougal, too, floated into unconsciousness. Beyond the tightly fastened Georgian shutters, the June morning was a brilliant glow.